Her Minder

BOOK ONE: THE DOCTOR

Her Minder

BOOK ONE: THE DOCTOR

Teddy Raye

Boscobel Books

Teddy Raye/Boscobel Books
118 Claridge Place
Belton, South Carolina 29627

Publisher's Note: This is a work of fiction. Names, characters, places, and incidents are a product of the author's imagination. Locales and public names are sometimes used for atmospheric purposes. Any resemblance to actual people, living or dead, or to businesses, companies, events, institutions, or locales is completely coincidental.

Book Layout © 2016 BookDesignTemplates.com
Book Cover Design: Rusty Apper@mintvision
Book Cover Art: Patricia Demoraes

Her Minder Book One: The Doctor/ Teddy Raye. -- 1st ed.
ISBN 13: 978-0999164204

This book is dedicated to:

Pam Martin for her amazing editorial skills, her inspiration, encouragement and friendship. Thank you for not giving up on me, even when I was ready to give up on myself. Pam, you are the greatest friend I have ever had.

Kela Hamilton, for challenging me to take up writing again and for medical continuity.

Special thanks to the following friends for their invaluable help and support:

Murphy McCall, for restoring my faith in myself and this story. Theresa, who is, and will forever be, my Angel. Mel, Marianne, and Jennifer, for initial read-throughs, encouragement and advice. Beth, for financial support, and to all my friends for never doubting me. Mike, the good Doktor, for his advice and expertise in the Kinkster world of BDSM.

Rusty Apper, for his incredible book cover design and his patience as I waffled like a waffling thing. Patricia Demoraes, for her amazing artwork and bringing Dahlra Gar to life.

Alan Rickman for the Voice.

My Precious Muse, the real, true Dahlra.
Thank you for reuniting with me.

The greatest healer
Stays in the background
Orders no one
Talks little
Loves Much.
If you do not trust those you serve
How will they trust you?
Share your heart,
It's all you have
And all they need to learn.
~~Haven Trevino (The Tao of Healing)

My Little Girl,

It's my duty to provide a safe-haven and it's your duty to accept that, knowing that as long as you're mine you're safe. Nothing will harm you. Not because you're weak, I've witnessed your bravery, but because I'll provide you with comfort when you feel overwhelmed and shield you from that which can cause you harm - your insecurities and negativity. The hand that guides and disciplines is the same hand that will tilt your chin so I may kiss you and it's the same hand that will pull you closer when you feel like falling apart.

~~ An opening gambit from her Dominant in the journal where His sub will record her highs and lows

That intoxicating moment when we first realize that someone we have yearned after with a helpless, hopeless, enduring longing feels the same way about us, when a dream is suddenly made flesh—living that moment is in itself a transformative experience. But what follows—that collapse of ego boundaries that comes with immersion in the waters of the beloved—is so charged with power, with the potential to nurture or to destroy, that it changes everything, one way or another.

~~Melinda Johansson

Bid me to live, and I will live
Thy Protestant to be;
Or bid me love, and I will give
A loving heart to thee.

A heart as soft, a heart as kind,
A heart as sound and free
As in the whole world thou canst find,
That heart I'll give to thee.

Bid that heart stay, and it will stay
To honour thy decree;
Or bid it languish quite away,
And't shall do so for thee.

Bid me to weep, and I will weep,
While I have eyes to see;
And having none, yet I will keep
A heart to weep for thee.

Thou art my life, my love, my heart,
The very eyes of me;
And hast command of every part,
To live and die for thee.

To Anthea, Who May Command Him Anything
By Robert Herrick
(1591-1674)

Excerpt from And Because Love Battles *by Pablo Neruda*

CONTENTS

Her Minder

THE DOCTOR

CHAPTER ONE

What Is Your Name?

In that golden, magic moment between sunset and dusk, Sydney Chapin strolled lazily down the long, deserted stretch of Holden Beach. The air was salty on her lips, the music of the beckoning tide a siren song. The water was cool on her bare feet, and the sweet sea breeze gently caressed her face with the tenderness of a kiss.

Occasionally, a stronger gust would lift her hair, until it streamed behind her like a banner. The shore was a warm carpet; now and again she would pause and dig in the sand with her toe, winkling up a crab or sand dollar with the ease of long practice.

A mile or so to the south was her beach house, a soft bed with crisp sheets, wine in the fridge, a rocking chair on the porch. It was getting late; she would make her way home and settle into her favourite rocker to sip her wine, gazing into the soothing, mesmerising waves until it was too dark to see them. Then she would fall asleep to the sound of their hushing, rushing lullaby.

As she approached the safety of the house, darkness suddenly descended, and the air grew cold and pitiless. In the secretive, moonless night, she grew disorientated and panicked. A desperate whine escaped her lips, and she tried to run, but it was like running in quicksand. The tide was coming in, and no matter how hard she ran, her safe haven, like that endless summer, remained forever out of reach...

She awoke with a start, heart-pounding, nerves jangling into consciousness. The lovely dream that had cradled her against her reality unraveled and dissipated like smoke, until she could barely remember it. This was no walk along one of the East Coast's prettiest beaches. There was no vacation home at the end of her journey. She was in one of the swampiest, dankest places South America could create, and the only thing waiting for her was a long day of suffering, torture and despair-if she was lucky.

She tentatively stretched her stiff limbs, and pain from a dozen points flared like struck matches. Disappointment flooded her chest with black desolation. Her eyes filled with tears, but she blinked them back, shaking her head to dispel the panic and the self-pity. Breathing through her nose, she warned herself, *don't cry, dammit! Tears only water your weaknesses. Think of the desert, think of anything else-*

Like an answering angel, numbers automatically bubbled to the forefront of her mind: *6, 13, 27, 4, 12; 6, 13, 27, 4, 12...* She could see them, tacked onto the frontal lobe, like the NPower bill on her kitchen fridge back home.

Home. She pushed away the image of her little flat in Oval very, very quickly. That was a no-fly zone. Thinking about a place she would probably never see again was painful enough. Sydney took a deep breath, held it for several seconds, and slowly exhaled. *I'm still alive. There's that.*

It was a shabby consolation prize.

Just for S's & G's, she tested her restraints. Nope. The straps holding her down were strong and snugged down tight. She felt a chary sort of pride that her captors still considered her enough of a risk to keep restrained, but in all truth, her muscles were now so atrophied she probably couldn't crawl out of there, much less attempt a daring, James Bond-esque escape. With a sigh, she glanced around her cell. Her prison might have once been a hospital, but sterile had not been part of its MO for a long time. Once, a lifetime ago, when she was still strong enough to plan such a daring escape, she had memorised the details of her cell should an opportunity present itself.

Now she could draw it blindfolded.

She calculated it to be ten by fifteen feet in size, with a door on the long wall. To her right, just in her line of vision, was a battered sink. The walls were dingy white, and the cabinets and cupboards above them were empty but for a few rolls of gauze, rubber gloves, boxes of hypodermic sharps, and bottles of alcohol, not that she could get to them.

Overhead, a bare light bulb swung lazily from a chain. And beneath it, she lay prone, strapped down on a narrow bed-cum-examination table in the middle of the room.

Aside from what she could see and hear and feel, the smell alone told her more than enough about her present situation. She wore most of it on her clothes. Since a dodgy stomach had been her constant companion since she had arrived, the state of her filthy hospital-issue gown told her entire humiliating story on that account. One of the guards apparently got off on that sort of thing.

Dimly, Sydney tried to focus on how many days she had been incarcerated. It all added up to somewhere around a month, but she could not be one hundred percent positive. She had finished her menstrual cycle a few days before her capture, and she had just ended another. She wondered if she had enough time left for one more. During regular intervals, she had been heavily drugged, drifting in and out of consciousness, but they had soon tired of that. Lately, they were really working her over. In addition to the days she did not remember, there were the increasing number of interrogation sessions, which were really nothing more than torture.

Any day now, someone would decide she was not all that much fun to play with anymore, and that they could really use the bed space. One of the guards would come in to her cell, cop a final feel, then put a gun to her temple. Before you could print the front page (*Agent finds miracle cure for PMS – a Sig Sauer!*) she'd be on the receiving end of an honour guard funeral back home, listed as MIA—Presumed Dead. It dismayed her that a large chunk of emotion pushing that thought around her head was relief.

Over and over she replayed the day it had all gone tits up. She had been so close. Perhaps she had grown too confident; perhaps she had taken too many chances. It should have been a simple snatch and grab; the enclave was backed by powerful friends, but they were sloppy and unorganised. Security was lax and the worker bees easy to bribe. Only one more week and she would be out of rotation and she could go home. One more reccie and her mission would have been complete and she could bail.

That day, however, she had known immediately that she was in trouble. Driving into work that morning, the guards at the security station had acted differently. She had been detained just long enough to realize the trap she had unwittingly stumbled into.

She had done exactly what she was trained to do should anything out of the ordinary occur. She was polite and cooperative, playing the compliant, scared civil servant, willing to go along in order to 'clear up the misunderstanding.' She felt confident her credentials were solid enough to convince them nothing was untoward. But the moment they dragged her from the car and started emptying the contents of her bags on the ground, looking for things she knew they wouldn't find, she was fairly certain she was screwed.

They had taken her to a holding facility within the group's compound; it was a former hospital, so she thought she might be treated at least as a political prisoner. They had only given her credentials a perfunctory glance before two guards walked into the interrogation room and slipped on the brass knuckles.

Then the real fun had started—at least for the guards. Even now, weeks later she still remembered the slow, methodical working over she had been given. As she had begged and screamed and protested her innocence, the numbers had popped in her head like they had been etched on the inside of her eyelids. Instantly, they calmed her panic and dampened her pain receptors down to something she could deal with.

While her voice keened against the cell wall, pleading for mercy that would not come, the mnemonic codes flowed into her mind, wafting like smoke. She was fascinated at the detached way her mind withdrew from the pain. She recited the string which allowed her to block what was happening to her, the numbers running through her mind like an anesthetic: *6, 13, 27, 4, 12; 6, 13, 27, 4, 12...*

Yes, it had hurt; she felt more degradation than she thought possible, but in truth, the overall feeling was of, *6, 13, 27, 4, 12; 6, 13, 27, 4, 12...*She could lock herself away with these numbers, and no one could get in. The combination to her own sanity safe; within, she could survive. She told herself this so much she almost believed it.

On that first nightmare of a day, the assault had been more about the sadism than the interrogation, and then that little greasy wad of an Intelligence Officer scuttled in and started his song and dance. Christ, she hated his guts. Every day he would come in and sit beside her, stroking his toothbrush moustache like a pet. Every day, he would ask the same questions. They were presented in different ways, in different tones of voice, even in different languages, but they always boiled down to: "What do you know?"

As far as she was concerned, she was a blank jump drive, with hidden files she could not see and no recollection of their contents or how to access them. They had no real evidence against her, they would not release her, and they were afraid to kill her in case she was part of the Nicaraguan government's own intel cell, because fuck knows they weren't going to claim her. That left the prospect of breaking her into confessing something she couldn't tell them in the first place. Thus far, she had not broken.

Every day she gave them the same answers. *My name is Geraldine Parker. I work for Venture Environmentals as an expediter. I have a husband and a daughter. I wish to speak to the British Embassy. Under the United Nations Universal Declaration of Human Rights you have no right to keep me here without proof of cause. When can I speak to my husband? When can I go home?*

The Intel Officer would write something down on his clipboard and leave, in spite of her whining pleas for mercy, to speak to the Embassy, to make a phone call. He would ignore her and call the guards. Little shit didn't even do his own dirty work.

Then the goons would come in, already grinning in anticipation. Sydney stopped fighting after the first week, and stopped asking for a bath after a fortnight. It was during that time some genius got the idea that the 'conventional methods of persuasion' were not working, so they started with her toes. The numbers managed to keep her from breaking. They could not prevent her from screaming.

During the past week, she got the feeling that she was an embarrassment to the Intel Officer. He had stopped questioning her every day. At first, she almost missed him, before stepping back and mentally hitting herself with a cricket bat. That was the Stockholm syndrome talking, and when that snagged in deep, you were done for.

The food was late today. The feeding schedule had become erratic, and though her internal clock told her it was almost noon, the cell was deathly quiet. Normally she heard noises, but not today. *Oh, great*, she thought. She was missing her captors. *Stockholm, here I come.*

To keep the crazies at bay, she tried to play her daily game of Top of The Pops. When she had first arrived, there were some nights she would sing until she had no voice left, until the melody was little more than a hoarse, hushed whisper. She sang every song she knew, then made up more. But every night she sang less and the silence grew. One night, soon, she would run out words and tunes, and that silence would mark the end of her.

She stared at the overhead light until the image burned her retinas. It was time to take stock. She had been lucky, for the most part. She was good at what she did, and had enjoyed a career she was proud of. She was not one for self-actualization, but she reminded herself over and over she had given this her best shot.

At the beginning of every day, her to-do list contained one objective: Stay alive. She told herself she still had a chance to survive. At nightfall, she congratulated herself on being able to tick the box one more day. *Just give me one more day past the one I'm living now.*

She was in the middle of 'Can't Buy Me Love' when the door opened, and an unfamiliar man stepped into the room. He was wearing a white medical coat; a stethoscope was tucked into his pocket. For a brief moment, stranger and prisoner sized one another up. Against the backdrop of this garbage-heap environment, he looked so sterile and surreal she burst into unwitting laughter. "What have you come as?" she cawed, unable to stop the hysteria from sliding through.

He turned to face her, his expression undefinable. It wasn't contempt, it wasn't indifference, but some strange place in between. At first, Sydney thought he was albino, with his white-blond hair and extremely pale skin, but something was not right about his colouring.

His eyes, for instance, were dark green; his eyebrows did not look right, either. They were bleached white, like his hair, and the entire effect was off-kilter and alien. He was tall, and might have even been considered handsome, but it was impossible to tell from the shuttered scowl on his face. His aloof, slightly disdainful countenance was in sharp contrast to the leering, lust-filled faces of the guards who brutalized her.

For a person who prided herself on being able to read most men, Sydney honestly could not get a bead on him. He was the first anomaly in a month.

"Do you know why you are here?"

"No, I don't. Please, umm, Doctor...?"

"Yes, you may address me by the honorific, 'Doctor,'" he replied. His eyes met hers; they were as cold as his voice. It was a deep baritone, with inflection and colour. Cultured, sophisticated, old money. He would know how to use it to get what he wanted. "Will you please answer the question, Ms Chapin?"

"I'm not this 'Ms Chapin'. That's what I've been trying to tell everyone! There's been some mistake. My name is Geraldine Parker. I work for Venture Environmentals as an expeditor. I would like to contact the British Embassy. Under the United Nations Universal Declaration of Human Rights you have-"

"According to the information given, you are in fact..." He leafed through the first few pages of the manila folder in his hand. "...Special Agent Sydney Chapin, and you are being detained on charges of industrial espionage."

"That's patently ridiculous-"

"Name?"

Sydney tried to swallow. Nope. That dry mouth of hers was not having it. Garnet Pinkerton, her partner at the Agency, had a saying: *When you can't produce your own spit, you're as royally fucked as Camilla.*

She turned the full weight of her eyes to him imploringly. "Please, help me, Doctor. I've been-" She paused for effect, and lowered her gaze submissively. "I've been beaten and...and raped. Repeatedly," she whispered, her voice thin with humiliation she no longer had to manufacture.

With a derisive snort, he tossed the folder on the table and brought his hands together in a slow hand clap. "Brava, Ms Chapin. It appears the theatre lost a great actress when you decided on a career in espionage. While I'm sure your little work of fiction is very entertaining, I would caution you not to waste time with further attempts to gain my sympathy. I assure you none will be forthcoming." He paused. "Name?"

Her initial shock at his reaction was minimal, which demoralised her far more than his jeering cruelty. "My name is Geraldine Parker. I would like—" Sydney stopped. Why bother?

"You would like... what? A bath?"

"What? Oh...yes, I would, but..." She sniffed and looked around. "I haven't been allowed to bathe in—"

"Yes, I can see that. I can smell it, too." His nose wrinkled in disgust, and she lowered her eyes at the odd mixture of contempt and pity in his voice.

She was almost sure he was playing a rather dour version of Good Cop; she had played it enough herself to know they were more dangerous than their opposite number. But she also believed in playing the odds, and she was almost certain she had heard a shred of genuine compassion in his voice. And that hair; she was certain it was a dye job. That suggested vanity, some way of setting himself apart–another weakness she could possibly exploit. If he was new to the game, and she could hold her nerve, perhaps she could find the means to snow him and still give nothing away.

"I'm sorry," she whispered, and allowed fresh tears to spill from her eyes.

Silently he stepped forward to unlock the restraints, then moved back to allow her to stand. Slowly, carefully, she pushed herself up into a sitting position, then gingerly swung her legs over the table. The moment she put weight on her legs, they crumpled beneath her as if they were made of overcooked spaghetti, and she stumbled forward.

The doctor reached for her, but he failed to move quickly enough to catch her. She fell painfully to her knees, landing in a heap onto the floor. Sick shame flooded her chest, and she sobbed for real, her lank hair swinging greasily around her face. From her vantage point, he seemed as tall as a mountain and just as unmoving. He put his hands on his hips, looking down at her with his unreadable eyes.

Finally, he leaned over and pulled her to her feet. His strong hands held her arms in a firm grip. "Ms Chapin, stop this. Stop this now." he demanded. "If you cannot stand unassisted, tell me and I will provide you with a chair."

Now she was sure she had seen a brief flash of emotion. "I'm very sorry, Doctor. I just want to feel clean. I want my husband and my daughter." His iron grip loosened, and she pressed on, "I want to know why this nightmare is happening to me."

The doctor was silent as he assisted her to the large tiled bathroom and turned on the shower. Two things struck her; he was actually waiting for the water to warm up, and he refused to look at her as he helped her out of her rancid clothing. He balled up the soiled hospital gown and tossed it into the bin.

His expression twisted in disgust. "This is revolting," he spat. "Can you stand in the shower long enough for me to order some new bedclothes?"

She nodded, and he left her in the room alone. She stepped into the shower, and tried not to hate herself for not making a run for it. A month ago, she would have been out the door, running starkers for the nearest exit. Now she was just too...what? Beaten, tired, weak, dirty? Hopeless?

The humiliation of it all rushed down on her, and for a moment, she considered giving up. Again. She gave up about a hundred times a day.

It was something she always managed to talk herself out of, but damn if she was not getting tired of that well-worn pep rally.

The water was tepid, but felt good running down her body, rinsing away the filth. Her parched, dehydrated skin lapped it up like a sponge, and she held her mouth open under the spray. *Get clean. Save your strength. You're still alive, aren't you?*

The door opened, making her jump. The Doctor's white-coated arm appeared; he had large hands, long fingers, no rings. He sounded chillingly calm as he addressed the unseen person on the other side of the door. "And get that room clean. I'm not going to work in an area covered in shit. While you're at it, bring some fresh clothes for the prisoner."

As Sydney listened, another wave of weakness passed through her like a hot flash, and in spite of her good intentions, she felt her knees noodle out on her again. She leaned back against the shower wall, hoping it would prop her up, but her feet slipped on the wet floor and she helplessly banana-peeled flat on her backside.

The crash landing reverberated from her tailbone up through her spine. Her head snapped back against the wall, and she saw stars. After a stunned moment, she barked out another harsh caw of laughter. It sounded nothing like her; it tasted bitter in her throat, like vinegar.

The Doctor loomed over her. "I fail to see what's so amusing." His prim disapproval made her laugh even harder. God, Garnet Pinkerton would have loved *this*. He lived for moments of unintentional slapstick.

She looked up into her captor's scowling face, and let the hysterical laughter spin away. *The Doctor isn't happy. Doctor Who? Number eleven or twelve? I'm going to be tortured by a Whovian nerd. Maybe he'll take me to the Tardis. Oh, Christ I'm losing it...*

She tried to get her legs back under her, but she was Bambi on ice, and once again the inappropriate laughter whistled from her breathless lungs. With something like a huff of disapproval, the Doctor shut off the water, and impatiently hauled her to her feet. She could feel his tangible displeasure in the air.

He turned away; after a moment Sydney heard water splashing in the tub. As it filled, she took the opportunity to study her new interrogator. His stony expression seemed oddly out of place with his downcast eyes. He seemed, in fact, intent on refusing to acknowledge either her nudity or her helplessness.

Trembling with effort, she managed to shuffle over to the tub and crawl in. The water was wonderfully, devastatingly hot, and she couldn't stifle a moan of comfort as the water rose around her. He let it run until it covered her shoulders, and for once she did not give a damn what his agenda was.

As Sydney lay immersed in the blissfully hot bath, what little energy she had in reserve bled out of her and into the water. She tried lifting her arms, but they felt as if they weighed five hundred pounds each. It was bad enough that her legs weren't working. Now she found herself too weak to do anything other than steep, like a teabag. She could accept being taken out and shot, but the idea that her own weakness would be her undoing... well, that *would* be failure.

A flicker of light overhead caught her eye, and she looked up at the CCTV camera in the ceiling. As it swiveled toward her, its lens flashed as light played across it. There was one identical to this one in her cell. So what if some asshole was in a monitoring station somewhere, getting his jollies off while she bathed? They had watched worse.

The Doctor was standing behind her, so she was unable to get a good lay of the land as far as his reaction. He was a professional, she was certain. They meant business this time, and she was pretty sure she no longer had the strength to face more rigorous interrogation. Hell, she didn't really think she could take the day-to-day crap she was used to anymore. She began to count. *6, 13, 27, 4, 12; 6, 13, 27, 4, 12...*

She jumped at a scraping noise behind her head. The Doctor had pulled up a chair, and was pouring warm water over her hair. He did this several times, until her hair was thoroughly wet. Sydney sat perfectly still as he worked shampoo into her hair.

His fingernails scrubbed at her scalp with surprising gentleness. Her eyes slid closed. *Oh, fuuuuck, that feels nice.* It felt more than nice. It felt orgasmically good.

"I thought you might enjoy this," he murmured. His voice was soothing, with a whisper of sensuality. His hands slowed, his touch deepened; her head lolled boneless against the edge of the tub.

Sydney's breath caught. He was playing her, using that voice of his. She could hear the jagged, chipped ice from before melting, turning into silk and chocolate. She let the sensation wash over her, before she realised she was buying what he was selling. *What the fuck, Sydney? Can you say, Good Cop, Bad Cop, boys and girls? Can you say, Stockholm syndrome, ladies and gentlemen?* She had to put that away fast. If anyone was going to do any seducing here, it was going to be her.

To block him, she began counting again, like a rosary: *6, 13, 27, 4, 12; 6, 13, 27, 4, 12....*

The Doctor's hands slowed their rhythmic scrubbing. "Ms Chapin-"

"Parker," She corrected him, her voice tight. "Mrs Parker. I'm married. I'm a mother of a four-year-old."

"As you wish. What were you saying before?" His fingernails scraped a little harder over her scalp, but by now her mind was getting back into fighting mode.

"I was praying." If he wanted to use this pleasure against her, let him bloody well try.

He gave her hair a perfunctory rinse and helped her to stand. As she dried herself with a thin towel, he looked away dismissively. That puzzled her, and she wondered why it even mattered. Normally she was praying for the guards to look anywhere but at her.

She turned to place the towel on a ledge, and caught a glimpse of herself in the mirror over the sink. She sighed harshly, sickened by what she saw. God, she was a mess. She had been in some scrapes before, but this was the worst. Seeing herself this battered actually frightened her. She had always been rather dismissive of her looks, but this was like observing a sick animal that had been brutally mistreated. Her chestnut hair, her one vanity, was now a wet, tangled mess. Cuts, contusions, gashes, scabs, teeth marks, purple and yellow bruises—almost every inch of her body was marred by pawing hands, careless boots, yellowing teeth. Her hazel eyes were swollen and bruised, her complexion sallow and jaundiced. No wonder every inch of skin felt as if it had been worked over with an industrial-strength emery board.

"Are you finished admiring your reflection?" Over her shoulder, she caught him staring at her. His eyes met hers, and again, she saw a flash of something she could not identify. She could not be sure, but a look like that always meant something.

He tossed fresh clothing in the sink. "Please change into these." He looked away as she slowly drew on the hospital gown and plain cotton knickers. Now that she was clean, she could think a little straighter. Under her breath, like a litany, she mouthed the numbers; she no longer cared about keeping them under wraps. They were more effective if she said them out loud anyway. "Six, thirteen, twenty-seven, four, twelve; six, thirteen, twenty-seven, four, twelve..."

"Eight, forty-three, two, twenty-nine, five," The Doctor mocked in a lazy drawl. "What do the numbers mean?"

As those five words drifted over her, something strange happened. Her head cleared, and she could feel calm stealing into her body. Giving up might just have to wait another day. *Score one for me,* she thought.

She answered defiantly, "Do you want to know the truth?"

"That would be a good start."

"I'm not allowed anything to read. I'm not allowed to do anything or go anywhere. And while I'll take boredom over torture any day of the week, I do miss a good Barbara Cartland now and then. So I sing, and I recite poetry, and I list numbers. Anything to hear myself do something other than scream. It's the only real thing I can control."

He scoffed. "Real, eh? Because you're all about real and truth, aren't you?"

She met his gaze, and he stilled, as if unwilling or unable to look away this time. *That's two for me,* she thought, dispassionately.

Two of the usual guards were waiting for them when they returned to the cell. They were here for what they euphemistically called 'Happy Hour.' Discovering a freshly-washed, pliant woman, they began pulling her clothes from her body. For the next two hours, while they 'interrogated' her, Sydney retreated deep within herself, and recited her numbers.

She cast about for something to focus her eyes upon, and spotted her new friend, The Doctor. He looked up only once, to find her staring defiantly at him. He dropped his gaze back to his notes, and refused to meet her eyes again.

Finally sated, the guards left, buttoned their trousers and boasting with one another as they sauntered out of the room. The Doctor waited until their voices had faded down the hall, then silently led her to the bath again.

Sydney scrubbed, but could not feel clean. He watched impassively as she tried to bathe the previous two hours away. She would have scoured the skin from her bones, but eventually he snatched the washcloth from her hands.

"That is enough. You are as clean as you can be. Rinse and dry yourself."

Once she was safely ensconced in her cell again, she found food waiting for her. They laced her meals with ipecac, but never in any discernable pattern and never two meals in a row. Eating was always a crapshoot. She ate everything on the plate quickly, even though the food was boiled to extinction and tasted tainted. If this meal was not sabotaged, she needed every ounce of nutrition she could digest.

She finished, and the empty plate was taken away, leaving her and the Doctor alone. Suddenly he turned to her, as if addressing her for the first time. "You are a spy."

She shook her head. "No, I'm not. How many times do I have to tell you-"

"In this cell, you will do as I say."

"Alright."

"My superiors lose interest in you with every passing day. If you want to stay alive, I suggest you obey me." He moved forward until he was looming over her in his most dominating pose. She recoiled, unnerved by the flat, cold look in his eyes.

"I've always cooperated-"

"Name?"

"Geraldine Parker. I work for Venture Environmentals..." A wave of nausea washed over her. Sweat popped out on her forehead, and as she looked up at him, the Doctor's eyes grew wide with alarm. He had just enough time to spin her around and bend her over the wastebasket before her lunch made its reappearance. She threw up quickly and violently, and the Doctor held her head as she emptied her aching stomach. He eased her back onto the bed, then turned away. She could hear water running

"How often does this happen?" He pressed a glass of water into her hand. "It's not drugged."

"Every other day or so. It's great for my weight loss program." She grimaced at the vile taste in her mouth. "Quite frankly, Doctor, if it was drugged, so what? You'd make me drink it anyway."

She took a large gulp, swished, and spat it into the wastebasket. Her throat felt as if it had been coated in Sterno and torched, her stomach still turned cartwheels. Vomiting had become just another form of assault; what was worse, her increasingly feeble hope always landed in the wastebasket along with her lunch. It took hours, sometimes days to claw that back to ground zero.

As the Doctor called for someone to come in and clean up her mess, she sagged against the bed, then climbed back onto her horizontal prison without being told. She hated herself for that. She laughed aloud, and it turned into a sob.

Don't cry. Tears water your weaknesses....my name is Geraldine Parker. My name is...I'm never going to see my family again. Jesus. She had talked about that husband and child for so long now she could actually imagine them, what they looked like; the kind of dress her daughter wore. She pictured them, waving goodbye.

That's when she realized the Doctor was probably going to win. Giving up almost felt like a welcoming friend. In spite of her original impulse to laugh at Dr Spic-and-Span's routine, the all too sobering truth was apparent. Whatever he had been sent to do, she was fairly certain she no longer had the courage or the strength to endure it.

Close on the heels of her self-pity was a small, burning pit of anger. Thirty days seemed an awfully short time to be thinking of writing herself off, though, not with her training and experience. She should be tougher than this; she should be stronger mentally to withstand this. She should have been clever enough to not get caught in the first place.

CHAPTER TWO

The Cell

For the better part of a month, the Doctor spent every day questioning her. His interrogation tool of choice was usually drugs, which he administered every morning. Every afternoon he gave his report to the Intel Officer.

Sydney's entire vocabulary was reduced to, "I would like to contact either the British or the American Embassies. I would like to contact either the British or the American Embassies. I would like to contact-" She spoke it patiently when she could, and screamed it when she could not stop herself. But she did not break. She could not have told The Doctor anything even if she had wanted too.

Her mission had been simple; to gather intelligence on a small but extremely well-financed enclave doing business in Nicaragua. She was to uncover proof of their ties to another organisation she was very much interested in taking down. Her preparation for the mission had been a complex and sophisticated form of self-hypnosis, involving numbers and word strings and mnemonic triggers. Once deployed, she would go deep undercover, and infiltrate the group.

The plan was to review each bit of intel, recite the specific 'combination' mnemonic, and the information would be stored in her subconscious, like a photograph. Consciously, she would remember none of it; once the mnemonic string had been called into place, the hypnotic suggestion effectively erased the data. All that was left behind was a footprint of knowledge that the information was there, just not what it actually was. It was only when she returned from her mission would she be 'deprogrammed' and hypnotised to recall the information she had gathered.

The possibilities of future use of this method thrilled and terrified the suits back at the Agency, but that was for the brainiacs to fine tune. The fact her superiors had used this method of espionage in the first place told her they suspected trouble. And holy crap, had she found it.

To Sydney, it was a brilliant opportunity to get the goods on an outfit she had been tracking for over two years. She had no intention of allowing another agent get the collar on it if she could help it, and she had come up trumps.

Every bit of intel she needed to accomplish her mission was now safely locked away in her head—even from herself. It made her virtually impossible to compromise; she could not tell them what she consciously did not know. It was a foolproof system.

Well, unless you got caught and were accused of being a spy. And that was just bad luck, karma, them ol' James Bond espionage blues, whatever.

She had once had the temerity to hope this would be one of those things you laughed about one day. That had been before the Doctor joined her team. Now, it was a pretty safe bet her knowledge would go no further than this stinking cell. Her mission had been reduced to dragging one more lungful of breath into her body, getting her heart to circulate her blood just one more time before it started to feel like more trouble than it was worth.

Each day, it was something different. One drug in particular made her body feel as if it were on fire. One made her violently ill; she struggled to breathe until he quickly administered the antidote. One made her skin break out in small blisters that itched maddeningly, reducing her to a howling mess until he slathered her with a salve that desensitised her skin. Another caused her to cry for hours. And always, The Doctor watched, assisting her when she reacted violently to whatever he was pumping through the IVs.

Through it all were the questions. Sydney told them nothing of importance, nothing incriminating, nothing the codes hid, deep within the vault in her mind.

Only the numbers kept her from breaking, ticking themselves off in her head, so that she could find them even through the haze of hypnonarcotics, fear and despair. It was strange; she had seen interrogations before. Hell, she'd performed them herself. And yet her reactions were much less extreme than any she had previously seen to these very same drugs. Were the codes really keeping the worst of the effects at bay?

It was at this point that it occurred to her that the guards had not molested her for quite a while. The last time they had even touched her was the first day the Doctor had arrived. And while she really ought to have been grateful, she was in no hurry to fall off her table with gratitude. The Doctor, while sparing her the more base form of rape, was far more dangerous.

"Why is it taking so long?" the weasel Intel Officer asked The Doctor.

He gave the greasy little man a look of contempt. "She's a professional. She won't break easily." He glanced at Sydney with chilling calm. "But she will break. In the end, they all break."

Sometime around the second week he was there, she noticed that the Doctor was growing irritable and restless. His cool exterior was showing stress fractures, and Sydney leaned on them every chance she got, because, to paraphrase Richard Ashcroft, the drugs didn't work. At one point, they were reduced to two trembling fighters; he from holding her down, and she from the effects of the latest serum being pumped into her. The Intel Officer had come down to check on their 'progress', and the Doctor was intent on proving he was making some.

She was sobbing and cowering and pleading for mercy. In truth, she actually felt groggy and would have loved to just lie down and sleep, but she wanted him to believe the drugs were causing the hysteria. If she copped a so-what attitude now, how high would the dosage be next time? How much shit would he pump into her to really send her into hell? So she whined and begged and writhed around and generally made a crying mess of herself, all the while begging him to please leave her alone.

With a menacing scowl, the Doctor leaned over to her. "You know, Ms Chapin, I would rather hear your pretty lies all day than the pedantic truths of my employers, but the fact is I have a job to do, and I require your cooperation." He moved in closer. "Tell me your secrets, Ms Chapin. It is inevitable. Sooner or later, you will tell me what I want to hear."

Something in his demeanour changed, as if her little performance was doing its job. His voice became feathery and light. Uncharacteristically, he reached out to stroke her tangled hair. From behind his head, Sydney saw the Intel Officer watching intently.

With his back to the camera, The Doctor looked down at her almost kindly, and he wiped the latest tear from her cheek with his thumb. His hand was large and warm. She actually leaned into it, as if seeking his comfort, and a ghost of a smile licked across his lips. His unreadable eyes softened, and he almost looked handsome.

"Let me help you," he soothed. His voice turned mesmeric, as soft as his caresses. "I don't enjoy watching you suffer. I'm not like them; I don't get off on seeing you in pain." He flicked his gaze toward the medicine cabinet. "I have all manner of pleasure-enhancing serums here. One quick jab and you will feel soooo good." He spoke the last words tenderly, almost seductively. "Tell me, something, anything—a word, a code. Anything, and I'll make the pain go away."

"You gave it to me in the first place." *Fuck you, doc. Just fuck you and your porn music voice. It's not working, it's not working... it's...*

He stroked her face, and leaned in for the kill. His eyes were large and green and lined with thick black lashes. "C'mon, Sydney," he crooned in a low, seductive purr. "You want this. Tell me you want this, and I'll give it to you."

She looked into his hopeful eyes and swallowed. "Six, thirteen, twenty-seven, four, twelve; six thirteen, twenty-seven, four, twelve..." Her whisper faded to silence as the numbers filled her head, and took the edge off the fire in her skin, the silk in his voice.

He looked around, as if to remind her that they were both being observed, and they were both failing. *Good. This is one "F" on your report card you earned fair and square, mate.* The Doctor's Barry White routine dropped like a hot potato. He rose to his full height, looking both frustrated and angry.

"You are a spy."

"I would like to contact either the British or the American Embassies." *6, 13, 27, 4, 12.*

"In this cell, you will do as I say."

"Whatever. I would like to contact either the British or the American Embassies." *6, 13, 27, 4, 12...*

"And since you insist on continuing this, you leave me no choice."

He placed his hands on her; one found a breast, while the other slid up her hospital gown to her thigh. Sydney felt her body flush with heat, but could not decide if it was from fear or some sick sort of head-warping arousal bollocks.

"Oh, fuck," she groaned, too freaked to keep her mouth shut.

He stepped back as if she'd pushed him. "Very well, Ms Chapin," he hissed. "Enjoy your afternoon. I will be leaving you in a vast amount of pain. You have only yourself to blame." He turned on his heel and left the room, with the weasel Intel Officer scuttling after him. The door closed with a soft click, followed by the slightly louder sound of the lock sliding in place.

Panting, waiting for the onslaught of the torment which was surely to follow, Sydney tried to breathe normally. When the pain came, it was not nearly as terrible as she had anticipated. This made her dread the next session all the more. He had failed; worse, he had failed in front of the boss. He wouldn't make that mistake again.

And he left her alone for the rest of the day.

That night, Sydney accepted her fate. She did the only thing left. She gave up hope. She had learned long ago that, to be a good agent, you had to believe your own story. Hers was walking into the sunset, toward that big The End.

She would die in the cell, tormented by this calculating, diabolical wielder of syringes. The guards could only harm her body. The Doctor was systematically fucking her head to death.

C'mon, Syd. You've been here before. This is just another blip on the radar, another mind-game. You can do it.

This time, her heart was not having it.

He had won.

The Doctor had observed this particular security guard every night since he'd arrived. The lazy pillock was sloppy, indifferent to his duties, bored, and he obviously hated the night shift. He came on at midnight and was relieved at seven am, and always fell asleep between three and five. You could practically set your watch by the snores.

The Doctor had developed the habit of checking on the prisoner several times during the graveyard shift. He almost always stopped by to speak to the guard, sometimes sharing a snack or cup of coffee with him. The coffee in the monitoring station was always hours old and had an oil slick on it. The guard claimed he needed it strong to keep him awake. There wasn't a coffee bean grown strong enough for that job; this work-shy arse would have needed jumper cables to keep him awake.

That night, the Doctor stopped by around two a.m. "How's our friend? Anything new on the jukebox tonight?" he queried, nodding toward the monitor. In the night-vision light, the prisoner's still form looked strange and ethereal, her long hair spilling over her pillow.

"No. Not a thing," the guard grunted, acknowledging the cup of coffee with a nod. "She's been sleeping since I came on duty. She don't sing no more," he said. There was a trace of wistfulness in his voice.

During the night hours, Sydney often sang to herself. At first, the guards had jeered at her, calling out requests. Since he had ordered the guards to inform him of any change in her behaviour, the Doctor had been told that during the last week, she had stopped singing altogether. On the surface, it seemed a minor change of routine. In reality, it was great cause for concern. When she stopped singing, he was afraid she had stopped being real to herself.

"Asleep, huh?" The Doctor grinned at the guard, and tipped him a leering wink. "Perhaps I might have to wake her up. You know, give her a little something to sing about."

The guard returned the lecherous grin. "Feeling a little... anxious, are we, Doc?" They both laughed.

"Let's just say that I feel a little justified in enjoying myself after hours—and where else am I going to find a little recreation in this monastery?"

"I won't tell if you won't." The guard grinned lewdly, and pointed at the monitor. "But you can't begrudge me having a watch."

"Watch all you want—just remember, it's been awhile for me, so don't critique my endurance."

"Hey, anything's better than the porn they ship in." The guard laughed again and finished the last of his coffee, yawning. "Enjoy yourself. Hell, I'm so sleepy this evening I may miss it all if you don't hurry."

The Doctor walked slowly toward the cell, calculating the amount of time it would take for the guard to start nodding off. It shouldn't take long. A good sandwich and a trip to the toilet usually did it for the pig.

He entered the cell without bothering to be too quiet; he wanted her awake.

The night lights came on with a faint electronic buzz. Sydney's eyes flew open, and she visibly shrank from him. "What do you want?" she whispered hoarsely. She was breathing rapidly; he could see the confusion in her eyes. He never came during the night; by now, any change in her routine brought on mild panic attacks.

He chuckled. "Oh, come now, Ms Chapin, or whoever you are, I think you know by now why I'm here, hmm? Didn't I promise I could make you feel soooo good?" He dialed a note of darkness in his voice, pitched with just enough purr to register as seductive to anyone watching.

When she didn't respond, he continued, 'Surely we can both agree I deserve a little reward for all my hard work on your behalf, don't I?" He roughly caressed her breasts through her hospital gown.

She looked away, accepting the situation without a struggle. He slid his left arm under her shoulders and lowered his head to nuzzle her neck, taking the opportunity to check his wristwatch.

With a heart beating so hard she surely must hear it, he pressed closer, and put his right arm around her waist. She felt as insubstantial as a dandelion.

"Ms Chapin," he whispered urgently in her ear, his lips barely moving, "You are giving up. I can't allow this to happen. I need you to keep fighting."

"I see. Is that what they teach in medical school these days? The beatings will continue until morale improves?"

He forced himself to look her in the eye. "Christ, Sydney. I'm not here for—" He stopped himself in time. "I want you to start living again. I want to help you."

"So you can make me—" She scoffed. "Feel better?"

"I've convinced them to stop raping you because I've told them I want you," he replied, his voice low and urgent. "I'm trying to give you time to heal. For Christ's sake, girl," he added, "sing, rant, scream, masturbate, even—something, anything, to make yourself care again!"

She turned the full battery of her protean eyes on him, and they glittered with the bright, hard gleam of calculation. "Oh, *that* kind of 'feel better'. And what will you give me in return, Doctor?" Her eyes flicked up toward the CCTV camera. "Can you make them leave me alone? Can you keep me alive?"

"I'll make sure no one touches you. I can't stop drugging you, but I can lower the dosage. As for the rest, that's up to you." A long silence stretched between them, full of things neither was quite brave enough to say.

Finally, she sighed. "It's not like I have any control over what you do, Doctor. You don't need my permission to rape me, do you?"

"I'm never going to rape you!" he hissed, sounding as desperate as he felt. "Don't you understand? I'm not like them. I'm not here for that."

"I don't know what game you're playing," she said, and he could hear her frustration. "I can't figure you out."

"Then just stick around until you do, Miss Chapin. That's all I want." He looked into her large, hazel eyes. "Whatever you think of me, know this: I'm not here to kill you." The confusion in her eyes gave him some hope. "Don't give up. I can't keep you alive as long as you're convinced I'm here to kill you. That's the last thing I want."

"Then what exactly *do* you want, Doctor?" she asked.

"To make sure you leave here alive."

As the Doctor walked from his car into the compound that morning, he sensed a change. He could see it in the furtive, worried way the guards looked at him. *They know. Oh, shit, the fuckers know it's today. Jesus, don't be stupid. How could they?*

He had readied everything as much as he could. In a few moments this hell would be over, one way or the other. Nothing had been left to chance. *Then why is everyone looking at me like they're afraid of me?* Close on the heels of that thought was one much more terrifying. *Have I said something, done something to give it away?*

He strode casually through the metal detector, obliquely observing the tense faces and clipped responses from the guards. His dread was a palpable thing, like the taste of heavy metal in the mouth. When no one tried to detain him, he headed toward the stairs to the basement, and froze at the door. From deep within the building he could hear her screaming.

He forced himself to stroll down the steps to the entrance and scan his security pass. When he walked through the door, it was the odours that met him first: the coppery smell of blood, the metallic stench of sweat, and the more corrosive stink of bloodlust.

In the antechamber beside her cell, a naked Sydney was surrounded by a gang of leering, laughing guards. Nylon rope bound her wrists; this was looped over a hook which hung from the ceiling. She had been cranked up, arms overhead, until her feet barely touched the ground.

One eye was swollen shut, and her nose and mouth were bloody. On a nearby table were a pair of pliers and several teeth. Sydney's face was frozen in a rictus of agony. Her gasping, uneven breaths wheezed alarmingly with each exhale, as tears coursed down her dirty cheeks.

While two other guards cheered him on, a huge man the Doctor did not recognize stood behind Sydney. In his hand was a slim, flexible metal rod. Flecks of blood decorated his trousers, his dirty shirt, his face, and the walls of the cell. As the Doctor stood frozen in the doorway, the man drew back the rod, throwing his weight behind it like a cricket bowler. He followed through as if delivering to an open wicket, and the rod sliced through the air with deadly precision toward its soft, vulnerable target.

The shriek torn from Sydney's throat was indescribable.

The Doctor forced his voice to remain impassive. "What's this in honour of?"

The man with the metal rod turned to him with a smile. His teeth were startlingly white; they stood out in stark contrast to his swarthy, blood-spattered face. "Stepping up interrogation." His companions laughed as if it were the funniest thing they'd ever heard.

"Why?" The Doctor ignored Sydney's bleeding form, as if she were of no more consequence than a bug in a pool of gasoline.

He shrugged. "Why not?" He turned back to Sydney, and drew his arm back for the next blow. "Get ready, doll."

Sydney wailed in anticipation. The Doctor caught the man's wrist mid-swing. "For fuck's sake, this is pointless. If you beat her to death, we still won't know anything, you idiot!"

The other men in the room turned their attention to him, their eyes wary and suspicious. One of them sneered, "Getting soft, Doctor? Or are you just keeping her for yourself?"

"It's not like you've left much worth keeping," he spat. "I can't get anything decent out of her half dead, and I won't be able to understand her if you pull the rest of her teeth." He pointed at the guards. "You two. Get her off that hook and put her on the table face down. I'll be back shortly."

For a moment, he thought they would defy him. He fronted them out, until the guard tossed the rod onto the floor, and commanded his resentful comrades to release her. They unceremoniously slung Sydney onto the table. She cried out with every movement; her body shook as if the table were vibrating. Her anguish was a tangible shimmer in the air.

One by one, the men left, until the last guard remained. He picked up the dripping metal rod, and casually wiped the blood onto his trousers. "If I were you, Doc, I'd be a little more careful about who I ordered around," he rumbled. "Or you might just find yourself on the hook next time."

"Get. Out."

The guard waited a beat, then left, slamming the door behind him. The Doctor paused only long enough to lock the cell door, then rushed into the adjoining bathroom.

He barely made it to the toilet before he vomited, heaving until spots swam in his vision. Bathed in sweat and breathing hard, he shakily crawled to his feet. Facing the mirror over the sink, he stared at the white, clammy face for several long, long seconds, loathing what he saw.

I'll make sure no one touches you. He had made that impotent promise less than a week ago.

He splashed cold water over his face several times, until his stomach finally settled, then rinsed his mouth and dried his hands. He quickly tucked his shirt back into his trousers, then left the room looking very much as he had entered it.

Now he could face her.

"This is going to be unpleasant, and I apologize," he said, deliberately forcing his voice to sound flat. She was bleeding profusely; some of the slashes were bone deep. His hands were shaking as he began to treat the worst of the lacerations on her back. He glanced at the clock every few minutes, calculating how much time he had left. *God, what a fuck up. Another twenty-four hours and I could have—*

Sydney's breathing was rapid and shallow. She was past shock now, and he was reduced to praying for them to get a bloody move on. Christ, he needed another pair of hands. He leaned closer to her face. "I notice you aren't counting, Ms Chapin."

Flat on her stomach, Sydney glanced up at him with the one eye that was not beaten shut. What the fuck was he going on about... numbers? The concept of counting spiraled away from her grasp. There was a white-hot, searing wall of pain between her and everything else. Nothing could scale it; he could have poured battery acid over her and it would not have made a difference.

The room was almost completely silent except for a soft plop-plop sound, which Sydney realized was her own blood dripping from the table. The only other sound was her raspy, gasping breaths. That's when it occurred to her. She was dying.

She was grateful.

The Doctor's white coat encroached on her line of sight as he leaned down to inspect the damage. "P-please..." she whispered.

"Why aren't you counting?" he repeated. "There is a place you can go to escape from this. You can't be touched with your numbers. Isn't that right?" His voice held a desperate tone.

She tried to speak, but the effort ate up the last bit of energy she possessed. She huffed, and a bubble of blood swelled in her mouth, then popped.

She had done all she could. Let someone else mop up the mess. She just wanted it to be over. *Sleep. Yeah. Sleep would do it...*

The Doctor shook her by the shoulder. His voice was harsh and loud. "What do the numbers mean, Sydney?"

When she did not respond, his voice rose almost to a shout. "What do the numbers mean? What. Do. The. Numbers. Mean?"

Something in the strident repetition of his tone cleared the fog of her fading mind, and big white letters, like chalk marks on a blackboard, appeared: *6, 13, 27, 4, 12; 6, 13, 27, 4, 12...*

The numbers began flowing from her swollen, bleeding lips again. "Six, thirteen, twenty-seven, four, twelve; six, thirteen, twenty-seven, four, twelve..."

His world narrowed down to the dying woman on the table. He worked desperately to contain the bleeding and stabilise her, but he was past kidding himself. She was in bad shape; as he looked down at her flayed back, the crushing thought zoomed into his brain; *I'm too late. She's not going to make it.* "Come on, Sydney," he whispered under his breath. "Don't give up. Please..."

As he taped large pads of gauze over the wounds, he heard distant thunder. Outside his small, focused world, he heard the sounds morph into the harsh cough of gunfire. It echoed and reverberated within the building, accompanied with the shouts of men. The shouts soon became cries, then screams of panic and agony.

He froze, his mind blank. A loud barrage of machine gun fire shocked him back to reality, and got him on the move again. He grabbed his bag from the counter and retrieved a small black case. Quickly he placed the contents in his breast pocket, his shirt, and his jacket pocket, his eyes never leaving the woman on the table. She was very still.

The noises in the hall were closer now—perhaps ten feet away from the cell door. He could hear the screams of the dying, and the curses of the invaders. He glanced up at the CCTV, and hoped this would be recorded properly, so the right people could see what transpired.

In the bottom of his bag was another, smaller black case. He unzipped it and looked at the contents; one loaded hypo, one empty one. With shaking hands he retrieved the loaded syringe. He took a long slow breath, and when he turned to Sydney and removed the protective cap from the needle, his hands were steady.

She watched his approach: a man walking toward her with a syringe. He pulled back her arm to expose her neck and shoulder to him. "It won't hurt," he whispered. "I *am* sorry."

Realization dawned in her glassy eyes, and the last vestiges of her self-preservation compelled her to pull away from him. She whimpered as he held her down. "Shh," he soothed. "It'll all be over soon. Don't try to fight it."

As the he drove the needle into the padded table beside her shoulder and plunged the contents home, she relaxed almost immediately. The Doctor's knees buckled, and as he leaned against the table for support, the empty syringe fell from his trembling fingers.

He felt a weak tugging at his sleeve, and he looked down at her. Her eyes flickered as she gathered the last of her strength. Then she smiled up at him. Her teeth were red. She took a long, painful last breath. *Thank you*, she mouthed, and her eyelids fluttered.

The door burst open and a male voice shouted, "In here!"

The Doctor looked up at the CCTV screen once more and held out his hands in surrender. A gun fired twice, and red bloomed from his chest and belly. He staggered back from the impact, and as he fell, he looked up in Sydney's face. A tall man in battle dress fatigues and sporting a military-issue AK47 strode into the room. He took careful aim and blew the camera into Humpty-Dumpty status. For a second, the compound was nearly silent as he searched the room for any additional monitoring equipment. Satisfied, he looked down. The Doctor was sprawled out like a fallen scarecrow, one leg slightly raised, as if trying to push himself back onto his feet even in death.

The commander of the Rescue Team sent to invade the compound and spirit away Special Agent Sydney Chapin spoke quietly. "The eyes are gone." He walked over to the prone woman and checked her pulse. "I can barely feel a heartbeat. Can you revive her?"

"Get us somewhere safe and I will."

The man Sydney Chapin knew as "The Doctor" was already checking on his patient even as he rose to his knees. Two large, red roses were spreading steadily across his shirt. The blood bladders, triggered to explode by an electronic remote, had worked perfectly. He ignored the viscous liquid dampening his chest; he was focused solely on Sydney.

Beneath the bruises and the beating, her skin was paper-white and clammy. Her pulse was almost nonexistent. If she was breathing he couldn't see it. Together he and another member of the team prepared her for evacuation. He scooped her extracted teeth into his coat pocket and began hastily checking his supplies.

He was stuffing the last evidence of his existence into a hazmat bag when the door opened again and two men entered, carrying a dead body. They carefully placed it in exactly the same position as he had fallen.

"Raise up his right leg more," the commander said. "It obscured his face from the camera."

As he started a medivac IV, the Doctor glanced at the body. His doppelganger's body looked uncannily like him. He was, however, completely unrecognisable; he had been shot directly in the face.

"Any other evidence that this isn't you is gone-fingerprints wiped, documents falsified," the commander explained. "Everyone who worked with you closely on a daily basis has been eliminated."

The Doctor shrugged; he had no time to ponder how or why this man had been chosen to take his place. At his signal, two men lifted Sydney and carried her between their shoulders like a sack of potatoes. She bounced against them roughly as they headed out at a trot.

"Be careful, for fuck's sake!" The Doctor bellowed. "She's severely wounded." The two men ignored him and kept going.

The commander looked at him with thinly veiled contempt, as if he'd just said the most moronic thing ever uttered. "As far as anyone is concerned, we're recovering a body of a fallen operative. You just concentrate on reviving her, Doc; we'll concentrate on getting you out of here alive." As if the commander felt he needed to explain, he quipped, "Once they're put in motion, you'd be surprised how easy these things go. That is, unless they don't."

Leaving turned out to be the easiest part of the mission. The team experienced minimal involvement, and those who engaged them died quickly and with a minimum of fuss.

Within minutes of leaving the cell, they were in a military mobile medical transport. As the vehicle started to move, Sydney was strapped onto a gurney, transfusions going, ECG monitors hooked up. The commander placed a stethoscope to her chest and listened carefully.

"She's coded."

The Doctor's heart started pounding, as if in sympathy.

As the commander readied a bag valve mask to place over Sydney's mouth and nose, the Doctor began CPR. He turned to the team's second in command. "Get that crash kit fired up now."

The entire squadron looked on silently as the three men worked frantically to resuscitate the woman on the gurney. The Doctor charged the defibrillator and called, "Clear." The other men stepped back as he placed the pads on her chest. The shock brought her body off the table, but there was no response. Her colour was changing from blue to grey.

He swore under his breath, as he continued CPR. Sweat ran into his eyes, but he did not wipe it away. "Come on, Sydney," he muttered. "Breathe for me, girl."

The Doctor applied gel to the pads and charged the defib unit again. "Clear." Again, Sydney's body fishtailed off the gurney. He placed the stethoscope to her heart, praying.

And there it was: a weak, feeble pulse, thready and faint, but there nonetheless. As Sydney took her first, struggling breath, he shuddered with relief.

His role had ended; his real work had begun.

CHAPTER THREE

Recovery

London, England is a sprawling, fascinating city—a perverse metropolis of all the best and worst mankind has achieved in civilisation. The most cataclysmic fire tried to destroy it right down to the banks of the muddy, putrid River Thames. The Great Plague wiped out one-fifth of its population. The most destructive war of the modern age was fought on its doorstep and reduced its streets to rubble. Roman soldiers and Twenty-first century terrorists have tried to bring it to heel, and every time, London has raised its two fingers and sneered at its invaders, "Is that the best you can do?"

It is a city vibrating with life and passion, but beneath its ancient and vivid extravagances, it is furtive, mysterious and austere. Tunnels, waterways and buildings run under the skin of London; the veins and arteries of this great beast bringing life to its vital organs. Each has its part to play in London's rude health; each has its own rich malleability. For every museum, point of interest, monument and artifact that London affords its visitors, there are twenty the average tourist will never see and the most ardent Londonphile has never even heard of.

Underneath Narrow Street, just south of Limehouse, is one such structure. Topside stands a nondescript building reported to house a minor insurance company, but its true purpose is revealed on a strictly need-to-know basis. It is an organisation whose origins began in the murkiest depths of MI6, and flourished to become one of the most well-oiled and respected institutions of its kind. It is known simply as The Agency, and most of River House's inhabitants are not even aware of its existence.

Twenty feet below this building, Senior Principal Inigo Lightoller strode briskly toward the Maximum Security Wing of the Agency Hospital, nodding curtly to those he passed. At fifty-eight, he was the Agency's youngest Senior Prin. He had Priority Clearance with the Prime Minister, the heads of state of most of the world's superpowers, and the Pope himself. He once quipped he could probably gain a private audience with God, should he need some ecclesiastical intelligence, oxymoron that it was.

He had been recruited almost directly out of Cambridge at the ripe old age of twenty-two, lured by his illustrious predecessor with promises of international intrigue, Ian Fleming-tinged adventure, and political manipulation. He had not been able to pass up such a tempting smorgasbord, and he liked to think in return he had given the Agency the best of himself. He had certainly given it the most of himself.

Inigo's rise in the ranks had been steady, if not stellar; he had never been an endorphin junkie like the majority of the juiced-up agents under his command. Instead, he had the gift of diplomacy and negotiation, making him the perfect buffer between the hotheads he supervised, the political snakes at River House, and the limp-wristed nobility within Her Majesty's government.

The combination of posh accent and preposterous name caused him a lot of grief around his working-class subordinates. At least he knew the cheeky bastards who answered to him weren't imitating him behind his back; the buggers did it right to his face.

From his immaculate iron-grey Gieves & Hawkes suit to his crisp dress shirt and club tie, Inigo was, even to his mind, a bit of a walking cliché. The part in his light brown hair was ruler straight; his blue eyes and square jaw remarkable only to his devoted, doting wife. He weighed the same twelve stone as when he played for the Cambridge University Cricket Club. He still bowled in the occasional friendly on those Sundays he wasn't working; in other words, less and less as the years went by and his position in the Agency rose.

He rounded the corner toward the ICU and picked up the pace of his stride. He stomach was churning from worry, as it had been ever since the previous night, when one of his best agents had been brought in from the field fighting for her life. It was not the first time he had entered this building to check on an injured operative, but it was one of the few times he was afraid of what he might find. As Sydney Chapin's immediate superior, Inigo was required to be concerned, but detached. As a friend, he was finding it difficult to keep his professional disconnect.

The Met Police had a saying when something unfortunate happened to one of their own: *If you can't take a joke, you shouldn't a joined.* He used to think it a very callous thing to say; a bit hard cheese all round. But as the years passed, he learned to appreciate the gallows humour of it. You recited that little ditty when the bad things happened, because when you did not, you froze, and that did not help anyone.

Sydney was good undercover, but it was not her forte. She was a proactive operative, one of his two best, along with her partner Garnet Pinkerton. But she had wanted the assignment, wanted to prove that she was more than just a button man, an attack-and-defend soldier. And she had been the best person for the job, full stop.

Sending Sydney on the mission had been the right thing to do; that she had been rumbled had not been her fault. Her cover had been flawless; she had cultivated it for months before going underground. Once in, she had been so deep, he had to dig to China to get any message to her at all. The fact that she had been incarcerated and tortured for the better part of two months was, as anyone in Inigo's position knew, a sickening occupational hazard.

His mobile chimed. He pulled the phone out of his breast pocket and checked his incoming messages. As receptors coded and decoded the message through twelve of the twenty-four random scramblers, ensuring the text could not be traced either at source or destination, he fervently hoped the message was from Garnet.

Dear Basil, the text began. Inigo rolled his eyes. After those silly Austin Powers films came out, Garnet had dubbed Inigo 'Basil Exposition.' Like all irritating nicknames, it had instantly and permanently stuck. *If you can't take a joke, you shouldn'ta joined.*

At that precise moment, Inigo did not mind—the impudent greeting meant Garnet was delivering good news.

Minor infestation eliminated. Your Friendly Neighbourhood Pest Control.

Inigo pocketed his phone with grim satisfaction. Garnet had taken Sydney's incarceration hard, and Inigo had been only too happy to let loose the dogs of war the moment she was safely back on British soil. The mole who had sold out Sydney Chapin was now part of the foundations of a new car park in Canary Wharf; such was the price one paid for shitting on one's own doorstep.

He knocked on Dr Gar's office door, then entered without waiting for an answer. Gar looked up with eyes that were still haunted and frayed around the edges. When he left England, his hair had been bleached white. Now, returned to its original dark brown, it threw into prominence a haggard face, gray with fatigue.

Inigo had a lot of time for Dahlra Gar. They had much in common; both were from upper-middle-class English families of good stock, in spite of their unusual Christian names. Both had attended Cambridge; both had excelled in their respective careers in the Agency.

Like Sydney, Gar had not really been the right person for the mission, but he had made up for his shortcomings with a determination to succeed. Inigo had been reticent at first, but the fact that Gar had completed the mission successfully made Inigo inclined to be charitable. He had shown remarkable dedication and skill as a physician, but he had made the amateur's mistake of becoming too emotionally involved, and that had almost cost them everything.

They shook hands and settled into the uncomfortable chairs. "Dr Gar, give me some good news. How is she?"

Dahlra Gar leaned his elbows on his desk and propped his chin on steepled fingers. He looked more tired than any man Inigo had seen this side of alive. "Critical, but fighting." He sounded ground down to powder; even his rich voice was threadbare. "I don't know how she's alive, but she's hanging on."

Inigo awarded the doctor a gritty smile of pride. "We'll talk about her condition later." There would be time for back-slapping and high-fiving once he had gotten what he came for. "Sorry to sound so cold-bloodied, old chap, but I need to know when we can access the information."

Dr Gar recoiled slightly. "Principal Lightoller, she's not a machine. Right now, the woman is hanging on by a thread. The only thing we can access is her vitals, and they aren't stable." Gar shifted uncomfortably in his seat, resentful for having to justify himself. "She coded twice on the trip back home—"

"Coded?"

"Her vitals crashed and she had to be resuscitated. She's in a drug-induced coma right now because the pain could be enough to send her back into cardiac arrest. She was nearly beaten to death! She has bone-deep lacerations on her back. She's had several teeth removed. Cracked ribs; both shoulders were dislocated. Aside from the blood loss and the individual injuries, there's the psychological trauma, not to mention—"

Inigo put up his hand to stop the lecture. "With all due respect, I'm not interested in your redemption, Doctor. Now give me the earliest estimate when her memories can be accessed. I need that information yesterday." He stood, his elevated position providing enough intimidation factor to get his point across. "Bring her to the surface, Doctor. You have every right to take a few days to catch your breath, but time is something I do not have. It won't take long to get what we need to know. After that, she can rest as much as required."

Gar stood up, towering over Inigo by a good several inches. His bright green eyes burned from behind the dark frames of his spectacles. "So, at the end of the day," he said, his voice cold and edgy, "you don't give a shit if she survives or not, as long as you get your precious information."

Inigo waited a beat before replying. "Let us get something straight right here and now, Doctor," he said, his voice as low and as quietly dangerous as Gar's. "I could have sent you into the compound to get the information and left her there. I could have sent in another agent and written her off as a lost cause the day she got captured. Instead, I sent you in to keep her alive and bring her back home so we could put her back together."

Gar tried to speak, but Inigo preempted his argument. "This was why she went there in the first place, Dahlra—to gather intelligence. If she could speak right now, she'd tell you exactly what I'm telling you: if she dies without imparting the information, all would be for naught."

Almost kindly, Inigo continued, "Of course it sounds heartless, but the bottom line is that she came out with important, far-reaching intelligence, and she would want you to dig it out of her, even at the risk of her life. So yes, I want that information; and if she doesn't make it, we can at least live with the knowledge she gave her life to ensure she made a difference."

He could see the emotions warring in Gar's face; protectiveness, proprietary respect. Inigo felt sorry for the man. After all, he, too, had suffered for what he had done; Inigo supposed the doctor could be forgiven for wanting to safeguard his patient – and expunge his own guilt.

"And in case you think it's all pounds, shillings and pence with me, Doctor, I'll tell you this for free: she's not just one of my best agents. She's also a friend, and in this business," Inigo paused, and allowed a rare glimmer of emotion to leak into his voice, "friends are as rare as rocking horse shit."

Gar sat slowly back in his chair and scrubbed his face, as if trying to force some mental *Control-Alt-Delete* to bring his flagging energy and resolve back online. "Give me twenty-four hours to bring her out of sedation. I'll do as much as I can, then I must insist we concentrate on healing her. Information or not, she deserves at least that much from me."

"That's fair enough. Thank you."

Gar smiled, and the ravaged eyes gleamed. "She was amazing, Inigo. I don't know how she did it. I've never known so much strength in one person."

"Oh, she's one in a million. Always has been. She'll be well compensated for this." He paused and gave Gar a pointed look. "And so will you."

"Thank you, Inigo," he said, his voice trembling with exhaustion and relief. Inigo thought, *oh, for fuck's sake, man, don't cry. You'll get me going, and then I'll have to kill you.*

He reached over the desk and shook Gar's hand. "I'd like to see her now." The Doctor bristled, and Inigo added testily, "Just to check on her, man!"

With a resigned sigh, Gar stood and led Inigo back into the hall. They paused at a closed door. "I'm not going to soft-soap it," Gar said quietly. "I've seen injuries like this throughout my career, but never on a living patient."

Inigo pushed open the door, and the sensors kicked on the overhead lights. The room was filled with monitors, each graphing a different component of Sydney's progress. Inigo focused his attention on the tiny figure lying in the hospital bed. He had to force himself to walk toward it. He had been prepared for... something. This was not it.

Sydney's breathing was quiet; her chest barely rose and fell. An oxygen machine hissed in a steady rhythm; an ECG showed the slow but consistent spikes that recorded her heartbeat. Her face was so swollen and bruised it was hard to believe this was the woman he knew. Three different IVs were pumping Christ knew what through tubes attached to her fine-boned, bruised hands. She was at least two stone lighter than when she left England.

Inigo was not a praying man, but if he had been, he would have asked for her to open her hazel eyes, just to make sure she was still in there. It was almost impossible to equate this pitiful, gaunt creature with the gutsy, wise-cracking woman who teased him about the dullness of cricket, who loved meeting his wife for overlong lunches she glibly charged to the agency, who could drill a twenty pence coin with a Glock 17 and give you 5p in change.

I should never have sent her. She should not have taken this punishment for my bad judgement. Inigo turned away. "You did everything you could under the circumstances, old man," he muttered aloud.

"Thank you, but it wasn't enough," Gar said, his voice rusty with remorse.

Inigo turned on his heel and left the room without another word. He did not have the heart to tell Dahlra Gar he had not been talking to him.

A quiet, insistent humming, like the sound of a distant lawnmower, brought Sydney to the edge of awareness. Groggily, she tried to open her eyes, but a nuclear sun blazed an inch from her nose, and she feebly tried to turn away from the piercing light. Her sludgy brain was having none of it. The droning sound became a disembodied voice. She wished it would shut up; it was annoying and she wanted to go back to sleep.

The voice grew in volume until it sound inches away from her ear. "Tone down the overheads." Almost immediately, the sun receded, but the persistent voice kept nagging her.

"Sydney, open your eyes. You are safe. You are in England, in the Agency hospital. You are safe. Open your eyes."

She moaned, wishing she had the energy to bat the voice away. Instead, it grew more insistent.

"Sydney, open your eyes and look at me."

Finally, to shut it up, Sydney tried to open her eyes, but her lids were weighed down with cinder blocks. She struggled a little harder, trying to make her leaden body move, but it was encased in amber, solid and unmovable.

The voice spoke again. It was familiar, comforting, and gradually the sounds Sydney heard started to make sense. It was the numbered patterns of total recall. Like a bobber rising through water, Sydney floated upward, her body and mind breaking the surface of consciousness. Another, less welcome bedfellow joined her—pain, jagged and deep, like broken glass sewn beneath her skin.

"Sydney, don't fight the numbers. Let them guide you."

"Hurts," she croaked, through cracked and swollen lips. The effort it took to say that one word exhausted her.

"I know," the voice soothed. "Five, two, nine, seventeen, three, six...Motorcycle, Oracle, Gymnasium, Roquefort, Landslide, Prosecute..."

For what seemed hours, numbers and words slipped and slid into her consciousness and she heard her voice answering. It sounded far away, like it was coming from a crappy 1970's transistor radio, scratchy and indistinct and having little to actually do with her...

Floating somewhere above, where the pain hadn't taken such a foothold, she heard herself droning away, like Jacob Marley on the piss: "Six points. London, Seoul, Beijing, Damascus, Washington, Beirut. Code names Snow, Maple, Oscar, Phonograph, Fortify and Cabernet..."

Video cameras and DAT tapes silently recorded Sydney's recall of detail after detail. Names, dates, weaponry, manpower, finances, and strategies. Everything was there - hard-wired into her brain by the mnemonics and hypnosis, and she repeated it back verbatim. For what seemed like days, she heard a voice urging her to stay alert, and when she was done she could once again sink back down into the beckoning darkness.

Conversely, the more she talked, the more alert she became. It was like holding down the reverse button on the past few months of her life. The recall started from the moment she awoke, then went back to her capture and confinement, then back to getting the information. It rolled her back to the embarkation point, her day of deployment, and beyond.

And that was when total recall meshed together into the big picture—the day she was programmed, when she had lain prone on the table and allowed a disembodied voice to fill her head with mnemonics, triggers, codes and alpha-numeric strings. The voice that brought her to this agony-upholstered surface was the same voice which instructed her to regurgitate all she had learned. It was the same voice that had planted the codes in the first place.

It was the same voice of the Doctor who had come to her in her cell. Doctor Dahlra Gar.

Five days later, an IV line containing her pain meds became blocked, and before anyone noticed or could clear it, Sydney awoke in disorientated agony, like a fist in boiling oil. The pain hit her from all angles, inside and out, top to bottom, sending her system into a tail-spin that lit up the vitals monitors like Chinese New Year. Her own shout shattered the lovely veil of unconsciousness, clearing her vision, and she saw a blue-clad figure, a nurse running from the room. There were excited voices beyond the wall.

She had always thought her pain tolerance was high; wrong-o. Anything she had experienced up to that point had been no more irritating than a spider bite. Then some pitying soul hit the switch again, and out went the lights. Sydney thankfully crashed back into unconsciousness, just as a man rushed into the room, hoarsely calling her name...

The next time Sydney woke, she was drowning in an acid bath of agony. It radiated inside her body and around the surface of her skin, and she could barely catch her breath against its onslaught. Someone was holding her over a fire, and her back was being burnt to a crisp; she could almost smell burning flesh.

The pain destroyed her mentally as well as physically, carving into her until she was reduced to a weeping bag of misery. She wanted to deal with it, ride it out, but this was a kind of damage that she simply could not climb on top of.

A gentle voice washed over her, trying to soothe her. It was beautiful, low, and sweet; an angel's voice. It reached out and blanketed over all the hard, jagged points of pain, and smoothed them.

When Sydney sobbed in misery, the voice answered with a tender, melancholy cadence that eased her. In her wretched state, she sought out the source of the voice, and a warm, gentle hand stroked her palm, the one place that didn't hurt. The hand was like the voice, and in her anguish, she grasped for it, desperate for it to take some of this crushing despair away.

Over and over, she surfaced, then sank back down into unconsciousness again. Caught in a net of nightmares from which she could not escape, she dreamt of pawing hands holding her down while men did unspeakable things to her. She saw a white-haired man looming over her, touching her, seducing her. Numbers and words and codes jumbled in her mind until they became a meaningless, useless tangle of sounds and visions.

Cool water bathed her face, and tender hands held her head upright and moistened her lips and gums with cubes of ice. Comfort was a pair of deep green eyes, dark hair, and a soft voice, encouraging and coaxing her to rest and heal. That voice was both a balm and a weapon; it soothed even as it rasped against her like sandpaper. It called to mind strong fingers dragging over her scalp, a soft caress, a command...

What seemed like a lifetime later, Sydney opened her eyes and thought she might be able to stay awake and focused. She felt hideous; there was not a part of her body did not have its own separate pain squad working overtime.

The change from sleeping to waking state must have triggered a silent alarm, because a huge black male nurse appeared, dwarfing the doorway. Sydney looked up in awe at the mountain of a man and slurred, "Am I going to live?"

His stern face transformed into a glorious, beaming sun, his perfectly straight, white teeth wreathed in a smile. "Yes, you are, Miss Chapin, and a lotta people gonna be happy about it," he answered, his lilting Jamaican accent as deep and rich as dark rum. His smile softened, and he put a large hand on her arm. "A lotta prayers have been answered. You made us believe in miracles."

Sydney looked at the man, and felt something shift within. The herculean effort to keep herself in control slipped, and the man's kindness undid her. Relief that she was home and safe was so sweet, her emotions rose up like bubbles in water. She was alive.

"I thought I was going to die," she tried to say, but her jaw felt as if it were unhinged, swinging free from the muscles of her face. The nurse touched her shoulder with astounding gentleness, and pressed a tissue into her hands. She mopped at her face, trying to calm down.

"You're going to be alright, Miss Chapin." Sydney looked up into his somber face. "I'm not gonna lie; if that doctor of yours hadn't been here, well, let's just say we might not be having this conversation, if you know what I mean..."

His voice drifted away, and she was asleep again before she knew she had closed her eyes.

The next time she awoke, it was a more natural transition from true sleep to lucidity, and she finally felt able to take stock of her situation. She was in a hospital gown, of course. This one was soft and clean, and she noted with a strange sense of amusement it had little flowers on it.

IVs snaked down from metal hooks into tubes taped to the backs of both hands. She could feel sticky, clammy ECG pads on her shoulders, chest and beneath her left breast. She had a sneaking suspicion she was hooked up to a colostomy bag, which was a whole other reason to be cheerful. Monitors behind her head were making soft humming, beeping and hissing noises.

She felt almost human, though the idea of getting vertical seemed a little beyond her. The pain had leveled off, from the *to-hell-with-this-kill-me-now* stage to the *please-will-you-anesthetise-me-until-this-is-over* plateau, and she thought this might be the beginning of actual recovery. With that thought, she allowed herself to review the events that had brought her to this moment. She thought about her last mind-bending moments in the cell before losing consciousness. Christ, she had been beaten all to hell. They'd done unspeakable things, oh God, they'd—

She took a steadying breath. She was not there now, and ramping up into a full-blown panic attack was useless as well as pointless. She was realistic enough to know the kind of trauma she had experienced would not go away overnight, but she could deal with that. She would not crumple under the weight of it. She convinced herself she would rise above it. She had a job to do; she would get herself healed up, spend some quality time with the Agency counselor to keep the PTSD demons at bay, and get back in the saddle as soon as they sounded the all clear. Because that is what you did in this job; you just got on with it. Like Garnet was fond of saying, *if you can't take a joke, you shouldn'ta joined...*

The door opened and the familiar figure of Inigo Lightoller sauntered into the room. For a moment, Sydney was so pleased to see him she felt the wimpy tears threaten again. He came to her bedside and took one of her hands.

"Sydney, my dear, you have no idea how happy I am you're back in the land of the living. I know you're in a right spot of pain, old girl, but can you stand to talk?" He gave her a genuine smile, not the counterfeit version he kept reserved for his trips to Parliament.

Sydney tried to speak, but her tongue felt three feet thick. "Wha' th' f—"

"Several of your teeth were pulled by your captors, and they had to be reset. You also have a hairline crack on the left side of your jaw, but according to Dr Gar that should heal on its own as long as don't put too much strain on it. Before you know it, you'll be right as the jolly old."

Dr Gar? She thought, frowning. Why do I know that name? What did...? Sydney's eyes widened. Oh. *Yes, that had been a right little leg pull, hadn't it?* It was one thing to know she had endured two months of torture; it was quite another to have the reset button reveal that the same Doctor who had tormented her in her cell was an Agency ringer she had been programmed to forget. The odds were unlikely that she would forget him now. By her way of reckoning, his groin had a date with her knee in the not-too-distant future.

After swishing her mouth several times with water from a pitcher on her bedside cabinet, Sydney felt a little more human. She ran her numbed tongue over her teeth with a grimace; her mouth felt like the Carlsbad Caverns, all stumpy tines and stalactites.

"Where is he?" Her voice sounded hollow, moving through the numbed-out hanger of her mouth.

Inigo's pally facade faded in the shadow of her resentful anger. "I know you aren't too happy about this, but there are a few things you need to understand before you go off half-cocked."

"He is going to be the one half—"

"Now see, this is what I mean, Sydney. Listen to me. Christ, you're as bad as he is." Inigo met her resentment with as solemn a look as she had ever seen him wear. "I'm going to be completely honest with you."

"I'm listening." Normally with Inigo it was two parts crap and one part bollocks. Heaven forbid he would volunteer anything substantial. It must be important, then.

He looked down at his immaculate nails. "There are a few things you must understand, Sydney. When we found out that you had been incarcerated, the word was that you were being tortured. We scrambled to put together a rescue operation, but we knew that would take time to coordinate in a way that would keep them off our backs. Even if we could get you out alive, they would either go underground or set off a political chain letter that we'd never get under control."

Sydney nodded. It was pretty much the same thing she had surmised. Mollified, Inigo continued, "In the interim, we knew it would be a matter of time before they cut their losses with you, and I refused to entertain that scenario. Then, we received extremely X4 intel that they were considering bringing on board a person or persons who specialised in more aggressive interrogation techniques. The kind that just might be able to break through your programming. That's when I decided the best thing to do would be—"

"Send in your own."

"Yes. The plan was to send in an operative posing as an Interrogation Expert working for our friends in South America. Gar was chosen for the assignment. We got him in after a month of intense infiltration.

"The problem was, for some reason, your captors were suspicious from the off. We discovered that the same mole who rumbled you was trickle-feeding poison about Gar. Not enough to completely wreck his integrity; too much information would have been traced back to the mole himself, and we'd have caught him sooner, more's the pity.

"But it was enough to make them wary. Gar was watched carefully twenty-four seven. Your cell, his study, even his quarters, were all wired for sight and sound. He was already viewed with suspicion. And don't forget; he was going in with a lot of knowledge that could have meant his own destruction. One wrong move, and he'd be the one strapped to the table.

"And before you ask, yes, his directive was to keep you alive at all costs, my dear. At all costs. I have his documented affidavits of every moment he spent with you. And no, it doesn't make for pleasant reading, but in not one way did he deviate from his objective."

Sydney had to grudgingly admit that it had been a nervy thing to do. Anyone sent in undercover would be even more vulnerable than her. He would not have the codes to hide behind if he was interrogated. Breaking him would have confirmed her as a spy, which would in turn have destroyed years of intelligence work; it would have caused an international incident and scandal to the Agency. In the grand scheme of world events, it was a very small situation with huge ramifications, had it gone tits up.

"As it was," Inigo was saying, "he went into this knowing it was essentially a suicide mission. He was told going in that if you didn't survive, he was on his own. He carried potassium chloride with him at all times."

"How did you get us out?"

"Bait and switch. We set up all the false information before Gar put one foot into the country. Fingerprints, voice IDs, retina scans. All faked. And let's face it; capturing you was probably the only intelligent thing those idiots were capable of doing. Nothing got checked; most of our covert work was overkill, in the end. I will admit, it took longer than we'd planned to infiltrate, because of the damage done by the mole. We had to keep Gar's cover clean, and that slowed us down.

"In the end, the monitor in your cell captured it all; well, all of the parts we wanted them to see. After we got you out of the country, their mop-up operation found the Doctor's mutilated body, or at least someone who looked like him, in the burned out ruins of the hospital."

Sydney had a brief recollection of seeing a figure lying sprawled on the floor, great roses of blood blossoming on his chest and stomach.

Inigo went on. "CCTV footage showed their operative The Doctor inject you with a hypo shortly before he was killed. The syringe found at the site contained potassium chloride, so as far as our friends are concerned, you're both dead as a very dead thing."

Sydney felt her body temperature plummet by about ten degrees. "You actually... saw the footage?"

"Yes. It has been analysed, and preserved as evidence. And that, my dear, is as A1 as they come." He waved his hand dismissively. "The last thing their organisation wants is Amnesty International breathing down their necks. Well, what's left of their organisation. We didn't leave all that much behind for the government to bury."

He smiled. "Don't worry, old thing. Only we know what happened after the CCTV cameras were destroyed. And every single man who laid a finger on you there is dead."

"Not every single one."

"Sydney, everything he did was under my orders. I won't apologise for that, and neither should he. And, if it makes you feel better, it nearly killed him. He arrived back here looking in worse shape than you."

"You can cry me a river."

Inigo pulled up a chair and made himself comfortable. "You yourself have done some fruity things in the name of this Agency, old horse. Just remember that."

Sydney could not argue with him. She had performed interrogations that made her feel so dirty no shower or bath could clean her for days afterward. She had inflicted her share of pain, played her mind games. But something about the doctor's behaviour struck her as different. She could not put her finger on it, but it felt somehow... personal. It was not just an operative following some less-than-lily-white objective.

Inigo allowed her a few moments alone with her dark thoughts, and patted her hand. "No point in remunerating, Sydney. Right now, you've got a bigger job. We need to concentrate on getting you back on your feet."

"Inigo? Did I...did you get what you needed?"

His smile looked oddly feral in that cultured, well-manscaped face. "Of course. It was as we suspected all along: the organisation was never anything more than a red herring. While they were busy trying to convince a certain country in Southeast Asia to bankroll their group to buy weapons and enriched plutonium, they were actually laundering cash in exchange for processing facilities and extra firepower for the drugs they were producing.

"Turns out they were a splinter group sanctioned by their own government, who was in turn slipping a few billion on the side as well to keep the lawyers, guns and money safe in Asia and the drug money safely inside their country. Except the money was actually going into bank accounts in Switzerland under assumed names, and no one was really getting paid but the splinter group—and Silverbirch, of course."

"All this plate juggling reminds me of the Generation Game."

"Indeed," he said, returning her smile. "Top drawer intel gathering, old girl. We sent that information down a corridor so sterile it still smelled of bleach when it reached Interpol."

Inigo preened and continued, "They contacted not only our sister agencies in the targeted areas, but us as well. The X4 info was distributed in so many pieces you'd have thought we found our bit on the back of a cereal box. No one was the wiser as where the information came from. It didn't take long for the status to change to A1, and seeing as everyone in the compound present on the day you were rescued is dead, including you, we simply sat back and congratulated Interpol for being so clever."

Sydney nodded, relieved. She had done it. It had been worth it. It had been so long since she had felt genuine happiness, it was a little hard not to feel overwhelmed by it. She saw his pride in her, and she swallowed hard, determined not to make a complete braying jackass out of herself.

"I'm sure you realise the work you did on this mission hasn't gone unnoticed by our superiors, Sydney," Inigo said, soberly. "To start, you've been given two year's full paid leave of absence."

"Two years? Why so much?"

He smiled. "Think of it as danger money."

"I'm sure I don't need that long to recover." She would go barmy sitting around for two years doing rock-all.

He fixed a baleful eye on her. "Yes, you do. I don't have to remind you that, at this juncture, you are believed missing, presumed dead. Your holiday gives us a little breathing room as well."

Sydney let this sink in before asking the one question he had not answered. "Was it enough to implicate Silverbirch?"

Some of Inigo's smug self-satisfaction faded. "I'm afraid our friends at Silverbirch did their own sterilising. It seems they learned a great deal from their past mistakes. We couldn't tie them to this."

The impact of his words hit Sydney like a physical blow. "Then it was for nothing. The cell, the intel, the Doctor, it was for nothing!"

"Calm yourself," Inigo insisted, and put a firm hand on her shoulder. "You don't want half this hospital in here, do you?"

"But Silverbirch—"

"Silverbirch will still be there, old girl. They're recruiting in the UK. Many of its top men remember you from the old days. Give us some time to get them back under heel."

"We can get them. Just let me—"

"No." He fixed her with a look none of his agents wanted to receive. "You don't want to quote chapter and verse to me about Silverbirch, Agent Chapin. And I wouldn't like to think you need reminding just how badly I want them taken down, either. You will put it behind you until I tell you otherwise. That's an order."

Sydney tried to front him out, but he had her dead to rights. Finally she lay back on her pillow; her bitterness cost too much energy.

Every agent she had ever known spoke wistfully about 'the one that got away'. The hard bastard who got off on a technicality, the intelligence that fell through due to one shoddy piece of investigation, the grimly-fought case that had to be abandoned because of political or personal flack. Silverbirch had been all those things to her. It had been the main reason she had taken this doomed assignment in the first place.

She was not happy with the situation, but she accepted it. She was not exactly in any hurry to raise her head above the parapet anyway. But dammit, two years—after six months of garden leave she'd be back here in the hospital, drooling over her porridge oats and keeping all her crayons inside the lines. She blew out her breath. Well, someone had to attend those macramé classes—

"Now that you've calmed down, I have some other, more pleasant news for you." Inigo's frosty glower melted into a faux now-play-nicely smile. "It is my profound pleasure to inform you that your performance in the field has merited a special commendation from the Queen. You'll be receiving an OBE, my dear. I use mine as a paperweight, but that's a story for another time."

She must have looked as gobsmacked as she felt. Chuckling, Inigo continued, "Additionally, in light of said performance, you have been promoted to the equivalent of Principal, with pending Minder Status."

It took Sydney a moment to parse his statement. Minder Status. Only Agency royalty were eligible for a Minder. It was the equivalent of handing out your own flipping commendations.

"I assume your reaction is one of stunned joy and happiness," he said. "You should be honoured. The first female agent in our history to qualify."

"Well, hell," Sydney said. "Commendation I pretty much counted on, but Minder status? I mean, the ones who have one don't even talk about them. I've heard the stories, of course, but..."

"Minders are a special class of government envoy, specifically trained to provide for all of the needs of the agents to which they are assigned. Only agents who have attained the highest level of security clearance and have exemplary performance records are granted Minders. You, old thing, have the Triple Crown—seniority, performance and commendation." The wording had that Mission Statement, boiler-plate feel about it, the corporate doublespeak that used a lot of words to say very little.

"Okay, but what does having a Minder entail?" she insisted. "What exactly are they supposed to accomplish?"

"Everything." Inigo looked a little abashed, as if he sensed he was treading into slightly murky waters. "A Minder is responsible for meeting all of the emotional, practical and physical needs of their charge. All needs," he finished, his voice neutral, but a slight smile on his face.

Sydney frowned. "I don't know if I want one."

"And how would you know? You didn't even know what they did thirty seconds ago."

"I'm a big girl. I can take care of myself."

"No one knows that better than I, Sydney. It's not a matter of saying you aren't capable of looking after yourself, it's saying you can now have access to a companion who can take care of your household. Minders are major domos. They are there to make your life easier."

They looked at one another for a long time. Inigo broke first. He brushed a minute speck of lint from his immaculate trousers. It was a tell he always used when avoiding an answer. "Well, it's not something that we have to pin down right now. Minder candidates go through a rigorous vetting and matching procedure. You can rest assured that your Minder will be so compatible to you that you'll soon wonder how you did without him."

"'Him'?" she echoed. "You mean you already know who it is?"

"No," he replied instantly. "Figure of speech."

Lying toff. She sighed tiredly, wishing her pain meds would kick in. "So, when do I get to pick out my Minder?"

Inigo glanced at his wristwatch, another sign he was being deliberately obtuse. "Look. We can discuss this in greater detail at another time, Sydney, but to be perfectly honest, I'm knackered. It was almost one o'clock in the morning when I left work yesterday, and if I don't get home tonight Pip's going to start believing I really do have a bit on the side." He patted her shoulder again. "Besides, you're tired, I can tell. We'll talk more about all this later, I promise. In the meantime, you need to rest and recover."

"How long have I been out of touch?"

"Almost three weeks. Today was the first real day you've been compos mentis, so I asked Dr Gar if you were up for a little company."

Something tightened in her chest at the mention of the Doctor. "Look, Inigo, I understand him a little better now, but I really don't want anything to do with that smug git."

His smile faded. "Sydney, he's your personal physician. Please try to understand—"

"Then replace him. Please," she added, her tone edging toward stubbornness.

He shook his head. "He cares very much for you, regardless of how you feel."

"So what?"

When he refused to take the bait, she admitted, "The truth of it is, I don't know if I can get past what he did to me."

"I must ask you to try, Sydney. He's worked very hard on your behalf to ensure your survival. If he had shown one speck of weakness, they would have killed him. And he knew that if he died, so would you. You can believe me when I say he took no pleasure in any of it. If he had, I'd have gladly let Garnet turn his intestines into a hammock."

At the mention of her partner, Sydney brightened. "How is Garnet?"

Inigo snorted. "The same as always, the objectionable, irritating toe-rag. Still treating me with a distinct lack of respect for my station."

"So, business as usual, then?" In spite of his penchant for getting up Inigo's nose, Garnet Pinkerton was one of the Agency's finest. After fifteen years as his partner, Sydney trusted Garnet with her life.

"He sends his love. He's been waiting for the all clear for visitation."

"Tell him I've got the all clear."

"That's Dr Gar's call."

"It's my call," Sydney insisted.

Inigo pressed his lips together in a thin line. "Sydney, I must ask you to please not fight me on this. Dr Gar is being protective of you for a very good reason. I don't think the man has gotten six hours of sleep since you returned home; he has spent day and night at your side. Your health and recovery is paramount to him, and he's committed to seeing that through until you are well enough to walk out of here." His expression relaxed a little. "He's done a great service to you and the Agency. We, and you, owe him your life."

He was right, of course, but so was she. And so was Gar, though it irritated the hell out of her to admit it. With a note of warning in her voice, she replied, "You're asking a lot, Inigo."

"I know. Think of it as his way of atoning. You need to find it in your heart to forgive him. He wants that as much as he wants to see you back in one hundred-percent form."

"I'll try. For you. I can't promise I'll succeed, but I'll try."

"Good chap." He beamed as if the subject was decided. "Now, you look as if you are flagging, and I know I am, so I'll go now and let you rest."

Sydney had long since passed from flagging and was moving deeply into full-on whipped territory. It was unnerving to think that a simple conversation would deplete her so much. Inigo's news notwithstanding, she was simply tired of trying to talk around the numbness in her mouth. "Thank you for stopping by, Inigo. It's good to see you. And thanks for the information. I'll think about it." She looked up at her Senior Principal; her mentor, her friend. "Thank you for bringing me home."

"Dr Gar brought you home, Sydney."

"You know what I mean," she huffed.

To her surprise, Inigo leaned over and kissed her cheek. For a brief moment, their eyes met, and Sydney could see the emotion in his shrewd, blue eyes. "I don't have the words, old girl. And besides, Pip would have never forgiven me if you hadn't come home in time for her next party."

As he turned to leave, she called out, "Inigo?"

"Yes?"

"You said something a moment ago about Gar coming forward for the mission."

"I did." His voice carried an undertone of wariness.

"Why would he do that? I mean, I understand how dangerous it was." She shook her head. "Why would he volunteer? More than that, why would you trust a civilian with such a dangerous mission?"

An odd, almost crafty look crossed Inigo's face. "Why don't you ask *him*?"

CHAPTER FOUR

Discoveries

Sydney sat up in bed, waiting in silent dread for another unwelcome dressing change. As her down time had decreased back to normal sleeping hours and her body had gradually come back online, the separate aches and pains setting up camp over her body ebbed and flowed, but one constant remained. Her back, which had been shredded like cheese during that last, awful beating, took up most of her misery quota.

The healing process was frustratingly slow, but as her favorite nurse Brody had explained, she was lucky to have any skin left. Because of the scale of the injury, skin grafts were next to impossible. Infection was the greatest worry, so the antibiotics being pumped into her through her IVs were some of the strongest a body could withstand, and the sterile dressing on her back was changed several times a day. She would be disfigured for the rest of her life. No more backless dresses or trips to Marbella in a bikini for her.

Dr Gar had not made his presence known for several days. Sydney wondered at first if he had voluntarily moved on, or if perhaps Inigo had changed his mind and replaced him. But when she had asked, Brody shook his head, his large, liquid black eyes full of compassion.

"Oh, the poor man is sleeping in one of the spare rooms. He collapsed yesterday. He made himself ill, working and worrying about you. He never leaves the hospital—never leaves this floor, come to think on it. One of the other doctors threatened to sedate him if he didn't get some rest." Brody sucked air through his teeth, his blunt-featured face full of pity. "Hard to see such a good man laid so low."

Sydney didn't respond. Instead, she pictured the tall man with his white-blond hair and his ice-chip green eyes, and then tried to imagine him vulnerable and weak because he was too busy taking care of her to see to himself. She didn't want to be comforted by the thought that he wanted her to get better. It was a struggle to realise these people didn't see Dr Gar the way she did, didn't know what he had done to her in the name of duty. To them, he was a gentleman physician who had brought on his own physical breakdown, looking to her needs before his own.

Sydney told herself he was worried for his own reputation; it had nothing to do with her. Like any medical person she'd ever met, he was undoubtedly more concerned with being spanked by the Agency if she didn't improve. She was not going to feel sorry for him. Never. No way. She had enough problems of her own in this fucking asylum they called The Agency Hospital.

With the exception of Brody, the biggest, gentlest man in the hospital, Sydney hated her nurses. They seemed to regard her injuries as if they were no more serious than a hangnail and she was a whining, ungrateful, fussy brat making life difficult for them. Their obnoxiously officious and patronising attitude made her long for her Glock just to thin out the herd.

And guess what? Brody had already finished his shift for the day. Sydney eyed the clock, groaning at the thought that the nurse she despised most would probably be in soon to change her dressing: Sister Madgerton, who made Nurse Ratched look like Mother fucking Teresa.

Sydney watched silently as Madgerton waddled in, bustling about in her overbearing way. Her round face and pug nose reminded Sydney of a bad-tempered Pekingese. It was a tribute to her complete and utter vileness that she was universally disliked by her fellow nurses as well, which meant her patients fantasised about crafting voodoo dolls in her image.

"Right, Ms Chapin," she huffed, her broad Mersey accent giving Sydney's name all sorts of unpleasant corners and edges. "You're my last task of the day and I'm ready to be done with you. Let's get this dressing changed."

Madgerton assisted Sydney in sitting up, and as she opened the back of her hospital gown, Sydney started taking deep, quick breaths, her calming numbers kicking in. Madgerton had never changed the large gauze dressings on her back before, but she'd certainly shown no sympathy for any of the other injuries she tended. As Sydney leaned forward, gripping the bedsheets in anticipation, Madgerton yanked the gauze away with an unceremonious ripping motion.

For a moment, Sydney thought what was left of her skin was ripped away along with the bandage. The agony that followed stole the breath from her, and she actually greyed out for a second. She came back to herself gasping, her ears ringing with pain, her eyelids screwed so tightly shut she could see her heartbeat pulsing behind them. There was a harsh, barking sound, and Sydney realise she was making it herself.

"I'm sorry, Ms Chapin, but you might as well get rid of it in one fell swoop," Madgerton was saying, her voice rising over Sydney's escalating cries. "If you'll just sit quietly this will all be over in a moment."

Sydney's full consciousness snapped back into place with a blast of *Fackinell*! She threw open her arms, striking Madgerton so hard the nurse actually staggered backward. Then the breath rushed back into Sydney's lungs, and she fishtailed to the end of the bed, frantically trying to get away from the nurse. Her back was a blazing surface of screaming agony.

Madgerton recovered quickly and tried to pin down the flailing woman. "Ms Chapin, I will give you a sedative unless you calm down," she said, trying to avoid the windmilling arms and legs. "You are reopening your wound and that is going to cause scarring—is that what you want?"

What Sydney wanted was a petrol-soaked Madgerton tied to a stake while she flicked a Bic. She fought harder, her cries reduced to a wheezing, breathless shriek, until the flustered nurse called over her shoulder, "Orderly! Bring restraints to Room Two—"

"Let go of her!"

The imperious voice rang through the hospital room like a clap of thunder, causing both Madgerton and Sydney to jump. Dr Gar was standing in the doorway, looking like he'd been run over by a dump truck. He was unshaven and bleary-eyed, and his face was stamped with rage.

Although his hair colour and style were different, Sydney would have recognised those eyes and that scowl on Mars. It was the first truly lucid time Sydney had laid eyes on him since the day she was rescued.

For a split second she was still, panting like an animal. Then the fight or flight reflex took over again and she lashed out, desperate to escape. Escape the cell, the hospital, the doctor, Lightoller—

Madgerton shouted, "This patient needs to be restrained—" Sydney backhanded the nurse squarely in the face, snapping her head back and causing the nurse to stagger back into the doctor's arms.

With a curse, Dr Gar dropped Madgerton like a sack of potatoes.

"This patient needs you to leave this room!" he growled.

Madgerton, unfazed by either the blow or his command, scrambled to her feet and continued to grapple with Sydney on the bed. The doctor forcibly pulled the angry, bleeding nurse away from Sydney, who had by now crawled toward the foot of the bed and was wildly ripping the IV from her arm. She had to get the fuck out of there, now.

As he tried to secure Sydney, Dr Gar turned to Madgerton, who was standing uncertainly at the foot of the bed. Catching his eye, she huffed and drew herself up to her full five-foot three. "Doctor, if you'll just let me call the orderlies—"

"If you've done anything to impede her progress, I will personally see to it you are struck from the nurse's registry. You'll be lucky to get a job cleaning toilets," he hissed, trying unsuccessfully to get his arms around Sydney. "I won't say it again—Get the fuck out of this room!" The little toad fled as if her pants were on fire.

"It's alright, Ms Chapin, she's gone—"

But Sydney was past listening. She fought against The Doctor's longer, stronger arms, knowing it was futile to fight, but helpless to stop herself.

"Shh, Ms Chapin, listen to me. You have to calm down." Her strength was waning; he must have felt her marginally slowing down, because his grip shifted. It became less restraining, more supportive.

Through the miasma of pain and rage, Sydney could hear him trying to calm her down with his voice, that same voice she recognised as the one that had comforted her in the early stages of her recovery. She must have turned blindly to him for help back then, knowing he had been a source of ease when she was fighting for her life. The thought humiliated her now.

Finally, exhaustion and pain won the battle. Her head fell forward, and she slumped in defeat, spent and brittle. Her back was singing the Star-Spangled Banner in the key of High Q.

I must look like a greasy spot on a dirt road, she thought miserably, *right along with that roadkill, Pride.* All she wanted to do was curl up into a ball and never straighten out again. She managed to scrape enough strength together to lift her head and look at him.

Gar was staring at her, misery and pity warring on his face; a faint trace of anger lingered as well. They were both breathing hard, and the wheezing, whimpering noises she made shamed and weakened her. As she looked up into his anguished eyes, his guard dropped, and he lowered his gaze, unable to hold hers.

He tested her balance by releasing her arms, and when she stayed in place on the end of the bed, he gave a little nod. Sydney looked at his downcast head, and something snapped, sending a spike of white-hot rage into the center of her pain-warped brain. It was one thing to acknowledge he had acted as her torturer before, but to insinuate himself back into her old world, pretending he was Doctor fucking Kildare—

She struck him with every ounce of strength she had.

The first punch caught him on the side of the head with a cracking sound that was very satisfying and hopefully set his ears ringing. He remained perfectly still as the second blow caught him across the mouth, and cut his lip. She took no pleasure in it; it was a necessary evil, like changing the dressing on her back, and the pain she felt with each blow had nothing to do with her physical injuries.

She punched at him until his eye was swelling and blood trickled from his mouth. Dr Gar remained passive through it all. The more she hit him, the more ineffectual the blows became, and the more she wept. It was only when she began to see black spots in front of her eyes that he caught her arms easily. "Please, Ms Chapin. Enough now. You...you have a lifetime to punish me."

She slumped over, too tired to reply. Tears streamed from her eyes, and topping it off, the adrenaline had fully drained out of her system. Her back had finished the National Anthem and was now having a crack at Wagnerian opera.

Dr Gar reached into his pocket for his mobile and speed dialed a number. "Brody, hiya. Are you still in the building? Can you come to her room, please?" His eyes met Sydney's. "I need some help I can trust, big man. Cheers."

He ended the call. "You trust Brody too, don't you?" He repeated the question twice before she managed a nod. "Good. I won't do anything without him here, alright?"

Another nod. In the silence, he sighed. "I know I don't have any right to ask, but I'm going to. Please, trust me. You must believe me. I'm on your side. I always was."

When she didn't reply, his hands stroked her arms soothingly.

"Please don't struggle anymore. No one is going to hurt you now. Not Madgerton, and not me." He spoke emphatically, as if hoping his words were sinking in. "As soon as Brody comes, we're going to have to place you on your stomach and tend to your back."

"No," she mumbled, shaking her head in protest. The thought of anyone touching her was unbearable. Self-pity waded into the emotional cesspool that puddled in her chest. It didn't help that Dr Gar was stroking her arm, his touch conveying his sorrow and shame as loudly as his battered face.

"Yes, I know it hurts. I'll be as quick and gentle as I can."

I hate you, she tried to say, but nothing came out. She hated him, and she hated the fact that somewhere between splitting his lip and blackening his eye, she had started to pity him. Somewhere in the midst of her little one-sided prizefight, he'd laid his pride and his life at her feet, and there was nowhere to go from there that didn't lead to forgiveness.

The door swung open, and Brody entered the room. He looked from the doctor's bloody face to the shaking, miserable woman. "What in the name of—" He shut his mouth with a snap. "I had a feeling I oughta hang around after my shift. What do you need, Dr Gar?"

Dahlra Gar watched her carefully, trying to gauge her reactions. Her expression changed as her emotions moved from anger to shame to reproach, but she never looked away from his eyes.

"Oh, Ms Chapin," he said. He stared at the ceiling tiles, wishing the right words might somehow magically appear. "Sydney, please don't do this again. At least until you're fully healed. After that, you can beat the shite out of me on a daily basis if you like, but right now you've just about sent yourself into shock."

He and Brody worked in silence, swabbing and cleaning her ruined back, taping new gauze over the wounds. Quietly, he added, "I deserved that beating and more—I don't deny it. I had to get you out at all costs, and I was fucked if I was going to let them kill you, even if I had to stand by and let them do those things. I don't suppose you really want to hear how much it hurt to sit back and watch those bastards, but I didn't know they were going to beat you that day. You must believe me. If I had, I would have taken it myself before I let them lay a hand on you."

He licked his split lip and winced as it stung.

"You have blood on your glasses," she announced tiredly, through clenched teeth. He looked at her in surprise, then removed his dark-framed spectacles to examine them.

"Why, yes, so I do." He retrieved a piece of gauze and wiped the blood away.

"Better not be mine," she replied with a sigh. Her eyes fluttered. She would be asleep soon, he thought, if only from sheer exhaustion. Shaking his head, he glanced up at Brody, who returned his look with a whole lot of it's-none-of-my-business. Any questions he had would go unasked, and for that, Dahlra was grateful.

Two days later, Inigo Lightoller was visiting Sydney when a discreet knock sounded on the door. "Come in," Sydney replied. Dahlra Gar opened the door and entered the room. He looked a great deal better. His face still carried the evidence of her Sugar Ray Leonard impression, but he was clean-shaven, and his dark hair was damp, as if he'd just come from a shower. He wore a pair of black trousers and a crisp, white dress shirt. Polished leather black Chelsea boots finished off the look. His silk tie was the only jaunty thing about his appearance. It featured a series of fractals in pink, purple, green and orange. The pattern was so lurid as to be almost hypnotic. It stood out like blues and twos in the sterile white room.

In spite of the cathartic beating she had given him the last time they met, Sydney still felt a thrill of visceral fear at the sight of him. He might have changed his hair colour and ditched the white medical coat for his Hermes boots and his trendy, eye-watering tie, but he could not change his face or his eyes, and they still carried with them the ghost of the Doctor. And as far as the unbidden feelings of pity and understanding she had begun to develop, well, she wasn't sure she wanted to go there anytime soon, either.

Inigo turned to the man in the doorway. "Ah, Dr Gar. I understand you were a bit under the weather a few days ago." He turned back to Sydney. "Good to see you up and about."

"It was nothing serious, but thank you." Dr Gar approached Sydney.

"How are you feeling, Ms Chapin?"

"Is this concern for my benefit or for my governor's?" she asked. He stiffened and looked away, but not before she saw the look of humiliation in his eyes. It didn't give her as much pleasure as she had expected. *Damn, now he's making me feel guilty.* "And what have you done to your hair?" she demanded.

Her non sequitur surprised him into reaching upward to touch his head. "I, uh, I dyed my hair for the—the mission." His disarming smile slipped a bit, and the tension in the room seemed to tighten a notch. "This is the 'real' me, so to speak."

"Sydney," said Inigo, looking warily from Gar back to her, "I have some very good news, old girl."

Dr Gar turned to look at Inigo, and a pleased look of pride and satisfaction flitted across his features. For some reason, Sydney didn't like the pally looks the two men were giving one another. Not at all. It spoke of too many private conversations with her as the main subject, too many decisions made about her welfare in which she had no input. If they thought they were going talk about her as if she was not in the room, these good old boys had another think coming.

"Okay. And what would that be?" Sydney asked. She shifted uncomfortably; her back was, as always, hurting. Dr Gar immediately leaned forward to settle her into a more comfortable position, adjusting the pillow and resting his hand on her shoulder. His touch was gentle, sure. Sydney rolled her shoulder out of his grasp and moved slightly away from him, not bothering to hide her unease at his presence. The gesture was not lost on either man. Dr Gar moved away, dropping his hands to his sides. *Aw, crap. He's doing it again*, she thought.

Inigo turned to Dr Gar. "Doctor, would you mind if I spoke with your patient in private? We have some things to discuss that are a bit confidential." He flashed his smarmy, conspiratorial smile. "I promise to call if your assistance is needed."

The doctor's face grew closed. Frostily, he replied, "Of course. I'll be outside if you need me." He glanced toward Sydney, and quietly left the room.

"You could be civil," said Inigo bluntly. "After all, the man did save—"

"Inigo, no offence, but if I hear one more time how grateful I should be to him, I'm going to jump out the window."

"An impressive threat, seeing as we're currently underground. As for Gar, you may resent him, but you can't change the truth."

"I'm getting very tired of being reminded that I owe him my life," snapped Sydney. "Dr Gar seems to be the only conversation we ever have."

"No, Sydney. Your survival and recovery is the only conversation we ever have. The only conversation I'm interested in having. And you wouldn't be alive to have that conversation if not for him. Full stop."

Sydney sighed harshly. She hated that she couldn't dispute him. Grudgingly, she acquiesced, "I just don't want to spend the rest of my life sucking him off in gratitude."

Inigo laughed, albeit unwillingly. "That's what I love about you Yanks. Always taking the high road."

"I'm sorry, Inigo. It's not just that I'm a little tired of hearing about the Great Dr Gar, from whom all blessings flow." She shifted painfully. "I'm hurting, I'm bored, and I'm sick of staring at these walls. I've read every book and watched every DVD Garnet's brought me, twice." She looked around the room in loathing. "I want to go outside for a walk. I want to go home. I want some fresh air and privacy and a little slice of normal."

His expression told her that, while he commiserated with her, he wasn't going to indulge her, either. "So, lay on me this good news, boss. New mobile, car or weapon? Or has the Queen decided to skip the OBE and recommend me for sainthood?"

Inigo chuckled again. "I can tell you're getting better. You're starting to sound like the old Syd again." He shifted slightly in the hospital-issue chair. "Do you remember the conversation we had shortly after you first came round? About your leave of absence?"

"Yeah. Well, mostly."

"Ah. Then perhaps you don't recall that you've been promoted to Minder status."

Sydney took in a deep breath and let it out slowly. "Yeeeaah. I do remember," she said warily. "All that stuff about having my own man-whore."

"Sydney, please."

She rolled her eyes. "Fine, fine. So, I take it that your good news is some poor sod has drawn the short straw and been assigned to me."

"Indeed. Totally unprecedented."

God, she hated being Inigo's straight man. "How so?"

"The normal procedure dictates that when an agent achieves Minder status, they submit a request to the Minder programme directors for an interview and compatibility testing," Inigo explained. "The application is reviewed scrupulously by said directors, who suggest three or four possible candidates. Once they finish interviewing the agent, they then decide which Minder is the most suitable for the assignment."

"Riveting," Sydney replied dryly. "And once the white smoke comes out of the chimney, we have a new Pope."

"Shut up. In your case, however, when it was made known that Sydney Chapin had been upgraded to a Minder-qualified agent, all the available Minder candidates petitioned the directors for consideration. That's twenty-five candidates, old girl. You should be flattered."

Sydney scoffed. "Oh, should I? I'm not a rock star picking out my groupie for the night. And I think it's barbaric that an agent has no say in who's chosen."

"An agent doesn't have autonomy for the very reason you just stated. You are *not* picking out your groupie. It's not a beauty contest. A Minder is a respected professional whose sole purpose is to make a real, lasting difference in your life for the better."

Sydney felt resentment oozing from several places in her head. She knew she was being railroaded, and she knew Inigo had sprung this on her while she was too weak and unable to take care of herself to disprove that she needed someone to do just that. And she felt queasy at the thought of some guy she had never clapped eyes on taking over her life.

"I suppose saying no is out of the question?"

"It's not in your best interest to say no, Sydney. You've been through hell and back. You need someone. You've earned it."

"It sounds like you're giving me some kind of concubine or indentured servant."

"I assure you, old girl, Minders don't view their role as such. They take immense pride in protecting the welfare of their agents." His gaze softened. "At least try to get to know him. You may find that he's exactly what the doctor ordered."

"Fine. Set up a meeting. I'll talk to him."

"I'll do better than that, old thing. He's waiting outside." Inigo leaned over and kissed her cheek. "Indulge me this once. Have a talk with him." He stuck out his hand. "Give it six months? Promise?"

Sydney felt like breaking the proffered hand. "I've already endured three months of confinement, Inigo. But for you, I'll give you another three."

"You drive a hard bargain, Sydney. Three months—" He shook her hand. "—from the day you leave hospital."

Sydney tried to remove her hand, but he held it firm. "Three months." When he didn't move, she added, "Fine. From the day I leave hospital."

"Excellent. I'll send him in. No time like the present, eh?" Without looking at her, he left the room.

Sydney lay back against the pillows and thought about this Minder she had inherited. It was like being given a puppy as a gift, when all she had really wanted was an African violet. But as her mind turned to the possibilities, she found her heart growing lighter at the prospect. Someone to act as a resource, a helper. Almost better than a partner— this person would be working for her. *A Minder is not just for Christmas—*

The door opened, and she looked up to see Dr Gar. But instead of striding into the room with his usual air of authority, he merely stood inside the threshold, as the door closed silently behind him.

Sydney gaped as cold realisation flooded her body. *Oh, no. Hell, no. Fucking Lightoller. I'm going to kill him.*

"Tell me I'm not crazy, Dr Gar," she said. "Tell me you haven't gone and done something monumentally stupid, like apply to become my Minder. And won the position."

Gar raised his eyes to her. *Holy hell*, she thought, *he's frightened.*

In that moment, staring into his familiar face, the words '*You will do as I say*' flashed in her mind. Except that, instead of hearing him speak the words to her, she was saying them to him. She felt a temporal shift in the ley lines; in those few seconds, Sydney finally ceased to feel like a prisoner. She was now the guv'nor, and he was the captive.

"Answer me," she said, her voice strong and sure. Again, something shifted between them so powerfully she could almost feel the bed move. "Are you my new Minder?"

"Yes, Ms Chapin," he answered. He stood perfectly still, and there was nothing in his demeanour that remotely reminded her of The

Doctor. *He's afraid of me*, she thought, and felt a thrill of power that was almost sexual in its ferocity.

I could break him in half, and he'd let me. She found the temptation to drive him to his knees pretty damn hard to resist. Make those three months she had promised Inigo such a ride on Hell's roller coaster, the poor bastard would never recover. Give him a taste of his own medicine, let him see how it felt to be molested—

He did it under orders. You'd be doing it because you could. Do you really want to live with that?

"Fucking hell," she muttered. She couldn't do that. Even though he probably expected it, possibly thought he deserved it, she couldn't indulge her payback-jones. Not with him like this, coming to her like a lamb to the slaughter.

She indicated the chair Inigo had vacated. "Please have a seat, Dr Gar."

He obeyed, moving gracefully to the chair and seating himself, sitting up very straight. Sydney regarded him thoughtfully. "You, know, I don't even know your first name. And I can't see us getting too far calling you 'Doctor.'"

He winced. "No." His eyes met hers, green and clean and sincere. "Dahlra. My full name is Dahlra Benjamin Peter Gar."

"That's a bit of a mouthful. 'Dahlra' seems a bit out of place next to all those biblical names."

He smiled shyly, and a dimple teased his cheek. "My father named me after an Indian physician who saved his life during the war. He thought 'DBP Gar' would look good on my business cards. He had rather high expectations of me."

"Sounds like a pretentious wanker," she replied. "Oh, shit, sorry. That wasn't exactly the nicest thing to say."

"Don't apologise," he answered mildly. "Actually, he was a bit of a wanker."

Sydney was surprised into rueful laughter. "Now my dad, he wanted a boy," she admitted, "so he named me Sydney, after his grandfather. Try being an eight-year-old girl with the only name in the world that rhymes with 'kidney.'"

"I imagine you were teased almost as much as I was."

The conversation suddenly ran out of steam, and the silence

stretched to just this side of awkward. Feeling a little desperate, Sydney said, "Still, your name is a change from the ordinary. When I first moved here, it seemed like every Englishman I met was either a Steve or a Paul."

"They do have a nice, anonymous ring, don't they?" he mused. "I hated the name Dahlra so much, I'd almost have preferred Basil."

"Sorry, taken. That's Inigo's nickname. I'm afraid you're out beside it."

"I suppose I'm stuck, then," he said. "But I'm glad I could at least make you laugh about it."

Sydney looked down at her hands, feeling as if he'd caught her out. *This is a business interview, Syd. Enough of the getting-to-know-you routine.* "Have you ever been a Minder before, Dahlra Benjamin Peter Gar?"

It was disconcerting to see him so unsure. "This is my first assignment as a Minder, but I have spent a great deal of time and training in preparation." he replied earnestly.

"As a Minder, what exactly will you do?"

Dr Gar considered his words carefully. "Well, what won't I do might be easier to answer. I will manage your household, act as your handler in the field and help you make decisions on your future.

"The first order of business is obviously to make sure you have a full recovery from your injuries. Then we see to making all the other aspects of your life comfortable. I take care of the minutest matters, from daily bill paying to food shopping. I'll act as an advisor and a counselor. I'll even help you make career decisions, if you wish to elicit my opinions. In the end, whatever you need, you should be able to turn to me and request it, and it will be done. The Minder credo is Practical, Emotional, Physical; Life, Soul, Body. My job is to make sure you are the optimum agent for this organisation."

Some of the old self-assurance flashed in his eyes. "We're very compatible, Ms Chapin. You still have a long way to go before you are restored to full health. You need help, and I know you won't ask for it, so I'm providing it." His easy smile returned. "Who knows? You might find it fun being cared for, and cared about."

As Sydney pondered this new development between them, she shifted absently, and her back wrenched sideways. She grunted, cursing her bad timing. Dr Gar was on it immediately.

"Look, you're in a great deal of distress right now," he said.

"I'm alright."

He sighed and pulled at his ear. "Ms Chapin, I don't think you are being entirely truthful," he said, not unkindly. "I can give you a pain reliever that's non-addictive and has very few side effects."

For a long moment, Sydney looked at him unblinkingly, breathing hard. She waited until she could think past the jolt of pain radiating from her spine. "Whatever. I seem to have no say in anything else."

"You have every say," he replied. "I know that Lightoller asked you to give the situation three months, but I'm committed for the long run." He reached for her hand. His were large and warm, and enfolded hers gently.

When he spoke again, his voice was soft and silvery. "I have so many things I need to tell you, but I don't want to totally overwhelm you. Just know that this is so much deeper than a physician caring for a patient. It's so much deeper than trying to make amends for things that I'm deeply sorry for." He looked into her eyes, guileless and hopeful. "Please, Ms Chapin. Give me this chance."

Sydney could detect no undercurrent of subterfuge, no hint of deceit. "Could we start with that jab, then?" she asked. "I could make a more informed decision if I could just think around this pain."

"Of course." He retrieved a small syringe from his pocket. Swabbing her arm with an alcohol pad, he administered the injection so deftly she didn't actually feel the needle pierce her skin. He tossed the spent hypo into the sharps bin. "You should start feeling better in no time."

As they waited for the medication to take effect, Sydney took the opportunity to truly study him. He wasn't as tall as she had originally thought; only around six foot or so. He was no spring chicken, either; he was at least five years older than her, maybe more. He had either taken good care of his face and figure, or inherited some enviable genes.

His black hair was thick and straight, and contrasted with his pale, porcelain skin tone. He had a good face, with well-defined cheeks and jaw, and his large eyes were pure green, framed with black lashes so thick Sydney felt a touch of envy. His mouth was finely drawn, with a perfectly-shaped upper lip curved in a slender cupid's bow; his teeth were white and even. Only his nose kept him from looking too perfect; it was large, with a diamond-shaped indentation on the bridge. Probably an old rugby injury.

There was no trace of the cool, hard calculation she had originally associated with him. So, he was handsome, he was solicitous, and he was eager to please. Would that be enough?

"It's going to take some time to reconcile you with the man in my cell," she admitted.

He sighed as he sat down again. "The man in your cell was terrified and under constant scrutiny. He had to do things that made him hate himself far more than you hated him. That man died in a hail of bullets, and I was glad. Do you believe me?"

"Yes, I believe you. But I don't know you any better than I knew him." Sydney could feel the effects of the pain reliever working its magic. "Actually, I probably know him better than I know you."

"In what way?" he asked, his eyes wary.

"I knew him enough not to trust him."

Sydney could feel sleep stealing her away from the pain, and with it the conversation, Dr Gar, Inigo, herself, everything. As she drifted off, she murmured, "Prove to me you aren't that man, Dr Gar, and I'll consider accepting your offer."

She was nearly under when she heard him whisper, "I will if you'll allow me, Sydney."

CHAPTER FIVE

The First Examination

After a cursory knock on Sydney's examination room door, Dr Gar entered with Brody close at his heels. The sight of him in the familiar white coat no longer triggered a feeling of dread, but it still unnerved her. The room was well lit and comfortable; a total contrast to the stark, filthy cell that had been her home away from home while she and the Doctor had played their warped version of Closet Land.

Sydney forced her expression to remain impassive as she sat, legs dangling over the side of the examination table. A glance at Brody made her feel a little better; Dr Gar's man he might have been, but Brody was intensely protective of her as a patient.

Gar gave her the professional, silent salutation that doctors seem to specialise in. "I realise that the usual protocol is to have a female nurse during an examination, but under the circumstances it was either the lovely Brody or Sister Madgerton." He smiled. "I hope you'll agree with my choice."

"Absolutely. Thank you."

He glanced up from her chart, an expression of pleased surprise lighting up his face. "Excellent. Let's see," he added, his eyes skimming over the chart in his hands. "How are you feeling today, Ms Chapin?"

Sydney took in his shy smile, his handsome face, his hopeful, soft-focus eyes, and wondered what he was thinking. "Do you know how a wild hawk is tamed, Dr Gar?" she asked.

He shook his head bemusedly. "I can't say I do."

A glance at Brody earned a shrug that was almost Buddha-like. "Don't ask me," replied the big man serenely. "Birmingham's not big hawk country."

Dr Gar turned back to Sydney. "Okay. I'll bite. How *is* a wild hawk tamed, Ms Chapin?"

"It's broken to the lure and trained to eat its meals only at the fist of its master."

"I—I see. I'll try to remember that." He looked so thoroughly flummoxed Sydney almost laughed.

He removed his glasses, rubbed his eyes, and proceeded with the usual exam: pulse rate, blood pressure, temperature, reflexes, eyes, ears, nose, and throat. He scribbled a few notes, then stabbed the final full stop on her chart.

"I understand you had some questions to ask about your progress. Your back is our primary concern right now, and it's healing at a steady, appropriate rate for your age and physical condition. Your physio starts in a couple of days, your stress counseling a few days after that. I think you'll start to see noticeable improvement, both physically and emotionally-"

"It's not so much that," Sydney said, steeling herself. For two days she'd been getting up the nerve to ask, and she was sick and tired of feeling like a complete wimp about it. "I wanted to know if ... if I'm alright ... internally."

To his credit, he didn't miss a beat. "Obviously there was injury, but it was not as severe as we initially ascertained. Of course," he said, suddenly quite interested in her chart again, "we can't be completely certain until a full gynaecological exam is performed, but-"

"Can you do that? I mean," Sydney mentally rolled her eyes. She sounded virginally awkward. "Am I in—in good enough condition to, um, have an exam today, just to make sure?"

He considered briefly. "I don't see why not. Would you like for me to perform the exam, or would you prefer another doctor?"

The question derailed her for a moment. Two days ago she would have said yes without hesitation. Today, she had to think about it. She had, after all, given Inigo her word.

"You're fine. I mean, I'm fine with you performing the examination," she finished, feeling like a complete idiot. She sounded like a middle-aged spinster trying to be cool.

Oblivious to her inner babbling, Dr Gar turned to Brody, who nodded and prepared to leave. "If you'll just get Sister Madgerton-"

"Not happening." Sydney turned to Brody. "I don't mind you giving me an exam, but I won't have that troll touching me. I'm more than happy for Brody to assist you."

Dr Gar looked at her searchingly. "Alright then. I need to fetch some equipment from another examination room, but we'll take care of it."

"Don't worry, Doc," Brody countered, already moving toward the door. "I'll get the equipment. Be back in two ticks." The door closed behind him, leaving Sydney alone with Dr Gar.

The silent stretched between them, feeling unnecessarily hard, and Sydney wondered if the fault lay with her own conflicting feelings. For the past few days, since they had tiptoed through their initial conversation about Minders, he had gone out of his way to be solicitous, careful and humble. He was never in her room without a nurse present, and he always kept their interactions efficient and professional.

The trouble was that Sydney didn't know how to trust this version of Dr Gar any more than she'd trusted the albino martinet in the cell. Intellectually, she knew she had no real reason not to, but it really was getting her nowhere. She had agreed to a trial period with him, but she just couldn't bring herself to warm up to him, no matter how gentle and patient and kind he was.

As she watched him, it suddenly occurred to her that he wasn't the only one whose situation had changed since the cell. When they'd first met, she was strapped down to a table after a month of steady, sadistic abuse. She had been weak and helpless. Even with the codes to keep her from going off the deep end, her frame of mind made Eeyore look like Mr Rogers in comparison.

But here, back at the Agency, she was in charge. She was stronger, mentally and physically, and growing stronger by the day. She was more than a match for any mind games Dr Gar might be tempted to play.

As her thoughts zoomed around, their eyes met. He seemed about to balk under her intense scrutiny, but then he relaxed his shoulders and met her gaze with a steady, level look of his own. *Whatever it is you're trying to decide,* his eyes seemed to say, *I'm willing to wait a lifetime.*

The moment was broken by a noise on the other side of the examination room door. Brody re-entered after a quick knock, carrying a wide metal tray of swabs, lubricant, specula, and other disturbing pieces of medical what-the-fuck. Sydney took in the various accoutrements and wished she'd never opened her big mouth about wanting this exam.

Dr Gar turned and smiled at Sydney, his professional manner firmly anchored back in place. "Right. Let's proceed, shall we?"

He helped her lie back onto the wedged pillow Brody had produced. "If it gets too painful to have this much pressure on your back, let me know and we'll try another angle."

Staring up into the ceiling, Sydney felt rather than watched the doctor place her feet in stirrups. She clenched her jaw. She had asked for this pelvic exam; she would deal with it. *Just be quick, Medic Boy. If I can't enjoy you setting up shop in my genitals, neither should you.* She snorted at her own thoughts. *Oh, well done, Sydney. You've just reduced your own body to the equivalent of a mini Cooper. It's good to see the feminine mystique is still alive and well and living in your pants.*

The silence stretched like a rubber band in the room. Sydney wished he'd show a little more of that inane bedside chatter most GPs used during this procedure. Most yacked it up like magpies, talking about weather, their kids, their vacations, their pets—anything to divert the patient from what they were actually doing. Sydney had an insane urge to break out in song, just to kill the silence.

His eyes met hers over her stirruped feet, and in spite of the situation, the awkwardness and the discomfort, Sydney laughed unwillingly. It was all rather absurd, wasn't it? Lying on a table, while a doctor sat in front of you like some deranged baseball catcher, waiting for God knew what to appear, like a rabbit from a hat. She laughed again and then groaned with pain, which made her laugh harder.

Encouraged by her reaction, he gave her a smile. "All right. I'm going to start now."

In the ensuing moments, the doctor took swabs and passed them to Brody; he checked her for any unhealed lesions or bruises. "Everything looks normal," he announced, as he collapsed the bills of the speculum and withdrew it. "Almost done. I just need to perform an internal probe."

A long, gloved finger pushed its way in and moved inside her, snapping Sydney out of her reverie. She looked up at his face; he was completely serious, completely professional, his attention focused solely on the map of the passage his fingers explored. "I'm sorry, did you say something?" she asked.

"I asked if you could feel this. Do you have any sensation?"

His fingers felt as if they were somewhere in the neighborhood of her liver. In a strained voice, she answered, "I think so. It might just be pressure, but I think I can feel..."

He began to probe deeper, and she felt as if he were pushing against a wall his fingers couldn't penetrate, and she tensed again. "Hmm," he said, a look of mild surprise softening his features. "You've developed a bit of scar tissue here. Feels like mini-hymen. Congratulations; you seem to be a virgin again." Dr Gar pressed down gently on her pelvis, just below her navel, and the sensation of stretching passed.

"Great," she replied, through gritted teeth.

"Relax, lower your bottom onto the table, Sydney. That's good," he said absently, his voice almost a whisper. "It's just a thin bit of tissue—hmm, oh, moot point now. There it goes." He looked at her carefully. "Did you feel any pain?"

Sydney shook her head. "Why?"

"I was probing it and it... broke."

Sydney quirked her eyebrow. "And you didn't even buy me dinner."

He ducked his head shyly. "Yes, well..." he seemed on the verge of saying more, but decided to play it safe and went on with the examination. While she tried her best to relax, her body doing its best Fort Knox imitation. Even as gentle as he was, he was going nowhere, and the journey was very uncomfortable.

"Doctor, I'm not sure I can—"

"Pant."

Sydney wasn't sure at first he'd spoken. She stared at him, looking down on her, his expression mild and patient. "What?"

"Pant," he repeated. "Pant, and bear down a little." He opened his mouth and breathed deeply and rapidly in and out several times to illustrate, his tongue flat against his bottom teeth. Sydney watched him, fascinated. "It will help you relax."

Thinking she had nothing to lose, Sydney obediently panted, and gradually she relaxed enough to allow him to proceed. Something slipped loose inside her, and the discomfort became something else. "There we go," he said, approvingly, his voice low. "Very good. Good girl."

The words escaped his lips before he was actually conscious of speaking them, and he stilled for a brief moment.

He called me that before, in the cell, in that exact tone of voice. It wrapped around her consciousness. His voice... like an instrument played for her enjoyment alone. Somewhere deep within, she rather felt she might do any number of things to hear that tone again. She twitched suddenly at her own thoughts. *Where the fuck had that come from?*

Finally, he gently lowered her legs from the stirrups. "Well, I'm happy to say that you're healing well, and overall your recovery is progressing at a very rapid rate. Of course, we'll have to check the smear tests, but early reports showed nothing amiss, so hopefully this examination has allayed any fears you might have had."

As Brody helped her to sit up, Dr Gar finished a note on her chart, then turned back to her, his expression friendly. "Well, that wasn't so bad, was it?"

"The highlight of my day." she said rather pathetically, but managed a tired smile.

"Always glad to help," he replied, and she shot him a quick look to see if he was taking the piss. He wasn't smiling, or even smirking ironically; in fact, he looked wistful, almost sorrowful.

"Thank you," she said. And for the first time since they'd met, she gave him a genuine smile, and meant it.

She had hoped to end the examination on a positive note; she was not prepared for the reaction she received. A look of stunned, pleased surprise stole over his face. His eyes lit from within, and he hit her with a slow smile so radiant it almost blindsided her. There was a boyish sweetness in it that was both touching and devastating, and the delight in his face transported him from a handsome man into an angel.

If that smile could be bottled, I'd never need a vibrator again. Close on the heels of *that* disturbing little thought, she added, *Oh, please, Dr Gar, please have a crooked toe or pick your nose, or eat like a pig and snore like an adenoidal bear. That smile is too perfect.*

"The top of your head's gonna fall off if you keep grinning like that," she quipped.

Brody laughed loudly.

CHAPTER SIX

Kensington

On a cool morning in September, Sydney was finally released from the Agency hospital. Several staff members gathered to see her off; even the battle axe nurses put in an appearance. To their credit, they had worked tirelessly on her behalf, sometimes in spite of her. One by one they shook her hand, and told her how privileged they felt to have been a part of her medical team. Sydney thanked each of them personally for their support and hard work, and hugged Brody for good measure. Sister Madgerton, she noted, was conspicuous by her absence.

She was bemused to see that many shook Dr Gar's hand and wished him well, since he, too, was leaving the hospital for an as-yet indeterminate amount of time. It gave Sydney a niggling feeling of frustration. Three months from now, the guy would no doubt return to his life here, but she would have another twenty-one months to fill until she was given the all-clear to return to work. She tried not to think about it.

Garnet had brought her some clothes so at least she didn't have to leave in a hospital gown. The beige jumper and old track suit trousers hung pathetically loose on her frame. Even her battered old Bass Weejuns felt loose on her feet.

By the time Dr Gar had ordered a cab and seen to her personal effects, Sydney was seriously faking the steady-on-her-feet routine. Just the tedium of red tape and paperwork required to check herself out of hospital left her feeling exhausted and edgy.

As they settled back into the black cab, the driver craned his head back for directions. "Twenty-eight DeVere Gardens, Kensington," Dr Gar instructed. "I've spent the last fortnight or so getting it ready for you. I think you'll be very happy there."

Sydney nodded. She'd already agreed to the new place, but... "I'm going to miss my flat in Oval, though."

"Oh, it's still there," he added hastily. "Principal Lightoller feels—"

"—and you agree with him," she answered. The effect was immediate and a little wistful. He tilted his head, his eyes searching hers carefully.

When he realised she was making a rather lame attempt to joke with him, he sighed with something that might have been relief.

"Yes, thank you, Mister Slope," he replied, then grew a bit more serious. "Well, you must admit, your old flat is rather small for two. Please understand, Sydney, all this has been done for your continued well-being."

"I know, I *know*. I'm not trying to sound ungrateful, Dr Gar—"

"Sydney," he interrupted, his expression one of patient frustration. "I realise you're making a real effort to go with all of this, and I appreciate that. But I think we'll get even farther along if we dispense with these formalities. Please." He smiled, and closed his hand over hers. "It would mean a great deal if you would call me by my Christian name."

She looked down at his hand. He had surgeon's hands; hands that had healed her, hands that had gently touched her intimately with surety and talent. She shook her head slightly to clear her mind of these treacherous, slippery-slope kinds of thoughts.

"I'm not trying to sound ungrateful... Dahlra," she began again, and was rewarded with a pleased smile and an encouraging nod. "I appreciate that concern for my welfare is probably somewhere in all this, but I'm just not used to having my *personal* life so meticulously looked after by someone other than me."

"I understand completely," he replied. "Lightoller was all for shifting you lock, stock and barrel here, but we managed to persuade him to take things a little more gradually."

"We?"

"My mentor and I. He lives just around the corner, actually, and since it's not far from the hospital, we thought this might be an acceptable compromise for the time being. I really think you'll be pleasantly surprised how nice it is here. Kensington is very-"

"Secretive."

"Pardon?"

She shrugged. "I don't know why, but Kensington has always seemed rather sinister to me. Probably because we've had to do surveillance work here so often. It seems like anyone and everyone with a dodgy past has a flat here, or uses one from time to time. I've always had this unsettling thought that some pretty unspeakable things could be happening behind those closed doors."

They turned down Queen's Gate Terrace, past houses of yellow flagstone. They flowed down the streets in unbroken lines, quiet and sullen. She hadn't been exaggerating; she had always felt uneasy in Kensington, with its air of privilege and superiority. The flats always seemed to be the preserve of those who had something to hide. They were frequently bought by well-heeled parents for their bored, privileged children to play house in after a hard day's work in the nearby museums and Harvey Nicks. They were used as love-nests for bored MPs, or safe houses for upmarket drug lords.

"Well, I promise you no acts of debauchery have been taking place in ours. At least, none that I'm aware of," he said, his expression clean, his tone devoid of any trace of irony "All I can say for our flat is that it is spacious, tastefully decorated, and the pantry's well stocked.

"There's a professional grade kitchen as well, a real gourmet's dream. In fact, I've planned a great meal tonight, if you're not too tired from all the closing ceremonies this afternoon."

"Oh, do you like to cook?"

He gave her one of his shy, self-deprecating smiles. "How do you think I put myself through medical school?"

"I suppose I just assumed it was daddy's money."

A shadow passed over his face, but it was gone in the next heartbeat. "You're only half right. Yes, my family had money. But my father believed that you have to work for what you want. Giving his only son money to put himself through medical school was a sure-fire way to encourage laziness and complacency. I paid my own way. I won't deny it was sometimes difficult, but in the end, I wasn't under obligation to anyone, especially him."

There was an undercurrent of pride in his voice, gilded in a delicate leaf of bitterness. Sydney had apparently touched down on the outskirts of a long-standing, complicated emotional outpost where Dahlra was concerned. Possibly an unspoken rivalry between father and son; perhaps the father had himself been denied an easy ride and believed sink-or-swim was a good parental philosophy to promote self-reliance.

Sydney had noticed that attitude in a lot of men of Dahlra's generation, especially in Britain. They carried within a grim satisfaction that they were beholden to no one for what they had achieved in their careers; they also shared contempt for those they considered to have 'ridden the coattails' of another's money or influence.

She could understand that. Her parents had been dead set against her going to Quantico, and hadn't exactly made her comfortable about it. It had taken them a good three years before they got it through their heads that their little girl wasn't going to be a teacher or a nurse or a housewife, and if they didn't accept that, the holidays were going to be a drag for all concerned. Eventually they had thrown all their support behind her with good grace, because they loved her and wanted to see her happy. Their devotion to her had ultimately destroyed them, but that was not something she was in any hurry to share with her new Minder.

Sydney turned away from that thought. Instead, she replied, "I only imagine how hard it was, fending for yourself in the British medical fraternity. Med school's never cheap, no matter how good you are."

Dahlra gave her a philosophical shrug. "I spent five years living in a grotty little hovel with four other medical students. We never had enough money to do anything other than pool our resources to scrape together a meal. Somewhere along the line I discovered I had a knack for combining ingredients that ended up tasting like something decent. Then I found I actually enjoyed it. From then on, if I wasn't cooking for my fellow students, I was working at one restaurant or another."

The cabbie chimed in, "Here we are, folks." They stopped in front of one of the many incongruous-looking yellow terraces, and Sydney peered out the window at the one marked '28'.

As Dahlra paid the cabby, Sydney let herself out of the taxi and glanced up the imposing street. She took in the shuttered windows and silent doors marching uniformly down the road, her agent's brain absorbing as many details as possible in her initial sweep of the area. There were plenty of parked cars, but no people. Except for them, not another soul was visible on the street.

It was poles apart from her flat in Oval, a miniscule third-floor apartment at the end of a hall, directly opposite the cricket grounds. This place was more than capable of hiding a few secrets. *We're one of them*, she thought wryly.

They were silent as they walked up the steps. Sydney heard the soft, metallic clink of keys as Dahlra unlocked the door. "After you, Sydney," he said, with an almost formal gesture of welcome. He ushered her into the flat, carrying her belongings.

She looked around in awe. This wasn't a flat; it was a Tardis. Doctor Who, indeed.

The front door opened into a long hall. Stairs marched upward to the first floor on the left side. She glanced in the first door to her left and saw an enormous front room. To her right was its mirror image. On the far side was another door leading to another set of stairs. Opulent rugs were scattered haphazardly over the gleaming hardwood floors.

The ceilings were high, and still bore the ornate crown molding that undoubtedly had been part of its new build one hundred and fifty years before. The flat smelled of floor polish and lemon oil.

Dahlra casually dropped his keys on a table just inside the door, and pointed down the hall beyond the stairs. "The dining room is off that way, and the kitchen can be accessed either through there, or through the right front room. This is actually two flats that were knocked through."

That explains the Tardis effect, then, thought Sydney. *This must have cost the Agency an absolute bomb. Inigo really means business.*

The house was tastefully and meticulously furnished, yet it still managed to feel comfortable. Dahlra gave her the grand tour of the ground floor, including the afore-mentioned kitchen, which stretched the length of the back of both flats combined.

They finally entered a sitting room, its walls lined with bookshelves. A black baby grand piano sat in the corner, like a large mastiff hoping to be noticed. Sydney drew her fingers across the keys. It was a nice, midrange model, nothing too elaborate. She played a few chords; it had a pleasing, dark, oily sound.

"Do you play?" she asked.

He shook his head. "Not even chopsticks, I'm afraid. Your partner Garnet told me you played, so I thought, perhaps you'd like to make use of it sometimes. I love..." He looked away shyly. "I love hearing you sing."

She played a final chord. "Thank you. Maybe I will."

Their eyes met, and Sydney saw a faint, yearning look in his eyes. "Well, why don't I show you upstairs? It's a pretty big place..."

"Dahlra." She paused before adding, "Look, if we avoid every subject that might remind one or the other of us about what happened in the cell, we're going to run out of things to talk about very quickly."

"You'll get no argument from me there." He cast about, his brow furrowed in concern. "Could we agree to make a fresh start, while still respecting what happened before? Would that be acceptable?"

Was it really that simple? She wanted it to be. She had never been one to brood over misfortune; she had very little to lose. Why not take this handsome man at face value, and start over?

Her long silence unnerved him, and he took it for reluctance on her part. His mouth became a thin, grim line; his eyes grew cold. "Sydney, do you honestly believe I took one moment of pleasure in what happened? That I enjoyed one damn thing about what I did?"

The breath left her chest in a gust, and anger flared in its place. "There was-"

"No, no, no," he said, shaking his head. His voice grew stern with warning. "I think if you recall, I wasn't the one in charge of *that*."

He faced her dead on, his gaze unwavering, and Sydney found she couldn't quite meet his eyes. They *had* done something, the last night before they were evac'd. And she *had* owned it then, dammit. He might have been her captor and she his prisoner, but she had choreographed every moment of that encounter...

Quietly, Dahlra continued, "I knew one of these days we'd have to face it. And I'm ready anytime you are. But we both know what happened that night was borne of desperation, not pleasure. For both of us. But if you want to put it on the table right now, I'm more than willing to dissect it right along with you."

For a moment, Sydney tried to front him out, but he had truth on his side and they both knew it. He was right. There was a lot to talk about, but not while the scab was too easy to pick. At the very least, they had a long way to go toward reading one another's motives.

"Alright," she said finally. "I don't want to discuss it now. One day, yes. Maybe."

She forced herself to look up at him, and saw he was just as tired and rattled as she was. "You're not going to dictate the way I live. I don't need a nanny."

"I...I'm not-"

"If you think you're going to boss me around and tell me what to do you are sadly mistaken," she added warningly.

Almost kindly, he replied, "I think *you're* the one who's mistaken, Sydney. The last time I checked, you were the boss. I'm the one following orders."

"Well hell." Sydney felt foolish and wrong-footed, and knew she couldn't blame anyone but herself. They couldn't pretend the past hadn't happened, but perhaps they could try to create some sort of future relationship in spite of it. And if they couldn't, well, dammit, she wasn't going to be the cause of it. She was through with thinking of Dahlra as a betrayal waiting to happen.

"Okay. You win," she conceded.

He looked surprised. "Sydney," he said softly, "it's not about *me* winning. It's about *us* not losing."

That hit her, right between the eyes. Once again she was reminded just how far they had to go. "Fair enough." She stuck out her hand. "Hi, I'm Sydney Chapin. I'm your agent."

Dahlra soberly took her outstretched hand and shook it. "Hello, Sydney. I'm Dahlra Gar. I'm your Minder."

"I'm pleased to meet you, Dahlra." For a moment they stood still, just looking at one another, and Sydney was struck with a swift ache, a longing. At that moment, she desperately wished they could have met under different circumstances - a party, a sports match, or a club; anywhere but that damned cell.

He released her hand. "I'd love to know what you're thinking about right now."

Sydney felt her face grow warm. "Probably the same thing you are. Tell you what: how about showing me the rest of the flat?" She glanced back at the piano. "Then maybe after dinner we'll see just how badly out of practice I am."

As they walked up the stairs to the first floor, Dahlra said, "Your bedroom is this first door on the landing." He opened it and stepped back, indicating for her to enter.

Like most of the flat, it had originally been two rooms, but the wall had been knocked out to create a suite. In the gigantic bath, there was even a whirlpool tub. Looking around, Sydney whistled in appreciation. "You could fit my entire flat in here."

Dahlra nodded in agreement. "I think the former owners spent more on this bathroom than I did on my first house. Still, that tub has some personality, doesn't it?" he smiled.

"If I ever want to get away from it all, I can always swim to the other side."

"At least I'll know where to look if you go AWOL," he answered.

The bedroom itself was furnished with rose-colored copper and RAF-blue accents, giving it a metrosexual vibe. The bed and wardrobes were a deep-brown mahogany, intricately carved, undoubtedly antique and most likely family heirlooms. Each piece appeared to have been chosen to harmonize perfectly and promote relaxation.

Sydney looked around quietly and then turned to Dahlra. He was watching her carefully, like he really, really wanted her to like it. It alternately relieved and irritated her to realise she did, very much.

"It's lovely, Dahlra. Really beautiful," she admitted. "I can see you've put a lot of thought into it, and I appreciate that."

She was rewarded with one of his side-swiping, thousand-watt smiles. "Why don't we finish the grand tour later on this evening? I hope you won't take this the wrong way, but you look seriously done in." He gestured toward the bed. "Now that we're here, why don't you have a bit of a kip while I make us some tea?"

Well, he had her there. Even though it was still early in the afternoon, her body pleaded for rest. When she nodded her agreement, Dahlra put his arm around her waist, and before she could react, he propelled her toward the bed. He pulled the covers back and gently pressed her shoulders down. "Sit. Please."

Obediently, she sat down on the edge; he knelt, and removed her shoes and socks. From the ornate chest of drawers he pulled out a long, cotton sleeping shirt and laid it next to her. When he attempted to pull her jumper over her head, Sydney stopped him.

"I can do this, Dahlra," she said, pulling the hem of her jumper back down over her torso. "Thanks, but I can manage."

"I don't mind helping you. That's my job, remember?"

"I hardly think a Minder should be expected to help me dress—"

"A Minder looks after all your needs. You *need* to sleep; ergo, I'm going to help you put on something to sleep *in*." His tone was chiding, but gentle. "Be honest with yourself, Sydney. You're so tired you can barely keep your eyes open."

Sydney sighed, wishing she could refute him, but in truth, exhaustion had seeped into her so quickly it was almost too much trouble to put up a protest. At her silent resignation, Dahlra quietly grasped the hem of her jumper and pulled it upward.

Sydney looked away as he tugged the garment over her head. He reached around her, unhooked her bra and pulled it from her shoulders with almost clinical efficiency, then immediately replaced it with the nightshirt. He waited until she pushed her arms into the sleeves before hooking his fingers over her track suit trousers and pulling them down her hips, silently indicating for her to stand so the trackies could slide past her thighs.

While he had seen her in various stages of dress and undress for months, it had always been in the confines of a hospital. Here, in the private setting of her bedroom, the simple gesture of allowing him to undress her made her feel distinctly unsettled.

Up close, his skin was creamy and smooth, like porcelain. His expression was carefully neutral as he picked up her discarded clothing, and when he caught her watching him, he shyly looked away. He pretended not to notice her discomfort as he lifted the bedclothes for her to swing her legs under.

Tucking her in like a parent would a child, he smiled down at her and gently stroked her hair away from her face. "There. You look better already."

For a moment Sydney had the distinct impression he was going to lean over and kiss her. Instead, he straightened, and walked toward the door. As he reached for the handle, he turned back to face her. His voice was as kind as his expression. "Have a little rest. If you need anything, pick up the phone and dial 'star-star.' It will ring into the kitchen."

"I'm impressed. It's just like Downton Abbey."

He laughed; it was a soft, disarmingly sexy sound. A glint of mischief lit up his eyes. "Will that be all, milady?"

She gasped out a short, startled laugh at his spot-on Northern accent. He gave her a smile of pure bliss. "Call if you need anything. I'll wake you when dinner's ready."

He softly closed the door behind him, leaving Sydney truly alone for the first time in almost four months. She looked up at the ceiling, which featured an ornate rose, surrounding an antique chandelier. It looked like a giant meringue, all curls and dollops and ridges of white plaster. She'd never lived in a place as nice as this; hell, she had never even *visited* a place this nice as a tourist. Living in a big, cushy house had never been on her bucket list; still, she could see its appeal, even though the sheer size of it threatened to overwhelm her a bit.

The massive bed was soft and deep and seemed to enclose her; hell, you'd need a Sherpa to find her in it, buried beneath its cloud of soft furnishings and down-filled comforters. She turned on her side, and buried her face against the pillow. It smelled faintly familiar. She sniffed. It was the same spicy scent she had noticed earlier, when Dahlra had moved closer to help her undress.

This had once been *his* room, but he had given it to her. She wondered if the room he'd appropriated for himself was this large and sumptuously furnished; she doubted it.

She thought of his submissive stance the day he walked into her room to announce himself as her Minder. He had been so afraid of her reaction. She recalled his delight at hearing her say his name, and his calm, professional, careful air as he undressed her. In the short time they had spent cautiously getting to know one another, Sydney was only truly certain of one thing: Dahlra Gar was committed to making sure she was happy. If he had two of anything, she would be given the larger piece. If they shared anything, he would give her the better half.

The Minder, he said, *takes care of all needs—Practical, Emotional, Physical.* She wondered if he expected her to start making demands on him. He certainly wouldn't make demands of her. Three months. She had three months to either get used to this, or walk away.

As she contemplated these things, her exhaustion, with help from the incredibly comfortable bed, took her over, and soon sleep's insistent call was too enticing to resist.

Ten minutes later, the door to the room opened, and Dahlra entered. He looked down at the sleeping woman, watching her measured breathing, slow and effortless and constant. She looked as peaceful and trusting as he'd ever seen her. Every inch of her was familiar, and beautiful and precious to him.

Her oval face was lovely in repose; her flawless, pale skin glowed with renewed health. She had without doubt the most lush, sensuous mouth he'd ever seen. Perfectly-formed, with a soft, plump bottom lip that had inspired more fantasies than he cared to admit.

She was long-limbed and graceful, and even though she was slender she was by no means boyish. Her hazel eyes seemed to change colour depending on mood, lighting, or the shade of the clothing she wore.

It was probably a good thing he had never been the kind to write poems; he probably would have written volumes about her beauty alone. Not that he would ever show them to her.

Dahlra Gar knew himself to be a hopeless optimist. *Time*, he thought. *Time, love and tenderness. That's all she needs.* She didn't stir when he gently touched his lips to her forehead.

He turned and left the room, quietly closing the door behind him.

Sydney woke up several hours later, feeling surprisingly human. When she followed her nose down to the tantalizing aromas in the kitchen, Dahlra looked up and smiled. "Ah! I was just coming to wake you. Hungry, I hope?"

"Famished. Whatever you're cooking, it sure smells like you're doing it right."

"I'll let you be the judge." He nodded toward the small breakfast table. "I'm just plating up, so we'll eat in here if you'd like. The dining room's a bit over the top for just the two of us."

He placed an oversized bowl in front of her, full of a chicken dish simmered perfectly with lemons and capers in a creamy sauce. This was generously poured over delicate handmade pasta ribbons. He was definitely more about portions than presentation; it was food enough to feed an army. It was on the tip of her tongue to tell him she would never eat that much, but when she mopped up the last of the sauce with a bit of garlic bread, she was glad she'd kept her options open. It was easily the best meal she'd had in years.

While she demolished her own meal, Dahlra ate with a bit more élan. His pleasure seemed to come from watching her eat his cooking with such relish, and his gaze rarely strayed from her face. He ate quietly, with elegant manners. His wine choice was tasteful and very classy, although Sydney, still on a cocktail of meds, had to content herself with mineral water.

After clearing away the plates, he placed a small ramekin before her, topped with a hard, toffee-coloured glaze as translucently beautiful as a tortoise shell. In spite of Sydney's full-to-bursting stomach, the little round morsel proved too great a temptation.

She tapped on its stained-glass window of burnt demerara sugar, and it gave with a satisfying crack. She dug down into the ramekin and spooned up a huge dollop of crème brûlée. It was the colour of clotted cream, speckled with vanilla beans, and it caressed her taste buds like a lover.

"Oh, my God. This is... oh, this is heavenly," she exclaimed. It was the kind of thing you wanted to shovel in your mouth until you were ill, but Sydney made herself shave the thinnest layer off the top in order to make it last.

"I'm sorry to be such a Philistine," she said between mouthfuls, "but this is one of the most delicious things I've ever eaten." She curled another sliver from the ramekin. "I think I'll be very sorry when I'm done."

He looked absurdly pleased. "A former girlfriend told me that a perfectly-executed crème brûlée was better than any aphrodisiac," he admitted, "so naturally I worked hard to perfect it."

"I don't know about aphrodisiacs, but I don't think I'd be upset if you made this for me every day. Well, my waistline would suffer, but I think I could live with it."

"I'll make it breakfast, lunch and dinner if you like. There's a workout room on the second floor," he said breezily, toasting her with his wineglass. As he brought the glass to his lips, Sydney stilled, and promptly forgot all about molesting her crème brûlée.

Without the almost constant self-consciousness, Dahlra Gar was simply stunning. There was something very masculine, and yet sensual about him that was so unfeigned, so natural, so *arresting,* that for a moment, Sydney just stared at him.

He held her gaze, and the emotion in it shook her right down to the floorboards. This time, she was the one to look away first, not because he had made her, but because she didn't want him to see *her* reaction. She had a nasty feeling she wasn't doing too good a job of hiding it.

Okay, he's attractive, he's sophisticated, and he can cook like Gary flipping Rhodes. Luck says he's hung like a hamster and has the staying power of the latest Britain's Got Talent winner. She grimaced inwardly. *Okay. That was just bitchy. And why am I even thinking about him in those terms? And am I fighting this because I'm too proud, or because I'm afraid of being weak?*

Desperate to change the subject in her own head, Sydney said, "You said my things had been moved from my Oval flat. Do I need to contact anyone about the power, phone...?"

"I'm arranging all that. As your Minder, one of my jobs is to take care of all household management. You truly don't have to worry about anything, except relaxing and making a full recovery."

She frowned. "Well, I still need to live in the world. I'm not going to be shut away."

"I should hope not. I'll be happy to take you wherever you want to go. Just tell me what you want and we'll do it."

Sydney pursed her lips. "Please understand, Dahlra, I appreciate your help, but I'm used to doing things for myself. It's a bit awkward to have someone doing everything for me."

"Not doing *for* you; assisting you. I realise this will take some adjustment, but it has nothing to do with any supposed inability on your part to do these things for yourself. The idea is to free you, to help you, and yes, to spoil you. It's only as awkward as you allow it to be." He leaned in closer. "Please give this relationship a chance, and I promise I will do everything in my power to make you content."

She frowned. "It's just... I'm just not used to doing nothing all day."

He sat back with a start. "I don't plan on us doing 'nothing' all day." He sounded genuinely surprised. "This shouldn't feel like being buried alive for either of us. I want us to have a normal, stimulating life."

It also occurred to Dahlra that thinking of him as her own personal chef in one moment, then resenting him for channeling his inner Jeeves in the next was the height of hypocrisy. One look in her eyes, and he got the feeling she was thinking the same thing.

"Besides," he said, with as much dignity as he could muster, "I don't plan on dying of boredom here. I happen to be a demon at Scrabble."

Sydney threw her head back and laughed, truly laughed. Dahlra sat transfixed, completely entranced as peal after peal of the most endearingly adorable laughter washed over him. Garnet had once told him that her friends and colleagues turned themselves inside out on a regular basis just to catch a rare outing of those delicious, bubbly giggles, and now he understood why. It was the sweetest and most infectious laugh he had ever heard, as moreish as sparkling wine. Dahlra was intoxicated by it.

Gradually, her laughter calmed, and she sat back with a contented sigh. "Alright, Scrabble Boy," she teased, "I hereby challenge you to an after-dinner game. Put your money where your mouth is."

Still spellbound, Dahlra managed to recover his composure enough to show a little savoir faire. "And I accept your challenge. We'll meet upon the field and do battle," he added, grandly. "If I win, you have to play a song for me."

She was already rising, her hands raised in surrender. "Fine, fine. You clear the dishes, I'll see if I can still play."

Within minutes, the sound of Scott Joplin's Maple Leaf Rag drifted in from the front room. By going their separate ways, Dahlra knew they were both trying to give one another a little breathing room, but somehow it didn't seem as awkward as he had feared. It didn't really matter who won the game. All he could think about was moving heaven and earth to hear that rare, sherbet scoop of laughter again.

Sydney moaned softly. "Harder, please."

"No." He used his best doctor-knows-best tone. "I can't."

"Yes, you can! Argh, this is torture!' She twisted around to look at him, her lovely eyes pleading. "Please?"

He sighed and increased the pressure of his touch. "All right, Sydney. You know how difficult it is for me to deny you anything."

She shivered and groaned with pleasure. "Ahhhh, yesss... oh, damn, that's good. More!"

"I'll hurt you. This is enough."

"No! More!"

"No more?"

"Dahlra!"

He chuckled as her pleas darkened to warning growls. He scratched marginally harder, and the growl softened to a relieved, shivery hiss of pleasure.

As her ruined back mended, the healing itch had grown maddening. Dahlra spent several minutes each night gently scratching her back. He was hesitant at first, and contented himself with deep tissue massage, but since scarring was already inevitable, and she had threatened to find the nearest tree and do it herself, bear-style, he gave in to her.

Each night, she sat on a small vanity stool, and he sat behind her on the bed, scratching her back. And each night, he would tell himself what a pathetic masochist he was, listening to her pleasure-drenched gasps and moans as he performed this palliative act. It was impossible to remain cool and detached, sitting so close, touching her so intimately. His traitorous body responded every night, growing increasingly more aroused.

He fought against his own desires, and when she begged him to 'do it harder' and 'give me more,' he threatened his own genitals with dismemberment if they didn't stand down. After all, Sydney wasn't talking to *them*.

"If I scratch any harder, I am going to undo all my hard work," he warned, reaching for the cocoa butter. It served a double purpose: it soothed the awful itching, and helped to reduce the scarring. She sighed as the cool cream touched her skin, and his large hands massaged the lotion deeply into the tissues of her back.

Every night he would spend as long as she would allow, massaging the emollient into her skin. Her back, even marred, was beautiful and warm and... and didn't that slick lotion come in handy after he had said his goodnights and raced back to his room?

In spite of the moans, the pleas, the sweet little sounds that caught on her breath and snagged into his gut, Dahlra knew the limits. His impatience had come close to destroying everything with this little scratch-and-massage bonding exercise, and he didn't think his heart could take another rejection like *that*.

It had been a good day together; they had gone shopping, eaten out at a nice restaurant, caught a film. That evening, they had shared a bottle of wine, and later, when he tapped on her closed bedroom door and gallantly offered his Minder services as Back Scratcher Extraordinaire, she had not refused.

As always, she had tucked a bath towel against her chest, leaving her back exposed. The scars ran deep, fanning outward from the centre of her back like the branches of a tree. It was all he could do not to kneel behind her and run his tongue over them.

Instead, he perched on the edge of her bed and drew his nails down each groove, across her back first up and down, then side to side.

Sydney, perhaps a little more relaxed than usual due to the wine, cooed blissfully. Her shoulders dropped, and she breathed deeply, giving in to the soothing, hypnotic motion of his hands. She unconsciously leaned back, and Dahlra saw her reflection in the vanity mirror, a smile of pleasure curving at the edges of her beautiful mouth.

Seeing her so open, so trusting, Dahlra's heart pounded. He leaned forward, and ever so softly he murmured, "Like that, do you? Would you like more?"

He had spoken close to her ear, his voice low and husky, and he saw the flesh of her neck pebble and prickle. She closed her eyes, and nodded. Her hands uncurled, and the towel lay loosely against her chest.

His blunt nails scored her ruined flesh, his slow, languid movements quelling the exasperating itch. She moaned, a soft, whimpering sound that lanced into his groin. His cock swelled and hardened. He forced his hands to remain steady, his voice to stay low and sweet as he crooned, "I'll make it better. Don't I always try to make it better?"

Caught up in the sensation, barely listening to the words, she nodded, and his hands continued their mesmeric seduction of her skin. The words he spoke were little more than just soothing, coaxing sounds of praise and comfort. His hands moved higher, ghosting over her smooth shoulders. Quietly in her ear, he whispered, "Relax, Sydney, lean against me and relax."

Finally, gradually, she obeyed him. He sighed, "Good girl. That's it...that's it... Hmm, what a good girl you are." In the mirror's reflection, he saw her eyes open slowly, luminous with the fiery beginnings of arousal.

God, he wanted her to want him. Seemingly of their own accord, his hands slid gently under her arms, his fingertips caressing the downy underside of her breasts. And then he was cupping their sweet, silky weight in his hands; they fit perfectly in his palm, warm and firm and smooth. His fingers closed on nipples already rock hard, and she arched against his hands. Desire flashed over him like heat lightning, and he pressed against, her, his erection straining, ready for her.

"Oh, yes, oh, sweet girl..." he moaned. His fingers rolled the tight nipples and she hissed, her head falling back against his shoulder. His mouth slid over the satiny skin at her neck and his tongue snaked out in a soft caress as he squeezed her perfect breasts...

She froze, then wrenched herself from his hands and wrapped the towel close to her chest. "That's enough!" she rasped, breathing hard.

Dazed and trying to think with what little blood still nourished his brain, Dahlra jumped to his feet, the fog of arousal burning away in a blinding rush. He croaked, "Sydney..."

She was staring at him with a terrible, soul-destroying combination of uncertainty and betrayal. "I really don't think we... I wasn't... I don't..." She looked feverish and angry. Her voice sounded choked, frightened, and the sudden plummet from desire to despair was such a deep, fast drop Dahlra felt slightly sick.

He raised his hands in a show of surrender. "Sydney, I'm sorry. I admit, I got carried away—"

"Y-you shouldn't have..." Her eyes still held the burn of desire, but it was tinted with shame. "I didn't mean to... I don't..."

Dahlra felt his own anger rise. The time to placate or bullshit her was long past. She had responded to him; he wasn't going to let her get away with pretending otherwise. Quietly, he replied, "Sydney, what is wrong with acknowledging desire? It felt good. You enjoyed it. I enjoyed it. You're obviously a sensual person..."

"That's not the point!" Her voice rang out in the room, hard and panicked.

"Then what is the point, Sydney? Tell me," he pleaded. "Tell me what you mean. I want you. And I think you want me—"

"I have to have some control." She took another step away, refusing to meet his eyes. Her voice and her expression were no longer angry; she seemed more sorrowful than anything. "Even if it's just over me and how I react, I have to feel like I'm in charge of something."

"I understand. I'm truly sorry I overstepped the mark, I—" He looked down at his hands, still slick with cocoa butter. "I knew you were enjoying it. I just... I want you to associate me with pleasure-not coercion, or pain, or humiliation."

"I know that. And I appreciate what you're doing. Truly. But you can't...you can't push this, Dahlra." She looked down at him, her eyes troubled, but determined. "If you care for me as much as you claim, and have any respect for me, you *won't* push this."

He stood, and when she didn't step away from him, he lightly placed his hands on her shoulders. "Take all the time you want, Sydney," he said. "I do care for you. More than you understand. And I won't push.

But I will not give up, either. I meant what I said. I will *never* let you fall. But you will never believe that, until you trust me enough to allow me to prove it."

Since that night, he had kept himself in check. No more limit-testing, no more flirtation. But each night she allowed him a little more freedom to explore.

He found a particularly hard-to-reach spot, and scratched harder.

CHAPTER SEVEN

Her Less-Than-Finest Hour

Dahlra made the same mistakes all newbie Minders did in the early days. The remit called for him to be all things and to meet all needs, but Agents were used to working without supervision or micro-management, and his behaviour felt like both.

From day one, Dahlra took every aspect of his Minder role very seriously. Sydney found it oddly touching that he kept meticulously organised notes on her preferences. She watched him jot down descriptions of her favourite colour, the way she preferred her eggs, that she bought shoes from this shop but preferred to buy her underwear from another. He knew her favourite snacks (Twirls and Twiglets), and remembered which ones to avoid (licorice).

He took her shopping; he went with her when she met up with friends. He drove her twice weekly to her sessions with the Agency's counselor. While Sydney could sense no malice in his actions, the mother hen routine got old after a while.

In his desire to be helpful, he erred on the side of over-protection. He followed her everywhere. And while he never attempted to inhibit her movements, he sometimes overstepped the mark. More than once she had to put the kybosh on the 'I-know-more-than-you-because-I'm-a-doctor' crap. He didn't *need* to hover. As she reminded him, she was not a supermodel.

He monitored her diet, but while he was making sure she got in her RDAs, he also tempted her with fabulous home-cooked meals that left her groaning in gastronomic joy. He knew how to make an egg taste like it was laid by the golden goose, and his chocolate mousse was only surpassed by his chateaubriand.

Dahlra was also one of the few good-looking men she had ever met who hadn't bought his own hype about his handsomeness. He had a shy, self-consciousness that some women found irresistible. Eventually he learned his lesson at her hair salon, where the stylists chatted him up so blatantly even Sydney felt sorry for him. He finally left her there out of sheer embarrassment, and promised from then on to simply drop her off and pick her up.

Of the two of them, he was the more sociable, and he had a gift for making people feel at ease. Garnet Pinkerton and Inigo Lightoller liked him very much. The three men formed a bromance over their shared love of football and cricket. Weekends at DeVere Gardens were spent with the house full of blue-shirted mayhem in front of Match of the Day while she and Inigo's wife Philippa wore the numbers off their credit cards at Liberty's.

And it wasn't that he didn't allow her privacy, or made her feel like a prisoner. He enjoyed spending time with her, and she found it more and more difficult to deny her own attraction to him. Perhaps that was why, when the opportunity presented itself, she did something so uncharacteristically stupid.

Dahlra had been called in for a consulting job at the Agency, and was scheduled to be away for the afternoon. When Sydney casually mentioned she would be going out without him, he acted so unconcerned she felt both lamely rebellious and guiltily disappointed.

"I'll check in," she offered, drawing an 'x' over her left breast. "Cross-my-heart-hope-to-die."

"Okay," he answered, frowning at his mobile. With hardly a backward glance, he added, "Be back soon."

He was out the door before she could say goodbye. She followed him out on the front stoop and sent him off with a wave like a right little June Cleaver, watching his car disappear around the corner. "Geez, you could've at least *pretended* you might miss me," she muttered aloud. Yep, they had truly become a couple.

She was about to go and fetch her coat, when she became aware of a singularly irritating problem. The door had automatically shut behind her as she walked out of the flat, and it had automatically locked as well.

"Fuck a duck," she said aloud. She was locked out of her own damn flat with no money, no keys and no phone. She tried to remember the last time she had done something that idiotic, and honestly couldn't.

"Ah, screw it," she muttered, and stalked down the steps. Dahlra would be back eventually; in the meantime she would continue with her plans. With any luck, he wouldn't raz her too much.

She headed down the street toward the shops, half-heartedly sussing out her own thoughts. Dahlra was on her mind, of course, and in ways that had nothing to do with his Minder duties. When she told him she was going out, he seemed uncharacteristically indifferent about it, and that bothered her. It bothered her even more that she was bothered about it. Whether he meant to or not, he was starting to fuck with her head again.

As far as she was concerned, her outing served two purposes; to prove to Dahlra she didn't truly *need* him to mother-hen her, and two, that she didn't miss having him around. And while she felt quite sure number one's objectives had been met, the jury was out on number two. No matter; by the end of the day, she was sure she would be able to work it all out in her head-maybe even to the point where locking herself out of the flat was all his fault. She smiled to herself; it was certainly worth a try, at least.

The day was cool, but sunny, and the shopping district was crowded with people as usual. Sydney decided to put aside pondering the enigma that was Dahlra Gar, and enjoy herself. She spent an enjoyable afternoon walking around the Kensington and Earl's Court areas, pausing to look into shop windows, trying on clothes she had no interest or money to purchase, and generally playing tourist.

Around four-thirty, a torrential downpour hit, catching her without an umbrella or raincoat. With most of the shops closing for the day, Sydney quickly morphed from urbane I-locked-myself-out-of-the-flat-on-purpose to soaked-to-the-knickers-drowned-rat in a matter of minutes.

She trudged back towards Kensington, cursing under her breath. She knew she could cadge a call from any corner shop and Dahlra would not hesitate to do the Parker routine and pick up Lady Penelope right at the curb. Hell, she could ring Garnet, or Inigo's wife, Pip. There were even Agency drivers who regularly acted as chauffeurs for the stranded operative.

But the thought of being driven home like an irresponsible teenager depressed her. She felt stupid enough without being given the big lecture about it. Dahlra was probably clucking so hard right now he would start laying eggs. Perfect Minder ammunition; he wouldn't want to let her out of his sight now.

She arrived at DeVere Gardens at dusk, breathless, dripping wet and shivering in the cold, October rain. The moment she knocked on the door she heard rapid footsteps heading toward her. A muffled voice within said, "Oh, thank fuck! Inigo, tell them to stand down. She's back."

Dahlra flung open the door, looking wild-eyed and disheveled. He all but yanked her inside, throwing his arms around her. "Don't *ever* do that to me again!" he cried, his voice harsh with worry. "I called you. No answer. I come home to an empty house. Your keys and phone are on the hall table. No one knew where you were. All I could imagine was you, lying in an alley somewhere. What were you thinking, Sydney?"

She winced. She had expected his anger; what she had not counted on was his anxiety. "I know. Dahlra, I'm sorry, truly. I locked myself out of the flat. "

"And you didn't think to find a phone-"

"Don't give me the big lecture, ok? I already feel like a complete idiot." She gave him her best pitiful face. "I know it was monumentally stupid—"

"Well, you'll get no argument from me on that account," he replied grimly. His large hands felt hot against her cold, wet face. "Well, you're home now. Come on. Let's get you out of these clothes and into a warm bath. You're a block of ice."

He hustled her up the stairs, his hand at the small of her back, urging her forward. "I'm sorry I was so terse. It's just... I'm relieved, and I'm cross and I'm worried. Promise me you won't do this again," he added, his quiet voice so fear-tinged it sounded like a plea. "I appreciate the cabin fever. And I know I've crowded you, and today I was determined not to. You *shouldn't* have to tell Uncle Tom Cobley and all if you want to take a walk. I get that, I truly do."

He caught her hand, and she turned to look down at him. "But I've been going mad here for over two hours. I was afraid to go out, in case I missed you. And it was killing me to just sit here, not knowing if you were safe or..."

He squeezed her hand so hard it hurt. "I don't want to sound like a thug and a bully, but this was childish thing to do, and I'm royally pissed off that you didn't at least think about your own health."

She found she could not meet his wounded, troubled gaze. He was right; she had behaved like an idiot. Worse, she had behaved like an amateur. She trudged up the remainder of the stairs and into her bedroom, with Dahlra following behind. "Look, I can only say I'm sorry so many times, but I am. And I promise the next time I'll be on the other end of a phone. Truly. I didn't do it on purpose."

"I know. But there are people out there who *think* you're dead. Sooner or later they'll know the truth. I'd rather have it later."

He stood in the doorway, arms folded across his chest. "Now, you will take a hot bath. Hot. Doctor's orders. And don't come out until you're a raisin."

"Aye, aye, Cap'n." She toed off her sodden shoes, and unbuttoned her shirt. For some reason, his fussing didn't get her dander up this time. Instead of hitting him with a standard-issue stubborn retort, she tried a different approach. "Hey. Do we have 'A Grand Day Out' on DVD?" she asked.

As she hoped, the non sequitur momentarily distracted him, but he caught on quickly enough. "If you're trying to charm me into changing the subject, it's almost working." He sighed. "Well, if we don't, we will by the time you get out of your bath."

"Good. I have this sudden urge to watch it."

"At least wear a coat next time, Sydney." His voice took on a bargaining tone. "And I'll buy you the entire Wallace and Gromit boxed set."

He wasn't smiling exactly, but looked as if he wanted to. Sydney felt a sudden, hesitant affection for him. "Deal." She was already shivering as she peeled off her soaked, clammy clothing.

As she turned on the tap, he called after her, "I knew if all else failed, pulling the W & G card would do the trick."

"Well, I hope your words are soft and juicy, Sydney," Dahlra announced, removing the thermometer from her mouth. "I'm afraid you're going to have to eat them, and I think your throat's a little too sore for anything sharp." A gentle probe confirmed swollen, painful glands at her neck.

"Ha bloody ha," she croaked, but that was about the extent of her rebuttal. Dahlra had heard her in the early morning hours, coughing and sneezing. He had entered her room just in time to see her staggering around drunkenly, and managed to catch her before she crashed into the door jam on the way to the loo. She had an inner ear infection and possibly the beginnings of strep. She grimaced each time she swallowed.

"I can't say I'm surprised," he added sternly. "Your body has taken a severe amount of stress and your immune system is shot. You were ripe for the first bug to come along." She stared miserably at him, obviously feeling too ill to summon a witty retort.

Attempting to respect her need for privacy, he left her to sleep off the aches and pains, but instead of dissipating, they grew worse as night passed into day. She was hot and groggy; he could barely rouse her to take her meds. Fever blisters bloomed on her mouth and her throat grew so inflamed it became too painful to swallow liquids. Her joints ached and all the nerves in her skin were raw; clothing felt like sandpaper against her body. He managed to keep her hydrated with IV fluids, but as the evening progressed into early morning, she showed no sign of improvement.

By the end of the second evening, Sydney's condition had worsened exponentially. Her temperature continued to rise despite the liberal use of antipyretics, and she fluctuated between feverish sweats and shivering chills. As the night fell, she started hallucinating, calling out to old colleagues and shrinking away from unknown attackers.

By sheer attrition, she fell into a fitful sleep, but Dahlra's continued efforts to decrease her temperature were unsuccessful. Looking down at her flushed face, her damp hair, he cursed his helplessness. It didn't matter to him that she'd brought this on herself; she was his responsibility, his charge. *His.* He shouldn't have let this happen.

It was time to call the Agency hospital and tell them to ready a bed for her. Better safe than sorry. He reached for his phone, but it was not in his trouser pocket. He must have left it in his room.

The mobile wasn't on his dresser. *I just had the damn thing. Of all times to wig out on my phone—*Out of the corner of his eye, he saw a white, ghostly figure flash past his door. Dahlra ran back to Sydney's bedroom. Her IV needle was lying on the bed; a bright spot of blood was spreading onto the pristine white sheet.

He raced down the stairs, searching each room, frantically calling for her. The ground floor was quiet; the doors locked from the inside. He stilled, listening intently. From high above, he caught the sound of her light footfall.

Dread ramped up into panic, and he took the stairs two at a time, calling her name as he dashed past the first floor to the second. The sound of painful, labored breathing reached his ears, and he looked up in time to see Sydney's bare foot disappearing through the trapdoor that led onto the roof.

His heart in his throat, Dahlra climbed after her and rushed out onto the top of the building. He frantically looked around. "Sydney! Where are you?" The tarred surface was still damp from an earlier rain. The cold night wind rifled through his hair. She was nowhere to be seen. "Sydney—"

"Sh-h-h." Dahlra whirled around. Sydney, clad in her thin white nightshirt, appeared by the front edge of the roof, shivering uncontrollably in the frosty air. Her hair, damp and tangled, fluttered in the wind.

"Don't give our position away," she whispered, glancing around with wild, staring eyes. "He's coming for me."

Dahlra took a step toward her. When she backed away, he replied in the friendliest tone he could manage, "Who's coming for you, Sydney?"

"The Doctor," she whimpered. Adrenalin shot into his bloodstream so fast his heart started skipping beats. She put out a hand as he took another step. "Don't come near me."

"He won't hurt you, Sydney. He wants to help you."

"No," she rasped, shaking her head over and over. "That's what he wants me to think. But I've been good. I haven't told him what he wants to hear. I'm so scared. I would have told them anything to make it stop, but I can't." Her voice broke, and she began to cry. "I don't know what he wants."

"Sydney, no one will hurt you ever again. I won't let them," he insisted, trying to keep the anguish out of his voice. "Come with me. I'll protect you."

She took another step back, toward the edge of the building. "I wouldn't tell. And then he..." She sobbed. "He lets them do things... and he *watches*." She pulled her hair around her face, as if to hide behind it.

"I never..." Dahlra cried out in spite of himself. It didn't matter that it was the delirium talking. "He always cared. You have to believe that. He had to stand by and let things happen so he would be able to save you later."

"I know." Her composure crumpled. "But, then he did things to me and made me like them. I didn't want to, but he made me like what he was doing... Don't touch me!" she screamed as he attempted to approach her again.

"Sydney, *please*," Dahlra begged, trying to pierce through the haze of the flashback. He edged slightly closer. "Come with me and I'll make sure he never does anything you don't want him to do."

"That's the problem! I wanted to do them. Can't you see?" she pleaded, her face etched with humiliation. "I'm so weak! I'm so ashamed!" she wailed, and turned toward the edge.

"Please, no," Dahlra whimpered, edging closer. She gave him a pleading look, as if he was the irrational one. For several seconds they were frozen in time: Sydney, looking at the ground forty feet below; Dahlra, desperately trying to find a way to break through the delirium.

"If I jump, it won't hurt anymore. I won't feel the shame anymore. I won't feel ill anymore. I won't be deformed anymore." Tears streamed down her fever-flushed cheeks as she took two more steps toward the edge.

"No! He won't let you jump. He'll stop you. He loves you." He put his hands together, as if praying to her. "*I* love you."

She paused, and her eyes cleared of their fever glaze. "No you don't," she whispered hoarsely, looking him straight in the eye. "All you do is watch."

She turned, and sprinted toward the edge.

Dahlra was on her in two long, leaping strides. He grabbed onto the only bits of her within reach, her hair and her gown, and yanked her back as hard as he could. He felt the cloth tear in his hands like paper; he heard her thin scream of pain.

Then they were spinning away from the edge, toward the centre of the roof. Dahlra lost his balance, and they landed with a crash as he fell clumsily on top of her. Sydney cried out at the impact. She struggled beneath him, but she was too weak to really put up a fight. "Please! Don't hurt me anymore!" she wailed.

"I'm not trying to hurt you, Sydney!" His fists were locked into her hair and gown; he had to consciously tell his fingers to relax. He staggered to his feet, and tried to help her to stand, but she was a struggling, fighting tangle of arms and legs.

She screamed as he held her close, and tried to fishtail out of his grasp. "I'll be good! I promise! I won't tell, I won't tell, iwonttelliwonttell..."

Her knees buckled, and Dahlra managed to catch her under her arms before she collapsed. Trembling with effort, he lifted her over his shoulder in a graceless fireman's carry, and made his way down the steps on legs that felt as if he had run a marathon. The heat radiating from her was incredible; he wondered how close her temp was to the protein-scrambling forty-one degrees that could fry her brain.

"Garnet!" she shouted, making him jump. "Watch your left side..." she trailed off, her words fading. Carefully descending the trap door steps, Dahlra made his way straight to his bedroom as quickly as his faltering gait would allow. He turned on the water in the large shower cubicle, letting it run much colder than his medical training told him was safe. Praying that it wouldn't send her into shock, he lowered her from his shoulder-crunching hold and awkwardly shuffled both of them into the cubicle.

They cried out in unison as the water sluiced over their bodies, and Sydney began to shake even more. She tried fruitlessly to get away from the frigid water, but Dahlra grimly held her under the showerhead. Her teeth chattered so hard he could actually hear them clacking together. "I'm sorry," he said, over and over, unable to think past those two words. "I'm sorry." Her breath came in and out in great wheezing gasps that broke his heart to hear.

Gradually, her cries dissipated to small whimpers. She looked up at him, mutely pleading for comfort, and he held her, kissing her flushed cheeks. As her body temperature slowly decreased, she relaxed against him, and he shut off the water. Holding her tightly around the waist, he managed to drag them out of the shower stall, staggering like two drunks pinballing out of a pub door.

He made quick work of removing her soaked nightgown, and wrapped her in a huge towel. After draping a second towel around her head, turban style, he removed his own dripping shirt. Then he picked her up in his arms again and carried her back into his bedroom. Her head rested against his shoulder like an exhausted child's.

Dahlra sat her down on his bed, rubbing her skin with firm, hard strokes, using the friction of the towel to warm her. He worked his way from her shoulders down, stopping when he reached her knees. They were scraped and abraded from the hard impact of landing on the roof; a tiny trickle of blood ran down her shin. *I did that to her*, he thought bleakly, adding yet another slice of guilt to his plate. *When am I going to stop hurting her?*

He rose, ignoring the twin pops of his knees, and headed back into the bathroom, shedding his soaked trackies and leaving them on the tiled floor. He moistened some cotton wool with Anti-Bac, and returned to kneel at her feet. As he carefully cleaned her wounds, she flinched, and Dahlra gently blew on the torn flesh to take the sting away. On impulse, he leaned forward, and gently kissed her scraped knee. Her eyes widened in surprise, but she said nothing.

He tried to smile. "Didn't Daddy ever kiss the hurt to make it better?" he asked softly.

When she didn't respond, he slumped in defeat. What a fuckup this entire thing had been. Suddenly he was sick of it all; the fever, the Minder crap, himself, even her. It was all too much. He rubbed his strained neck.

Sydney was still staring at him. Then, she touched his face, and whispered, "Thank you."

His heart flooded with tenderness, and he exhaled in a great, exhausted gust. His gaze leveled on her feet dangling off the side of his tall bed. They were pale, and slender, and achingly vulnerable. He could see the deformation of the nails, where some sadistic bastard had tortured her.

He clasped them in his hands; they were like ice. He rubbed them gently to warm them. She jumped slightly, but it was more a reflex than any conscious attempt to pull away. Without stopping to think, he pressed his lips against her white, soft foot.

"I would do anything for you," he said, his breath warming her flesh as he spoke. "I would do anything to show you..." his voice broke awkwardly, and he didn't bother finishing the sentence. He chanced a glance at her face; she was watching him as if she had never seen him before.

They were both shivering; Dahlra knew if he didn't get dry, he'd be the one with pneumonia. He sat back on his heels. Sydney was still shaking uncontrollably. To hell with it—tonight, he wasn't going to leave her. If she didn't like sleeping with him, too bad.

He quickly toweled himself dry. "Sydney, I'm going to get some things for you to wear. Please don't get out of bed, okay?"

She looked up at him blankly, as if he were speaking a foreign language. He put his hands on her shoulders "Sydney darling, lie down." She continued to stare at him, uncomprehending.

He watched her anxiously as he exchanged his soaked boxers for a dry pair. She was clocking his movements, so he knew she was at least lucid, but she just didn't seem to parse what he was saying.

He walked over to the bed, but just as he reached her, she obediently laid down, her eyes locked with his. "Good girl," he said, with a smile he hoped didn't look as scared as he felt. "You just stay there, love. I'll find you something to wear."

He quickly rummaged through his dresser, trying to find something comfortable for her to sleep in. He grabbed an oversized Queen t-shirt that he had bought while Freddie was still alive; it was faded and frayed at the collar, but soft from a thousand washings and long enough to cover her knees.

Sydney was exactly where he had left her, curled up on the bed like a wounded animal. The sight of her shivering tore at his heart, and he tossed the t-shirt on a nearby chair and quickly climbed into bed with her.

"Come here, Sydney. Let me get us both warm." He threw the heavy duvet over them both, wincing as cold skin met colder skin. "Shh. It's alright." He pulled her as close as he could, briskly rubbing her arms. As warmth gradually began to seep into her, she looked into his face. She was still shivering and miserable, her eyes huge and wet in the dim light.

With a voice laced with shame and exhaustion, she whispered, "I wet myself in the shower. I couldn't help it."

"I'm pretty sure I did, too." His statement drew a ghost of a. He brushed her drying hair from her face. "It's alright, Sydney. It was very cold." He could feel her body temp rise again, but it didn't feel like the shocking fever it had been.

Against his chest, Sydney whispered tiredly, "I understand what you did, and why you did it. I forgive you. And I..." She sighed. "You did the right thing. I can't help it that I'm angry. I'm trying, Dahlra. I'm really, really trying to accept it."

The night after Dahlra entered the cell and told her he wanted to help her, he came to her again. She tensed as she saw his tall form silhouetted by the light in the corridor. He closed the door, and stood for a moment to allow his eyes to adjust to the darkness.

She watched intently as he produced a syringe. Her expression changed from uncertainty to terror. *She thinks this is it*, he realised. *She thinks I'm here to kill her.*

After swabbing an alcohol pad on her arm, he quickly injected her, then tossed the spent needle into the hazmat bin by the door. "Oh, God," she whispered. Her eyes were wild with fear. "Okay. Okay. Numbers, I could really use some numbers right now." She closed her eyes and took deep breaths, counting feverishly, as if the numbers were Hail Marys. Dahlra felt so full of guilt and self-loathing he wanted to cry.

"I would have thought what I'm going to do would be obvious by now, Ms Chapin, but I fear I'm wrong. I'm not here to kill you," he said softly. She stared at him in shock, and the realisation that he hadn't given her a cyanide chaser made her go limp. Perhaps she was glad. Perhaps she was disappointed. In a way, it made what he was about to do even more important. He only hoped that one day he could make her understand why.

He lay down on the bed, almost on top of her, and slightly to her right. A look of growing apprehension rose in her eyes; then they shifted out of focus as the drug began to take effect. This was not one of the vials of interrogation juice he had been using on her during the day. This was something he had saved for just such an occasion. He lay still against her, praying he was doing the right thing for the right reasons. "I need you to do this. I need you to enjoy this."

She cut her eyes back to his, clearly nonplussed. He leaned forward and nuzzled her neck. His hand drifted downward and grasped her hospital gown. As he slowly gathered the material in his hand, the hem crawled up her legs, and she began to struggle.

"I'm not going to hurt you." At this whispered declaration, Sydney examined his face closer. With the drug taking effect, she was obviously trying to understand what was happening, but she couldn't seem to grasp it. When the bottom of the gown reached the top of her thighs, his fingers brushed between her thighs, across the opening of her sex. She jumped as his hands slipped inside her knickers and caressed her.

"The monitors are on. We're being watched," he whispered. He could barely hear his voice over the blood pounding in his ears. "The guard thinks I'm here to—to molest you."

She made a low, soulless sound, like a laugh, or a cough. "Oh, you think? If it looks like rape and feels like rape it must be cole slaw Do you actually think this is exciting me?" Her voice shook with anger and humiliation.

He pressed his forehead against her temple. "It *is* exciting you. You can couch it any way you like, Ms Chapin, but your body doesn't lie," he whispered, his mouth close to her ear.

She turned away from him in disgust. "Oh, my mouth says no but my eyes say yes? How fucking cliché! Is this how you get all your women to go to bed with you?"

"Only the ones I want to keep alive," he said, his own voice harsh. "Listen to what I'm telling you."

"Fuck. Off..."

As her last words faded away, her eyes fluttered for a moment, as his fingers found the soft, dormant bud at the entrance to her sex. In spite of her anger and denial, Sydney felt a sudden, unwelcome bloom of arousal, and hated herself for it. His fingers expertly teased her flesh, urging her body to respond against her will, the juices she produced smoothing the way for him to stimulate her further. She looked into his unsmiling face. His eyes were anything but unreadable now.

She turned her face away and stared up at the ceiling. "You've humiliated me in every way possible," she whispered back, "Now this? Is this part of your, 'let's make her feel better' regime?"

"I need you to feel alive again—I need..." he whispered, kissing her temple almost feverishly. "This will help."

He smelled good; an enticing mixture of fresh, spicy soap and clean male. She thought of the rank, unwashed bodies of the men who had abused her. The Doctor smelled like a lover.

"I'm not a performing monkey," she spat, but she could hear the uncertainty in her own voice. Try as she might, she could not quell the deep pressure in her core that called for her body to orgasm.

I've been raped over and over here, she told herself. *This man has tortured me. This is another mind-fuck, Sydney, Stockholm central, and girl, you can't do this. You hate this fucker! You hate this—*

Oh, holy fuck, he knew what he was doing. His touch was too feather-light, too knowing, and aided by the drugs, she felt the slow burn build within, that tightening pull deep inside that was the Get Out Of Jail Free card for her libido. Soon, short of jabbing herself in the leg with a shiv, nothing would stop her body from climaxing.

He must have sensed how close she was. "Good, good. That's it. Don't fight it, Sydney," he coaxed, his voice low and insistent. "Let it happen. Get good and angry. Hate me all you want—just let it go."

Her senses overloaded with arousal and shame, coerced by his talented, knowing fingers. She was going to come. "Oh, no," she groaned, as if her denial had any power to stop it.

"That's right, love," he crooned. "There we are, all ready to go—you can hate it all you like but let it go—" Under his breath he moaned through gritted teeth, "Come on, Sydney, come on—"

She stiffened suddenly, and found her release. Her body strained against his fingers, and he felt her breath, hot and moist, on his neck as she gulped for air.

He stayed with her, working to take her as high as the waves of her orgasm allowed. She took a large breath, then let it out slowly, like a tire deflating. Her limbs slackened as she came down from her climax. It had not been the spectacular release he'd hoped, but perhaps it was enough.

"Well done. What a good girl you are," he praised. He kissed her damp forehead as he lowered her gown back in place. He turned his face away from the camera and waited until he got his own breathing under control before he whispered, "Do you want me to take you to the toilet to clean up?"

She gave him such a look of pure hatred that he recoiled from her. "And what are we going to do in there for an encore, Doctor? Act out the Kama Sutra? Jesus, I thought the guards were bad," she slurred, her face contorting with disgust.

He smiled mirthlessly. Her fire was still there—smoldering, tamped down, but there, nevertheless. "Good. I deserved that."

"Oh, you think?"

"As long as you are feeling something, I can keep you alive, Ms Chapin," he countered. "If you can remember pleasurable stimuli, you'll stay alive. So remember how much you hate me, and *stay alive*."

He glanced at his watch. "I have to go."

Her eyes were hard in spite of the relaxant. "Thank fuck for that."

He turned and swung his legs off the table, and stood. He walked over to the door and switched the lights to infrared again. "Pleasant dreams."

As he reached the door, she hissed, "The Good Cop-Bad Cop routine doesn't work if you play both parts, you know."

He turned back to her. "And which part am I playing now?"

Long after he had gone, Sydney lay awake, eyes shut, breathing deeply. She was completely flummoxed over this latest development. She knew she was missing something vital, but she was still stoned, her head as muzzy as if she'd spliffed up.

As hard as she tried, she couldn't pull all the pieces together. Her body still faintly hummed from the release he had all but dragged out of her. Instead of feeling violated and dirty, as she always did when molested, she just felt pissed off.

And which part am I playing now?

Good question. *Perhaps he was right*, she thought. *Perhaps I shouldn't give up just yet.*

The next night, he returned. Silently, he crossed to her bed and quickly unbuckled her restraints. "The guards think I want you for myself. I've made them leave you alone. But nobody's watching right now. The guard is asleep, so do what you need to do. Do you understand?" he asked. She nodded her reply.

"Good girl." He straightened. "You have about thirty minutes before the watch changes. I'll be back just before then to replace the restraints. Don't try to escape; don't do anything stupid. I'll be on the other side of the door."

He turned and left so quickly Sydney could have almost believed the whole incident a dream, except that her arms and legs were blissfully free—and she was wonderfully alone, if he was to be believed. She stretched deeply and turned on her side, curling up into a fetal position.

She considered the entire situation. He might be lying about the guards. But, so what? With one eye on the CCTV camera Sydney swung her legs off the table, and furtively tested her weight. When she found they would support her, she took a brisk walk around the room, studying it carefully, looking for anything that could be used as a weapon. She found nothing; even the hazmat container of old sharps had been removed. The Doctor had planned this little picnic with care.

She stretched and flexed her muscles, trying to work a little strength back into her atrophied limbs. It felt good just to move around. She did a few squats and kicks; she was horrifically weak. She was just been about to break out in song when the door opened again. The Doctor waited in silence as she dutifully crawled back on the table. Only then did he cross the room, and place her hands and legs back in the straps.

"What did you do with your time, Ms Chapin?"

She looked up into his face, but it was a blank, solemn mask. "What do get from all this, Doctor Who?" she demanded softly. "What do you really want?"

He seemed on the verge of answering, but instead, turned and left. Only the faintest trace of his cologne proved he had been there at all.

The next night, he entered her room as before. This time however, after he removed her restraints, he left wordlessly. This time, as the door closed behind him, Sydney wasted no time. She instantly jumped from the bed and began another series of calisthenics. It felt glorious to move of her own accord, to strengthen and stretch her weakened muscles. As she arched her back, she unconsciously stroked her arms, her belly, her breasts. Her nipples were hard. Sydney had a flashback of the Doctor's hand slipping inside her, his voice low and sensual as he caressed her.

She remembered what it was like to enjoy sex, but hell, a good mile run and a sauna provided the same endorphin high. She had never been one to fantasise much, at least not about anything she'd share with anyone else. It was hard to come up with the goods, so to speak, that would get her body motivated.

Standing still, she closed her eyes and sighed as her hands drifted over her breasts. She rubbed her stiffened nipples with her open palms. They did feel very sensitive...

Her eyes flew open and she looked around. She felt too exposed in this room. With a glance at the door, she turned away from the CCTV, toward the back wall, and closed her eyes again. She unbuttoned her gown. As she caressed her nipples, she was amazed how hard they were; how good it felt to touch them. After the past few weeks, she suspected she would never want to touch herself or be touched ever again. Yet, even now, she could feel heat stirring, and without conscious thought her hand slid between her legs.

Sydney felt a sharp, sudden pang of arousal lance into her core. *Oh shit,* she thought. Her arousal faltered, and fell over. She growled softly in frustration, feeling like a complete head case.

She tried to recapture it, telling herself she was an adult; she could do this. She took a deep breath and thought of that voice again, the whisper of his cologne. She touched herself, feeling the wet, slick heat between her legs. Her fingers found the engorged nub at the top of her sex and began to circle it rhythmically.

It felt surprisingly good; good enough, in fact, to feel a little dirty. That excited her more. Her breathing became deeper and the heat in her belly grew, crowding out her inhibitions. The image of the Doctor came into her head, his velvety baritone voice urging her on. "Good girl, come for me..."

Her orgasm caught her by surprise, causing her legs to buckle. She grasped the table for support and held her other hand over her mouth to stifle her cries. The climax seemed to last forever. She leaned against the bed, breathless, feeling exposed and ashamed.

The door opened, and she wrenched away from the table, keeping her back to him. With shaking fingers, she misbuttoned her gown, breathing deeply to calm her racing heart. She would be damned if she was going to give him the satisfaction of seeing her like this, panting and sexed up and fantasising about him.

Unfortunately, he didn't give her any time to collect herself as he purposefully crossed the room to where she stood. "Ms Chapin. On the table, please," he commanded quietly.

She looked up at him, still breathless from her orgasm, and mutely dared him to say anything. Silently, he re-buttoned her gown properly and pulled it down over her knees.

He turned away, and she heard water running. He returned with a warm flannel, and carefully cleaned her hands of any evidence of her actions. With the same gentle handling, he returned her wrists and ankles to their restraints. Sydney watched him carefully, but he would not meet her eyes.

"Who are you, Doctor?"

He looked at her then, and Sydney was stunned at his expression. Either he was a hell of an actor, or her pet tormentor was almost in tears. Suddenly he bent his face close to hers. He smelled of basil and toothpaste. "Don't give up." He left without looking back.

For six nights in a row this was their ritual. Sometimes the monitors were online, sometimes they were not. He never explained what he told the guards or what they thought they were seeing, but she suspected he had fed them a lot of shite about voyeurism and conditioning. At the end of the day, it didn't really matter.

On the nights they were watching, she played with herself, or pretended to. On the nights her cameras were dead, she ran laps around the room. On one memorable occasion, she sang at the top of her voice until she was hoarse. She found she didn't care if they were watching or not.

When she actually masturbated, it was furtive and quickly done, not particularly satisfying for anyone watching. But every night's performance was on her terms. During the day, wielding his drug du jour, the Doctor neither chastised nor praised the previous night's performance. This vaguely pissed her off in a way that gave her a twisted sort of pleasure beyond the endorphin rush. She *was* starting to care again.

On the seventh night, he entered the room, and removed the restraints. "The monitors are down tonight," he said by way of greeting. Instead of leaving, as he had always done, he backed away until he reached the far table, and stopped. His expression was hard to read, but his eyes told their own story. They were large and luminous; almost glowing in the dark. This time, the Doctor wanted a piece of the action.

Sydney turned on her side, facing him, and their eyes met. Something in his stance and the look on his face stirred a current of lust in her loins. She felt strangely drugged, as if his presence were the equivalent of a hit of E or a really good spliff. Showtime, folks.

"If I ask you to leave, will you?"

"Yes." He nodded slowly, as if he, too, was drugged. His voice was soft but there was something pleading in it she had never heard before. "But I don't want to."

Sydney smiled. That tiny bit of power she had over him seeped into her veins like a spider's poison. It wasn't enough to do any damage, but now it didn't seem to matter too much. And the monitors were off.

"Okay, Doctor. You can stay. But I want something from you."

"Yes." He didn't hesitate, not even to draw breath.

"You want to watch, Doctor?" She rolled onto her back, reaching for the buttons of her gown. "Then so do I."

His eyes glinted as she slowly parted the sides of the garment, revealing her breasts. She was thin from her incarceration, so she arched her back to make them look fuller. She caressed her nipples until they were hard and taut. The Doctor stared at them like a starving man ready to devour a banquet. His mouth parted in a soft gasp. "Oh…" he all but groaned.

Arousal bloomed in her core, surprising her with its yearning ache. She closed her eyes as her hand drifted over her taut nipple, and she moaned softly as she rolled it between her fingers. The Doctor leaned his head on his arm against the cabinet beside the door. His erection was obvious even in the half-light. He was breathing hard, a loose, open expression on his face. He slowly licked his lips, and her core flooded with wet heat.

His eyes followed hers down to his crotch, and hesitantly, he stroked himself through his clothing, a gasp leaving his lips unbidden. Sydney thrilled at the feeling of power she had over him at this moment.

She kept her eyes locked onto his as she slid her hand down her belly and into the waistband of her knickers. Her eyes closed involuntarily as her fingers found her sex slick and primed.

"Take them off." Her eyes flew open. He was still standing against the wall, but his presence had grown in the room, asserting his dominance again. He nodded toward her knickers, his eyes burning hot enough to incinerate them. His voice was hoarse and quietly urgent. "Take them off."

She gave him what she hoped was a rich smile, full of promise. "You didn't say the magic word, Doctor." she whispered with a soft moan.

He turned his face away, as if to master his desire. "Please," he ground out his voice tight and angry. "Please."

"Well, since you asked so nicely." She slowly peeled her underwear from her hips and kicked them onto the floor.

Their eyes met again as she began to pleasure herself. He watched her fingers moving against her turgid flesh, and with each moan from her lips his breathing grew more rapid and uneven. She growled petulantly, "You know what I want. A deal's a deal."

Obediently, he unzipped his fly and took himself in hand.

Something changed. At first, it was just the thought of him actually abandoned enough to masturbate in front of her, but as Sydney felt her body gathering itself for release, she knew it was more than that. It was a need within, a desperate longing to see him lose control, and to lose control with him. If she could make him do that, perhaps she could gain more control over him. If he obeyed her once, he would do it again.

She turned her head back to the ceiling, and he rasped, "No! Look at me. I have to see your face." He hesitated. "Please."

Close to the edge, Sydney turned back to him. Their hands seemed to be moving at the same urgent speed. "Why?"

He moaned and stroked harder. His words came out in a rush of desperation. "I want to see the look on your face. I want to be part of it. I want you to come for me. Just for me, Sydney, please, it's got to be soon, it's got to be now—"

And oh, God, if that rasping, low, pleading voice didn't excite her more than anything she'd ever experienced in her life. She uttered a harsh curse and she could feel herself going, and her back arched as she reached the peak. "Then tell me to come. Make me come for you," she demanded, and her broken words seemed to break something in him as well.

The Doctor rushed toward her, blazing down on her like a cobra preparing to strike. In a deep and commanding voice, he choked, "Come. Come for me, Sydney. Do it now!"

Pleasure bloomed from a pinpoint in her groin, then rushed through her. With a guttural moan, the Doctor found his own pulsing, hard release. They came together, their bodies wracked with spasms, their soft gasps and moans an erotic duet.

Wave after wave of pleasure crashed over her, hitting her hard, allowing her to come up for air, then plunging her into ecstasy again. The orgasm seemed to last for years. And the entire time, her eyes were locked onto his.

At last, she fell back, mewling little cries of relief. He sagged over the table, panting like a runner. In his blissed-out state, he was totally open, and as if to prove it, he made a soft, whimpering sound of completion.

It took him several minutes to compose himself, but when he did, he stumbled away from her, toward the sink. She watched the movements of his shoulders as he washed his hands, cleaning away all the evidence of his unpardonable loss of control.

Still breathless, Sydney rolled onto her side, facing him. She thought wryly of the mess he'd probably made in his trousers.

"Why?"

He turned his head to the side, but didn't turn around. "Why what, Ms Chapin?"

"Why this? Why tonight?" When he didn't reply, she pressed on, "Are you lonely? Missing someone back home?"

"I... I don't know."

"Did you do this? Did you wank the first night you forced yourself on me?"

He dropped his shoulders with a soft sound, but didn't reply.

"Well, did you?"

He shut the water off and dried his hands with a towel, but didn't face her immediately. His voice sounded nearly normal again when he answered, "No."

"Why not?" She pressed, hoping to rattle him a little while he was vulnerable. "I would have thought a red-blooded male like yourself would have gotten off after that little performance. My smell on your hands—"

"Please, Ms Chapin." He sounded weary and spent, and not in a good way.

He turned around and returned to her table, still holding the flannel. He didn't seem angry or upset. In fact, he looked stricken, as if the moment they shared had truly been something sordid, unworthy, like a tryst with a prossie in a cheap hotel room.

He looked down on her for so long that she began to feel self-conscious, and tried to turn away from him.

"No." he said. His voice was soft, with a touch of accusation. "You wanted this. You will accept the results. Cause and effect." He buttoned her gown and retrieved her discarded underwear. He dressed her fully again. He then grasped her damp hand and washed it meticulously.

He was gentle in his ministrations, his face set and intractable. And while he didn't meet her eyes, he was as careful with her as he had ever been. There was something strange about the look on his face; he seemed more saddened than sated from his climax.

She allowed him to restrain her, too wired up and tangled in her thoughts to really notice what he was doing. It wasn't real, she told herself. It was all a pretty illusion, and crediting him with any other motive was dangerous.

He is playing you like a cheap violin, and you're just affection-and-compassion-starved enough to buy this 'I'm the only chance you have' crap. This is one of the oldest interrogation techniques in the book, and you're falling for it like it's the first time it was ever used. Grow up, girl. The only way you're leaving this cell with him is in a body bag. He is the enemy, and the only real chance you have is to play him right back.

Still snagged in the conflicting thoughts running through her mind, she called softly, "Doctor?"

"Yes, Ms Chapin?" He answered over his shoulder, as if he didn't trust himself to look at her again.

"I don't mind if you watch. If you come here every night, I'll let you watch."

He turned and faced her, a twisted, stricken look marring his face. "For God's sake, Sydney ..."

"It's okay, Doctor," Sydney replied consolingly. She didn't bother to hide the triumph in her voice. "I'll keep you sweet. Like you said, you're my only chance."

The next day the Evac Team arrived, and Sydney did indeed leave in a body bag of sorts, just not quite the way she had expected...

"I really *do* understand. Why you did it, I mean," Sydney repeated, as her body convulsed with cold.

Dahlra wrapped his arms around her so tightly he could hear her gasping for breath. The heat of his skin eventually warmed her, and her teeth ceased their uncontrollable chattering. Gradually, she relaxed, and her breathing slowed.

She eased against him, seeking comfort. As she nestled her face against his, he breathed heavily, as though his heart would burst. "I'm sorry for everything, Sydney. I hated myself. I still do."

"I hated myself, too," she confessed, and tears moistened her eyelashes. "I hated myself for getting caught. I hated myself for giving in. And I hated myself for blaming and manipulating you into...into doing things."

"Will you ever be able to stop hating me, Sydney?"

She looked at him for a long time, and placed a cold, trembling hand on his face. "You were so scared, weren't you?"

"I don't have any right to ask, but please, Sydney—"

"I forgive you, Dahlra. I really, really do."

The relief of her forgiveness broke him utterly, and the tears he had tried so hard not to shed overwhelmed him.

Sydney looked alarmed at his emotional outburst. The more he tried to get himself under control, the more he fell apart. He wept helplessly, for all he had done and the shame he had carried with him like a burden he was not allowed to lay down.

"Hey, it's okay," she said soothingly, wiping the tears from his face. "Dahlra, I forgive you. I have to. How else can I forgive myself?"

"Oh, God," he sobbed, holding onto her tightly, but she didn't complain. "I wish I could make you feel whole again—"

"I believe you. Why does it hurt so much to cry?" she asked, her tears flowing in unison with his.

He kissed her forehead again. "It only hurts when we try to hold it back," he replied with a sniff. "Let them go, Sydney. You'll feel better if you do. Getting ready to cry is worse than crying itself."

Later, she lay curled against his shoulder, exhausted and tear-spent. Dahlra held and comforted her, and finally, lulled by his soothing whispers, she fell into a deep sleep. Gradually, he relaxed, but sleep was the last thing on his mind.

He chastised himself, not for the first time, that he was being totally selfish by insisting that she accept him as her Minder. A voice inside his head, which sounded suspiciously like his mentor's, told him she would probably be a lot better off without his daily presence serving as a reminder of the hell he had helped her experience. He knew the voice was probably right. But he couldn't bear the thought of not having her in his life. If that made him a selfish bastard, so be it.

Three hours later, he awoke with a start and bolted upright, wide awake and terrified. He had been dreaming. They were back on the roof, but instead of grabbing Sydney at the last minute, her shirt melted away as soon as he tried to grasp it. Impotently he screamed as she fell, watching her fall to her death. Watching her, always watching and being

able to do nothing—

Sydney lay beside him, perfectly still. Too still; too pale. Alarmed, he placed his fingers at her neck, then sagged with relief. She was drenched in sweat; her fever had broken. Her pulse was strong and steady beneath her cool skin. Dahlra sent up a silent thanks to a deity he had not prayed to since his exam days.

He wicked away most of the sweat using a towel, pausing every few seconds in case he awoke her. He needn't have worried; he could have probably dumped her in the tub and she would have slept through it. Satisfied, Dahlra crawled back into bed. Sydney nuzzled against his neck, and he stroked her back fondly. As she slept peacefully enfolded in his embrace, he found his own dreamless sleep at last.

Sometime later, Sydney drifted awake to find herself snuggled against a soundly sleeping Dahlra. He made a very comfortable, warm pillow. When she stirred, he pulled her closer with a possessive little rumble, and whispered her name. In the pre-dawn light, his skin looked like marble, smooth and constant and firm. His chest rose and fell rhythmically, his exhales almost but not quite turning into snores. She could see his eyes moving beneath his eyelids in REM sleep.

I wonder what he's dreaming.

Looking into his sleeping face, Sydney felt safe for the first time since returning to the UK. *Why not accept this handsome, caring man, indeed?*

She snuggled deeper into his arms, trying them on for size.

CHAPTER EIGHT

Dreams

In the days that followed, Sydney recovered slowly but steadily, thanks to Dahlra's insistence that she follow his instruction to the letter. His better-living-through-chemistry approach with antibiotics and Vitamin C kept the recovery going in the right direction. She even managed to dodge the strep infection bullet.

Knowing that he would dig in his heels at the first sign of any insurgence, and not exactly eager for more hands-on experience with the joys of delirium, Sydney gave in graciously, letting him mother hen her to his heart's content. And if she were totally honest with herself, it *was* nice to loll about in bed sucking on crushed ice, while Dahlra padded around, fussing over her and spoiling her with crème brûlée and any other soft, easy-to-swallow food he could persuade her to eat.

Oh, yes, everything was going swimmingly. Until bedtime.

The nightmares, which had faded since leaving hospital, returned with a vengeance. Each was more terrifying than the last, as old fears resurfaced and old enemies regenerated. Sleep heralded a nightly Hit Parade of the most hideous moments of her capture and torture.

Dahlra figured prominently in many of the dreams. In the worst ones, he would be the one inflicting pain, while others like Inigo looked on. She would see him standing by the wall, watching as she suffered at the hands of her captors. Sometimes he would be smiling, as if he were enjoying the show. There were mornings when she felt such unasked for animosity toward him, he would avoid her until after lunch.

The nightmares struck Sydney as textbook Freudian. During her incarceration, she had constantly dreamed of home, the beach, her old life before the Agency. All those safe haven dreams that tormented her with their normality, their security. It rankled that she wussed out with a nightly case of the heebie jeebies over dreams that, in the cold light of day, were about as scream-worthy as a Bela Lugosi B-movie. She could bitch all she wanted that her dreams were so clichéd as to be boring, but at one-fifteen in the morning, her screams were loud enough to wake the dead. Never had she been so glad to live on an end-of-terrace house with no neighbors on either side.

She stoutly refused any sedatives or sleeping aids, believing the nightmares ultimately served a purpose, like lancing a wound to purge it of poison. One day, she was convinced, the nightmares would release their hold on her system. In the meantime, she suffered them with grim determination.

Dahlra agreed with her in principle, although it made for hard times for the both of them. Their sleep-wake patterns grew unstable as they snatched catnaps during the day, saving their strength for meeting the horrors in her head at night. Dahlra never faltered, never strayed from his post, never left Sydney to fend for herself. Even as she cursed him and flailed in the bed, trying to get away from unseen hands, he was there to calm her. Each night it was his voice calling her back to the surface as she drowned in the clutches of her nightmares.

It was Dahlra who soothed her when frustration and sleep deprivation left her restless and strung-out. He would ease her awake when the twitching alerted him to the impending dream, then settle her back to sleep again, staying with her until she drifted back off, always watching over her, steady and compassionate, in spite of his own exhaustion.

As Sydney tenaciously held out against sedatives, they tried more inventive ways to combat the dreams. She exercised daily, running herself into the ground on the treadmill in the work-out room. They took walks that lasted hours. He fed her traditional torpor-inducing foods: turkey sandwiches, chocolate chip cookies, cups of Rooibos tea, hot milk and cocoa.

He read dull, dry books aloud, trying to drone her to sleep. They tried hypnosis, Neuro-Linguistic Programming, mnemonics, hot baths, stone massage, lavender oil and soft music. Sydney embraced every new attempt with grim hope. She would have tried voodoo if it would have stood a chance against the nightly Shock Theatre routine. But the nightmares remained the enemy, and sleep the battleground.

If she had trouble settling down again after a particularly bad one, she and Dahlra would sometimes sit up in bed, watching mindless telly or just talking into the wee hours. He was only too happy to oblige; he hoped their quiet conversations would lull her to sleep. Sydney hoped they would keep her awake.

They told one another about their lives growing up. They swapped war stories; they talked about books and music and theatre; they discussed the films they had enjoyed and the meals they had eaten. They talked about everything except their time in the cell. That particular conversation was unnecessary; Sydney relived it on a nightly basis.

The nightmares continued for a month. During the last two sleep-deprived weeks, Dahlra spent each night sitting in an armchair in her room, grabbing what little sleep he could until the cycle started again. He would come to her then, and gather her to his chest, rocking her, calming with his deep, soothing voice, and she would clutch at him like a drowning woman.

One morning, Dahlra was interrupted by Sydney's strangled cry of distress. He came flying into the room, toothbrush in hand, to find her staring at her reflection in the mirror. A strand of her hair on the right side, from root to tip, had turned white.

"It doesn't matter," he said, tenderly stroking the offending hair. "It doesn't change the fact that you're beautiful. You know that."

She refused to be comforted. "I look like Lily Munster." No amount of reassurance could convince her otherwise.

Her nightmares ended abruptly, after one of those sun-breaking-through-the-clouds revelations that, if she had seen it in the movies, she would have dismissed as being trite and hackneyed. By that time, they knew everything remotely interesting about one another; all those getting-to-know-you facts all couples shared in the early days of a burgeoning relationship.

Dahlra had an older sister living in Australia; Sydney's parents had been straight-up American middle-class conservatives from Kershaw, South Carolina. Dahlra's father had been a physician; Sydney's a small town dentist. His mother had been a housewife and by all accounts a beauty. Hers had been the secretary at her elementary school, ostensibly so she could spend the summer vacations with her daughter and thus avoid having to pay a babysitter.

She also discovered Dahlra did not, as she had once predicted, have crooked toes or snore like a pig. He seemed more than capable of filling out his boxers, and he was constant and good natured about everything except losing at Scrabble.

That night, their talk had turned to secrets—harmless little confessions of things few others knew about them. "So, you know

Freddie Mercury, from Queen? I was crazy about him in high school," said Sydney. They were propped up in bed, listening to Debussy and eating chocolate chip cookies dunked in milk. She licked her fingers. "My friends gave me hell about him. I used to spend hours arguing with them; I was convinced he was straight," she added, with regret.

"Yeah," Dahlra replied, "I know how you feel. I had this thing for Toyah Wilcox. I told myself her lisp was actually quite sexy for a punk."

Sydney gifted him with one of her lovely laughs, and he pretended to be hurt. "You're laughing at a dearly held, cherished belief."

"I'm flattered you would share it with me."

He smirked. "As am I, regarding your secret love affair with Freddie Mercury."

"Actually," she began, and darted a quick glance his way. Hell, *nobody* else knew this one. "One night, when I was still in college, I went to this club and got totally trashed. I mean, completely rat-arsed. I saw this pretty girl in the toilets, and..." She stopped, feeling heat flush over her face.

Dahlra eyed her curiously. "And...?"

In for a penny... "Well, we sort of hit it off, and before I knew it, she had backed me into one of the stalls and we had steamy hot, monkey, girl-on-girl action."

Dahlra gasped, and choked on his cookie. "Wha—did you actually—I mean, was she—"

She pounded him on the back. "Let's just try finishing one of those sentences, okay?"

It took a large gulp of milk to settle him down His cheeks were curiously pink. "Well, it's just I didn't take you for the—I assumed you preferred—"

"I'm going to put you out of your misery, okay?" Sydney said, amused and rather charmed. "It was a one-off. I was absolutely blotto, and curious, and afterward I felt pretty *meh* about the entire thing. I find women incredibly sexy and attractive, but when the rubber meets the road, I'm about as hetero as they come. Better?"

He toasted her with his milk and uttered a silent laugh. "Well, I'm relieved to hear *that*," he replied. "Blimey, I'm afraid I don't have anything to top that."

She thought back to the time she had taunted him about 'Mrs Doctor' in the cell. "Were you involved with someone before...well, before?" The moment she asked, she felt like kicking herself. After all they had been through, and as far as they had come, did she really want to hear about his love life?

"I was married for almost seven years."

It was Sydney's turn to be shocked. "When was this?"

"Oh, it's been awhile back. I've been divorced over five."

"O-oh. Okay. What happened? Did you just grow apart, or...?"

"She was having an affair." His smile was bitter, and rather sad. "Caroline wanted to marry a doctor. Turns out I was the wrong doctor."

"Jeez, Dahlra. That sucks. I'm sorry." She felt surprisingly angry on his behalf "What happened?"

"Caroline's father and mine were partners in the same surgery. They decided we'd make a good match, and for some reason, we believed them. Her father promised a huge wedding and all the trimmings. And she was pretty, and everyone raved about what a handsome couple we were, so..." he shrugged diffidently. "She never loved me. I discovered she was seeing someone else. A friend, or so I thought."

"Damn. That's cold."

"I tolerated it for longer than I should have. She was very blatant—even to the point of encouraging me to find my own 'bit on the side'. As far as she was concerned, cheating was alright as long as both of us were doing it. But that didn't make it right, did it?" He shook his head ruefully. "But I was proud, and I didn't want the world to see the horns. So we trudged along, her sleeping around, and me, the weak fool putting up with it." His tone brightened, overly so. "But, then I found a reason not to put up with it anymore, and I ended it."

Sydney pondered his choice of words, his sudden, closed expression. There was something important he wasn't telling her, yet her instincts told her he had left the door open for her to guess.

"Well, I suppose you got tired of feeling used," she offered. When he didn't reply, she tried again. "Has there been anyone else since then?"

"No. I've spent the last five years...training to be a Minder."

He was still trying to tell her something, but she didn't know enough of the facts to get at it. "You mean, you've been in some sort of limbo for five years, waiting for an agent to get Minder status?"

He turned those large, green eyes on her, then raised his chin, as if he had made a decision. "Isn't it obvious, Sydney? I was waiting for *you* to achieve Minder status. *You* were the reason I joined the programme."

If she had been surprised before, she was utterly gobsmacked now. "Me? Why me?"

He inspected the contents of his glass. There was a bitterness in his low voice. "You know, sometimes I ask myself the same question. I entered the programme for the sole reason of becoming your Minder, and the first thing I do when I get the opportunity to help? I alienate you to the point where you can barely tolerate being in the same room with me."

Realisation flooded Sydney's body. Here at last was the final piece of the puzzle that was Dahlra Gar: the inexplicable fact he had volunteered to infiltrate her cell and watch over her as best he could until an operation could be laid on to rescue her. This was the answer to her question to Inigo, *Why did he do it?*

Suddenly it all made sense: his fanatical devotion, his conflicting sexual signals, and above all, the peculiar choice he had made to leave his medical practice and take this crazy leap into a whole new venture to become her Minder. It was all for her, all so he could try and be there for her when she needed him most.

She knew she had to say something, but for the life of her, she didn't have the first clue where to begin. Finally, she decided on the truth. "It wasn't so much the physical stuff, Dahlra; it was the head fuck. I didn't know you were trying to be there for me, and you were sending out too many mixed signals. I feel like an idiot for not seeing this sooner. Looking back, I can see you took too many risks. You gave yourself away too much. But at the time I only saw you screwing with my mind."

"Playing Good Cop and Bad Cop," he answered, with a nod. "It didn't matter which. You would always see one of them as a liar." He kept his eyes locked onto his plate. Tightly, he added, "I never should have gone. I was the wrong man for the job. But I just thought I could make sure you were safe." He ran a hand through his dark, spiky hair. "I couldn't freeze you out, and I ended up hurting you worse than if I'd never tried to help.

"And then I thought, if I could just get you here, if I could show you how much I wanted to bring joy to your life, then I could make up for the shit I put you through. But I've messed that up as well."

Sydney felt a pang of sympathy; ever since their return to England,

Dahlra had done everything in his power to make her happy. He had never asked for more than she was willing to give. It brought her no joy to realise how little she had willingly given to him. "You haven't messed anything up," she replied. "You don't have to try so hard, Dahlra. And I haven't been as cooperative as I could have been. But that's not your fault."

"Isn't it?" He looked up at her, his face sad, his eyes bleak and exhausted. "I wanted you to enjoy yourself. I wanted you to enjoy having a Minder."

Quietly, she asked, "Do you enjoy it? Being my Minder?"

For a long moment, she thought he wasn't going to answer. His voice was painted with sadness. "Sometimes I wonder if I made the right decision. For your sake, though, never for mine. But it's been a lot harder than I ever dreamed it would be." The haunted look in his eyes made her stomach clench. "How can I enjoy it, Sydney? How can I—knowing that, as much as I want you, you don't want me?"

"I don't know what I want anymore, Dahlra. I mean, we've been here, what, a few months? And we're just getting around to this conversation? We're still walking around on eggshells here. But that's not to say that, with time..." she halted, unsure of exactly how she wanted to finish that sentence.

He put a hand over his heart, as if to shield it from her pity. "My head knows you may never accept me, but my heart won't give up hope. So I hang on, even though it kills me a little more every day, knowing you're unhappy."

"Have I ever said, 'I'm not happy with you'?"

"You didn't have to—"

"Have you ever heard those words coming from my mouth?"

He looked at her with immense dignity, in spite of the sorrow in his eyes. "Don't say things just to make me feel better, Sydney. I have to live with it, so I would appreciate the truth, even if it hurts."

"Dahlra, I promise I won't ever lie to you. I owe you that much. I owe you *so* much."

"Don't think about me that way!" He stood, and paced the room, breathing hard. "You were so fucking sick of hearing Lightoller exult about how much you 'owe me.' So was I. You don't owe me anything.

"We have to start at ground zero. We have to forget the cell, and the Minder shite, and the Agency. We have to start at you and me."

He sat down heavily, as if his painful bout of passion cost every ounce of energy. His shoulders dropped, as if he were too tired to go on. "If we can't do that, I'll leave tomorrow, and you can choose another Minder, if that's what you want."

Sydney felt a sliver of ice pierce her heart, like a pin in an apple. "That-that's not what I want," she stammered. "I'm just not sure I'm worth all the grief I've put you through."

He clasped her hand fervently. "*I'm* sure. I'm surer of that than anything else I know." He brought her hand to his lips and gave it a searing kiss. With a contrite smile, he added, "Look. We're both running on empty right now. This is too heavy a conversation to have while we're both suffering from a deplorable lack of sleep. We can talk about replacing me when you're stronger."

The icy feeling in her chest radiated outward, making it hard to breathe. *We can talk about replacing me.* In a rush of sudden, sleep-deprived clarity, those words sank in and snagged deep, as if she were hanging by them through a hook buried in her spine. That was the *last* thing she wanted.

"I'll—I mean, if you really think..." She floundered, feeling sick, and as she sat up, a sob escaped her. "Oh dammit," she choked.

"Sydney, what is it?" The loving concern in his voice only made it worse, and like a weak, pitiful idiot, she burst into tears. Without a second's thought, Dahlra pulled her into his arms. He was warm and solid and smelled of good cologne and chocolate.

"Shh. Don't cry, it's okay. It's alright, darling," he crooned, cradling her head against his shoulder, rocking her gently. His sweet, unselfish comfort only made her cry harder. "I've upset you, and I'm so sorry. I say stupid things when I'm this tired. Everything will be alright. *We'll* be alright."

She put her arms around his waist, feeling his firm body caged around her, and a sudden, desperate fear hit her, a fear that had nothing to do with the coming night, or the fucking dreams. That was pussy stuff compared to this.

"Don't go," she whispered against his chest. His chin rested on the top of her head, and she could feel it moving back and forth in an emphatic *no* motion.

"I shouldn't have said anything. It's the exhaustion talking. I'm not going anywhere, Sydney. As long as you need me, I'll be here. Dahlra's here."

"Promise?"

"I promise."

When she sagged in relief, he kissed her forehead, and rose from the bed, heading into the loo. He returned with a flannel and bathed her face, his sweet crooning as welcome as a lullaby. He held her, stroking her hair, until the tears were spent. Her emotional outburst left her even more drained and edgy, and Dahlra eventually settled her into a thin, uneasy doze.

As Sydney drifted into deeper sleep, Dahlra went to his room to change into more comfortable clothing. A wave of crippling exhaustion crashed over him, so debilitating that his hands dropped from his half-buttoned shirt, his arms too heavy to lift them. He struggled to climb on top of it, but it was so sudden and intense he was surprised by its voracity. If he didn't get eight straight hours of sleep soon, he was going to be so flaky he'd be of no use to anyone. As if their last, disastrous conversation hadn't been indicative enough, he was also pretty sure he wasn't exactly doing his own peace of mind any favours, either.

He yawned so widely his jaw cracked, and he stretched, trying to get his blood pumping a little. He wondered if a B-12 jab might help. He rolled back onto his bed, boneless and limp. Oh, that felt almost sinfully good. As much as he told himself he needed to sit up, stand up, and go back to Sydney's room to check on her, his body just would not respond. Maybe in five. Just five minutes...

He was jangled awake with a start, his heart beating like a military tattoo. He was at Sydney's door before his brain registered why he was even on his feet. All he knew was the sound of his name being shouted, over and over.

"Dahlra! No! Dahlra!"

Four dark figures entered Sydney's room. They were composed of black; black combat trousers, black turtleneck shirts, balaclavas and gloves. Nothing resembling skin was visible, and they loomed in silent malevolence like giant wraiths.

She tried to demand, "How did you get in here? What do you want?" But her tongue was a dead thing in her mouth, stiff and useless. Panic dumped gallons of adrenaline into her bloodstream, making her skin ache and her heart hammer.

Silently, the men drew close enough for her to smell the stench of their unwashed bodies. They parted, two to the left, two to the right, and a fifth man entered the room. The Doctor's white-blond hair gleamed in the moonlight.

Bile rose in her throat, and she swallowed thickly, shuddering with fear. This was a dream. Dahlra would wake her soon. *Soon. Hurry, Dahlra, hurry and wake me...Oh, shit, wake up, wake up!*

Her intruders faced the bedroom door, listening, waiting in anticipation. It was then she realised she'd made a terrible mistake. She was the bait. These men weren't here for her; they were here for her Minder.

The door flew open and Dahlra burst into the room, blazing with righteous, protective anger. Sydney tried to cry out a warning, but her voice was nothing more than a whistle of sound coming from lungs that couldn't take a deep, solid breath.

They attacked Dahlra from behind. One delivered a vicious chop to the back of his neck, and the other kicked his feet out from under him. Seeing them bearing down on the man who had tried so hard to keep her alive filled Sydney with fury, and she fought with all her might to get out of bed and help him. Her traitorous body was leaden; she could not even raise her head from her pillow. Moaning in frustration, she tried to push the covers from her legs, but it was as if they were buried in the mattress.

She found her voice and cried, "Leave him alone! He's a civilian!" Trapped and terrified, she could hear the keening wail of protest in her head as they began to beat Dahlra with merciless, sickening deliberation.

And all through the horrific beating, he was silent, his eyes fixed onto hers, his expression accepting, as if he'd anticipated all along this would be the retribution he would suffer for what he had done to her in the cell—what he had *allowed* them to do to her.

Sensing his sorrowful submission, she howled in protest. "You don't deserve this! You don't have to take this—" She fought like a tiger to jump start her limbs, but she might as well have been dead for all they acknowledged her.

Finally, the Doctor pointed to Dahlra and growled, "Pick him up." His voice sounded unnaturally deep and demonic. His silent colleagues obeyed, hauling Dahlra to his feet between them. His head lolled helplessly.

"What are you going to do with him?" Sydney demanded, but they ignored her. "Don't hurt him, please!" she begged, her voice sounding ineffectual and childish. She had to make the Doctor stop hurting him. *She* had brought this on. He wouldn't be in danger if not for her. They had just come to an understanding. They had turned a corner. The Doctor wasn't part of her life anymore.

One of his attackers dumped Dahlra onto the end of the bed, and the Doctor approached, slowly removing a flat, glinting object from his coat. Sydney saw the flash of light on metal; it was a large meat cleaver. A table appeared as if by magic. Understanding dawned, making her fear ramp into a screaming tailspin.

"No! Fucking leave him alone! Don't you touch him, you—" At last, the leaden weight lifted from her body, and Sydney lunged toward the Doctor. One of his men caught her in a choke hold, blocking her air. As she struggled, two of the attackers grabbed Dahlra's arms and quietly forced his hands, palms down, onto the table. His battered eyes met hers, and a red-tinted tear rolled down his bruised and split cheek.

"For you," he whispered. "I should've taken the beating for you."

"No," she sobbed. She tried to look away, but the man holding her forced her head forward.

"This time, *you* will watch," The Doctor demanded, his low, dispassionate voice terrifying in its own right. Unable to shut her eyes or look away, Sydney saw the glint of the cleaver, and heard the sickening clang of metal striking bone as Dahlra's left hand was severed from the wrist. His eyes flew open in shock as his nerve endings sent their horrible message to his brain, and his scream made Sydney's stomach roll with horror.

The Doctor wrenched the cleaver from the table, and lifted it into the air. The sound of the blade severing Dahlra's right hand was indescribable. His cries of agony and terror were the only constant in her brain. "My hands! Oh, God, my hands—" The sounds unraveled into animalistic screams. She tried to reach for him, but she could not move, could not help him. He was bleeding to death, and she could do nothing to save him.

"I'm sorry," she sobbed.

One of the men casually gathered up Dahlra's white, severed hands, and the Doctor and his men began to laugh. Still, she could not help Dahlra, who rose to his feet and staggered toward her, blood pumping from the bleeding stumps where his hands had been. His life's blood soaked the bed, and his face was contorted in insane fear and agony. The taunting laughter of the Doctor rang in the room, distorted and carnal.

"It's not enough!" The Doctor crowed, laughing at Dahlra. "It will never be enough!"

Sydney reached for Dahlra. Panic and grief warped into something too great to bear, and she wailed in terror, knowing he was going to die. He was going to die because of her...

"Sydney! *Sydney!* It's another nightmare! For Christ's sake, wake up! *Wake up!*"

"It's too much! Your hands! He took your hands—Dahlra! The Doctor took—"

"Sydney!" Dahlra was shaking her roughly. "Nobody's taken anyone's hands, see?"

Full-on lucidity rubber-banded Sydney, snapping her fully awake, her scream dying in her throat. Dahlra was there, unharmed. Breathing hard, Sydney looked down to see his large, finely-made hands, his fingers laced with hers, locking him to her in a vise-like grip.

It had all been a dream, every bit of it. Dahlra's hands had not been chopped from his wrists with that shiny cleaver. Relief flooded her, and she leaned against his shoulder, so damned glad he was alive and whole. She felt his fingers tighten around hers, encasing her in his solid, constant presence.

"I—I can't get my fingers to work," she mumbled. "I can't let go."

"That *is* quite a grip you have," he replied with a quiet smile. "It's okay. You can hold on as long as you need to."

"My hands are cramping," she admitted. "Help me."

"It's alright, Sydney. Just relax. Now, take a deep breath, dear, and we're going to let go together, alright? Ready? One, two three..." With an effort, Sydney loosened her grip and released him. She stared at his hands; they were smooth and large, sitting gracefully at the end of his elegant wrists. She touched each one tenderly. They were still very much attached to him.

She glanced up into his face. His emerald eyes were dark and soft with concern and affection. Without hesitation, Sydney raised her arms and twined them around his neck. She grasped the back of his head, pulled him down to her, and placed a swift, soft kiss on his lips.

She felt his shoulders tighten in surprise, but he wasted no time in pulling her closer. His hand caressed her tangled hair, and he murmured, "My darling girl." It fell on her ears like a benediction. He reluctantly let her go only when her arms slid from his neck.

She cleared her throat quietly. It was dry and raw from all the yelping she'd done in her sleep, but she had to ask. "Are you okay?"

"Am *I* okay?" He rewarded her with a smile that would have melted chocolate. "Oh, Sydney, I'm fine."

"I've never had a dream like this. It felt almost prophetic, like a premonition." She shuddered. "That was the worst yet."

"Say the word, and I will give you something to help you sleep without these damn dreams."

"No," Sydney said stubbornly. "Please, don't think I'm trying to be a hero, but I'd rather just deal with it. They won't last forever. They *can't*."

"Alright. But the offer stands." Dahlra gently stroked the hair from her damp forehead. "I'll bet your blood pressure has hit the ceiling. You are absolutely drenched with sweat."

Sydney closed her eyes, reveling in the feel of his fingers ghosting over her skin. She had been unconsciously kneading the folds of his shirt against his chest, as if to assure herself he was okay. She could feel his life's drum beating in his chest, steady and strong.

"To tell you the truth, I don't feel so bad now. Not like I usually feel when I wake up from the nightmares."

"I take it from your reaction that..." He hesitated, as if he were entering delicate territory and wanted to tread carefully. "That somehow, I was *not* okay in your dream."

The vivid image replayed itself in her memory: the gruesome sight of the blade singing through the air and his scream— "No," she whispered.

"Well, thank goodness it was a dream, then."

"I—a terrible thing happened to you in the dream. It was my fault. I couldn't bear the thought of losing you— that way." Almost the moment the words left her lips she wished she had couched them in a way that sounded less melodramatic.

Dahlra's hand stilled, and almost imperceptibly he moved closer to her. "Does all this concern mean that I'm finally growing on you?"

She pressed her forehead against his chest. She was shattered, but also hyper-aware of the man sitting on the bed with her. For weeks he had held her, soothed her and nursed her through the worst of her nightmares, but she had been too wired up to fully appreciate his tactile, caring nature.

With her eyes closed, she took in the scent of him. It was a familiar, welcoming smell; it contained traces of the starch in his shirt, the spicy note of his shampoo, the touch of patchouli in his cologne. All this was layered against the warm, natural smell of his skin.

His shirt was half-undone, and impulsively she placed her palms against his chest. He enveloped her in his arms, and she stilled, a thrill of anticipation washing over her. In that moment, she decided that whatever move he made, whatever action he took, she would welcome it. This was not the Doctor in the cell; this was not her Minder. This was a man who wanted her, a man she could admit to herself she had come to care about.

Gentle fingers tilted her chin, and Dahlra leaned forward until his lips touched her forehead. A ribbon of excitement wound around her spine. She remained still, as he lightly kissed the delicate curve of her eyelid. His touch was feather light, and Sydney shivered as arousal bloomed inside her. As he released the kiss, her eyes fluttered open, and a tear broke away from her lashes. Dahlra caught it with another kiss, then licked his lips, as if savouring her salt.

For a moment they simply held one another's gaze. Sydney could see the desire in his face. It shone in his luminous eyes, his full, parted lips. He hesitated, as if his hope was still tempered by a fear of rejection.

The time for rejection was passed. "Don't stop," she breathed.

He smiled. "Never." He cupped her face in a warm hand, stroking her skin with his fingertips. "You have such a lovely mouth." he whispered, his voice low and indescribably beautiful.

He lowered his face to hers for their first real kiss. It was tentative, almost chaste. He made a soft, boyish sound that was unbearably erotic, and Sydney whimpered her reply. His hand slid around to the back of her neck, and he pulled her to him. She melted against him, her body pliant, as if all her inner framework had loosened a quarter turn.

Dahlra's soft, suckling kisses drew her in, each kiss intensifying on the heels of the one before. He parted her mouth with his tongue, its velvety tease and retreat coaxing admittance to this sweetest of all penetrations. When she opened herself to him, he gave a deep, ragged moan, and hungrily plunged into her, sucking her tongue into his mouth. It was an invitation she could no more resist than her next breath.

For a divine, soul-searing moment, it felt as if her entire body was in her mouth, being stroked and pleasured by his warm, soft lips, and the silken, wet muscle within. She clutched at his arms and sucked his lower lip between her teeth, sweeping her tongue across it as he explored her mouth, plundering its secrets. Each kissed fueled the next, flooding her body with arousal that seemed to grow hungrier with each breath.

Gradually, Dahlra's kisses grew slower, lighter. Their passion ebbed as naturally as it began, until the kiss gentled into an affectionate, soft nudging of lips. Finally he loosened his hold and pulled away.

Bewildered and bereft at the loss of him, Sydney finally opened her eyes. He was looking at her with a stunned, happy expression on his handsome face. "I hope I don't sound like the biggest muppet on the planet, but that was undoubtedly the best kiss I've ever had."

She laughed shakily, too unraveled to think straight. "If you're Kermit, I'm Miss Piggy."

They smiled at one another shyly, like a couple of teenagers. Dahlra tenderly kissed her forehead; it was a kiss of boundless gratitude, with just the remnants of the feverish desire they had ignited moments before.

He looked down at their entwined fingers. "Are you going to be alright?" he asked. "Would you like a cup of tea or anything?"

She smiled and shook her head. "No. I'm really okay now. I think I'll see if I can get some sleep," she said.

He walked toward the door and then turned back to face her. "I'll be right here if you need me."

"I know. Good night, Dahlra."

"Goodnight, Sydney."

She continued to stare after him for a long time. Finally, she touched her fingers to her lips, and her body rekindled the heat from their kiss.

It made so many promises—promises that Dahlra seemed perfectly capable of delivering. Sydney had been ready; if he had pushed her back onto the bed, she would have opened herself to him without a second thought. And she knew he had wanted her, too. That large outline in his trousers was not merely for decoration. But he had not pressed her.

As she drifted off to sleep, she pictured the Doctor—not the laughing ghoul of her dreams, but the uncertain man in the cell. In her mind's eye he morphed into Dr Dahlra Gar, the man who would gladly have taken any punishment, any risk to keep her safe.

Suddenly, she saw the white-haired man in the cell as a friend, not the enemy. Something in her head rang out like a chime, and anxiety and dread dissipated, like smoke drifting away. In that moment, she knew that the nightmares were over for a while.

CHAPTER NINE

The Heart To Heart

Sydney woke up with a strange sense that bags of time had passed. Blearily, she glanced at her clock; it read 9:04, but the light in the room was wrong. It should have been bright morning, but it was pitch black dark. She had slept all night, all through the next day and into the following evening. With nary a dream in sight, much less a bad one.

She heard a soft rumble and rolled over. At the end of the massive bed, Dahlra was sprawled out, dead to the world and snoring softly, his long legs dangling over the edge. One arm lay across his chest, the other was flung out over the duvet. He looked like he'd been dropped from the ceiling and fallen asleep where he landed.

She nudged his hand with her foot. "Hey, sleeping beauty," she said hoarsely.

Dahlra opened one bleary, bloodshot eye, and raised his head with such supreme effort Sydney felt guilty for waking him.

She patted a pillow next to her. "Lie down like a real person. Your back will thank you in the morning."

It was testament to his exhaustion that he didn't even reply. With heavy, uncoordinated limbs, he laboriously crawled into bed beside her and was asleep so quickly Sydney wondered if he'd actually woken at all.

She turned on her side and watched him for a moment. He slept like he did most things; no muss, no fuss, no tossing and turning, just peaceful repose. She drifted back to sleep watching the steady rise and fall of his chest, as constant as his heartbeat, as comforting as his voice.

They would spend almost forty-eight hours of nearly uninterrupted, healing sleep.

They say when a person is ill they forget how it felt to be well, and when they are well, they don't remember how miserable they were when ill. Sydney's captors had tried sleep deprivation early in her incarceration; this had been much worse. She had nearly forgotten how lovely 'normal' felt.

Sitting across the breakfast table from Dahlra, seeing how refreshed and rested he looked, she realised just how close she had come to sending them both to the nuthatch. He caught her eye over *The Guardian* and smiled. "It's so good to see you looking like yourself this morning," he said.

"Not half as good as it feels." She dropped her shoulders, reveling in the warm heaviness of her muscles. "There were times during these past couple of weeks when I felt like eating my Glock," she confessed, pouring them both a cup of tea.

"There were times during these past few weeks when I was tempted to cook it for you. I hated seeing you so miserable." He lowered the paper and clasped her hand. "Sydney..."

His mobile rang, and he glanced down at the caller ID. "Excuse me. I need to take this." He pressed the button. "Hi... yeah, much better, thanks... oh, okay..." His face lit up. "Great! Yeah... yeah, I will... I promise I won't... yeah, yeah, fine. That's super. What name are they under? Excellent! I owe you one. Or three. Cheers." He ended the call, looking very pleased.

"That sounded like good news."

"It is. I've been trying like mad to arrange a pair of tickets for a special concert at the Royal Albert Hall tomorrow night. Holiday Music by the BBC Radio Orchestra and Chorale. The concert was by invitation only, but I got lucky." He added wryly, "I thought perhaps some pre-holiday music might cheer you up."

Sydney beamed at him. The Albert Hall, with its beautiful architecture and stunning acoustics, was one of her favorite venues in the world, especially for music.

Dahlra carefully watched her reaction. "Does this please you?" he asked softly.

"Very much. Thank you."

"Good. Apparently it's a very formal affair, black tie, lots of celebrities, that sort of thing."

She bit into her toast thoughtfully. "Sounds pretty swish. I suppose a little retail therapy is in order. I wouldn't want to look dowdy."

"As if you could. Well, how about tomorrow? I had a text waiting on me this morning. The hospital has requested consultation on a case. It should take two or three hours at the most. You can shop, and we'll meet for a late lunch after. Deal?"

"Deal," she replied. "I'll swing over to Sugarbags; they usually have something I like, and Jules has been known to give me first crack at the new stuff before they make it available to the general hoi polloi."

He gave her a bemused look before returning to his paper. "Sugarbags, eh? Good. I'll—"

"But you better be thinking long and hard about what *you're* going to wear," she interrupted archly. "I'm expecting something elegant and tasteful. I can't abide overstuffed dinner jackets and bowties."

She had meant it as a joke, but he looked at her so levelly she thought for a moment she'd somehow offended him. "Hmm. I shall endeavour to do my best, Ms Chapin. It won't do to disappoint you."

Sydney poured milk into her tea as he returned to his paper. While his voice had been as lightly teasing as her own, the message was clear: they still weren't quite on the same page. Dahlra was the same solicitous, happy-to-please man as before, but Sydney now felt a growing sense of anticipation, of waiting between them.

She glanced back at him and found him watching her again, his eyes dark with yearning.

As if on cue, they both spoke at once.

"Dahlra, I—"

"Sydney, do we—"

They both stopped. "You first," he prompted.

"We need to talk about... this."

He folder the paper and laid it aside. "Alright. Where do you want to begin?" His voice was calm, but she could see a flicker of concern in his eyes.

"This whole Minder thing," she said. "Things have changed—"

"And I couldn't be happier," he replied. She knew he was also thinking about their full-on, snog-your-knickers-off kiss.

She opened her mouth twice to speak, and shut it again. Dahlra leaned forward and took her hand. "Hey, Sydney," he said, his voice was intimate, tangible. "It's just me. After all we've been through together, I would hope you know you can be totally candid."

She looked at him for several heartbeats, trying to come up with the best way to approach her misgivings. "Dahlra, I'm not sure what I'm supposed to expect from you in this Minder thing, but what happened the other night: are we breaching some sort of protocol? Don't get me wrong," she added hastily, then faltered. God, she was making a mess of things. "That kiss was incredible."

"I thought so, too," he answered quietly. With a smile as soft as sin, he continued, "I have to admit there's been little else on my mind since I woke up."

"First of all, I'm so grateful..."

"Grateful, Sydney?" The smile faded. "Is that all that kiss was about— gratitude?"

"I..." She sighed, frustrated. "You know it isn't. But it has to be said: you've been patience itself. And you've given me so much."

"FYI—'Minder,' remember? It's my job, dearest. It's what I enjoy doing. It's what I've been trained to do." His eyes were soft. "It's what I want to do."

"And I'd be the lowest scum on the planet if I didn't acknowledge that. I appreciate it, too. And I'm not going to deny that I find you attractive, or that I haven't thought about... well, us. But I can't help but wonder if you..."

She plowed on. "You see, I can't help but wonder if you're doing this more out of feeling guilty because of what happened. I don't want you to feel obligated, because you feel sorry for me. I don't want manufactured passion because you're afraid you'll lose the job because I've compromised you—"

"A pity fuck? Is that what you really believe?" He looked as if she had punched him in the stomach. "After all the time you've spent with me, do you honestly think of me as some sort of prostitute hired to service you in recognition of your merit with the Agency? That I left my career as a physician and pursued Minder training for the sole purpose of throwing myself under the bus for Lightoller?" He gave her a look of reproach. "Do you honestly think I somehow fabricated that passionate kiss? I think we've already established that I'm not that good an actor."

"I told you, I don't even know if I'm worth the trouble..."

"Don't say that, Sydney. That's patent nonsense," he replied, his tone firm. "I know perfectly well what I found in that cell. What I'm still not sure of is what you think you saw of *me* there."

Sydney took a moment to gather her thoughts, unused as she was to having to explain herself or her actions to anyone. "We met a very short time ago, in extreme and horrific circumstances. And no, I'm not counting the time when you first programmed me, because I was already under hypnosis and I didn't remember you at all. By the time I knew your full name Inigo was readying us to move in together."

"Ah. So, you don't remember the first time we *actually* met, do you?"

Deep inside, an inner bell rang, and in that moment, Sydney knew he was about to tell her something very important. Something, she thought, that might just forever change her perception of the man sitting before her.

"Well," she replied, hesitantly, "would you care to give me a clue? If not, I'm afraid we'll be reduced to playing twenty questions."

He waited until he was sure he had her full attention. "The attempt on Vasily Gregorin."

"The assassination attempt?" Her head snapped back, and she gaped at him, eyes narrowed, as if she were truly seeing him for the first time.

Vasily Gregorin was old school; he had made his KGB bones years before the words *glasnost* and *perestroika* entered the Western consciousness. On Christmas Day, 1991, when the Soviet flag flying over the Kremlin was lowered for the final time and replaced by the new Russian banner, the Cold War was all but over, and Gregorin found himself effectively out of a job. He spent the next fifteen years free-lancing the highest bidder, playing so many ends against the middle he resembled a Catherine wheel.

Lightoller hated his kind; mercenaries were notoriously disloyal and unfaithful bedfellows, but Gregorin had a wealth of contacts and old friends. In those days every 'Made-upistan' freshly carved from the defunct Soviet block was taking their first baby steps toward counter-intelligence, so Gregorin barely noticed a change in income. At first.

He developed a well-known habit of burning his bridges like a cheating lover, and the steadily decreasing number of agencies who trusted him meant he could no longer afford to be choosey about who signed his pay packet. Following a botched mission in which he was critically wounded trying to burn that particular bridge, Inigo persuaded him to come in from the cold.

It was one of the few mistakes in judgement Inigo would make during his illustrious career; Gregorin was a deep-set and very wily dangle, who went on to double-cross the Agency five years later, and the repercussions of that betrayal would eventually land Sydney in the cell.

While he was in the Agency hospital recovering, a small-scale attempt was made on his life. It had been a Charlie Foxtrot from the word go. The hired assassins infiltrated the hospital with more dumb luck than skill, killing a security guard in the process and sending the entire hospital on high alert. Sydney, Garnet Pinkerton and another fellow agent, Ross Bullard, had been called in to repel them and secure the area. Each agent approached from a different level; Ross coming from the floor above, Garnet from the floor below, and Sydney coming in on Gregorin's floor.

Sydney and Garnet took the stairs together; he stopped at the entrance to the fifth floor, and nodded to her. "My back to yours."

"My back to yours, Pink. Don't get dead."

"Right. Off you go, then." Sydney grinned as she sprinted past him up to the sixth floor.

She was creeping in the shadows when she spotted two quick-thinking doctors wheeling Gregorin's hospital bed into a small but relatively unnoticeable alcove at the very end of the hall. It had been a good move, but it also unfortunately meant the doctors were now cornered. They froze when they saw her moving toward them, low and soundlessly, her weapon drawn. Silently, she signaled for them to stay hidden. That was when it all kicked off.

The assailants came charging down the hall, firing at anything that moved, screaming like banshees to make themselves sound bigger and scarier. Ross Bullard took a hit; Sydney heard him curse as he fell. Breaking cover, Garnet took out two of the group, and alerted Sydney through their earpiece that a third was coming her way.

She stood on the blind side of the alcove, her back to the charging gunman, facing the two doctors. In the dark, recessed area, they were well camouflaged, but Sydney didn't plan on letting anyone get much closer. She glanced up and caught the eye of one of the doctors. She took a mental snapshot of *tall, dark-haired, forty, scared.* She stored the info in her mental file, then looked away.

In the glass of a small cabinet to her right, Sydney watched the reflection of the assailant heading in her direction. Six feet away, he stopped and turned to give a signal to his compatriot. Sydney spun out of her hiding place, aiming on the move, and caught him with one killing shot. She leapt back behind the wall before the man even knew he was dead. She did not bother to check when she heard him drop to the floor.

A bullet ricocheted off the archway on the other side, and she grimaced as flying plaster grazed her cheek and drew blood. Garnet popped the fourth gunman, but it was a messy shot, and chummy went down screaming, clutching his belly.

From behind him, a fresh barrage of gunfire erupted. Afraid her presence had already called too much attention to the men in hiding, Sydney prepared to abandon her cover.

The younger of the two doctors, a ginger-haired man, broke from his hiding place and shouted, "Don't leave us!" A bullet caught him on the side of the head. His face disintegrated, and he spun toward Sydney. A bright blue eye looked at her reproachfully from the ruin that had once been his face, and the man fell dead.

Sydney heard a metallic clink, and something rolled to a stop against her foot; it was a tear gas grenade. Without hesitation, she grabbed it and lobbed it down the corridor as far as her pitching arm would send it, shouting, "Gas! Incoming—" As she turned back, the final attacker grabbed the remaining physician around the throat and pulled the doctor close to his chest.

"Drop your weapon!" he cried hoarsely. He was deathly pale beneath his olive skin, and shaking so badly he could barely hold the gun against the doctor's temple. He could not have been more than twenty-five years old, obviously inexperienced and completely horseshit with fear. He had just watched three of his fellow goons die in a matter of minutes, and could hear the fourth one screaming as he tried to hold in his own intestines.

"I s-said drop your weapon! I-I'll k-kill him," he stammered, blinking sweat out of his eyes.

Sydney calmly walked toward the man, her own gun steady and trained on the assassin's face. "Put the gun down and let him go—"

"Back off! I will kill him! I'll do it!" He jammed the muzzle hard against the doctor's temple. "I'm not bluffing."

Sydney noted absently the hostage was doing the right thing—not struggling, but not exactly helping, either. She glanced down at her watch as if checking the time. From the corner of her eye, she saw the gunman's eyes drop as well.

In a flat, bored voice, she said, "You know if you kill him, you'll be dead before he hits the ground. That's how it works. The rest of your companions are dead." She nodded toward his hostage. "Let him go. It's the only chance you have to survive."

"Shut up!" wailed the gunman. He was in tears. "I'm not fucking around here. Back off or I'll kill him."

With a disinterested shrug, she said, "Then kill him already. I'm missing *Midsomer Murders*." When the gunman froze in confusion, she pressed. "Look. I've got my period and I'm cramping, so hurry up. I've had a shit day and I'm pissed off. You have two choices. Let him go and you get arrested. You'll go jail instead of the morgue. You kill him, I'll do you, too." She glanced back at his companion, lying in a spreading pool of blood, screaming his lungs out. "It won't be *that* clean, I promise."

"Shut up!"

The hostage's eyes met Sydney's. They held the stunned, detached look of a man who expected his own death at any second.

Sydney cocked her head slightly to the side, then sighed impatiently. Giving the gunman a look of withering contempt, she scoffed, "Your safety's on."

He gaped in surprise, then moved the gun away from the doctor's head to check.

In that split second, Sydney fired. A neat, round hole appeared in the dead centre of the gunman's forehead; a four-foot-wide bloom of blood, bone and brain fanned out on the wall behind him, like grisly pop art. He dropped like a bag of rocks, and the physician stumbled away, his expression frozen in horror.

Sydney holstered her Glock and called out, "Pink? Ross? You boys alright?" Over the fading wails of the last living invader, she heard Garnet's laconic, disembodied voice.

"Fine. Ross is down, but what's new?" A low groan wafted from down the corridor, and Sydney suppressed a rueful grimace. Ross Bullard was notoriously accident-prone. "It's not serious, anyway. You?"

"I'm good." She knelt to check the ginger-haired doctor's vital signs. "We have one civilian casualty." She turned her attention to the remaining doctor, who was ashen and quiet. He had produced a snow-white handkerchief and was wiping his forehead.

Sydney queried, "Is Gregorin alright?" The doctor nodded numbly.

"Are *you* alright?" she asked, and received another nod. "Good. I'm very sorry about your colleague." When the doctor didn't respond, she noted the greenish pallor of his skin and added, "Look, why don't I help you cover him?" She went to one of the cabinets, found a white sheet and started unfolding it.

The doctor roused himself and silently caught one of the edges. Together they covered his comrade, giving him his dignity. They both ignored the fallen gunman.

As they straightened, Sydney said, "There will be other agents arriving shortly to debrief you. You may feel a little depressed for a few days, but that's just a sign that you're getting over the shock." With a soft huff she added, "Then again, you're a doctor. I'm guessing you already know that."

She turned to join her colleagues when the doctor finally found his voice. "Do you need me to check your face, Agent?" he asked. His voice was very deep and rich, and there was a touch of wonder in his tone, as if the reality of what had happened was starting to hit home.

Sydney watched silently as he brought a hand up to examine her cheek. She gingerly touched her own face. The cut was shallow; it had already stopped bleeding. "No, thank you."

A ghost of a smile crossed his lips. "What about some paracetamol?" At her blank stare, he ventured, "For those cramps?"

"What? Oh." She laughed shortly. "No, I'm fine, thanks."

"You ready, Syd?" Garnet asked.

"Yeah, hang on. I'm coming." She gave the doctor another tight smile, then turned and headed toward Garnet, who was filling in the debriefing unit. From behind, the doctor called out again.

"What is your name, Agent?" He shrugged. "I'd like to know the name of the person who saved my life."

"Special Agent Sydney Chapin," she replied.

He started, his eyes widening in surprise. "*You're* Sydney Chapin?" he asked.

With a curt nod, she turned and walked away. As the distance between them lengthened, she heard his mellow baritone as it floated softly toward her.

"Was it really on?"

Sydney turned back, puzzled. "Was *what* on?"

"The safety."

"No." When the silence between them stretched into five seconds, she turned on her heel and left him standing in the alcove.

"Well, hell. I do remember. Ironic, isn't it? If they had accomplished their mission and Gregorin hadn't survived, he wouldn't have sold me out, and I wouldn't have gotten captured." She shrugged. Gregorin's body was now propping up some important building in Canary Wharf, to hear Garnet tell the tale. "We wouldn't be having this conversation."

She whistled appreciatively. "And that was you! Jeez, that was... that was at least five years ago," she murmured. "Hey, that was right before you left your wife."

"More to the point," Dahlra replied, his voice light, almost cheerful. "It was the *reason* I left my wife."

"Wha-? Why?"

"I wouldn't have even entertained the idea of becoming a Minder. I had no inclination up to that point. If you hadn't saved my life, I never would have started training. I never wanted to become a Minder for anyone but you."

At her startled look, he added, "I had heard of the famous Sydney Chapin, but until that night, I'd never seen so much as a photo of you. Tell the truth, with the name 'Sydney' I always thought you were a bloke. You hear gossip, of course, about certain agents. But people talked about you and Garnet differently, like a couple of rock stars. I think I envisioned you two as the Mick and Keef of the Agency."

She laughed, and he continued, "So I started asking questions about you, and that led me to hearing about the Minder programme. By then I realised just how important you were in the Agency, and I knew one day you would be eligible for Minder status. You were too good not to. So, I entered the training programme the next week. Knowing who you are, what you do, it brought out every protective instinct I have."

He added quietly, "You know, I didn't go into medicine to follow in dear old Father's footsteps. I did it because I like taking care of people. It was never a career choice to me. It's a vocation, a calling.

"The Minder programme seemed tailor-made for someone like me, who wanted to see that you took care of yourself and had a comfortable environment to come home to. So, I watched your career zoom up into the stratosphere, and I waited.

"And as time went on, if I heard of a job that went well, or you were given special commendation for a particular mission, I would feel this absurd pride in you. I wanted you to succeed because you were so strong and brave and good. I was your secret cheering team."

Sydney had not given that night a serious thought in years-and she had certainly never associated Dahlra with the frightened doctor. She'd been too juiced up to remember much past the spilled blood and the adrenaline high. She had a sudden wish that the floor would open up and swallow her.

"I'm sorry, Dahlra. It doesn't exactly show me in the best light, but I never made the connection. I do remember Dr Stone, though." They both unconsciously bowed their heads in tribute to the ginger-haired doctor who had been killed. Stone and the security guard had been the only civilian casualties. In any situation, the death of the innocents was hard to accept, and Sydney always remembered the ones who fell on her watch.

To lighten the mood, she added breezily, "And I remember that chunk of plaster that nicked me." She smiled. "Bloody thing took forever to heal. I was sure it was going to leave a scar. Garnet says all good agents should have scars. It makes us look windswept and interesting." She sobered. "I must be the most windswept and interesting woman on the planet now."

"Stop that." Dahlra did not join in her laughter. "Do you know what *I* remember?" When she shook her head, he continued, his voice laced with awe. "I remember touching you—just there, on your cheek." His fingers brushed softly against the skin beneath her right eye. "It was like touching a live wire. You were fresh from the fight and your eyes were blazing and you were electric. I could feel the heat from your body. I could smell your perfume. I was utterly enthralled."

Dahlra turned the full force of his emerald eyes on her, and caught in their incandescent glow of remembrance and longing, she saw herself through his eyes. The understanding of it shook her right down to her foundations.

It was the reason *I left my wife...you have a lifetime to punish me...I have so much more to tell you... I was your secret cheering team...*

Compassion seeped into all the cracks of what was left of her armour. He wasn't some agent groupie; he wasn't the male equivalent of a Bond

Girl. Here was a man who had lived with the same horrors, felt the same relief in freedom she had known.

At a time in her life when any real thrill had long since gone from her job, her life, the meaning or purpose of her *life,* she had stepped between him and certain death, and became his hero.

"Oh, Dahlra. I wish I had known." She thought back to the last awful night, when he offered to leave. If he left, who would it benefit? Certainly not him. And not her, either. She had the chance to be his hero once, and he had repaid her. There was no reason for him to stay out of any obligation; they were even.

Staring at the bashful, complicated mess sitting across from their kitchen table, Sydney realised that, in all likelihood, she truly didn't deserve Dahlra Gar. And she had about five seconds in which to decide what she should do about it.

She reached for his hand. "You're a good man, Dahlra. You're handsome, and you're talented, and you're a great cook and good company." The words snagged and caught in her throat, not because she didn't want to say them, but because she had never had cause to say them before. "I think I could have done a lot worse, Minder-wise."

She cursed under her breath. "Yeah, great. Way to go, Chapin. That's a wonderful way to put it. He'll be begging to stay after that—"

Dahlra leaned forward and kissed her, cutting off her rambling. It was not like their first kiss, that stone-melting crash of heat lightning and storm. It was, if anything, a swift rap on the knuckles kind of kiss. The kind of kiss that said, *shut up while you're ahead, kid.*

She chanced a look into his face. The open and honest love in his eyes enveloped her like the heat of the sun. He stroked her face. "Oh, little girl, just being here with you, sharing your life—it's all I want in this world. I did it all wrong, but I don't regret it."

For a sweet moment, she thought he was going to kiss her again, properly this time, but instead, he released her, and sat back. Sydney took a drink of her cold coffee, more to give herself some breathing room than from any real thirst.

It was on the tip of her tongue to ask him why he had not just circumvented this whole Minder shite and sought her out. If he *had* walked up to her at one of the Lightoller's parties and introduced himself and asked her to dance, she knew herself well enough to know she would have taken him home and shagged his brains out. Wryly she thought, *and he knows it, too. And he wanted more than that.*

She remembered what he had said about his father, and his wife Caroline. Two people he had trusted had hurt him badly; Sydney couldn't blame him for being wary with that big, mushy heart of his. A Minder could be a more cautious solution; after all, it was a fait accompli. If he got in, it was more likely he wouldn't have to suffer another person he cared about rejecting him.

Softly, he murmured, "The day the news came down that you had been captured, I was told to do anything and everything possible to save you. I was put on extensive, fast-track prep. I thought to myself, 'here's my chance. I'll rescue the fair damsel and slay the dragon, and become *her* hero."

His voice took on a sorrowful, bitter edge. "But the moment I arrived, I knew I was in over my head. I have never felt so frightened of failing in my life. Not for me, but for you. I really don't think I could have lasted much longer than I did. By the time the rescue team arrived, I was a wreck. I was unable to keep most food down, when I could force myself to eat. I couldn't sleep. The only thing that kept me going was the determination to keep you alive, and get you home."

His eyes grew dark, and haunted. "And then they finally rescued us, and I couldn't revive you. I was so tired. I thought I had killed you because of my incompetence..." He paused. "When you took that first breath in the evac transport, I felt like I was taking mine."

Sydney opened her mouth to reply, but he rolled on, as if he had to get it out or choke on it. "You know, when we returned to the UK, if I wasn't in your room watching over you, I was working on getting the house ready for us. I thought, 'if I can just bring her here and show her how much I want to make her happy, she'll forgive me, and we'll be on track'.

"They had this ridiculous induction do; all Minders are thrown one. It's like a graduation ceremony for the programme. My mentor literally dragged me out of hospital for it—said he refused to let me skive off my own party. By then, every trainee in the programme knew you were already taken."

Sydney shifted uneasily, but Dahlra didn't notice. "You should have seen their faces when I was named as your Minder—if they weren't cursing me my good luck, they were patting me on the back, envying me..."

Suddenly, something that Dahlra had said in passing chimed within Sydney. *Not just in name only... a bit naïve... you were already taken...*

Her growing trepidation must have showed in her face. "Sydney?" he asked. "What is it?"

"Are you telling me that you were named my Minder *before* you—before the cell?"

"Yes. It was part of the terms of your mission."

"Meaning what?" She felt a little ball of ice forming in her solar plexus, and it was growing bigger and colder by the minute.

"Meaning that, when you were selected for the mission, Lightoller approached me and told me you were elevated to Minder status and I was chosen."

"Before or after you gave me the mnemonic codes?"

He thought for a moment. "Before."

The realisation of it all struck Sydney with such anger she felt a pang in her side. "That smug pimp! He used you! And he lied to me! I should have known that smarmy git would do something like this."

Dahlra looked alarmed at her outburst. "Sydney, what are you talking about?"

"Inigo. He told me I qualified for Minder status *after* I came home. I asked when I would interview Minders, and he said he'd already picked one. But he didn't say he'd picked one before I even left for the fucking mission."

At his baffled expression, she continued, "Think, Dahlra! You've made no secret of the fact your agenda in the Minder Programme is me. Inigo needs someone to perform this new, innovative, memory recall procedure on one of his top agents. He promises you the flippin' moon on a stick, as long as you do all his dirty work. You're compromised, and you don't even know it! The procedure itself is untried, potentially damaging psychologically. If you screw up my head, he can say that, as my Minder, you acted negligently. That means scandal and jail for you."

"But I—"

"Then I get incarcerated, and he knows you're just the type to volunteer to go in and get yourself killed to get me out. If you succeed, great; if you don't, well, he doesn't have to worry about you anymore. All his debts are paid. He used you, and endangered you, and that pisses me off!"

"Wait, Sydney. That can't be right," Dahlra said reasonably. Placing his hand on his chest, he said, "I wanted this. I accepted this. You can't be angry at him for giving me what I asked for."

"Yes, I can. All that crap Inigo fed me about careful vetting, all that stuff about checking through all the criteria to find the most compatible match... it was all bullshit."

"No," Dahlra said, firmly. "I had already been vetted. We *were* the most compatible. It was decided that making it a *fait accompli* before you left the UK would save time upon your return."

For a moment, Sydney could not believe what she was hearing. She had no doubt that Dahlra was telling her the truth, but—

"It doesn't make it right! He knew when you volunteered you weren't ready to go in undercover. I... what?"

Dahlra looked troubled; what's more, he looked strangely sheepish. "Please don't get me wrong, Sydney. Of course, when I was told you'd been captured, I wanted to do anything to save you, and I would happily do it again. But I can't sit here and have you think of me as some self-sacrificing fool with a death wish. That's not exactly how it happened."

Sydney heard Lightoller's voice: *Gar put himself forward for the assignment.* Not exactly lying; just bending the truth. Suddenly, all the little clues in his behaviour in the cell clicked into place.

With a sick feeling in the pit of her stomach, she asked quietly, "He *made* you go, didn't he? It was part of the T's & C's of your Minder assignment, wasn't it? If anything happened to me, you would participate as part of any follow-up mission. He ordered you to go in there, knowing if I died, so would you. Then he lied to me and said you'd volunteered."

"I *would* have volunteered. All I knew of the mission was that you had been deployed, and even then I wasn't told until a week afterward. The next time I saw Lightoller, he was putting me on a plane to Scotland to attend training at the Holyhead facility."

His expression was placating but unapologetic. "Look, I'll admit that on the surface, you're right; yes, you were lied to, and yes, I did allow myself to be used. What else was I supposed to do, put myself in the candidacy pool and take the risk that I might be passed over because the selection board was in a bad mood? Watch you handed over to some jammy bastard who really *would* see you as a trophy? I couldn't let that happen!

"When Inigo made the offer, yes, I jumped at the chance. I did a year's training to perform the procedure and implant the codes. And it's true, I was told I'd be the one sent in if anything happened to you. But it made sense that I would. And I wanted that, Sydney. I was already acting as your Minder; you just didn't know it."

She rose from her chair, breathing fire. Dahlra caught her wrist. "I don't really understand why you're so upset! Who cares how it came about? The results are the same."

"Fait accompli, remember? I care because I'm pissed off that you were used like a disposable pen, and I was the prize slipped under the table in payment. So he lied to me; what's new? You know Inigo's lying—his lips are moving. But he sent you into an environment you weren't prepared for, to do a job you hadn't been adequately trained for, and that placed *both* of us in danger. And he sent *you* because he knew you would do anything for me, which made you cannon fodder.

"Did he give you any idea of what would have happened to you if you hadn't been able to keep your cover? At least I had the codes to protect me. You had nothing but your word against the mole who was trying to discredit you. You didn't *win* your Mindership. Inigo gave it to you in a poisoned chalice and convinced you it was wine."

Fuming, Sydney tried to leave, but Dahlra stood and blocked her dramatic exit. His eyes were flashing with emotion, but his voice was calm. "No. I don't want you to walk away until I have a chance to explain myself." He placed his hands on her shoulders. "Please hear me out, Sydney. This is too important."

She wavered, then sat down again. Dahlra pulled his chair closer until they were sitting knee to knee. He took her hands in his, and kissed each one tiredly. "Oh, Sydney, why must every step forward with us result in three steps back? Why can't I make you see what seems as obvious to me as the sun in the sky?"

When she didn't reply, he sighed. "I won't deny I was infatuated with you at the beginning. And on the surface, it might appear I was bit on the obsessed side."

She had to smile. "A bit?"

"Touché." He gave her hands a gentle squeeze. "While you were gone on the mission, I would work double shifts, holidays, anything to keep myself occupied. When I didn't, all I did was worry about you. Wondering if you were safe, if the codes were working, if anything I had done was enough to save you.

"And then Lightoller told me you'd been rumbled, and were in a hospital being tortured. He told me what I would have to do, and I knew I wasn't the right man for the job." He sadly shook his head. "But I had to be, didn't I? I had to shut off my emotions; if I didn't, I'd be the one who got you killed.

"The first time I saw you in the cell, my heart nearly stopped." Sydney tried to interrupt him again, but the bleak, stunned grief in his eyes stilled her tongue. "I was supposed to play the part of the enemy, the torturer. All I wanted to do was take you in my arms and get you out of there, and I couldn't. I had to watch the woman I cared for being raped, and I had to let it happen. The best I could do was prevent them from doing it again.

"And then you started giving up, and I was out of my mind, trying to find a way to make sure your codes held and you didn't break. That's why I..." He stopped himself. Even though they had already crossed that minefield once, he could make himself double back over it again.

"That's why I kept asking, 'What do the numbers mean? What do the numbers mean?' It was a trigger, you see, meant to block pain receptors and help you to calm, and focus.

"By the time we returned to England, being your Minder was the last thing I knew you would want me to be. So I told myself that, as long as you were alive and well, I could learn to live without you. That would be my penance for the hideous things I'd been forced to do. But Lightoller insisted that I continue as your Minder. I think in his own strange way, he thought he was doing me a favour. I couldn't make him see that all you associated with me was pain and betrayal. And I should have walked away, and let you heal, and let you forget about the Doctor. I know I should have."

His soft, voice was achingly tender. "But I couldn't leave, knowing there was the slimmest chance you might one day understand, and find something about me you could live with."

Sydney looked down at their hands. While he was speaking, his hold on her fingers loosened, relaxed. A romantic, idealistic softie Dahlra might be, but Sydney didn't know too many men who would have had the balls to walk into the belly of the beast, half-trained and frightened, brave enough to keep her alive and unbroken, even though he had to stand aside and watch them almost kill her.

And all the while, he never blew his cover.

She looked into his troubled face, too overwhelmed to put together a coherent thought, much less a logical sentence. She was trembling, but she didn't know why. She rose to her feet, tugging on his hands to encourage him to stand. When she took him in her arms, he relaxed against her, and let her support *him* for once.

She whispered in his ear, "You kept me going when I had given up. Okay, maybe it was a messed up way to do it, but you made me care again. It was a damn heroic thing to do."

He shook his head. "I'm nobody's hero. I was terrified," he answered softly. He pressed his lips against her temple.

"We're all terrified, Dahlra." She laughed shakily. "You should see me now."

"I see the bravest woman in the world," he said, his lovely voice washing over her like spring rain. "I see the woman who saved my life, in every sense."

Even as she held Dahlra close, Sydney felt a wave of fierce protectiveness. Inigo had used him like a tool. He hadn't deserved to be sent over the top, nor had he deserved the burden of duty and obligation Inigo had manipulated him into feeling. The Agency had held him cheap; it was up to her to make sure Inigo acknowledged his worth.

CHAPTER TEN

The Tube

"Yes, I'm angry with you! I'm fucking furious at what you put Dahlra through. He was a civilian, Inigo! Aside from that, you sat in my hospital room, looked me in the eye and told me I'd qualified for Minder status *after* the mission, not before."

Lightoller sat quietly behind his desk, fingers laced over his lap. He had not moved from the moment she had barged into his office unannounced and started shouting.

"How are you two getting on?" he asked abruptly.

"Oh, don't even *think* about changing the subject—"

"And your injuries? Healing well? You're certainly *looking* well, old thing."

Sydney felt like chucking his paperweight at him. "I thought you foisted the man on me after what had happened in the cell. I couldn't understand why you were forcing us to be together, after what we'd been through. I thought you were rewarding him for being so good at torturing me! Why didn't you just tell me about all this Minder crap before I left?"

"Because it could have jeopardised the mission," he replied evenly.

"The mission?" Sydney closed her eyes as a bomb detonated in her head. "Bugger the fucking mission! You could have told me the truth. I wouldn't have liked it, but I could have accepted it."

Her voice grew in volume and pitch, but she didn't care. "Instead, you pulled out the Big Book of Lightoller Bollocks and quoted chapter and verse about how Minders were carefully vetted and tested and matched with compatibility measures that would make genetic modification look like a crap shoot." Inigo tried to cut in, but she plowed ahead. "And it wasn't just him. What about me? He was a liability from the start."

Inigo steepled his stubby fingers and peered over them. Sydney knew a stone wall when she saw one, but she couldn't stop herself. "Why couldn't you just tell me that you'd discovered the one man who not only wanted to be my Minder, but who would also gladly and willingly stride into the seventh circle of hell for me? I could have protected him as well. At least I wouldn't have hated him."

"You were *supposed* to hate him. It was crucial to his cover. Remember, he was compromised enough by Gregorin's poison."

"Don't you think I know he was? It still wasn't right, sending him into that cell with barely any training and zero means of protecting himself should he be discovered, which you yourself admitted was days away from happening." She began to pace. "He was so scared, Inigo. You nearly broke him. You know, I'm not the only one who—"

She stopped abruptly. Inigo prompted, "Not the only one who what, Sydney?"

She winced. This hadn't been what she had meant to say at all. "I'm not the only one who suffered, Inigo," she admitted. "You might take advantage of your agents with impunity, but what I can't stomach is what you did to a civilian. You pushed all of Dahlra's buttons until he believed it was his duty to do things that shamed and degraded him—to the point where I couldn't stand to be in the same room with him. And after all that, you told him he won the lottery and lost the ticket."

"Ah," he remarked, sitting back, "I think I'm starting to get the picture."

"Well, bully for you," she snapped.

Inigo held up a hand. "I've listened to you. Now you will return the favour. I'm going to let you in on some home truths. You've made such a great to-do about pointing out Gar's 'civilian' status. Would you like to know what he did during the past five years? He was training."

"I know that-"

"He was subjected to every kind of physical, psychological and emotional assessment the Agency gives any potential agent, including *you,* and he passed with flying colours. I was convinced he was a man of integrity and intelligence and mental stability before I even set up an interview with him.

"Now, I may have played a little fast and loose with the truth, but he knew exactly what he was getting into, and he was ready and willing to do whatever it took to protect you as an agent, even if it meant earning your hatred. The aftermath was not what he wanted, but he was prepared to accept those consequences as well, as long as you were home and safe and alive."

"You could have saved us both a lot of trouble if you'd seen fit to inform me." Sydney knew they were covering old ground, but she hated letting him have the last word. "Dammit, Inigo. You can be so cold-blooded at times."

"What do you want from me, Sydney? An apology?" He raised his hands in a gesture of surrender. "Very well. I'm sorry I offended you. But if you want me to apologise for not compromising this mission, for doing everything I could to ensure you had what you needed to stay alive, well, you'll be waiting a bit longer, old horse."

They fronted one another out, Sydney fuming, Inigo calm. Finally, he cleared his throat. "You know, you're an intelligent person, so I didn't think I'd have to spell this out for you. The whole situation had been the perfect storm. You were an agent thirsting to prove herself, he was a talented physician who particularly wanted to be said agent's Minder."

"With the qualifications and unbreakable loyalty required to embark on a mission that was one part glory and two parts suicide," Sydney added, quoting chapter and verse with contempt. "You gave the agent the mission, and then promised the physician a one-way ticket to hell if he couldn't retrieve said agent. It didn't hurt that such an incentive had the added benefit of being an offer he couldn't refuse."

"You both have a difficult shared history to overcome. But because Dahlra was, first and last, the best man for the job, there was nothing for it but let you two work it out, together or separately." Inigo smiled his politician's smile, "But I am jolly glad you *did* work it out. You're a good match.

"Now, you've chewed my arse to a bloody rag, and I've apologised. All is forgiven. Let's put this unpleasantness behind us, and concentrate on enjoying the rest of your leave, yes?"

When she didn't reply, he sighed impatiently. Testily, he asked, "Are you unhappy? Are the two of you not getting along? You agreed to a three month trial with Dahlra; that's coming to a close soon. A deal's a deal—say the word, and I'll remove him as your Minder right now."

"Fuck you, Inigo."

"Jolly good. It saves me a mountain of paperwork. And at the end of the day, even you must admit you make a nice couple."

Inigo stood, signaling the end of the conversation. Sydney muttered, "I still think you're a dick, Inigo."

He laughed. "Quintessential Sydney. Cut the Gordian knot by

skipping any dialogue and moving directly to insults. However, in this case, you're absolutely correct, old thing. Last I heard, one of the Senior Principal's prerequisites is to be a complete bellend. Part of the swearing-in oath."

She gathered her coat and shopping bags, and he ushered her to the door, saying, "Do give my best to Dahlra. Pip and I will see you at the New Year's Eve party. Cheerio, old thing."

"Cheers, Basil," she replied acidly. It had been almost worth it to catch his involuntary wince.

She strode down the hall, stuffing her unruly temper back into its cage. The entire interview served to remind her that in the great crap shoot of her career, Inigo and the Agency, like any profitable casino, always won. If she had been in Inigo's place, would she have moved the chess pieces on the board any differently? Would she have confided her plan to the agent in question?

Most likely not. Although it gave her no pleasure to admit it, she knew if she had treated Dahlra any differently in the cell, his cover could have folded, and the rescue attempt would have lost its already narrow window of opportunity for success.

As Sydney approached the door of her old office, a familiar voice within caught her attention. She sidled up to the threshold and heard, "He wha—? Lemme get this straight. Bullard got stabbed with a fork? Did she eat him? I swear, if that muppet was any more stupid—"

"—they'd have to water him twice a day," Sydney quipped.

Garnet Pinkerton glanced up from his doodle-covered notepad, and a delighted smile broke over his sallow, gaunt face. He spoke into his phone, "Look, I gotta go. Cheers, mate." He slammed the headset down on its cradle and jumped up from behind his cluttered desk. He was so tall he had to practically fold himself in half to reach her.

"Syd! 'Ello darlin'!" he crowed, in a voice gruff with East End glottals and diphthongs. His bearish hug of welcome squeezed her like a tube of toothpaste. "What the hell are you doing, slumming down here with us plebs?"

"Pink, my old china," she replied breathlessly. She plopped onto the battered green leather sofa in the poky little office they shared. "I was in the neighbourhood, and I thought I'd check in and see what you were up to, besides clocking in all that fake overtime."

"You malign me, my dear. I'll have you know that overtime was totally legit! I was having our office redecorated by Laurence Llewelyn-Bowen. No expense ... spent."

They laughed together, and some of her anger and frustration bled away. Garnet Pinkerton, born hugga mugga to the sound of Bow Bells, was a wiry yob of a man, thin as a shadow and strong as an ox, with wispy brown hair and a goatee beard. He had the hair-trigger reflexes, ropy muscles and battered pug nose of an ex-boxer. His bright blue eyes, hard as sapphires, shone with intelligence and keen wit. He looked and sounded like an extra on The Sweeney, but Sydney had never been fooled; beneath his hardnut exterior beat the heart of a gentleman, as well as a lion.

They had met at orientation, both green as grass and nervous as hell. Garnet was the East End wide boy made good, and Sydney the strange American bird with the funny accent. They were paired up straight out of training, with less than auspicious results.

From the start, they had clashed horribly over almost every aspect of every case they worked together. Garnet was hot-headed and gobby; Sydney, stubborn and insular. Eventually they went to Inigo and asked to be reassigned, but Lightoller, with his unerring nose for talent, sensed this unlikely duo could be the dream team he had always needed, if he could just teach them to play nicely.

Time and experience eventually turned their unwilling partnership into one of mutual trust and respect. They quickly earned the reputation as the two best agents to come up through the ranks in years. One of their peers christened them Syd and Pink, the Floydian Slip.

Together, they gained celebrity status within the Agency; some of their early exploits were told and retold until they became the stuff of legend among the rank and file.

And Lightoller took all the credit, of course.

They became more than partners, more than friends. They commiserated on one another's bankrupt love lives; they fostered one another's careers. Even while convalescing in the Agency hospital, Sydney had gotten phone calls or visits from Garnet every day, regaling her with Agency gossip and the latest cases. He was a frequent guest at DeVere Gardens; he and Dahlra never missed Match of The Day when

Chelsea was playing.

He eased back into his office chair, shirt sleeves rolled up to his elbows. A navy suit jacket was hanging from the sagging coat tree behind him; his shoulder holster peeked beneath it.

"Hey, good news. I got a note from Basil this morning, Syd. I'm coming up for Minder eligibility meself,"

"Hmm. If I know Inigo, it's a done deal." She filled him in on her conversation with Dahlra about the entire Minder fiasco, followed by the impotent meeting with their boss. Garnet looked solemn but not surprised. They'd both worked with Inigo for too long to be shocked at anything he did in the name of his precious Agency.

"Ah, don't be too hard on our fearless leader, ay, Syd? As for me, I'm hoping for a five-foot-two, eyes-of-blue little blonde bird to come and take care of me in me old age." He fixed her with a look of mock-severity. "And I don't want you queering the pitch when it comes to me nomination—"

"Goddammit, Pink, this is a Minder you're talking about, not a sex toy!" A fresh wave of pissed-off hit Sydney between the eyes. "These are real people with genuine feelings, you know..."

Her words trailed off. Here she was, having a go at Garnet for treating his as-yet-unknown Minder without feelings or consideration. But hadn't she spent a good portion of her early time with Dahlra doing the same thing? In the beginning, she had treated him like an unwanted puppy she had gotten for Christmas. A different man would have told her to fuck off months ago. Hell, no one but Dahlra Gar would have bothered to take her to DeVere Gardens and set up house with her. Anyone else would have done a runner while she was still laid up in hospital.

When Inigo had offered to replace Dahlra, she had felt the same panic as before. The idea of not living with Dahlra Gar was now completely unacceptable. However uncomfortable the last three months had been, they *had* got through it together. She had to know where the two of them were going from here. A proverbial ton of bricks fell on her head. She could be living with another Minder right now. Bloody hell. *She could be living with someone other than Dahlra Gar.* Her stomach roiled at the thought. *No.*

All this time she had concentrated solely on what Dahlra wanted.

Maybe it was time to determine exactly what *she* wanted from her Minder. Whatever that was, she had a pretty strong suspicion he would fit the bill exactly.

Garnet mistook her contemplation for anger. Contritely, he said, "Jeez. Steady on, gell. I didn't mean anything by it."

"I know, Pink." She rolled her eyes. "It's not you. I haven't exactly been the easiest person to live with these past three months, and I haven't always been fair to Dahlra." She sighed. "It took me finding out what Inigo had put him through to realise what *I've* been putting him through. I'm surprised he didn't cut his losses before now and tell me where to stick it."

"But he hasn't," Garnet replied. "Truth to tell, I'm a little jealous."

"What for?"

"Well, you were lucky he was so mad to be your Minder." He gave her a sly look. "Dahlra's a good looking guy, innee? I'm a straight-up bloke meself, but even I'm tempted, nut mean?"

"And they say James Bond does anything with a pulse."

Pink waggled his eyebrows suggestively. "I mean, think on, Syd; you coulda done a lot worse, couldn't ya? He's smart, he's a good cook; he's 'andsome, and he's crazy about ya." He made a self-deprecating gesture. "I'm wondering if I'll be that lucky."

"According to Dahlra, this Minder thing is pretty water-tight. Even with Inigo meddling, they make sure your Minder is the best person for you. It's not just about how much they want to be your Minder; it's about how well matched you are."

Sydney heard her last words as if someone else were repeating them back to her. Well, wasn't this just a day for revelations?

Garnet answered cheerfully, "That's what I've heard. Fancy them finding someone willing to put up with my ugly mug. She'll have to be either very accommodating, or very shortsighted."

"You know what? I don't think Inigo would've told you about the Minder thing at all unless he *did* have someone in mind. I'll bet your Minder has already been chosen." She smiled. "I think all that stuff about us earning the Mindership has a lot more to do with the perfect match more than just it being 'our turn,' Pink."

Garnet made a moue of consideration. "Yeah," he replied. "Look, I know Baz shoulda told you the truth. I'll grant you that. I mean, I realise that Dahlra did some seriously demented shit to keep you two alive. But things between you and him are alright now, yeah?"

He chucked her on the chin. "Cheer up, mate. It might never happen. You gotta look to the future, not the past. You know the old saying." He raised his eyebrows in challenge. "'If you can't take a joke—'"

They finished together, "—you shouldn'ta joined.'"

Sydney entered the Agency Hospital shortly after one o'clock. As she walked down the corridor, she scanned the faces, looking for Dahlra. It was then it occurred to her that she had missed him this morning. She had always cherished her freedom, her solitude and her quiet time. *Oh, screw that. Is it so pathetic to admit it? I've had a great morning. I've nailed my boss to the wall and he more or less took it with good grace. I'm not needy, I'm just—*

The door at the end of the hall swung open. Dahlra appeared from the exit, his mantle of authority sitting easily on his shoulders, like some genetic code all physicians carried. He headed straight for her, rocking a casual, masculine stride, leaving a bevy of stunned nurses in his wake.

As his long legs ate up the distance between them, he broke into a slow smile that put the sun to shame. Sydney felt heat blast into her like a furnace. In that moment, the impact of her realisation was almost physical. Everything she'd said to Inigo and Garnet this morning boiled down to one thought: Somewhere between chewing on Lightoller's ears and speaking to Garnet, she had accepted Dahlra Gar lock, stock and barrel, and she wasn't going to let him get away.

A shiver, part thrill, part terror, ran down her entire body. Hairs on her arms stood on end, and goosebumps pebbled her skin. She wasn't sure the sudden, sweet urge in her belly was to turn and run for her life, or to run to him and throw her arms around him.

Oblivious to her epiphany, Dahlra kissed her forehead in greeting. "All done? How about some lunch? I'm starving." He took her coat from her hand and helped her on with it, looping the handles of her shopping bags onto his arm. He placed a large, cool palm against her cheek. "Is everything alright? You look a little flushed."

With what little oxygen she had left in her brain, Sydney replied, "How about we just head home? It's been a rather strange morning."

"Of course. You're sure you're alright?"

"Yeah. I'm fine. Just, you know, Inigo: hours of fun. Nothing new. I'll tell you all about it later." She couldn't get him out of the building fast enough.

As they waded through the throng of holiday tourists milling around the Tube Station, she slipped her hand in his, and squeezed it gently. He looked at her in pleased surprise as they started down the steep steps toward the platforms.

"Sydney, do you remember when we first moved to the flat?"

"Of course."

"And your back was itching so badly from the healing. Do you remember what happened?"

Oh, hell, did she ever. She had almost swooned the first time, it had felt so good. *Like that, do you?* he had murmured in her ear, and even though his voice had been soft and sweet, it had carried an edge of something that had made her entire body burn. Then his large hands were cupping her breasts and his long fingers were lightly teasing her rock-hard nipples and—

At that time, the reality of who he was and what he was doing had been like a bucket of ice water dumped on her, and she'd nearly hurt herself getting away from him. His eyes had been hot and enormous with the same arousal that was whizzing around in her stomach, and she had wanted to run from the flat, crying foul. She hadn't wanted to want him, but she had.

Dahlra kissed her hand, snapping her out of her reverie, and when she looked up, those eyes were now soft and full of hope. "I've been doing a lot of thinking this morning. You know, all I have *ever* wanted is to be the part of your life you associate with pleasure. Every move I make is to achieve that. I'm on that launching pad, Sydney. All I'm waiting for is the countdown."

"That's an impressive metaphor. You got all that *and* did a consultation this morning?"

"I can multitask."

"So...was that a very frilly way of saying you're going to take me to the moon and back?"

Instead of returning her teasing banter, he gave her a heated, level look. "There's nothing frilly about it, my girl. If you let me, I *will* take you there. And unless I'm very much mistaken, Sydney Chapin, you're going to enjoy the ride."

Sydney stared up at him, but he was leaning forward, looking ahead. "Ah. Speaking of rides, our carriage draws nigh, my lady," he said, as a clattering behemoth of old Circle Line rolling stock rumbled into view from the mouth of the tunnel.

As the carriage wheezed to a stop, the ever-chipper voice of Emma Clarke announced, *"This is Tower Hill. Change for the District Line, DLR from Tower Gateway and National Rail Service from Fenchurch Street. Exit for the Tower of London, Tower Bridge and Riverboat Services from Tower Pier. The next station is Monument. This is a Circle Line train, terminating at Edgware Road..."*

The train was packed with holiday makers and commuters heading for home, pub and party; it was early Friday afternoon, and many were skiving off work to get in one more day of Christmas shopping. In spite of the weather, it was stiflingly hot in the tunnel. They politely threaded their way inside the packed carriage as soon as the doors opened, burrowing into the middle of the train.

Sydney grabbed onto one of the upright support poles, surrounded on three sides by the suited backs of junior executives and salesmen. Behind her, Dahlra reached around and grasped the pole for balance.

There were so many people crammed into the small space, it was almost suffocating. Clad in her coat over a light jumper and skirt, Sydney could already feel sweat trickling down her back. She managed to shuck off her coat and throw it over her arm, the shopping bags on his arm jostling her hip.

As the train jerkily pulled away, he leaned in close and whispered into her ear, "I have a question for you, Sydney."

"Yes?"

"Have you ever met anyone like me before?"

Sydney tried to turn and face him, but he was too close, the carriage too packed. His body molded against hers in a way that felt right. "No," she replied softly. "I've never known anyone like you. I mean it."

Some of the tension left his body. "I know you do. You never say or do anything you don't mean. And neither do I."

His lips drew closer to her ear, and his words came out swiftly with a sudden urgency that surprised her. "After all I have told you and everything we've been through, you must see how much I care for you— what you mean to me."

His arms surrounded her, and she could feel his breath tickle her ear. "Ever since the night you saved my life, I've felt that you owned it. I've spent all my time preparing for the day I could turn it over to you to do with it what you will. But I want to be more than that. I trained so I could study *you*, to understand how your mind works, what challenges and excites you.

"And I'm not telling you this because I'm trying to make you feel beholden, or because I feel like I'm entitled to anything. I did it because I wanted to make you happy. I've tried in every way I know how to make you feel comfortable, content and pampered. I love taking care of you."

There was a sinuous gloss on the surface on his words. "There's only one aspect of our lives together we haven't explored, and I think we're both ready. But I have to hear it from you."

His lips brushed against the delicate shell of her ear as he murmured, "Are you ready for me, Sydney?"

As those six words torched her spine, Sydney grew weak-kneed. How, in a matter of heartbeats, had their playful teasing morphed into this?

He whispered, "I would like you to answer me, Sydney. Aloud."

She thought it must be his voice. It seemed to grow at once darker and gentler, compellingly indefinable. Whatever it was, it defeated any last vestiges of doubt.

"Yes," she whispered. "I'm ready."

As reward, he pressed a gentle kiss against her ear. "Thank you, my darling girl. And I want you to know you can trust me." His voice grew more intense. "Ask me, Sydney. Ask, 'why should I trust you, Dahlra?'"

Sydney could barely breathe in the fetid carriage. The hand on her waist tightened. "Please ask me the question, Sydney."

Sydney whispered, "Why should I trust you, Dahlra?"

He expelled his breath sharply, as if he had been holding it. "That's my good girl. And because you've done what I ask, I'll tell you.

"You can trust me, because my only concern is you. I will never hurt you; I will never be unfaithful to you. Whatever we do is because you want it to happen. There is no fantasy, no taboo, no hidden desire that I cannot make real for you."

He pressed closer, and she felt his erection rising against the cleft of her bottom. His voice took on a solicitous tone. "You can tell me anything and everything; I will be your father, your brother, your priest.

If you want a slave, I'll kneel at your feet. If you want to punish me, I will humbly take your pain, and thank you for it.

"Do whatever you want to me, and I'll plead for more, and I'll *mean* it. I'll cry for you, beg you, submit to your will completely. You can beat and humiliate me, if it will give you pleasure."

He seemed to roll the word in his mouth, as if tasting it before offering it up to her. The arm around her waist slid toward her pelvis, and when she yielded to him, he pulled her closer. Urgently, he hissed, "Command me, and I will get down on my knees in this train to prove my submission. I'm yours for the taking. Has any man ever said those things to you before?"

Sydney was as still as a statue, hypnotized by the whispering, purring cadence of Dahlra's voice.

"Answer me, pet," he murmured, and a shiver traveled down her body from her spine into her core.

"No."

"No, no one has ever knelt at your feet. And I truly don't believe you want that. Because you don't see me as a slave, do you?" he asked. He waited a beat. "And you don't even have to ask this time, because I think I already know, and so do you." His voice was soft, cool and dangerously mesmerizing.

"You want a Master, Sydney."

She stared ahead, unseeing, breathing hard.

"You see, my love?" he purred. "You're becoming aroused now—my voice is exciting you."

Her body felt so hot Sydney was amazed the man in front of her didn't turn to locate the source of the sudden temperature spike. Dahlra chuckled softly in her ear, a low sensual sound. He was indulging her; playing the part of a dark, menacing stranger on the train, seducing her with words alone.

His accent became more pronounced and drawling, his words no louder than glottal stops and hisses overlaid on a sweet bed of sexsound. "I've paid attention; I've listened and watched. You want to be commanded. You want to surrender yourself to someone you trust enough to dominate you. You want to explore, but you want to feel safe. And I will never judge you, or use anything against you, or try to force you into doing something you don't want. You can tell me all the dirty little fantasies and I will make them come true."

A thrill of recognition raced through her, as if she had been waiting to hear those words all her life. In that instant, everything changed, as if Dahlra had awakened a primal, uncharted part of her brain. It was awful and needful and inarticulate; compared to this exasperating itch, her back had been nothing.

This epiphany had not merely struck a nerve, it had cold-cocked it. It pulled the stopper out of the whirlpool of her frustration and regret. She was overwhelmed, both at his declaration, and her newfound understanding of herself.

"Look at you, my darling girl." His voice was enticing, wolfish. "Look at you, writhing like a naughty schoolgirl, all wet for teacher."

"Oh, fuck," she whispered, then turned her head to the side, abashed that she'd actually spoken aloud.

He hummed his approval. "Hmm, would you like *that* fantasy, *Ms Chapin*?" His words fondly caressed her like knowing fingers, searching out those places that she had always kept so well hidden from herself. His tone became intimately scolding, smoky with lust. "A naughty girl such as yourself must be punished. I suppose I'll have to place you over my knee and spank you."

"Jesus, Dahlra," she rasped helplessly. She was going to come on the train if he kept this up.

He was relentless. "You want that, too, don't you, my dirty girl?" He relaxed a little, as if some male hunger inside him had at least been *promised* a good meal. "So, now that we've determined what you want, Ms Chapin, ask me, 'what do *you* want, sir?'"

"What do you want, sir?" The words tumbled out of her mouth so quickly he actually laughed aloud. His hand slipped beneath her jumper, and his warm fingers found bare skin. He hadn't so much as touched her below the waist, but she was already wet. Sydney glanced furtively around the carriage, but no one was paying them any notice.

"I'm very pleased," he murmured. His voice was pure sin, velvety and dark. "I'm so pleased with your obedience, little one. And so, I'll reward you again."

Hidden beneath their coats, his hand slid beneath the band of her skirt, until he was caressing the lacy edge of her knickers. Sydney lowered her head, not wanting anyone to see the look on her face, and widened her stance. "Good girl," he whispered. His fingers ghosted over the fabric between her thighs, his touch light, teasing, promising.

In the softest, most tender of whispers, Dahlra began. "I want to undress you slowly, and worship every inch of your body with my mouth. I want to lick, and suck, and bite you until you beg me to take you. I want you to be my virgin so I can gently deflower you, and show you what it's like to taste real love for the first time. I want to fuck you until you come screaming my name. I want you to be wild and wanton for me, and I want to tie you to my bed and screw you like an animal. And afterward, I want to hold you, and pet you and stroke you and sleep with you in my arms."

His fingers slipped lower, and his voice took on a darker note that was almost obscene, making her wetter with every word. "I want to bathe you. I want to feed you from my hand. I want to wrap your hair around my cock and masturbate with it. I want to strap you to my examination table and fondle you until you beg me to come.

"I want you to call me Master while I spank you."

Sydney no longer bothered to mask her stuttered breathing, her pulsing arousal. The train slowed and emptied, then filled again and took off, ticking off station after station, but Sydney was only peripherally aware of any of this. Holding onto the pole, remaining upright …that was all she was capable of doing.

She felt exposed and vulnerable, as if he had languidly undressed her with his words. She was completely unnerved, not because of what he had said or done, but because of her own reaction, her own realisation that she wanted what he had offered—wanted it more than anything she had ever coveted. There was no hiding from him, and she realised she no longer wanted to.

As she felt his warm mouth caressing her throat, his teeth nipping at her earlobe, she knew he was waiting for an answer, and she needed to tell him. *See, Dahlra? You were right. I want it all. And it's not just about the knock-down, drag-out grudgefucking sex, either. I want to pay it forward; you deserve a little of that pleasure as well.*

The train lurched as it began its final pull towards the station. "We're almost home, little one. Say the word, Sydney. It's such a small word. Say yes, and we can start properly. Forget about the Agency. Forget about the Mindership. They aren't important. Tonight, we'll be in my bed, or I'll bend you over my knee, or we'll play dirty little games, or we'll make love with enough fire to make the angels envy us—or all of them at the same time. I only have one request."

Automatically, Sydney whispered, "What is your request, sir?"

She could hear the smile in his voice. "You are a good girl, aren't you? So responsive.

"My request is this: you will give yourself over to pleasure, and you won't hold anything back from me. You'll allow me to take you to all those places you've never been."

Sydney lowered her head against the pole. Her head was spinning with the possibilities of his offer.

"Say it, Sydney." The arousal, the desperation, the need in his voice was undeniable. "Tell me what I want to hear, my girl."

"This is South Kensington. Change for the District and Piccadilly Lines. Exit for the museums and Royal Albert Hall."

The train stopped, and the doors were already opening. "This is our stop," Sydney marveled, her voice thin and quavering. She tried to swallow, but her throat had dried up. All the moisture in her body, it seemed, had headed south.

Dahlra removed his hand from the waistband of her skirt and quickly jammed it into his pocket. The mob in the carriage shuffled as one unit toward the door, the trundling crowd propelling them both onto the station platform. Dahlra held Sydney's hand so they would not be separated, surreptitiously checking to make sure her skirt was not in disarray. She looked up at him and squeezed his hand encouragingly, but he did not return her shaky smile. He was the one rattled now. He felt as if he had aged five years on that train journey.

As they silently headed for the stairs, Dahlra felt a light tap on his shoulder. "Pardon me."

He turned, and was met by a young woman in her mid-thirties, a typical English Rose type, with pale skin and rosy cheeks. Her fine, blond hair fell limply about her shoulders, and her clothing was lackluster and wilted from the heat of the carriage, but she smiled timidly up at him.

She pressed a piece of paper into his palm, at the same time shooting Sydney a disdainfully dismissive glance. "If she doesn't say yes, here's my number ... *sir*." English Rose gave a flirtatious little bow and turned away, leaving Dahlra swilling in mortified disbelief. For a moment they stood frozen, staring at her retreating back.

Dahlra felt so embarrassed he wanted to throw himself onto the third rail. He risked a sheepish glance at Sydney, fully expecting her to be indignant at the very least. To his surprise, she burst into helpless laughter. They laughed until they were breathless, although Dahlra wasn't sure if it was from humour or hysteria. Every time one would settle and gain some measure of control, the other would be off again.

It was a good minute before they could speak coherently. "Flippin' heck," crowed Sydney, wiping tears of mirth from her eyes. "It's like being in a Lynx advert. Should I be doing the 'boom chicka wah-wah'?"

Arm in arm, they chuckled all the way up the stairs to the street. The slip of paper fluttered, forgotten, to the platform below.

They arrived at the flat twenty minutes later. Along the way, they chatted amiably, though they both seemed in mutual agreement not to mention the one-sided conversation on the train. Dahlra was relieved; things had gotten a little too real on the Circle Line. While the interruption by English Rose had broken the tension, it had served a deeper purpose; it had allowed them to reboot, to gain some perspective. Back at the flat, they separated at the first floor landing. Sydney paused at the door of her room, her hand on the knob.

"Dahlra?"

Something in her tone told him she had made up her mind. He searched her face for any signs of her decision. This was a crossroads in their relationship; he had declared this the new ground zero, and he would have to live with the consequences of that declaration.

There was no going back from whence they came, and it was totally up to Sydney how they would move forward.

"Yes, Sydney?" He was relieved how calm he sounded. His heart was pounding in his chest. The air around him felt heavy.

Sydney ducked her head for a moment, and then raised her eyes to his.

No fear, he told himself. *Show any fear, and she'll eat you alive.*

She gave him a fragile smile that carried relief and acceptance and hope within, like jewels encased in a bubble of amber. It was a smile that held him to his promises, and to Dahlra, it felt as though all the trash had been swept away, and all his work validated.

"Yes. My answer is yes."

Without waiting for a reply, Sydney turned back to her door. It was then Dahlra brought all of the talents of his voice to bear, and it stopped her dead in her tracks.

"I have a request, Ms Chapin. You do not have to obey it; refusal carries no punishment. But if you choose to honour it, I will take it not only as an indication of trust, but also proof that all future requests and commands will be honoured as well."

There was the slightest of hesitations. "And what is this request, sir?"

"No underthings tonight, Ms Chapin. No bra, no knickers, no stockings, no suspenders. I want to explore you tonight—whenever I want, however I choose."

"Okay. Yeah, okay," she whispered.

"Would you care to repeat that, Ms Chapin?" While the words were softly spoken, they carried with them a sinister promise that was crystal clear.

"Yes, Dr Gar... sir." She rewarded him with a shiver that caught on his heart like a passing flick of barbed wire, making his blood sing with desire.

"Very good. Such a good girl," he whispered.

Sydney didn't turn around or even glance over her shoulder. She left him on the landing, and disappeared into her room, softly closing the door behind her.

CHAPTER ELEVEN

Albert and the Bentley

The flat seemed eerily quiet, as if he were the only one there. Dahlra stared after her for a long moment. Then he exhaled as he leaned heavily against the wall. He held himself still for a moment, then uttered a silent, relieved laugh. She had done it. She had accepted him. Trust Sydney to turn an ordinary day out into a life-altering event.

He replayed his words to her on the train. They had come out of his mouth without conscious thought, and when all was said and done, he still didn't know where half of that monologue had come from. He didn't know whether to feel elated or horrified.

He pushed himself from the wall, tucked his shirt into the waistband of his trousers, and took a deep, steadying breath. He could do this. He would play the game she wanted; he would dominate and command her. But in the end, they both knew Sydney was the one truly in charge.

In his room, he speed-dialed a number. For several moments, he conversed with the party on the other end, then ended the call. Rising to undress, he caught his reflection in the mirror. He saw a dark-haired man in his forties, tall and well built. His was a handsome face, although he regarded it as nothing special. It wasn't as if he had earned it, or spent a fortune to acquire it. It was his, owing to good genes and the occasional dab of moisturiser.

He thought back to the nondescript woman on the train, her bold offer. He remembered the women his mentor had tried to set him up with during training. And even though some of them were heart-stoppingly gorgeous, obviously not averse to his attention, and certainly not desperate enough to proposition him on the District and Circle Line, he had turned them all down. Why should he settle for empty, physical pleasure, when he could have Sydney?

He undressed and headed toward the bath. He had a lot to do in very little time, and he wanted everything to be perfect. This was the moment he had planned for since the day Sydney had saved his life. All of his hard work, dedication and patience were finally going to pay off.

As Sydney diligently prepared herself for the evening, her mental state fluctuated between knee-knocking arousal and first-date jitters—which was really stupid, when she thought about it. She had lived hand-in-glove with the man for almost four months now, had eaten meals with him, played endless rounds of Scrabble, drunk countless cups of tea, played music, even slept with him.

But this was different. Tonight, they were going to become lovers.

Sydney had never been one to indulge in deep, forbidden fantasies. She understood the dynamics of Dominance and submission quite well, but she had never entertained the notion of them pertaining to her, and her submission to a Dominant man. Hell, she had never met a man she trusted enough to remotely consider relinquishing that much power over her mind as well as her body.

Dahlra had recited her litany of fantasies as if she had presented him a list of her darkest secrets, neatly printed in fourteen-point font, only to find they were no longer dark nor secret to him. They *had* been living the wrong roles. The idea of surrendering herself to Dahlra excited her like nothing else she had ever experienced with a lover.

He had said he wanted to explore her. The idea of Dahlra indulging in a little exploratory op made her worry that she might end up with a damp patch on her dress. It certainly made the 'no knickers' rule a bit of a challenge.

After taking more care than usual with her hair and makeup, Sydney brushed out her long chestnut hair, pleased to see that it was looking healthy and alive again. It had certainly been a mess when she had first returned to the UK. Thick, shining, and gleaming, it had been her one real beauty, as far as she was concerned, and she had always worn it at least shoulder-length. Now it reached down to the middle of her back, framing her oval face, setting off her large, hazel eyes. The strip of glaring white hair that streaked down the right side of her parting no longer bothered her. Somewhere in the past few days, she had stopped thinking of it as a war wound and started regarding it as a trophy. She had certainly earned it.

The dress she had bought for the occasion was a floor-length, matte silk sheath of deep burgundy, with a high back and long, fitted sleeves.

The plunging neckline accentuated her breasts, but was not so low as to court disaster.

Subtle, but intricate iridescent beading swirled in a complex, whirling pattern, beginning at the top of her left shoulder, curling down across her abdomen, finishing below her right hip. The covered toes of the slim, matching pumps hid her disfigured nails, just as the high back of the dress shielded her scars from prying eyes. Emerald-cut garnet earrings, a graduation gift from her parents, flashed at her earlobes.

Taking a last look at her reflection, Sydney decided she didn't hate it. In fact, she thought she looked pretty good. Close on the heels of that thought was the memory of Dahlra's voice, whispering his desires in her ear. The kernel of arousal that had taken root in her belly on the train had grown like something radioactive. For a moment, it was so all-encompassing she swayed on her feet.

There came two soft taps on her bedroom door, causing the butterflies in her stomach to ready their wings for takeoff. "Ms Chapin? It's time to leave."

Sydney exhaled through her mouth in a rush. It was as if they were making up a play as they went along; each word taking them further into a fantasy of their own creation. It was exciting, unbearably so. She smirked, and murmured to herself, "Well, Dr Gar, if you want to play games, let's play them right." Reaching for her purse, she took a deep, bracing breath, and opened the door.

Dahlra was waiting, his hands clasped behind his back, one foot slightly in front of the other. He had dressed with care and originality. Instead of a typical dinner jacket, he had chosen a long, Edwardian-style frock coat and matching trousers. The fabric was so black, it appeared cut from negative space.

An innumerable row of buttons marched down the front of the coat, almost to his knees. The Nehru collar was high, accentuating his graceful neck; a precise half inch of snowy, white shirt peeked from the collar and wrists. His long legs were emphasised by the faultlessly creased trousers, which fell perfectly over black Hermes Chelsea boots. The whole effect, down to the dark frames of his glasses, was severe and elegant; he was playing his role to perfection.

He took in her appearance in one appreciative glance, from her hair to her kitten-heeled shoes. His eyes settled on hers, and she was heated by the fire she saw in them. "You look absolutely lovely."

"Thank you. You look... great," she stammered. *Oh, Gordon Bennett. I'm blushing.* "Sorry, I *am* actually over sixteen, in spite of evidence to the contrary." She turned toward the stairs to hide her embarrassment.

"Wait." Sydney froze at his imperious command, and remained motionless as he approached her from behind. She could hear his even, quiet breathing as he slowly lifted the hem of her dress, exposing her naked flesh. He released the skirt abruptly, and it fell back into place with a soft whisper of silk.

He then gathered her hair in his hands, and draped it over her shoulder. Tugging at the long zip on the back of the dress, he drew it down with the same languid anticipation.

As he parted the dress to reveal her back, it took every ounce of Sydney's self-discipline not to flinch. It was impossible to prevent the flush of discomfort, and the moment seemed to lose some of its other-worldly glamour.

"I know what you're thinking." He was so close she could feel the warmth from his body against hers. "You find your scars an embarrassment. You think no one could possibly find them attractive, that the sight of them would quell a man's desire for you. That *is* what you're thinking, isn't it?"

Stiffly, Sydney nodded, too discomfited to lie.

He placed his hands on her shoulders. "You must understand that this is not true, especially not of me. I watched every stripe being made, I watched every tear you cried for it, and I added my own tears, as I healed it."

The emotion and the sorrow in his voice felt as palliative as a balm. How many hours had he spent gently scratching her back, when she herself would have gladly clawed it bloody again, just to stop the itch? How many times had he slathered her ruined skin with cocoa butter and unguents to reduce the hideous scarring? Had she ever thanked him?

He pulled the back of the dress together, and zipped it closed. Then he gently slid his hands around her waist, and drew her back against his chest. It was a gesture that carried more comfort than passion.

"I'm afraid of you, Sydney," he whispered, his mouth close to her ear. She could hear his naked vulnerability in every word, and her inner sense told her he was laying his bared soul at her feet. "I'm afraid of your power and your strength. There is nothing, *nothing* I won't do to prove my love for you."

Sydney turned to face him, and took his hands in hers. "You know, there was a time when I might have used that statement against you. I would have had you on your knees, and you would have let me do it, wouldn't you?"

"Yes." He lowered his head. "I still would, if that's what it took." He turned those incredible eyes on her, and there was a ghost of a smile on his lips. "Don't be fooled by my games. I may be the slave here, but I fought tooth and nail for that privilege."

Sydney looked up into his face. It was as if everything she'd ever wanted in a companion was standing before her, and on the heels of that thought came the certain, oh-my-God knowledge: *I am going to have sex with this man tonight.* The butterflies in her stomach upgraded to hummingbirds.

Suddenly, all her doubts seemed pretty unimportant, and she felt one-hundred percent sure she was ready for this new ground zero of his. There was no point in going back and revisiting the past. They were not the same two people they had been before the District and Circle Line dumped them off at South Ken Station this afternoon. They would reinvent themselves, starting tonight. It was an exhilarating thought; almost as thrilling as the erotic litany he had recited on the train.

"Dahlra Gar, I accept you completely." Impulsively, she took his hands in hers, and kissed them. "Be my Minder, in every sense of the word. That's all the proof I need." His smile was so perfect, so beautiful, it took her breath away.

She released his hands. "But you were right, Dahlra. I don't want a slave. Not tonight, in any case. I want a *Master*. And I want that Master to be you."

With her last words, she stepped away from him, and turned to walk back to the top of the stairs. She bowed her head just slightly, and waited. *Your move, Dr Gar.*

For a moment, he was perfectly quiet behind her; her senses, finely tuned as ever, clocked every movement, every sound around her.

With his delicious, baritone voice, the first sexual instrument he would ever use on her and *her favorite*, he murmured quietly in her ear, "You will make us late, Ms Chapin. With tardiness comes reprisal."

"I'm sorry." She started down the stairs, only to feel his hand twine in her hair.

"Ms Chapin. I should like you to try again." His authority was unquestionable, and Sydney felt those hummingbirds all but drowned out by the low throb of desire settling into her belly. She bowed her head in what she hoped was a gesture of contrition.

"I'm sorry, sir."

They joined the swelling number of other well-dressed patrons milling through the Great Albert Hall, indulging in a bit of A-list watching as they sipped mulled wine. Sydney's inner menagerie gradually settled a little, and by the time Dahlra placed their wine glasses on the bar, took her hand and lead them to their seats, she was almost back to normal.

They had been given a Grand Tier box smack in the centre of the circle, affording them the best view and acoustics in the house. They shared the box with three young women, who looked and sounded like a raucous pandemonium of parrots, in brightly-coloured holiday party frocks. They gave Sydney a cursory glance as they entered the box; they gave Dahlra a slightly longer, cooler appraisal as he took Sydney's thin wrap from her shoulders and draped it across the empty chair beside his.

As the orchestra tuned up and the last of the patrons filed in, the lights dimmed. After the obligatory round of applause for the conductor, the orchestra burst into life with a flashy rendition of Happy Holidays. The trilling, fluttering notes of the woodwinds twinkled like a handful of glitter flung over the melody. It was stirring and exciting, and usually, Sydney would have been transfixed on the music. Instead, she was only marginally aware of it. As the music whizzed around them like fireworks, she wondered if Dahlra was as hyperaware of her as she was of him.

Of course he was. The man missed nothing about her. He always sensed the slightest change in her mood and temperament, as if his inner barometer was on the highest sensitivity setting. It was undoubtedly calibrated to maximum tonight; she could feel the quiet thrum of his energy as his left leg rested lightly against her right. He was so intensely, implacably *there;* his very presence drowned out the music.

She thought she had learned everything she needed to know about him, but this commanding, handsome, silent man sitting in the dark next to her was someone else altogether. It was incredibly arousing; waiting, knowing that when the music ended, he was going to take her home and then—actually, she had no clue what was going to happen next. She only knew this anticipation and seduction by silence was part of it.

Well, hell. You'd better have a plan, Dr Cool, because if we're improvising, we might give these girls the shock of their lives. Christ, when did I become such a randy bitch?

What *would* he say, if he knew she was seriously thinking of crawling into his lap, taking his Cupid's bow upper lip between her teeth, and kissing him until he lost the very last vestiges of that calm, unruffled demeanour? He had lost it only once, and oh hell yes, she wanted to see *that* again.

She was honest enough with herself to admit that, layered over this damn-the-torpedoes-full-sex-ahead lunacy, was desperate, nail-biting nervousness. It was all well and good daydreaming about giving him a lap dance in time with Jolly Old Saint Nicholas; in reality she felt like the prom queen, getting ready to lose her virginity to the captain of the football team.

Sydney had purposely embarked on a career in which she rarely had to justify her actions. She did what was required, she apologised if necessary, and grew selectively hard of hearing when the 'Why?' question was asked. It was, as far as she was concerned, a no-win kind of query. 'Why' rarely satisfied anyone, especially herself. So asking 'Why are you so nervous over Dahlra Gar?' was not a question she was in any hurry to investigate.

She had never been one to indulge in self-delusion, either. Before Dahlra came into her life, she had intentionally engaged only in disposable relationships. Being an agent provided very few opportunities for getting to know someone on any kind of intimate basis. She had often sensed the possibilities of mind-blowing sex, and in those lonely, horny moments, experienced idle yearnings for it, but she had never had a lover who even *talked* about sex.

During that mind-bending ride on the Tube, he had made love to her using only his voice. Every erogenous zone she had, plus a few she was only discovering, felt alive, clamouring for friction.

She forced herself to calm the hell down. This sudden craving to throw away her own formidable self-control was a new kink; she had never had a lover reach into her psyche, break through all of her carefully constructed defenses and read her with such detailed scrutiny. Dahlra Gar had gotten in her head like a new drug.

You can do sweet FA right now, no matter how many fantasies you have about jumping him between The Holly and the Ivy and Chestnuts Roasting on an Open Fire. Concentrate on the bloody music, she told herself, *before you get so wet it shows through your dress.*

She stole another glance at Dahlra. He was listening intently, completely engrossed in the music. *Damn him for being so cool and for making me want him and then ignoring me as if he were above it all and completely unaffected.* She smiled in the dark. *Two can play this game, Dr Gar.*

It might have amused Sydney to know that Dahlra was feeling anything but cool at that precise moment. Sitting next to her in the dark, with this intense anticipation stretching between then, he was as nervous as a schoolboy. His hands were sweaty; Christ, he'd been less nervous the night he'd lost his virginity to his parents' maid, *and why the fuck am I thinking about that now?*

As it was, the escalating, anticipatory tension had his stomach rolling like a snowball into a tar pit. He had written a spectacularly large cheque today on that tube train; tonight he was going to have to cover it.

He also felt an obscene amount of pleasure from the memory of watching other men watching Sydney. Their eyes had followed her as she walked by, and they had glanced at him with envy. Smirking to himself, he had thought, *look all you want lads, but this one is going home with me.* As the music played, he stole occasional glances at her lovely profile. Every so often she would shift in her chair. Once, he noticed that she even winced slightly as she moved.

She glanced in his direction more than once, but he forced himself not to acknowledge it. He had never seen her so restless or unguarded. To reassure her, he took her hand in his, and brought it to his lips. He reveled in the softness of her smooth, cool flesh against his mouth. She didn't overtly acknowledge the gesture, but her fidgeting increased.

He repressed a chuckle, then turned her hand over and touched his tongue to her tiny palm. He heard the soft intake of her breath. He smiled against her hand, kissed it again, and then lowered it to rest on his thigh.

"Are you uncomfortable, Ms Chapin?"

"No, sir." She stroked the soft wool of his trousers, which made it necessary for him to count the round baffles in the ceiling. Three times She lifted her hand from his thigh as if to remove it, then slowly settled it slightly higher on his leg, closer to his crotch, gently caressing the inside of his thigh with her fingertips.

"Are *you* uncomfortable, Dr Gar?" she whispered innocently. He risked another glance at her, but her eyes were firmly locked upon the stage.

"Wicked little girl," he hissed.

Thus they sat, tense and restless through the remainder of the concert. Even before the much-needed glass of wine at intermission, they had both given up even pretending to listen to the music. He had never before engaged in such an exquisite form of foreplay.

As the applause followed the Finale, Dahlra finally spoke. "If you have no objections, Ms Chapin, I would prefer to leave now. I see no need to wait for the encore." He gazed into the middle distance, his tone silky, almost bored.

Good, she thought. *Or I'm going to spontaneously combust into a cloud of orgasmic confetti.* "Sir? Did you not enjoy the concert?"

"I would rather be enjoying *you* at this precise moment."

Out of the corner of her eye, Sydney registered the shocked faces of the three girls sitting behind them. Inwardly, she rubbed her hands in glee. The game was afoot. It would be swift, and aggressive, like tennis, and he had just served his opening volley

"Of course, sir. Your command is my wish." It was said playfully, but with a hint of insubordination.

He smirked as he adjusted his cuffs. "Impertinent, Ms Chapin. You will be held accountable for your conduct," he drawled, each word pronounced with elegant, tongue-tip precision. He was just playing with her now. That layer of badass juxtaposed with his cultured, handsome figure was, quite frankly, sexy as fuck. *Love, all, indeed.*

"But you promised to show a *little* leniency, Dr Gar." A furtive glance showed the enthralled faces of the college girls. They were now straining to appear nonchalant, but it was obvious they were existing for the next words out of Dahlra's mouth.

He didn't disappoint them; he gave her a smile that was sexy as sin and magnetic as north. "I don't plan on showing any leniency at all, Ms Chapin." His smile was darkly sensual, his tone like chocolate. "Your sweet little cries for mercy will only make me spank. You. Harder."

If sound were a gateway drug to sex, she was pretty sure he had just lined up the powder on the mirror and handed her the straw. It would have been torture, had it not been so damn much fun.

He offered his arm. "Shall we?" He assisted Sydney toward the exit, steering her with a hand at her elbow. As an afterthought, he turned back to the young women.

"Good evening ladies." He coolly raked his eyes over them, then swept Sydney out of the box, leaving the girls staring open-mouthed at the tall, mysterious man, leading his woman toward her fate.

"Jammy cow," one of them muttered under her breath.

It was all they could talk about for a week.

The temperature had dropped during the evening, and the drizzle that had accompanied them to the Albert Hall changed to patchy sleet. Sydney shivered in her light wrap as they walked through the icy rain. To her surprise, Dahlra eschewed the row of black cabs lined up against the curb, and steered her toward an elegant Bentley parked at the corner.

It was a classic motor, black and sleek, a car proudly disdainful of its garish stretch limo cousins. Well-heeled families hired cars like this to take wedding couples to receptions, or peers to Parliament. A man in chauffeur's livery stood by the door. He was heavy-set and dressed like an old school villain, complete with long black coat and gloves, but his smile of welcome was friendly.

"But I thought we were going to..." Sydney stopped, unsure what to say next. It seemed like a lot of trouble for a quick drive around the corner to their flat.

"You're quite correct, Ms Chapin. We *are* going to..." He let the sentence hang in the air. Sydney shivered again, but not from the plummeting temperature. Dahlra put an arm around her. "Come now. Let's get out of this cold and wet. I don't want you to catch a chill."

The driver touched his hat in greeting. "Good evening, miss, sir."

"Good evening, Terry. Sydney, I'd like you to meet an old friend of mine. Terry Whitely, this is my lovely girl, Sydney Chapin."

Terry gave a courtly nod, and rumbled, "Pleasure to meet you, miss."

"And you." They shook hands, and Sydney pulled her wrap around her more closely, not so much to protect from the chill, as to hide the rock-hard nipples punching through her dress. Terry helped her into the Bentley's back seat, then held the door for Dahlra to join her. As they settled in, he shut the door, enclosing them in the dark.

As they settled back into the plush seat, Sydney took a surreptitious look around. It was easily one of the cushiest cars she'd ever seen. Polished walnut trim gleamed with wax and care. The floor was carpeted in fine black wool; the door panels were trimmed in the same expensive buttery cowhide as the seat. The car *smelled* of devotion; it was babied it shamelessly.

Resting in the middle console was a bottle of Dom Perignon, nestled in a silver ice bucket. Drops of condensation sweated on its surface, glittering like diamonds. Two silver champagne goblets sat in a little velvet-lined box beside them. They were smooth, with clean lines, and very heavy. Around the rim of each goblet, a sentence was engraved in a florid, fading script: *Presented to Reverend David Peter Gordon Gar, from a grateful congregation. 25/12/1898.*

Dahlra moved to the middle of the seat and pressed a small button on the door console. An opaque black glass window rose between the front and back seats of the car, blocking them from the chauffeur's view. The small space they shared grew darker and warmer. When the glass was in place, the sounds outside their own little world grew muffled, and unimportant.

Wordlessly, he passed her the goblets, before turning his attention to the Dom Perignon. With more panache than she could have ever managed, he unwound the wire cage from the bottle, wrapped a snowy white linen napkin around the neck, and popped the cork like a sommelier. Sydney's hands were a little unsteady as he deftly poured the bubbly into the silver cups.

"To us." The goblets made an expensive sound as they made contact.

"To us." Sydney took a grateful sip. The champers was perfectly chilled and absolutely delicious. The tiny bubbles seemed to dance on her tongue, and the buttery, crisp flavour was unlike anything she'd ever imbibed. She drank with more haste than the excellent vintage deserved, so it was no surprise that it went straight to her head.

When the bottle was empty, Dahlra took her goblet along with his own, and returned them to the caddy. He settled back in the seat as calmly as before, but even with the alcohol buzzing in her system, Sydney was too nervy and impatient to relax. She was fairly crackling with anticipation.

Dahlra patted her hand, which almost made her jump out of her skin, then pressed another button on the console. Terry's gruff South London voice came through a speaker overhead. "All settled in, Dr Gar?"

"I believe we are, Terry. Whenever you're ready."

The Bentley's engine revved with a deep, reassuring throb, and the big automobile majestically pulled away from the curb like a luxury liner from its berth. As they headed into the flow of traffic, Sydney glanced around, puzzled. They were definitely heading in the wrong direction for DeVere Gardens.

"Where are we going?"

Dahlra turned and looked at her, as if finally noticing the distance between them on the seat. He beckoned to her. "Come closer, dear," he invited. "I won't bite."

No worries, there, Doctor Love.

They rode in silence for several minutes, sitting close enough to touch, until the undercurrent of expectation nearly propelled Sydney into the ceiling. *Start as you mean to go on.* "May I speak, sir?"

"You may." He turned his attention back to the windscreen, his gaze impassive. His relaxed hands rested lightly on the tops of his thighs.

"Would you tell me where we're going?"

"If I asked you to trust me, would that be answer enough for now?"

Trust. There was that word again. A friend had once told her that trust was a Dominant's greatest treasure, and a submissive's greatest gift. All the sexual tension aside, she thought about the Minder mission statement – Mental, Emotional, Physical. Well, it was all about the trust, wasn't it?

She tentatively placed her hand over his. It felt solid and safe. "I trust you, sir."

"Good girl." The praise made her stomach flutter.

The Bentley pulled onto the M25; they were now officially off the map, in every sense of the phrase.

Dahlra unhurriedly unbuttoned his coat. Sydney could not tear her eyes away from his long fingers as they pushed the buttons through their holes: 7... 8... 9... 10... 11... 12... It seemed to take hours to unbutton them all. The crisp, brilliantly white shirt beneath looked luminous in the inky darkness.

When he was done with this erotic little striptease, he reached into the pocket of his trousers and withdrew a small black case. Inside rested a pair of short-nosed, long-handled surgical scissors, the kind physicians use to cut away bandages... or clothing.

Sydney watched raptly as he retrieved the scissors, then closed the case and set it aside. In the dark, his voice startled her. "There've been lots of little defiances tonight, haven't there, Ms Chapin? Little defiances, requiring little punishments." He placed his hand on her shoulder. "Be still now, little girl. We don't want any mishaps, do we?"

"No, sir." *You like this adrenaline buzz, and he knows it.* It made their magical mystery tour into the dark territory of Dominance and submission all the more electrifying. *You're safe, this is just for fun. Enjoy it—*

"Close your eyes." Sydney heard the *snick* of the scissors as they cut through her dress, like a fin through water. The cool edge of the blade licked her skin as he slowly, methodically snipped upward.

She rested her head against the back of the seat, and she relaxed into the sensation of full surrender. This was foreplay, and the metallic sound of the scissors, along with his quiet breathing, were merely part of the soundtrack of his seduction. He was stripping away her inhibitions as effortlessly as the scissors sliced through the fabric.

He stopped cutting just under her arm and she felt the loss of his heat as he moved away. In the silence, the ratcheting tension grew, until she was afraid the moment he touched her she would squeal like a girl being tickled on a first date.

She heard the soft click of the scissor case snapping shut. Time spun out, still and tense. The longer he made her wait, the faster her heart pounded. The anticipation grew so heavy it dwarfed the small space, and the air grew thicker and close—

Cool fingers touched the bare flesh of her ribs, and this time she did jump. Dahlra laughed. "My, my, aren't we sensitive." His hand slid beneath the silk dress, and gently cupped her breast. She whimpered softly, arching her back to meet his palm. "What a lovely sound. A man could get addicted to that little cry." His mouth was close to her ear as he sighed the words, and she felt his tongue flick gently against her earlobe. She gave another helpless mewl, and he responded by nipping the lobe sharply.

His fingers found a nipple, taut and aching, and he rolled the tightly furled flesh between his fingers, then scratched across the tip with his nail. Her entire body felt open and hungry, drinking in this slow seduction like some vital nourishment. She made herself remain still, her arousal dancing on tiptoe, waiting for those knowing fingers to find other, more needful parts of her to play with—

"How very obedient of you. You are intoxicating when you obey me." His voice held a touch of suave menace that made her feel deliciously submissive. Obey? She would have probably shredded the dress herself at this point, if he meant he would just move a little lower...

"All night I've been thinking about you sitting beside me in the Albert Hall, wearing nothing underneath this pretty dress." He gave her nipple a playful pinch, then soothed it by rubbing the flat of his palm against it. He nestled his chin against her shoulder and drew her closer. "There you were, playing the innocent, all the while stroking my leg, higher and higher. You were teasing me, you wicked girl. Weren't you?"

Sydney glanced up at him; he was breathing harder now, his expression loose and heavy with arousal. He teased her aching nipple with slow, rolling tugs. "Was it all for show, or were you making yourself wet for me? Were you fantasizing about me fondling you while we sat there, unable to touch?" The hand slid down, past her ribs, past her stomach, down to the waiting, yearning part of her. Her thighs parted like water, and he teased the soft nest of curls between her legs. "Did you think about me doing *this*?"

"Yes, oh, God, yes." She had given up any pretense of fantasy or role-play or flirting. There was only one conclusion to what he was doing, and she needed to get there, *right now.*

His long, middle finger parted her cleft, and they both hissed as he found the little bud, hard and slick. Sydney shuddered as her hips canted forward, allowing him to slip inside.

He circled her clitoris delicately, his touch a tantalising whisper. "You're deliciously wet, my girl. I don't think I've ever felt anything so lovely." He placed a soft kiss on her check. "I want to play with you until you come on my fingers, until you can't see or hear or feel anything but the pleasure I want to give you. Would you come for me? Would you let go and orgasm for me?"

"Yes! Please!"

His touch grew insistent, relentless. He bit at her throat, the stinging, nipping kisses sparking an unbroken current between her nipples and her cunt, playing a counterpoint of pain and pleasure that built as his talented fingers found that perfect spot and teased it over and over and *over oh shit yes—*

Her climax was poised at the edge, ready to make empires fall in its great rushing explosion. She buried her head against his shoulder, feeling that delectable, rushing sweet heat blooming in her core, and slurred, "Oh God, I'm gonna come..."

"No." His stern voice cut coldly through the lust-coated buzz in her head.

"You can't stop!" But he had already withdrawn his fingers. She could see his fingers glistening with her juices. "No, goddammit, you made me—"

"You will come when I am ready for you to come, and I'm not ready." He sat back, his calm expression back in place, the cap on his control screwed down and locked tight. "Interruption, Ms Chapin, is a very powerful aphrodisiac."

"Dammit—"

He pulled her close. He spoke swiftly, almost like a litany. "Have you not agreed to trust me, obey me, to believe that I have your pleasure in mind with every move I make?"

Sydney felt as if she'd been dangled off the edge of a building, only to be yanked back up seconds before she was to fly. "Yes, sir."

"Good girl. And I promise your reward will far outweigh your frustration. You may, however, show your appreciation if you wish."

He sat back. "Now, lie across my lap. On your stomach."

"Pardon?"

"And you seemed so eager to obey me." He patted his leg invitingly. "Do as you're told. Lie down across my lap. Now."

With trembling limbs, Sydney crawled clumsily across his knees, stretching the complete width of the car seat. She lay there panting, waiting. He ran a large, firm hand down her back and over her bottom, then eased the fabric of her dress aside, fully exposing her. She could feel the cool air as it ghosted softly over her bare flesh, in counterpoint to his erection, hard and hot, against her ribs.

"That's better." His fingers drifted over her skin, in a gentle caress, and the sensation caused her skin to goosebump. "So soft," he murmured. He cupped the globes of her bottom in his large warm hand. "You have the most gorgeous arse, do you know that? It's like a perfect little peach. I've been dying to do this all day."

The smack rang loudly in the car. While the blow was neither hard nor exactly unexpected, Sydney cried out in surprise. Her backside flared with heat, as if all the blood in her body had rushed to fill in the imprint left by his hand.

She waited for the next blow, but his fingertips once again kissed the edge of her sex, charging her up like an electric current. "Such a naughty girl, getting wet from her spanking," he cooed, in what could only be described as the most lecherous baby talk she had ever heard. It flipped a switch deep inside her head, flooding her with the dark, secret whisper of the forbidden, the unspoken, the taboo.

He spanked her again, harder, skidding her entire body into a tailspin of sensation. He smacked her once more, hard enough to make her cry out. He toyed with her, his touch whisker-sensitive over her needy flesh. No matter how she moved, he never intensified his caress.

"Please... more," she whispered. "Please..."

"Begging. Yes, I quite like hearing you beg."

She growled, too desperate with lust to weigh the consequences. She was past caring if the chauffeur heard them, past trying to control herself. "You bloody tormentor! Don't stop—"

"You're forgetting yourself and your manners, Ms Chapin," he admonished, punctuating his words with another sharp spank. "More," he sneered, his voice laced with power and desire. "Beg. Me. More."

Sydney tried to speak, but her voice seemed caged in her throat. She was so caught up in the fantasy, so primed for him, so frantic and over-stimulated she was ridiculously close to tears. She was on fire, aching with a desperation she had never experienced —all because this man was spanking her in the back of a car.

"Please... sir, oh fuck..."

He pulled her tighter onto his lap and delivered ten more ringing smacks in quick, relentless succession. With each blow, she drew up her knees until she was kneeling rather than lying over his lap, crying out with each gasping breath. Her hands worked furiously in the fabric of his magnificent coat, clutching onto the garment as if it was a lifeline to her sanity.

As she lay poised over his lap, panting and lightheaded, he wrapped his arm around her waist, and leaned forward, brushing his lips against her cheek. "Would you *really* like more?" Once again, his voice was her undoing.

"No. Yes. I mean, I don't... I want you to—I need you to—"

"Shh. Calm, little girl."

Sydney grasped his hand, and began to lick her moisture from his fingers. His breath caught in his throat, and he moaned. "Yes, my good girl... oh yes... lick my fingers clean... lick them for me... lick me..."

His calm Dominance crumbled; he pulled his hand from her grasp and brutally kissed her. This fusion of mouths was nothing like the first deep kiss they had shared. There was nothing tender or sacred about this. It was feral and ravenous and so out of control Sydney tasted blood. She greedily sucked his tongue into her mouth, savouring her essence on his lips.

He dragged his hands through her hair, pulling her closer, his kisses full of more pent-up passion than any man should have to carry. It tasted of punishment and reward and possessive, feral ownership, and Sydney glorified in it.

Gradually, he slowed the kiss down to a sensuous dance of tongues and teeth, slanting her head until he was drinking from her mouth, moaning low, teasing and nipping in slow, measured caresses, gently biting her bottom lip, then soothing it with his velvety tongue.

They broke from one another as if pulled apart by unseen hands. For a moment, neither spoke, but merely faced one another, breathing hard. Dahlra's lush mouth looked tender, bruised, and he was holding her so tightly it hurt. She moved to kiss him again, but he stopped her with harsh growl.

"No. My game; my rules."

Sydney smiled; he might have been in charge, but his breathless, ragged voice told a different story. He must have thought the same thing, because he sighed heavily, and pulled her into an embrace that was as tender as an apology.

"Perhaps we both have a lot of work to do on the issues of discipline and reward." She could almost *hear* the smirk in his voice. "I'll have to buy you another pretty dress to destroy."

Sydney leaned in close, stroking her cheek against his starched shirt. "If you kiss me like that again, I'll let you cut up everything I own."

His pleased laughter was the sexiest thing she'd ever heard. "You are a delicious little girl," he murmured affectionately. "You make it very difficult to say no."

"Then don't."

"And what kind of Master would I be, giving in to your every whim?" His fingers slid down her neck possessively. "No, I don't think I will allow you to come yet."

Her crestfallen expression made him laugh again. "Don't pout," he cajoled, then leaned forward and gave her a hard, swift kiss. "Seduction. Dominance. Isn't this what you wanted?"

"I do want it. I want you even more," she confessed. She dropped her guard completely, and shook her head in amazement. "Bloody hell, Dahlra. I want you so badly I can't make a fist. I've never felt so much desire," she whispered. "I don't think you understand how much I want you."

Dahlra took her face in his hands and kissed her gently. They sat back, and she rested her head on his shoulder. He stroked her back lazily. "In all seriousness, I don't want our first time to be in here. Not even in a car as sexy as this. It's too important, and you're too precious for that."

Sydney opened her mouth to reply, only to have it pre-empted by a yawn so epic her jaw cracked in protest. "Excuse me." *If I'm this exhausted by the foreplay, I'm gonna be comatose tomorrow.* "Wow, I'm— I'm just a little bit..."

"I understand, love. We have an hour or two before we reach our destination. Would you like to have a little sleep while we're travelling? You could rest your head in my lap if you like."

During the first hour or so of the journey, he touched her constantly, stroking her face, her hair, sliding his hands down the curve of her hip, kissing the hand that entwined trustingly in his. These caresses were not designed to enflame, but to engender a sense of bonding. Sydney knew he was marking her. In her own way, she was marking him as well.

CHAPTER TWELVE

The School Master

"Sydney." From the depths of a dreamless sleep, Sydney's instincts immediately took over, and she reacted with visceral, immediate force. She was instantly on the move, and before she was even aware she was doing it, she had grasped his shirtfront.

A strong hand caught her wrist. Dahlra wrapped an arm around her waist and pulled her tightly against his chest.

"Flippin' 'eck, I'm sorry—"

"It's alright." There was laughter in his voice. "It was my fault; I was trying to wake you as gently as possible. We've arrived."

Sydney blinked and rubbed her eyes, waiting for her heart to stop tripping along in her chest. *Arrived where?* she thought blearily. *Damn... I must have really conked out.* Bewildered, she looked up at Dahlra. "Have we..." They were still playing their game, weren't they? She tried again. "Will you please tell me where we are, sir?"

"We're just outside of Windsor, so not as far as the drive would lead you to believe," Dahlra explained. "I had Terry take the scenic route before bringing us here."

She peered through the Bentley's tinted windows, but it was impossible to see anything but vague shadows outside the car. "But where is here?"

"Home, Ms Chapin."

The door opened, and light and cold rushed into their warm, private little world. Dahlra got out of the car first, then turned and held out his hand to assist her. Sydney slowly unfolded herself out of the vehicle, still feeling stiff and a little groggy.

A moisture-laden, icy wind blasted around them, and with it came the promise of more snow or sleet. A cold finger of air slipped into the open side of her dress. Dahlra draped his black coat over her shoulders. She pulled it around her like a cape, burrowing into the warmth and scent he had infused into the folds of the garment.

He turned to their driver. "Good night, Tel, and thank you."

"My pleasure, sir," he answered, and tipped his hat in salute. "I bid you good evening, miss."

Sydney studiously inspected the Bentley's bumper to avoid any look Terry might be tempted to slide her way. After what they had done in the back seat, she could barely make eye contact with Dahlra, much less the chauffeur.

They watched the car as it disappeared from sight, its tyres crunching over the gravel drive.

When it was nothing but a light flashing against the distant trees, they turned toward one another, and Dahlra took her hand. "This is our real home, Sydney. You could say, I have been waiting for this moment since the day you saved my life."

Sydney looked around, stunned. The Bentley had deposited them on the circular driveway. All around them, Sydney saw dense woodlands and rolling meadows shining brightly green in the misty winter moonlight. Standing in the middle of this beautiful English landscape was an enormous house, four stories high, built of grey stone. It looked like a photo op for one of those poncy magazines like *Architectural Digest* or *Posh Weekly*, or something with the same general toffery. It was statelier than many fine hotels.

Two distinct wings, like turrets, flanked either side of the main entrance. Warm lights shone invitingly from the windows, and it had the look of a house that would be cozy and homey on the inside with the right furnishings and colours. Holiday wreaths and garland festooned the windows and front door. She stared at Dahlra, bewildered to the point of speechlessness.

He offered his arm, and together they walked up the steps to the entrance. He produced an Abloy key from his pocket and unlocked the large, ornate front door. As it swung open, he scooped her up into his arms and carried her across the threshold. Inside, he gently lowered her back on her feet, and the door shut behind them with the rich, echoing sound of a bank vault.

Sydney gaped as she looked around, so gobsmacked she momentarily forgot Dahlra was even there. The house looked like something out of Downton flippin' Abbey. Paneled walls and iron balustrades gave the manor the feeling of a grand hunting lodge, or some Lord Muck's private library. Even the enormous and lavishly decorated Douglas Fir Christmas tree taking pride of place in the sitting room spoke of class, of care in the choosing of each ornament.

The house smelled of sugar cookies, fresh cut wood and furniture polish. The dark floorboards gleamed with wax. So much thought had been put into every inch of space, as if the house itself wanted everyone who came through its doors to feel at home and welcome.

Sydney looked up... and kept on looking up. *Holy crow*. She could see all the way up to the fourth floor. A chandelier the size of the London Eye hung from the middle of the ceiling, its elaborate and decorative crystals flashing in the soft light. Each floor had a balcony that ran the entire circle around the open centre, and looked down into the front room.

"I had planned for this to be a Christmas surprise, but I decided to move up the timetable this afternoon." His eyes followed the huge, ornate staircase that wound up to the second floor. "This is where I promised myself I would bring you if you ever...If you ever accepted me as your Minder. So, while we've been at the Albert Hall, most of our belongings have been moved here for us to take up permanent residence."

All the breath left Sydney's lungs in a gust of disbelief. "You're shitting me."

"I shit you not."

She laughed shakily. "Do I want to know how you did all this in a matter of hours without witchcraft?"

"I have good friends. Friends who have a lot of manpower on hand."

"And a fuckton of moving boxes," she answered absently, noting the familiar knickknacks, books and pictures from Kensington, already arranged on the tables, shelves and walls of the large, welcoming front room.

He took her hand. "Friends who really want you to feel at home here. A few items are still back at Kensington, but enough of our possessions are here to make it feel familiar. The piano, I'm afraid, won't arrive until next week. It was either the piano or everything else, and I made an executive Minder decision."

She looked up at him for a long time with what she knew was a big, sappy grin on her face, but she couldn't help herself. Trust Dahlra to once again make an incredible shift in their lives and do it so seamlessly. And she had to admit, there were worse places to call home.

"But, who does it belong to? The Agency?"

"It belonged to my grandparents. It's called Maidenvine. My grandfather deeded it to me on my twenty-fifth birthday."

"Wow. All my grandparents gave me on *my* twenty-fifth was a toaster."

He laughed and gave her waist an affectionate squeeze. "It's not quite as simple as that, unfortunately. Grandfather promised it to me on the condition that I would finish medical school and establish my own practice. I officially inherited it when I turned thirty, but I've never lived here until now."

That surprised her. Remembering what he had said about his ex, Sydney was sure Caroline would have loved playing lady of the manor here. "Why not?"

"Well, for one thing, the place was a mess when I inherited it. 'Stately pile' just about sums it up. The inheritance tax alone nearly killed me. It took me ages to get it on the National Register as a listed building. And it took another six years to secure the funds to circumvent the register's restrictions on alterations to their listed buildings. It took up most of my time and money just making it habitable again."

He looked down at her with a smile. "It's really only had its finishing touches since last summer. I signed off on the work the day I left England to start the rescue mission. I wanted to show the universe that I believed that one day, I would bring you home."

Sydney reached up to brush a stray hair from his forehead, and he leaned into her touch. "You have a lot of faith, Dahlra."

"I have a lot to believe in, Sydney," he murmured. Suddenly he turned and placed his hands flat on the huge front door on either side of her face, pinning her down. A look of intent momentarily darkened his features.

"You know, our nearest neighbors are several miles away." He gave her a slow, rich smile. "So there is no one to complain when I make you scream."

His voice could have given lessons to silk on how to slide against skin. She could feel his erection, hard and insistent, against her belly, and she put her arms around his waist to draw him closer.

"Is that what you're planning on doing tonight, Dr Gar?" Breathing hard, she rose on tiptoe, her lips close to his. "Making me scream?"

His smile faded, and the look in his eyes made her body grow hot.

"Oh, yes. You're going to scream and beg and cry. And afterward, I'm going to teach you how to make me scream as well."

Then his mouth was on hers, his kisses long and slow, stoking the conflagration in her body to furnace heat. He suckled her mouth, his lips impossibly soft and warm as they drank her in with indolent, deep pulls. As his hand closed over the back of her neck and angled her head to draw her closer, his tongue flickered against her lips.

"Open to me," he whispered against her mouth. With an answering moan, Sydney obeyed him, and his tongue eased between her lips with such languorous penetration her knees buckled. It dipped and teased, but every time she tried to reciprocate, he broke the kiss.

With a knowing smirk, he lowered his mouth again to hers, his tongue more insistent, but when she moved hers to entwine with it, once again he pulled away, denying her. He laughed, a deep rumble that vibrated against her chest and sent waves of desire rippling through her.

"So greedy." He bit at her bottom lip, sucking it into his mouth. "Such hungry, *fuckable* little lips."

Sydney pressed against his chest, needing to be close, needing to feel him from mouth to ankle. It was more than just his intoxicating kisses. It was more than this little game of Teacher's Pet they were playing. It was the knowledge of him, Dahlra Gar, she found thrilling. Whatever she wanted, he was going to make happen.

As if reading her thoughts, he gradually pulled away from her and placed a final, chaste kiss on her forehead. "But let us not get ahead of ourselves, my girl." He turned back and brushed his finger across her swollen lips teasingly, his eyes dark and hot. "While the thought of taking you against the front door is tempting, I have something a little more suitable in mind."

He walked back to the foyer and retrieved an object from the hall table. Returning to her side, he handed her a huge iron key hanging from a green velvet ribbon. The key was so old, and the bit so intricate, it looked like it must fit the lock of some great treasure chest.

"There is a room on the first floor, Ms Chapin." He plucked his coat from her shoulders. "I would assume you would like to change out of that dress into something more... appropriate."

Aye, aye, Cap'n. "Yes, sir. Which one..."

"You will know." He glanced at his watch. "I think thirty minutes is sufficient time to prepare yourself."

Oh, bloody hell. Too much time, more like—

"Oh, and I would suggest you use the loo while you are there. You will not be allowed to leave the room once I come to you. I will wait here, and join you shortly." He nodded toward the base of the stairs. "Up you go."

Sexed up to the eyeballs and feeling like Alice in Wonderland, Sydney started up the stairs on trembling legs. She could almost feel the heat from his eyes as she made her slow, sinuous ascent to the first floor. The heavy key, hanging from its wide ribbon, swung like a thurible as she moved. Halfway up, she paused and turned around.

Dahlra had moved to the foot of the stairs, leaning on the railing. He was watching her expectantly. He raised an expressive brow questioningly. Impulsively, Sydney brought the key to her lips and kissed the ornate bit. His mouth parted, and his eyes grew heavy-lidded and dark. Smiling, she turned and resumed her walk up the stairs. She didn't look back again, but she thought she might be forgiven for putting a little extra sway in her hips for his benefit.

On the first floor balcony, she spotted her destination immediately. At the end of the hall on the right, a massive door stood sentinel. It was positively medieval: a great, oak slab with black iron bands, like something out of a castle—or a torture chamber. It was obviously older than the house itself, and had been added to the architecture at some point. It was a door that made her seriously wonder if she should be afraid of what lay behind it.

She placed the key in the keyhole and turned the heavy lock. Even though it must have recently been oiled, it took a bit of muscle to trip the tumblers. It took even more strength to push the door open. Suddenly she couldn't wait to see what was inside.

It was a bedroom, a massive, cavernous space that covered most of the first floor. Sydney gasped aloud, and the sound echoed in the room. On the far wall from the bed was a fireplace large enough to stand in. Sometime during the evening, their movers had built a fire, and its smouldering embers filled the room with golden light.

To her right stood the largest, most elaborate four-poster canopy bed she'd ever seen. It was so tall that a small step ladder was needed to mount it. The mahogany pillars were as thick as a man's waist and practically groaned under the weight of their intricate carvings of swirls, leaves, vines and other flora and fauna for which Sydney had no name. The headboard was lavishly wrought with heavy iron scrollwork. It looked like something Greek gods would have frolicked in.

Sydney closed her eyes, and imagined gripping that iron headboard while... Dahlra's voice came to her unbidden: *I want to tie you to my bed and screw you like an animal.* She wondered if he'd ever lain in this bed and thought those things, wondered if he'd been thinking of this bed when he said those things to her. God, she hoped so. A vision of him naked on the bed, writhing as he took himself in his hand, made Sydney's entire body flush with raw lust.

Lying on the duvet was a long, grey jumper of the softest, purest cashmere. Next to it was a pleated skirt in a darker grey plaid. He may have planned the move, but this fantasy was something he could not have anticipated. *He had arranged this. All in the matter of hours. You have to admire his attention to detail.* She hurriedly slipped out of the wrecked dress.

The cashmere jumper was warm and soft as sin. It felt exquisitely sensual against her bare skin. The absurdly short little skirt fit perfectly, though its hem barely reached the tops of her thighs. Sheer, over-the-knee tights and dainty ballet flats completed the ensemble. At the last moment, Sydney perversely left off the shoes, and padded around in her stocking feet.

She checked the clock; ten minutes had passed. Nervously she headed across the room toward another door she assumed to be the loo. She paused at the entrance, looking around in wonder. It was an Art Deco dream, all shining chrome, black and white subway tiling and chunky, symmetrical fixtures. The claw-foot tub promised hours of long, hot soaks in fragrant oils. Fresh-cut orchids stood in tall vases, as stark and beautiful as sculpture. At the far end of the room, another door with a glass window hinted at a sauna.

Sydney hastily used the facilities, washed her hands, and brushed her teeth. Feeling a little less travel worn, she inspected herself in the mirror. As she turned, the little skirt flared out, offering a glimpse of her bare arse peeking from underneath. *Not exactly innocent school girl*, she thought, *but just wicked enough to rattle the cage of a certain doctor below.*

She left the bathroom and checked the clock again, marveling just how elastic time could be. Only ten minutes left, and the butterflies in her stomach were bashing around like lightning bugs in a jar. To give herself something besides her libido to focus on, Sydney took in as many details as she could tally.

Next to the fireplace was a simple desk and chair—a desk fit for a school master. Besides the things one would expect to find—books, pens, letter openers—a single book sat alone: a volume of love poems by Pablo Neruda. Curious, Sydney picked it up. The book was well-worn, dog-eared; lines had been circled and little notes in Dahlra's handwriting were jotted down in the margins.

The book naturally fell open; it was obvious that Dahlra had read this particular poem often.

About me, nothing worse
they will tell you, my love,
than what I told you.

What more can they tell you?
I am neither good nor bad but a man,
and they will then associate the danger
of my life, which you know
and which with your passion you shared.

And good, this danger
is danger of love, of complete love
for all life,
for all lives,
and if this love brings us
the death and the prisons,
I am sure that your big eyes,
as when I kiss them,
will then close with pride,
into double pride, love,
with your pride and my pride...
...And I in these lines say:
Like this I want you, love,
love, Like this I love you,

as you dress

and how your hair lifts up

and how your mouth smiles,

light as the water

of the spring upon the pure stones,

Like this I love you, beloved....

...You came to my life

with what you were bringing,

made of light and bread and shadow I expected you,

and Like this I need you,

Like this I love you,

and to those who want to hear tomorrow

that which I will not tell them, let them read it here...

Jesus.

She reread it, picturing him here, reading these passion-drenched words long before she even knew who he truly was. If any man embodied that kind of love and devotion, it was surely Dahlra Gar. He must have marveled that the ink was dry.

In that moment, she understood him at last. A man like Dahlra only gave his heart to one person in his lifetime, and that person was her.

Sydney closed the book and placed it carefully on the table. She thought of the millions of little things he did for her every day, never questioning whether or not she was worth it, believing in their relationship enough for the both of them.

This went beyond obsession, beyond arousal, beyond lust, beyond the Dom/sub UST he had orchestrated tonight with the same military precision as this move to his own personal Manderley. This was a pure emotion, and it enveloped her as sure and as closely as his embrace. She looked around the beautiful room, and knew that the next time she saw him, he would be coming to her as her lover.

She looked at the clock again; twenty-seven minutes had passed. He would soon be coming for her. *He's somewhere in this house waiting for me,* she thought, and the impact of that knowledge was like a physical blow. A delicious thrill of anticipation, mixed with this new, terrifying emotion, licked over her body, making her nipples tighten and her heart race. In every sense, they were playing a dark, erotic game of hide and seek.

He could be anywhere in this massive house, and I'd have to look for him. But he knows exactly where I am. She closed her eyes. *He's coming for me. My lover is coming for me...*

The heavy door swung open, and Dahlra soundlessly entered the room. He had rebuttoned his coat and removed his glasses. His expression was solemn; he looked at once younger and more intractable. He completed one turn around the desk, slowly pacing around her, his hands behind his back. She could feel his complete and total attention on her, rocking on a knife-edge of Dominance and control. She was so keyed up her adrenaline was pumping painfully against her skin.

In a rush of movement, he grabbed her chair and spun it around, facing him. The speed and ferocity of his move startled her into a huff of nervous laughter. He lightly grasped her chin in his large hand, and entreated her to look up at him. "Something funny, Ms Chapin?" She allowed him to lift her head, but she still kept her eyes lowered—one of those little defiances that seemed to excite them both.

"No, sir."

After a long, edgy moment, he let his fingers slide away. He leaned toward her, his hands gripping the arms of the chair, until his face was inches from hers. She could almost feel him smirking at her. "Ms Chapin, something has come to my attention."

"Sir?"

He squatted down, trapping her in the chair, his expression cool and austere. He placed his hands on the sides of her thighs and slipped them slowly under the skirt. "It has come to my attention that you are not properly dressed for your lessons." She watched, fascinated, as the skirt rose until it bunched against her waist.

"Well? Do you have anything to say, Ms Chapin?" His expression grew dark and lecherous as his eyes slid down to the small triangle of curls between her thighs. His eyes flicked up to meet hers, and his head tilted almost flirtatiously. "Oh, my. We seem to have forgotten more than just our shoes." He looked up at her face, and she saw in his eyes a powerful lust that more than matched her own.

Without preamble he parted her thighs and leaned forward, his face close to her. He was just toying with her now. "I'm afraid, Ms Chapin, you are getting my chair quite damp. What punishment would you recommend for this little infraction?"

Oh, shit, he wants me to talk now? I can barely breathe. "I...I don't know, sir."

Dahlra stood up slowly, and tilted her chin upward with his long fingers. He leaned closer. "Do you *want* me to... punish you?"

She glared up at him, and his eyes widened. "Yes, Doctor."

His reaction was immediate. With one sweep of his hand, he pushed the books and ephemera from the desk. He pulled her from her chair into a tight embrace, and sat her on the desk, stroking her back with slow, languid caresses.

"Now, now," he murmured, his tongue flicking out to nibble her earlobe. "You must tell me what you really want. What is it my naughty girl desires? Tell me."

She laid her chin on his shoulder, whimpering. Fantasies weren't supposed to be *this* good. "Please, sir."

"Please what, little one? You'll have to be more specific than that."

With indecent slowness, he peeled the stockings from her legs and carelessly tossed them over his shoulder. Another quick tug, and the skirt slid from her waist. It, too, was thrown somewhere in the vicinity of the bathroom. He pulled the jumper over her head, then rubbed it against his cheek, his eyes never leaving hers.

"God, you are beautiful," he whispered, and then his large hands were cupping her breasts. His warm mouth closed over the puckered nipple, and he moaned against her flesh in time with her own soft cry of pleasure. He nipped and licked and suckled the tight bud, until her sex pulsed in time with her pounding heart.

With a hard tug, he released her, replacing his mouth with his long fingers, rolling and pinching until she was grinding her body against his, ready to promise him the moon if he would just—

Gently but firmly, Dahlra forced her down onto the desk. "Open your legs," he commanded. "Let me see you. I want to see all of you."

He slid his palms up the inside of her thighs, pressing them apart. Using his thumbs, he delicately opened her like a priceless book. The sound that escaped her lips was so helpless and abandoned he laughed, an irresistible, carnal sound that spoke of damnation and the devil.

Her hips rose from the desk, urging him on, but he gently forced them back. "No, no. I want you down on the table. There we go," he crooned, as her body relaxed. "Oh yes... I've been dying to taste you," he hissed as he lowered his head. For a second, he was still, poised, ramping up her anticipation to an unbearable level.

An incredibly warm, velvety wetness rimmed the lips of her sex. Sydney went rigid, her entire body locked into place by the point of his tongue. "Oh *fuck,*" she whimpered, her voice tiny and quavering.

He hummed rapturously, and nuzzled a little deeper, his lips lightly gliding over her wet folds. Capturing her clitoris between his lips, Dahlra's tongue flicked playfully over the pearly button. Then he drew it in his mouth and released it with a wicked little popping sensation that sent electricity sizzling up her spine.

He dove in deep, plunging his mouth against her drenched sex, burrowing into her with a growl of lust so voracious Sydney felt it vibrate into her belly. He consumed her, his talented lips and tongue fluttering hard over the little swollen knot, flooding her entire body in pleasure. "Don't stop, oh, *Goddammit,* right there, right there..."

And, oh, fucking hell, he stayed *right there.* His lips and tongue were magic. Dahlra knew exactly what he was doing, and did it like he loved it. He rolled his head sensuously, mapping out every good, sensitive part of her, memorising her responses and learning her body with every flick of his tongue. The flat of his tongue lapped at her fevered flesh, varying the pressure and rhythm, teasing her with promises that only his sinful mouth could possibly satiate.

She felt a tightening in her lower back, and lost herself to the steady, intense fire that was driving her closer and closer to the edge. His fingers did not merely thrust; they pumped, hard, unerringly finding the spongy little ring within, and Sydney cried out as the orgasm he sought from her grew in mind-shattering intensity.

The heat and ache and the glorious blooming of her orgasm arced wider and higher, until the pleasure and pain rushed together in devastating accord, and she was going to come, oh yes, she was going-

The orgasm shot through her like an arrow released from a bow. She howled as wave after wave of pleasure crashed over her, each burst of it wrenching a sobbing cry from her lips that sounded feral in its intensity.

She cried out his name until it became her mantra; prayer and incantation, angel and demon. It took her deeper and deeper into its depths until it was too much, until she thought she would die of it, until it was all she was and nothing else mattered, not even the next breath. She had never climaxed so hard and so long; it was never going to stop.

And still, Dahlra's wicked hands continued their insistent thrusts, and he bore down on her, filling his greedy mouth with her. Sydney's thighs began to jerk involuntarily, as her body's pleasure and pain receptors overloaded.

"Stop! Dahlra, you have to stop!" she moaned brokenly. "I can't take it..."

He held her in an iron grip. "You can take it. You *will* take it," he growled triumphantly against her body. He laved her burning, aching sex again, she began to shudder uncontrollably. She answered his loud moan of with her own wail of inarticulate ecstasy, as he brought her to that second little death he had promised with his voice, his fingers and his blissful tongue.

It was, he told her later, the most erotic moment of his life. Gradually, he slowed, and gently eased back from her body. The aftershocks of the second climax left her trembling; the muscles of her thighs shivered and clenched with each tremor of her inner walls. "You are fucking perfect," he growled possessively.

He lifted her upright; she was rag-doll limp and breathing hard, her gasps threatening to turn into sobs. He murmured soft little crooning comforts as he held and stroked her. Looking into her glowing eyes, Dahlra was so overwhelmed he felt lightheaded. He recalled with a start that this was, in all likelihood, the first orgasm she had experienced since the last night in the cell months before.

"Thank you."

With a look of awed pleasure, she answered, "I think I'm the one who's supposed to thank *you* at this point."

"You're welcome."

Her voice was slightly higher in pitch than normal. "I mean it. I've never experienced anything like this in my life." Her eyes were shining.

He kissed her deeply, pouring all his love and affection into that single gesture. As he broke the kiss, he brushed her hair from her face. "Not to put too fine a point on it, my love, but we're only really just getting started here."

The smile she gave him was as beautiful as the dawning sun, full of affection, and arousal, and absolute trust. He fell blind, stupid, drunk in love with her over again. "Get used to it, Sydney."

CHAPTER THIRTEEN

Going To Eleven

He carried her over to the bed, and climbed in beside her. They lay side by side, facing one another. Sydney felt dazed and dizzy; her throat was parched. Between her thighs, her sex buzzed and tingled.

Dahlra's eyes closed, his long black lashes like ink strokes against his pale skin. As if he had an eternity in which to explore her, he lowered his mouth to hers in a slow, deep kiss that torched her to her foundations. His lips moved over hers like silk, raw and elemental.

She brought her hands to his face and held him, inviting him in. With a soft, purring moan, he teased and stroked, his kisses suckling, sipping, sure and capricious. She could still taste her essence on his lips, and she hungrily opened herself to receive him, to be filled by him. He eased his tongue into her mouth with staggering sensuality, and every brain cell she possessed melted in a torrent of incendiary lust.

They were both breathing heavily, hands tangling in hair, bodies grinding against one another. Sydney's arousal passed from urgent into painful; it pulsed throughout her body, demanding and desperate as he drank his fill of her with his draining, torturing mouth. The civilised Master fantasy was forgotten.

He finally broke the kiss, gasping as if coming up from a deep submersion. "I'm becoming impatient for you."

"Good," she gasped between his kisses. Impatience was so three hours ago for her. Sydney slipped her hand between them, giving his erection a hard, deep stroke. She teased him, rubbing him through the cloth of his trousers, and he arched against her hand like a cat.

"Ah, you delicious thing," he breathed. "Do you want me to fuck you, little girl?" His voice was so power-drenched she whined in desperation. "Yes?" She nodded helplessly. "Then show me. Play with yourself while I undress."

Dahlra hungrily watched as she obeyed him. Not once did his eyes leave her writhing body as she pleasured herself for his benefit. "Oh, fuck," he growled, voice slurry with lust. "That's it. Just like that." He undressed quickly, pushing buttons through holes, dropping his beautiful coat to the floor in a careless crumple. His shirt quickly followed.

A thin line of black hair formed a perfect T-shape between his caramel-coloured nipples and down his sternum. The treasure trail teasingly disappeared below the waistband of his trousers. There was the occasional grey hair, which oddly enough, excited Sydney even more. He stilled, trapped in her high-octane stare.

"Disappointed?" His tone was level, but there was an underlying note of doubt.

"Not at all." She trailed her hand over his taut abdomen. "Dahlra, how old are you?"

He hesitated slightly. "Forty-five."

Suddenly, it wasn't just that he was a new lover. He was a new, slightly older, more experienced lover. *Okay, yeah, that's sexy as fuck.* Her internal thermostat ramped up another two or five degrees.

His expression grew uncertain. "What? Too old?"

She could feel the silly grin smearing over her face. "Oh, no. "I'd say you were just right. I told you I thought you were beautiful. I meant it. I like what I see."

His face grew calm. "Everything you see belongs to you, Sydney."

She caressed his cheek, and leaned forward to press a kiss against his warm chest. "My Dahlra Gar," she whispered against his pale skin.

"Your Dahlra Gar."

She leaned forward and pressed warm, open-mouthed kisses across his chest, and when her nails scored teasingly down his belly, he made a low sound in his throat. As she toyed with his belt, Sydney's kisses slid gently over his smooth jaw, and onto his throat.

Dahlra's reaction was instant, and surprising. He froze, then, with a helpless little sound of arousal, he pulled her closer, and rocked his hips against her. "Oh, that feels incredible. Do it again..." She nipped at his throat playfully, and he moaned raggedly, "Oh, fuck, don't stop..."

Drunk with power, Sydney obliged him, running her tongue over the column of his throat, leaving soft, biting kisses in her wake.

Dahlra kicked his head back, his handsome face transported with ecstasy, at once submissive and commanding. "Finish what you started," he whispered raggedly.

Sydney unbuttoned his trousers and lowered the zip, but her slow strip tease proved too much for him. Impatiently, he pushed his trousers and boxers from his hips and kicked them away, leaving him gloriously naked. She stared at him in wonder as he climbed back into bed beside her. *Oh, holy hell.*

His cock was large and uncut, and long enough to light her head up. It was also exquisitely hard. "You've been hiding your light under a bushel, Dr Gar."

The twin globes of his sac hung like a heavy suede pouch beneath it, dusky and potent. She cupped them in her hand; they were warm, and tight. He made a delicious sound, somewhere between a whine and a moan, and she gave his balls another tender stroke just to hear it again. Taking his cock in her hand, she slid lower onto the bed, impulsively rubbing her cheek against the shaft, reveling in the feel of velvety flesh covering stone. She gave it a good, deep stroke; it was feverishly hot.

"Oh, *fuuuck,* that feels good," he slurred.

She nuzzled against the black, wiry hair that ringed the base of his cock, breathing in, loving the clean scent of him. The head was smooth, apple shaped, glistening and ready for her. Her tongue flickered out, brushing against him, and he clutched the bedsheets like a lifeline. His hips rose in a silent command, but she smiled, unable to resist teasing him. "Sir, may I -"

"Fucking hell, girl," he moaned. "Put your mouth on me..."

Sydney twirled her tongue around the head of his cock, then planted a wet, open-mouthed kiss on the head. She took as much of him down her throat as possible, and he uttered a short, barking curse. His fingers braided through her hair, moving her face against him.

She glanced up at his face; he was drinking in her movements intently. His mouth was parted in an *O* of pleasure, his heavy-lidded eyes burning like green fire. He was totally, helplessly enthralled with what she was doing, and this excited her as much as anything he had done all night. His unraveling control was proving to be seriously moreish. Oh, yes, making him come apart was going to be an enjoyable hobby.

To reward him, she gently parted the tiny slit and fucked the entrance with her tongue. She felt his desperate groan of pleasure as much as she heard it.

"Oh, fuck," he rasped. "Do you—" he stammered as her tongue worked its magic on the sensitive head of his cock. "It's so good, do you...?"

Sydney pulled away, sucking hard. "Do I like doing this? Is that what you want to know?" He nodded, and she flicked her tongue against the underside of the sensitive glans. "I fucking *love* it, Dahlra. I love sucking you."

He pushed her head closer. "Then do it."

Dahlra could feel his orgasm primed and ready to burst from his cock, especially when she massaged his sack with an experienced, strong hand. He was so close to abandoning himself to her, to thrusting in that hot, rosebud-shaped mouth until he exploded. Then, by some miracle, a sliver of sanity permeated his lust-saturated brain, and he found the strength to back down. He pulled at her shoulders. "Sydney, stop."

She ignored him, until he grasped her head and gently pushed her away. "Stop now. I mean it." His voice sounded warped to his own ears. She released him reluctantly, letting go of his shaft with a sucking pull that nearly made him change his mind.

He rolled them over, until she was beneath him again, her arms wrapped around him in a possessive, hungry grasp. Her lips were wet, swollen, her nipples tight and hard, and the scent of her nearly sent him into orbit. She smiled up at him, and he saw everything he had every hoped for in her magical eyes. Desire, impatience, contentment, affection.

"I want you more than I've ever wanted anything in my life," he growled softly. His mind cleared of everything beyond the thought that he had to possess and tame every molecule of her slender, tensile body, her tough, ruthless heart.

"Take what you want." She writhed against him, nipping at his throat to excite him more. She reached for him, taking his cock in hand, trying to pull him to her. "No more games, Dahlra. I'm done playing. I can't wait..."

Neither could he. She sighed with relief he grasped the base of his shaft and teased her by sliding his cock along the seam of her core.

"I've waited so long for this," he growled. "Look at me when I make you mine." His large cock quested at her entrance, and he opened her slowly and deliberately. They stilled, waiting for her body to accept his penetration.

"Dahlra—" she whispered, and for a split second, she sounded frightened. Then her hips surged to meet his, and he slid sweetly home. They both cried out with shock, and held onto one another.

He drew back slowly, and the sensation of that sweet friction nearly blinded him. "Sydney, you feel so fucking good. I have to move, I have to—" He thrust, hard, causing them both to shout, and he rasped, "Do you like that?"

"I've never... oh, dammit, Dahlra. You're so big."

He uttered a harsh laugh. "You're like a vise. So wet. So tight..."

"Oh, God, don't stop—"

"You couldn't make me stop," he promised. "I'll never stop. You *belong* to me."

He wanted to savor this moment, but as he drove into her with another deep thrust, she uttered a sweet cry that destroyed his last shred of self-discipline, and he rose up on his forearms, drunk with lust and power. "You cry, little girl. Cry for me while I fuck you..."

He curled and churned his hips, finding their perfect rhythm. He fucked her with abandon; it was hard and fast and oh so sweet and Sydney was rocking beneath him, hot and wet and tight and she was holding him, calling him her darling, her angel, and she was fucking him and he loved her oh yes he loved her, he loved her—

He could feel her clenching around him, and he could not tear his gaze from hers. He locked against her until he could feel her from her collarbone to feet, and she was wrapped around him, pulling him in greedily.

"I'm so close," she moaned. He hooked her knees over his arms and began pistoning his hips against hers. He now knew how a man could become addicted to a woman, addicted to her pleasure. He succumbed to his addiction, allowing his body free rein, pumping into her relentlessly as she held onto his arms. Nothing had ever felt this good; no woman had ever been so perfect...

Suddenly he couldn't bear for it to be over. His struggled to hold himself back, to make it last. Then, she seemed to pull away from him, gathering herself inward like the ebbing tide of the sea.

Her orgasm burst from her with a feral scream; she threw back her head and howled his name over and over. As she cried out her inarticulate wail of release, he released her thighs and fell against her, his hips pumping, slamming into her until he felt pleasure burn in his groin like molten lava.

He came in a sudden, painfully sweet rush, shattering in every direction, each thrust an orgasm in and of itself. For one terrifying, soaring moment, he was blind, deaf and dumb to everything but the sweet, agonising bliss of his climax.

He collapsed against her, stunned, and breathless and sated. For several minutes they lay entwined, their gasping breaths harshly rising and falling in tandem. *Five years*, he thought dazedly. *Worth every second and more.*

As his pounding heart gradually calmed, Dahlra looked down at Sydney. Her eyes were tightly closed, a tiny furrow between her expressive brows. She was trembling all over, still clenching him tightly within, reeling in the grip of her powerful climax.

He gently pressed his lips against that furrowed line, and it smoothed away as if by magic. He kissed her beautiful, swollen mouth as he settled into her arms. Surely no one could condemn him for pressing her tender body into the mattress; he couldn't have crawled out of bed if the house caught fire. Finally, he tried to rise, but Sydney possessively cradled him to her breast. "No, Dahlra, not yet. Don't get up. Stay with me."

He nuzzled against the downy pillow of her breast. "I'm not going anywhere." He rolled over, carrying her with him, and Sydney looked down at him. The expression on her face was one he couldn't identify. Concerned, he gently touched her cheek. "What is it, love? Is something wrong?"

"Oh no, no..." Sydney shook her head. "This wasn't....This wasn't good sex. I mean—oh, God, what am I saying? Of course it was good sex. It was *great* sex." She rolled her eyes. "I mean, I've never—this wasn't just..."

Dahlra understood. "We were making love." When she didn't reply, he pressed his lips to hers. "Haven't you ever-"

"Not if that's what making love feels like." A smile teased the corners of her lovely mouth. "But I'm glad you were my first."

He rewarded her with another kiss.

She glanced around the room. "All of this. Everything. Becoming my Minder, the flat, this amazing house, even the—the cell." She looked young and vulnerable and somehow fragile. In a stunned, tight voice, she breathed, "You've been making love to me for years. That's what you've been trying to get through my thick skull all along, isn't it?"

Dawn was breaking as they finally reached the point of total exhaustion. Sydney was sweat-soaked, hoarse from screaming, sore from being pummeled in all the right places, and shaken to her foundations. Her arms were locked around Dahlra's back. She knew she needed to let go, but she was pretty sure it would mortally wound her to release him. Dahlra was a heavy, powerful weight on her, panting heavily into her ear, and she could barely breathe, but still she pulled him closer.

Finally, with a groan of exhaustion, Dahlra ungracefully fumbled up onto his elbows and rolled onto his back. Clumsily, he wrapped his arms around her, and pulled her close. Even replete and almost dozing, he held her like something cherished.

Sydney looked down at him, sapping out a little. In the snow-pearled morning light, with his eyes closed and a loopy smile on his handsome face, Dahlra was the very picture of a well-fucked, happy man. She wanted to keep this moment close, and never forget she had been the one to put that look on his face.

She nestled contentedly against him, resting her head on his shoulder. "You know, I fit really well in this little place between your arm and your shoulder. Sir," she said.

"And so you should, Ms Chapin," he rumbled, sounding sweet and sleepy, like a little bear. He placed a warm, slow kiss on her forehead and pulled her closer. "Grow old with me, Sydney Chapin. Stay with me, here at Maidenvine, and I'll make you crème brûlées, and you'll sing me to sleep, and I promise I'll make you happy every day for the rest of your life."

Sydney looked up into his face, her body suffused in happiness, and thought how his statement would have worried the hell out of her as little as a few days ago. Now it just eased her into sleep.

CHAPTER FOURTEEN

Stone and Clay

Over the coming days and weeks, Sydney found Dahlra true to his word; he was open to anything. Sex with him wasn't just an act—it was a ceremony, a rite performed for the gods of passion and adoration. He paid attention, treating each thrust and cry as a learning experience to be filed away for future use. He had a true understanding of umami, the perfect blend of sugar and spice.

There were times when he was explosive and carnal, and Sydney felt like a pagan sacrifice as he towered over her, doing and saying things that bordered on the profane. Those were the orgasms that left her screaming, as if giving tongue to them was the only way to ride them out without losing herself. And there were moments of breathtaking tenderness, when he made love to her slowly, with deliberation and purpose, as if he could go on for weeks.

And while he might at first give the appearance as the poster child of the tightly button-downed British male, Sydney found him to be one of the most heart-on-your-sleeve men she had ever met. He was compassionate and tender-hearted, but with a playful streak that was both charming and guileless.

Sydney joked that acting out their intricate fantasies was perfect training for her undercover work, but in reality it felt as if she had only just learned what fantasies really were. With a lover like Dahlra, fantasy had a way of becoming reality, and reality morphed into another fantasy. Exploring their mutual sexuality with him was like starting over again on a new, infinitely more pleasurable status quo.

At first, Sydney had felt rather ridiculous confessing her fantasies to him, thinking in the cold light of day they sounded puerile or mundane. She cringed her way through her first confessions, her face hot with embarrassment. Dahlra, ever sensitive to her needs, devised the habit of having her sit on his lap, and whispering her secrets in his ear. He never judged, never questioned her motives, never scoffed.

"If you want those things, I can give them to you, my darling girl." He gave her a tender, encouraging smile. "There's no need to feel ashamed. All you have to do is trust me." What remained unsaid, but what Sydney understood immediately, was that Dahlra had given years of thought to these moments.

It wasn't just that the sex was the best she'd ever had in her life. It was his commitment to her pleasure. It was his all-encompassing need to take care of her, to let her soar when he finally let her go, to hold her when she needed to come down. And in teaching her how to lose her inhibitions; he was teaching himself, giving himself permission to take the reins and drive. It wasn't some sort of ego trip for him; even in his rawest, most out-of-control moments, he always made sure she came first, in every sense of the phrase. Denial was not in Dahlra Gar's personal remit.

In those moments, with his intense concentration focused solely on her, there was nothing between them; no cell, no baggage, no Minder, no agent. It no longer even bordered on Dominant/submissive. They connected on a visceral level neither felt the need to analyse.

He patiently guided her into the deeper waters of Dominance and submission without causing a ripple in their daily lives. At first, she was reticent to initiate their love making, thinking that, as the submissive in their relationship, it was not her place. He quickly set her straight; in order for him to Dominate her, she had to allow it to happen. He could not be her respected, gentle Master unless she chose to submit to him. It was a fascinating concept, giving the Dominant permission to Dominate.

Far from being helpless or powerless, Sydney found the role of submissive to be a very strong position within their relationship, and he eased her into the more extreme and intense aspects of the lifestyle with patience and respect. Theirs was an equal partnership.

The enormous bed became their first playground. More than once he tied her to the iron headboard using silk scarves or handcuffs, which turned out to be very exciting to them both for very different reasons. At times, they switched. Not only did Dahlra enjoy being Dominated, but Sydney found his submission blazingly erotic. When he submitted to her, he was nothing short of breathtaking. It was like stroking a fully-grown male lion: beautiful and intense, tame because she demanded it, and explosively passionate when unleashed.

Sydney was intrigued with the idea of leather and paddles and blindfolds, and Dahlra enjoyed wielding them. He did things to her he heretofore had never considered himself capable of doing with anyone.

Sydney bloomed and reveled in his Dominance. Her acquiescence and growing understanding of submission gave him carte blanche to be as creative and adventurous as he wished. She freely gave him control over her fantasies, and in turn he gave her the freedom to explore her own sexuality.

He was the first to admit that, in reality, she was the likelier candidate to be the Dominant one. Her personality and her proficiency in her chosen profession seemed to naturally foster it. The act of relinquishing her will to someone she could trust became the catalyst for her submission. Her growing affection for him gave him a feeling of purpose and fulfillment like nothing, even medicine, had ever afforded him.

In the mornings, he allowed her to shave him with a straight-razor. It was something she had always loved to do, but few men would allow anyone outside a professional barber to do the Sweeney Todd routine on them. It became a daily ritual that grounded them.

In the same vein, Dahlra would brush Sydney's long, thick chestnut hair as she sat as his feet. Sometimes, if she had been 'a very good girl,' he would place her over his knee and spank her with her hairbrush. This particular bonding exercise usually culminated in being taken doggie-style on the floor. She quickly grew conditioned to love the sight of her hairbrush in his large hands.

At first Sydney could not understand how they had made the effortless shift from the stilted, awkward conversations they had first shared to the limitless streams of consciousness that now flowed easily between them. She wanted to justify it by some other means beyond their sex life, which, fair enough, resembled something out of a Cosmo article. At the end of the day, it was all about trust, honesty, and affection. Once she had decided to trust him, the sticky, uncomfortable silences melted away.

"You actually expect me to believe your Minder training included courses in—in sexual technique?" They were lying in bed, feeding one another wedges of cheese and biscuits.

"I do, and yes, it was a bit uncomfortable at first for a reserved British doctor like myself to openly discuss in open forum." He favoured her with a self-deprecating smile. "My Mentor apparently saw this as *the* most important aspect of my training, and wanted me to be prepared."

"Well, hell," she mused. "Who... what... how did you practice?"

"How do you think? Test dummies, of course."

Sydney honestly couldn't tell if he was joking or not. "So... you're fantastic in bed because of a *sex doll*?"

Dahlra threw back his head and laughed. "Oh, Sydney, you are priceless." He kissed butter and crumbs from her lips "If I'm any good at sex, it's because I had five years to fantasise about all the ways I wanted to make love to you."

He piled slivers of Wensleydale cheese on top of melba toast. "And, not to put too fine a point on it, I may have spent the last five years celibate and the preceding seven monogamous, but I wasn't exactly a monk while I was single."

Sydney looked into his calm, open face, and he raised an eyebrow which plainly said, *I'll willingly answer any question you ask, but are you really sure you want me to quote chapter and verse about my sexual history? And quid pro quo—would you be willing to answer the same questions yourself, Sydney?*

No. Some roads weren't worth the bother of traveling, and Dahlra's expression told her that he felt the same. "Well, hell," she marveled softly. Sydney stroked his belly, and his emerald eyes slid closed. "Maybe I should do some training for you," she teased, sliding her hand down over his crotch.

Kensington had been about re-orienting herself. To Dahlra, it had been nothing more than a halfway house. Maidenvine was his manor, literally; he was more relaxed, more at home, and he taught her to relax and learn to play as well. It was where they truly came to know one another. After they celebrated the holidays, they settled into a new daily routine, and Sydney set about acquainting herself with Maidenvine.

The sheer size of it staggered her; almost ten thousand square feet of house sat on thirty acres of mostly meadow and woodland. It had rooms on the ground floor that could easily hold a small army and still not feel crowded, and the front and back gardens were landscaped with the help of several enthusiastic lads studying horticulture at the local technical college.

In the kitchen, a door with rough-hewn boards and heavy iron bands led to a huge basement with partitioned walls, complete with a large but unfortunately empty wine cellar. There were countless little alcoves and secret rooms and corridors that led to unexpected parts of the house. Once, while investigating a tiny, cramped space that looked like a priest hole, they discovered a subterranean tunnel that led into the back garden. Beyond the L-shaped orangery, the meadows and fields undulated in patterns of green and gold, stretching as far as the eye could see.

The piano arrived just after the New Year, and they housed it in a bright, multi-sided, multi-windowed room Dahlra christened the Conservatory. Sydney loved this room most of all. In the afternoon, seated on the piano bench, she rediscovered her keyboard chops while Dahlra performed his culinary magic on the AGA range cooker in the kitchen.

It was all black enamel and chrome, like a cross between a pipe organ and a Rolls Royce. Sydney christened it Orson Wells, because it glowered from beneath its tiled alcove and looked as if it chased young maids around when not in use. Orson gave off a constant, stupendous heat which kept most of the ground floor warm without any other heat source. The kitchen was also equipped with a stainless gas hob and a conventional oven for use during warmer weather.

The house whispered its understated good taste to the world, and Sydney grew to understand how growing up in that sort of rarefied atmosphere could breed a man like Dahlra. Museum quality portraits lined the stairs, ancestors of his stretching back to the age of Napoleon.

Compared with some she had seen at the National Gallery, they were a better-than-average looking group for the most part. Among them was the stern countenanced Reverend David Peter Gordon Gar, whose champagne goblets had toasted their first night as lovers.

Dahlra dutifully pointed out each relative with the careless deference of a boy schooled in the importance of family history, but not necessarily defined by it. One day, while looking through a box of photographs, they came upon the picture of a boy, around eighteen years old. He was standing alone, dressed in cricket whites, leaning on his bat. He was tall and lanky, with scruffy dark hair and a nose the rest of his face had not quite caught up with. He wore a look of patient, unsmiling resignation; a self-conscious kid who hated having his photo taken, but was too polite to refuse.

Sydney realised with a rush of affection that the awkward kid squinting into the sun was none other than her Minder. He was one of those guys who was never going to make a handsome kid; it took a few years for men like Dahlra to grow into their looks.

And had he ever.

Whether it was because it had been the first fantasy they had played out together, or perhaps because it was so appealing to both of them, they spent many hours as teacher and student. Dahlra was ingenious at finding ways to act out this fantasy, and it became his persona when instinct told him Sydney wanted to submit to a stern or demanding Dominant. It was indecent how quickly she became aroused at the sight of him in that long coat.

If they drove down to London to attend a play or concert, he almost always wore that suit, or a similar garment in a deep charcoal grey. Sydney loved the sight of him, darkly, austerely beautiful, surrounded by others who often found him just as fascinating.

The Bentley was often at their disposal, and thankfully Tel the chauffeur was a man of the what-happens-in-the-back-seat-stays-in-the-back-seat variety. Many a night she and Dahlra sat entranced by the beautiful music that surrounded them, sharing contented smiles. There would be other nights when she would turn to see him watching her like a predator, his eyes blazing with lust. Sydney would find herself suddenly urged from her seat, almost carried outside to the waiting Bentley. She would be ready for him by the time they left the building.

On those nights, nothing would do but for her to open his clothes and straddle him as they drove back to Maidenvine. Nothing would do but for her to take him on a slow, sweet ride, kissing his throat until he was moaning with need and desperation.

For a man who was essentially modest and a trifle shy, he had a devilishly wicked mind; when it came to Sydney's favourite kink, no one could talk dirty like Dahlra Gar. Sydney would often mentally replay some of the things he said during sex, and become so hot nothing would do for *her* but to interrupt dinner, to have a little ride of her own.

He never seemed to mind.

During his Minder training, Dahlra's mentor had explained that there comes a moment during the best sex play when a submissive willingly, joyfully, completely surrenders to her Dominant. It took the most astute Dom to suss out the catalyst for it, and even then it didn't always happen. But when it did, there was no more erotic or rewarding proof of a submissive's love and trust, or her Dominant's skills and power.

"When this happens, it's more intense than even the sex that follows," his Mentor had lectured. "It's that moment when they totally let go, and their arousal and trust and anticipation merge. They give themselves over to you, and release any self-consciousness or fear or responsibility. You see it in their eyes, you feel their body change. In that moment, they are yours, perhaps forever. That's when they're ready for you to take them to the absolute edge of everything they know, and push them just one inch beyond it. Even the most seasoned Dominants get off on it. It's the best, most addictive high.

"But a true Dom will understand the importance of using that power wisely. You have to be careful: when they reach this point, no limit is too hard, no pain is intolerable. They'll yield to anything. The predators in our world will abuse that trust, but the best Dominants only use it to send their submissives to pleasure beyond anything they've ever experienced before.

"That, my friend, is the essence of Domination—taking them where they've never been, and bringing them back safe and unbroken."

Dahlra faced his severe, black-clad image in the mirror, and studied the implement in his hands. It had arrived in the post today; another memorable gift from his mentor. He closed his eyes, and breathed deeply, willing his body to relax, his heartbeat to calm.

He had promised to take Sydney to places she had never been. It was time to cash in that promise.

Sydney was sitting on their bed, drying her hair, when she heard the large oaken door swing ponderously open. She looked up to see Dahlra standing just inside, looking cool and impeccable, and as sexually charged as if he'd been plugged into a socket.

He was holding something by his side, and as Sydney's eyes lowered to his hand, he smiled, and slowly tapped a long birch cane against one black-clad thigh. His voice sounded calm, its hypnotic, sensual tone compellingly smooth. "I think it's time we took your submission to a new level, pet."

They had spoken of this in recent days. Part of submission to a Dominant included the facets of disciplining and reward. Even as Sydney's trust grew, she admitted that the idea of being disciplined as a bonding exercise both excited and frightened her. Neither could forget the last time she had been struck, their first night in the Bentley not withstanding. They were both determined that this demon, too, could be exorcised by replacing it with a different act, one in which she had ultimate control.

"Jesus," she whispered. She could almost *hear* her nipples stiffen.

His eyes traveled slowly over her body. "If you are ready, remove your clothing, Sydney."

Obediently, she stood and shucked her dressing gown, revealing her naked form. He leaned against the door jam and crossed his arms imperiously, the cane jutting from his fist. "Good girl," he drawled.

Sydney didn't really want to know what it said about her and some kind of Daddy issues kink, but *fuck* if she didn't get wet when he called her that.

With a brief nod of his head, he gestured to the writing table by the sofa. "Bend over the table. I am going to cane you until you come."

Breathing hard, Sydney leaned across the table, keeping her feet flat on the floor. Bent over the cold surface of the desk, Sydney listened to his slow measured steps, their only accompaniment the sound of the cane absently tapping against his thigh. He circled her like a bird of prey, tasting her anticipation, savouring her obedience.

She didn't raise her head, but just inside her vision she saw the buttons of his coat, the white cuffs of his shirt. The contrast of white against black always sent her arousal Himalaya-high. There was the smallest frisson of anxiety; she was, after all, very exposed. But he had laid her down on that same desk the night they became lovers, and she knew in her heart she had nothing to fear.

He tossed something onto the desk, mere inches from her face. It was a small black bundle, and it smelled of leather. "Open your mouth," he ordered, in that same gentle commanding voice, and when she obeyed, he placed the cane in her mouth like a riding bit. "Now close."

Compliantly she bit down on the cane's slender length. Sweat trickled down her temple, but she wasn't sure if it was from trepidation or anticipation.

The black bundle revealed itself to be a pair of gloves, made of fine, buttery kidskin. She heard the smug creak of leather as he slowly drew them onto his hands. He spread his fingers apart and flexed them, and they looked like two large spiders, strong and menacing. The thought of those gloved hands on her body... she shifted restlessly.

"Open." He removed the cane from her mouth, and it was only then that Sydney realized she had been clenching her teeth so tightly she had to drop her jaw to relax it.

"Sir, may I ask..."

He cupped her face in his large palm and tipped it upward toward his. Sydney could smell the leather of the gloves, and the clean, male scent that was uniquely his own. His thumb stroked across her bottom lip, and she licked it, a small moan of lust curling from her throat. His lidded eyes and parted lips were a sign that he was completely into what he was doing.

This was no aloof, detached Dominant. "Ask."

"Have I done something to... to displease you?"

He sneered, a predatory look of power and possession, and pushed his thumb into her mouth. The taste and scent of the leather swirled around her tongue. "Why, I'm your *Dominant*, little girl. I don't require an *excuse*."

He pulled his hand away, and walked around the desk. "However, today's lesson is about trust, about sensation. I know you're a little afraid, but you don't need to be, do you?"

"No, sir."

In his lecturer's voice, Dahlra explained, "Disciplining is all about trust, about taking you to the farthest edges of your sexual limits. Yes, it might hurt a little. It might hurt a lot. But I will never *harm* you."

His hand came to rest on the soft curve of her bottom. "Regardless, I will require your acceptance. Will you submit to my discipline, my lovely girl, knowing I only want to ultimately give your pleasure? Will you trust me? And will you say your safe word if you cannot continue? There will be no repercussions, of course."

In spite of the intensity of the situation, Dahlra might have been asking her which wine she wanted with her meal. It all sounded so fantastic; it all sounded so ordinary. And ultimately, even now, she could stand up and walk, and he would be the same gentle Dominant he'd been. But if she stayed, what rewards would she be given?

"Yes, I accept," she replied.

For a moment, he continued stroking her lovingly. "Oh, such a good girl. I'm so pleased with you." He stepped back, and she heard the whistle of the cane in the air.

The first blow was a sting that slashed right across the very tops of her thighs. The shocked cry that was wrenched from her caused him to pause. He braided his fingers through her hair and eased her body backward towards him. "I think ten switches will do, don't you?"

When she did not answer, Dahlra said gently, "Have I been mistaken? Do you wish for me to stop?"

Oh, God, do I want this to stop? she thought. The stinging sensation warred with acute, painful arousal. He held her still, waiting, until she rasped, "More, sir. Please."

"I'm very pleased with you." He pressed a tender kiss against her nape. He lowered her against the desk, then stepped back again. "I can feel the heat radiating from you. Such a *naughty* girl, panting for teacher." His voice curled around her body like Eve's wicked serpent.

"Bad little girls get spanked, Ms Chapin," he purred, his voice barely above a whisper. "Are you my bad little girl, hmm? Did you grow wet listening to me say dirty things to you? Let's make you wetter, shall we?"

Something within her snapped, like a guide rope from a mooring, and Sydney melted against the table in an ecstasy of surrender. "Do it," she moaned. "Oh, God, please do it. Do whatever you want."

He answered by lightly flicking the tip of the cane over her backside, whipping the rod back and forth in a switching, stinging motion.

He varied the force he used, sometimes giving little more than a sharp switch, and sometimes a more intense smack, just hard enough to make her clutch the desk and mewl helplessly. The overload of sensation felt like a million little points of pain-pleasure dancing over her backside, hot and pulsing with her heartbeat.

Tears spilled from her eyes, but they were tears of release, not pain. She was breathing hard, but there was exultancy in her heart, a still, certain pride. She reveled in her own acceptance of the act as much as the act itself. Each time the cane struck her flesh, Sydney whimpered and writhed and moaned and begged for another.

Dahlra gave her the promised ten switches. As he applied the cane, watching Sydney accept and absorb his disciplining, he was aware of an addictive, sexual power mounting within. At that moment, he knew even he was capable of taking things too far. This, then, was what his mentor had been trying to explain—the true Dominant's power; the power to know when too much was too much and when the limits had been reached, and when to leave a submissive craving more.

He stepped back, his eyes locked on Sydney's pale, beautiful body. Faint pink welts bloomed on her luscious backside. Dahlra removed the gloves and tossed them onto the desk.

"I was told there is nothing more beautiful than a willing submissive being disciplined, my darling girl. And it is true." Dahlra gently stroked her cane-warmed flesh. "Your arse is gorgeous when it's covered in my stripes."

The sight of her naked body against his clothed one was beyond erotic, bordering on debauched. He opened his trousers, and thrust his cock into her wet, tight sheath, filling her and stretching her fully.

She was shockingly hot, and Dahlra held himself very still, lost in the delicious feel of her. Sydney tried to force him to move by clenching her inner muscles, and he uttered a juicy curse and lightly spanked her arse.

"Oh yes, you like this, don't you, you dirty little girl?" He thrust into her again, and she pushed back against him, growling like an animal on heat. "Cat got your tongue, Ms Chapin? I want to hear you, girl. A man needs to know he's appreciated – oh, fuck, yes, I can feel you coming—"

Sydney cried out as the orgasm slashed through her. Each powerful thrust wrested another scorching cry from her throat, driving Dahlra mad with lust. "Nothing makes me want to fuck your tight little quim more than hearing you cry for me." His voice faltered as his groin filled with hot, molten pleasure. He no longer cared about this fantasy; all he knew was taking her, owning her.

"This is for making me wait," he rasped. "This is for not letting me have you sooner, all wet and sweet for me. Don't ever," he gasped, "ever

... make me wait...again!" He roared with pleasure and slammed home so hard the table scooted forward. His body shuddered over and over as he climaxed, his hips jerking as he came.

Panting like a runner, Dahlra salvaged just enough presence of mind to lock his arms so he would not collapse on Sydney's tender, caned bottom. When he trusted himself to stand, he shifted his heavy weight from Sydney's shuddering body. She was limp and her breathing was heavy and tear-clogged. The welts on her bottom looked redder now, and he wondered if he'd taken things too far in the heat of the moment. He was sure she would have stopped him... wouldn't she?

"Sydney?" She raised her head and slowly turned to face him. Her lovely face was flushed, her eyes swimming. But he saw so much more in those startled, enormous eyes. He saw wonder, and the fire he had kindled inside her. He saw his woman, his Sydney, looking at him with a new appreciation. Dahlra gently pulled her upright, and she held out her arms to him. Relieved, Dahlra enfolded her in his embrace. Her arms encircled him, strong and sure, even as she trembled.

"Easy, love... shhh... Don't work so hard. It's alright... you're alright..." He picked her up and carried her back to the bed, crooning comfort as he went. Sydney curled up in his arms, and in a few moments, she completely relaxed.

"Dahlra?"

"Yes, love?"

"Am I the most degenerate woman in the world that I seriously got off on that?"

He laughed. "What do you think?"

"I think I want more."

CHAPTER FIFTEEN

Ramcat

The caller ID on Sydney's phone flashed, *"Basil Exposition."*

"Inigo. What a surprise." She leaned back in her armchair. "I thought you'd committed yourself to leaving us alone at least until Christmas."

Inigo's voice oozed into her ear like melted butter. "Sydney, old chap, I hope you're well, happily buried at Twelve Oaks, as it were. How are you and the good doctor faring in the land of tweed caps and tugged forelocks?"

Sydney looked over at Dahlra, who was lounging in his favourite track suit bottoms and an old Guinness t-shirt. His bare, slender feet were propped on an ottoman while he read the Telegraph and drank his tea. He glanced up, and cocked an enquiring eyebrow.

"Oh, you know, bearing up under the strain and all that. What's on your mind, Inigo? I can't imagine you're just calling for S's and G's."

"Quite right," he drawled. "I'm calling because I wondered if you might fancy doing a little *ad hoc* consulting work while you're on leave."

"Maybe." It never paid to show Inigo too much enthusiasm at the prospect of a job; it only gave him the upper hand in negotiations. "What's it about?"

"Silverbirch."

Sydney's heart rate graduated from a canter to a trot. *Silverbirch.* Mentally crossing her fingers, she asked, "Is the case being reopened?"

"At present, no. Well, not *exactly.*"

"Then what *exactly* is not going on with Silverbirch?"

"There's been ... some activity. If we keep a very low profile, we might actually go the distance this time, providing the evidence is supportable."

Sydney's excitement kicked up another notch. "What do you need me to do?"

"I need you to pay a visit to your special friend in Wiltshire. She knows a lot of people, and no doubt would be privy to information that would take us much longer to research without your intervention."

"Do I take it that a few agents have come back with their tails between their legs?"

"I haven't sent any other agents. We both know Clara would shut down anyone else."

"Fine. Courier me with the new evidence. I'll arrange everything from here."

"Good show. But Sydney, this must be said." His voice lost some of its oily sheen. "I realise this case was your Holy Grail, but you are still on leave and will remain so for at least another year. I'm only asking this one visit as a favour."

Trust Inigo to give you a shiny thing to play with, then make you give it back just when things got good. She replied tersely, "I'm going to ask one more time. Does this interview mean the case *is* reopening or am I just doing a little dirty work on your behalf?"

"Possibly the former, depending on the information you acquire. And your work is for the Agency, not me."

"I thought that amounted to the same thing."

"If that's supposed to be flattery, tell Dahlra he needs to give you some more lessons."

"You want flattery? Then try this on: Sod off, and get one of your minions to do it, if Clara will grant them an interview. I'm not going to put either myself or Dahlra in the firing line again just to let all the credit go to some subaltern."

Inigo had the decency to sound affronted. "I would never do that to you, Sydney. The bottom line is that Silverbirch might or might not be reopened, based on new evidence which has recently come to light. I'm merely asking you to do this, as you were always a favourite among the denizens of the dark."

Sydney huffed. "Now whose flattery leaves a lot to be desired?"

"I don't flatter; I inspire."

"Christ, Inigo—"

"Look. You are known at Ramcat; Clara likes you, she trusts you. These are not people who give their trust lightly to outsiders. I don't want to undo your past good work by sending in some ham-fisted junior agent now, nor would you want me to. You said yourself: you threw yourself under the bus for this investigation; it's only fair you see it through, garden leave or not." He hesitated, then added, "Of course, I will keep you abreast of any developments. Your expertise is vital to this case."

"Fine. Once I get the reports, I'll set up an interview."

"Good show."

"How much should I tell Clara?"

"Enough to let her know what's at stake," he replied promptly. "She's an extremely intelligent and discreet woman; she can add two plus two."

"Why Inigo, now that *did* sound like a compliment." Sydney smiled.

"Good show. I'm as eager as you to wash the taint of Silverbirch away for all concerned. Keep me informed at all Stations of the Cross, and give my regards to Clara. Tell her I am delighted she's feeling better."

"Will do."

"And convey to Dr Gar my felicitations."

"I'll see what kind of felicitating I can do for him." Dahlra gave her a quizzical look as she ended the call.

"What did Lightoller want?"

Sydney sat in his lap and kissed him. "I think Inigo has decided to give us our revenge for the cell. Throw on your best suit, love. We're going hunting."

Even as an owner of a country manor of no small size, Dahlra was impressed with Ramcat Estate. As they rolled up the long gravel drive to the house itself, he whistled, awestruck. "Good Lord, what a monster. I've heard about it, but—"

"Oh?" Sydney stole a glance at her Minder. Even now he had the ability to surprise her. "What do you know about it? Oh, let me guess. Your *mentor* told you all about it."

"I think his exact words were, 'It's probably the closest you can get to an X-rated Alton Towers for adults.'"

"You really must introduce me to this mentor of yours soon. He sounds like an interesting character."

"You have no idea," he replied absently, angling the Audi into the drive. "How on earth do they keep this place up? Is it listed?"

In a Fraightfully Naice, Received English accent, she retorted, "Why Doctor Gar, how *arwfully* middle-class of you. I thought posh families like yours didn't sully themselves with *pindes*, shillings and pence."

"If they didn't, there soon wouldn't be any *pindes*, shillings and pence left to sully."

Dahlra paused to speak to the gardener, an elderly gentleman in green overalls weeding the flowerbeds that lined the drive. Sydney ran lightly up the steps, where a handsome black man in footman's livery obligingly took her purse and jacket. He led her into the elegant, sumptuously-furnished drawing room where Clara Liggon, their hostess, waited to welcome them to Ramcat Estate.

She greeted Sydney with a smile of welcome as sunny as the rays of afternoon light streaming in the window behind her. She folded Sydney into an A-frame hug, "Sydney, you pretty thing, it's so good to see you!"

"And you! You look like a good time, you do."

Clara rewarded her with two smacking, red-lipsticked kisses on her cheeks. She took Sydney's hands in hers; a diamond the size of a peach pit sparkled on her left ring finger. "Just like a Southern girl, turning my head with your charms. I've been beside myself, waiting for you to get here and explain what's going on!"

Clara had been famous as a stunning beauty in her youth. Now, in her late fifties, she was still a force of nature to be reckoned with. She was a quintessential cool blonde, Grace Kelly type, adorably petite, and beautifully proportioned from her heart-shaped face to her delicate ankles.

Her deep crimson dress made her skin glow with renewed health, while showing off her slender but curvaceous figure. The dainty little pointed shoes on her number-four feet looked edible. Her short hair, newly regrown, was smooth and shining. Her deep blue eyes sparkled with intelligence and warmth.

She swiped her thumb across Sydney's cheeks to remove the traces of lipstick. "You could have knocked me over with a feather when I got your Mr Lightoller's call. We've set aside the entire weekend to devote to you."

"Thank you, Clara. We really appreciate it."

"Besides, I might even be able to suggest a few diversions for you while you're here," she added with a knowing wink.

"Well, you know what they say, Mistress: All work and no play."

"Said no one, ever." Clara's laugh was surprisingly husky for such a tiny woman. "So where is this handsome fellow who's stolen your heart? And don't pretend otherwise. Good Lord, girl, you are positively glowing."

"He's outside with your gardener, discussing the care and feeding of ash trees, I think," she replied. "We have one in the back garden that's looking a bit puny."

"Clovis does have a tendency to get carried away when discussing the care of flora and fauna. We might have to send a rescue party, or they'll be out there all afternoon." Clara pulled a nearby bell cord as they settled on the Louise Quinze sofa. "While we're waiting for tea, catch me up. It's been ages since you've been to visit," she added, with a teasing pout. "So what have you been doing with yourself?"

A handsome woman of Sydney's age appeared in the doorway. She was in full uniform; real Upstairs, Downstairs stuff, complete with the frilly little hat. The only anomaly was a black leather collar around her slender neck. "Yes, Mistress?"

"You can bring in our tea now, Reilly. And please let me know when Mister Jason arrives."

The woman dipped a quick curtsey. "Yes, Mistress," she replied, and left as silently as she had arrived.

The clock chimed three. "It's later than I thought. Jason should be here any moment. He only went into town for some shopping, but I'd hoped he'd be back by now."

"How is Jason?" Clara's husband and submissive was second-in-command at Ramcat; most of the management of the estate was in his capable hands.

"He's good as gold, like always," Clara replied, her voice fond and indulgent. "In fact, there's something I'd like to discuss with you regarding Jason. You see—"

The door opened and Reilly entered with the tea on a silver tray. "Pardon, Mistress, but Mister Jason wishes to speak to you. I have him on the house phone."

"Thank you, Reilly. I'll take it in my study." Clara turned to Sydney with a warm smile. "Excuse me, dearest. Won't be a moment." Sydney watched the older woman cross the room, walking rather stiffly, and wondered if she was completely out of the woods yet.

Except for the ticking of the massive grandfather clock, the house was incredibly quiet, though Sydney knew it was occupied with many guests. She glanced about her, thinking of the juxtaposition of the elegant, somewhat staid appearance of Ramcat, and the private activities that took place behind its gilt-edged doors.

Ramcat Estate was a place of great secrets. Clara Liggon was one of the most famous Dominants and purveyors of the Fet-stroke-BDSM lifestyle in England—perhaps Europe. She was legendary for her philosophy on the method of training Dominants and submissives.

Clara had met her first husband in the late eighties while he was visiting the University of New Orleans, where she was a fresh young psychology professor. It was, as Clara explained, "lust at first sight." He brought his lovely bride to England to his family's estate, where they lived in happy eccentricity until he was killed in a car accident.

Of course, the locals whispered behind her back that she was a fortune hunter, a gold digger, and worse. She blithely ignored the wagging tongues and set about remaking Ramcat to be "the Roissy of Great Britain, without all the petticoats and bad hair styles."

Throughout the world, the name Ramcat was soon known and respected by the most organised and exclusive of the kinkster/fetish societies. It was to this opulent den of sin that she had first arrived, working on a fledgling case codenamed Operation Silverbirch.

Its purpose was to investigate a small band of extreme fetish clubs that staged 'hunts,' using mostly non-consensual human prey. Sydney, Garnet and Russ Bullard had been assigned the case from the beginning, and Sydney's role in the early stages of the investigation was researching Britain's kinkster communities to discover where these hunting societies were hiding, how they did their recruiting, and who was protecting their members. Inigo Lightoller himself had personally arranged for Sydney to interview Clara Liggon, the doyenne of Ramcat estate.

They had struck up a warm and lasting friendship. With Clara acting as a goodwill ambassador, Sydney met others who took her deeper into the confidences of these communities than she could ever have gone on her own.

At that point in her life, Sydney hadn't been curious about BDSM at all; she had actually found it incomprehensible. She had approached Mrs Liggon with her wealth of prejudices and misinformation regarding the lifestyle firmly established. Clara had quickly educated her, but had never quite sold her on the idea of taking it out for a test drive.

Due to the fact that Ramcat was a cultural centre for all things

Kinkster, Clara was privy to many confidential activities. She became an invaluable resource regarding the Dominant/submissive, BDSM and kinkster/fetish communities in Great Britain. She knew everyone who was anyone in the lifestyle; she understood their hierarchies and customs.

Unfortunately for Clara, the men who did their dirty deeds knew her as well. They were dangerous men, and they seldom saw the need for either morals or scruples. The wider the net, they correctly assumed, the harder it would be to pinpoint the source. The individuals the Agency tried to prosecute had powerful friends, and the potential for scandal proved more than even Downing Street was prepared to risk. Just as Sydney and her team were on the brink of a serious breakthrough, word came down from on high to shelve the investigation.

It had been a bitter pill to swallow, especially as some of the men involved were caught so red-handed they looked like they had been dipped in paint. Sydney had protested, argued and bullied, but the brick wall was up and whitewashed, and the investigation was shut down.

It had infuriated Sydney so much she had even seriously considered resigning from the Agency and going after them solo. She had busted her chops for them; it rankled that her organisation was so hamstrung by the political fat cats they were hired to protect and serve.

Shortly after Operation Silverbirch folded, Clara was diagnosed with cervical cancer. She had undergone a series of aggressive chemo treatments, and as of the previous fall, the cancer was in remission. The strain, however, had taken its toll. She had reluctantly entered into a state of semi-retirement, making Ramcat available as a sort of conference and cultural centre for the fetish communities of England and beyond.

Sydney glanced at her watch. Knowing Clovis and how he loved English country gardening, he was probably boring poor Dahlra into a coma. Perhaps it was time to go fetch him. As Sydney stood, a soft, masculine voice sounded behind her.

"Well, hello there."

A tall, handsome man stood in the doorway. He had even features and warm, golden skin that spoke of Scandinavian heritage, but he dressed more like an Italian. His silver grey suit was of an excellent cut, set off by a white shirt and icy blue silk tie.

Long, white-blond hair, tied back in a sleek queue, completed the look, and gave him the louche air of a dandy. In spite of his immaculate appearance, there was something off-putting about him. It was in the way his eyes slithered over her, as if his very psyche was coated in slime.

"Hello, yourself," Sydney replied warily.

"I don't believe I've seen you here before." Dominance radiated from him in palpable waves; this was a man used to being bowed to. "Are you new to Ramcat?"

"Not really. I just don't come here that often."

"I see." His gaze swept over her rapaciously. His eyes were as slate-blue as the North Sea, and just as cold. "You know, I can't quite make up my mind about you."

"Oh yeah? What about, then?"

"I can't decide if you are a Dominant, because of your bearing, or a submissive." His eyes did another slow ride up her body. "For the simple fact that I would *love* to play with you."

"Why don't you just call me a friend of Clara's, and let's leave it at that?"

"You're very cheeky for a submissive."

"I suppose it's a good thing I'm not one, then."

Far from being rebuffed, the blond seemed amused. "Of course, we'll have to do something about that attitude, but we all have to start somewhere, don't we?" He held out his hand. "My name is Silas Markham. Here I am known as *Master* Silas."

Yeah, I'll just bet you are, she thought. After the slightest of hesitations, Sydney put her hand in his. He caressed it more than shook it; his hand was coolly unpleasant to the touch. Sydney moved to pull her hand away, but he kept it locked firmly within his own.

"So what is it to be, little one?" He enclosed her hand in both of his. "If you're here to play, I have one or two games in mind—"

"Sorry, love. Clovis and I were so engrossed that the time simply got away from me." Dahlra walked in, but stopped short when he spied the two figures. "I trust everything's alright, Sydney?"

Sydney pulled her hand free, fighting the impulse to wipe it on her shirt. "Everything is fine, *sir*. I was just chatting with Silas here."

"So I see." He held out his hand, and when she gratefully took it, he pulled her close.

Silas scrutinised Dahlra carefully, then turned his attention back to her. "Sydney... Chapin? You should have at least told me your name."

"I was just about to."

"And therefore you must be the famous Doctor Dahlra Gar," Silas added, extending his hand. His smile stopped somewhere just south of his eyes.

Dahlra took Silas' hand and shook it perfunctorily. "I am Dahlra Gar, yes, but I'm afraid you have me at a disadvantage."

"Indeed. I'm Master Silas. Perhaps you've heard of me." He looked Dahlra over, as if measuring him. "I've heard all about you. Elwess is an acquaintance of mine. I gather from him you've become quite the 'Daddy'. And this exquisite creature is your 'little girl.'" Charming. And fortuitous. I was just inviting her to one of our little play evenings here at Ramcat." His voice was so slathered with condescension Sydney wanted to punch him.

If it bothered Dahlra, he didn't show it. "Thank you, Master Silas, but that's not really our thing."

"Perhaps you should reconsider. When in Rome—"

"We're not in Rome." While his pleasant expression did not change, Dahlra's voice feathered with a sudden frost. "We're not here to play with anyone."

Sydney's reflexes went on alert. Dahlra had a very high dander threshold; it took a lot to get it up, though it mollified her somewhat that his instincts mirrored her own.

Silas' face grew shuttered, his eyes angry. Something definitely unpleasant was surging between them. "All submissives play, Master Dahlra." His emphasis on the word *Master* was deliberately patronising. "Whether they want to or not."

"Not where I come from, Silas," Sydney retorted. She moved back, making herself a shield between the two men. "I'm what you might call a one-Dominant submissive."

"Really? I thought that was called being more trouble than you're worth." His glacial eyes bored into hers. "Does your Master always let you fight his battles, submissive? Or is *Master* Dahlra merely your service top?"

The temperature of the room seemed to drop a few degrees, "I wasn't aware we were engaged in a battle of any sort, Master Silas," Dahlra answered, his voice as cool as vapour on ice. "I've never been one to pick a fight with someone I've just met."

Several heartbeats passed. There was a dawning trace of apprehension in Silas' expression. His voice grew tight. "I can see you both have a lot to learn about being a submissive. *And a Dominant.*"

Sydney stepped up in Silas' grill so quickly he took an involuntary step backward. "You want a teacher? I'll—"

"Sydney." Dahlra's voice was iron and eiderdown, the warning in it unmistakable. It was the audible equivalent of uncocking a gun: *stand down.*

He placed his hand on the back of Sydney's neck. "Come, pet. We mustn't monopolise any more of *Master* Silas' time."

Sydney felt torn. To ignore Dahlra's command was to undermine his authority; to obey him meant this arrogant bastard got away with his insulting, patronising bullshit. *What the hell,* she thought. *It's not like I'm ever going to see this little toerag again.* She stepped back into Dahlra's embrace and felt his body relax ever so slightly.

Silas, watching the silent battle for Dominance, gave her a look of withering contempt. He managed to claw back some of his dignity by adding, "Well, then I'll leave you to your 'training'. Enjoy Ramcat." With a voice that could have buttered bread, he added, "And do give my regards to Elwess." With a final sneer of derision, he turned on his heel and left the room.

In the ensuing silence, Sydney turned to Dahlra. "Mind telling me what that little alpha-male pissing contest was all about?"

Dahlra exhaled hard through his mouth. "I'm not sure, to be perfectly honest." Almost to himself, he added, "And I'm not exactly thrilled that Elwess shared our business with someone like this Silas character, either."

Sydney started. "Elwess? Are you-"

"I'm so sorry, darlings." Clara breezed into the room. "Jason needed to ask me about some estate business that couldn't wait. By the time we finished discussing it, he was pulling in the drive. He'll be in any moment." Clara turned her full attention on Dahlra, and seemed to drink him in.

"So this is the famous Dr Gar I've heard so much about! Welcome to Ramcat, my dear."

"Thank you, and please call me Dahlra, Mistress."

"Oh, enough of that *mistress* tosh, my dear. We're all friends here. Please call me Clara," she entreated, her lovely blue eyes warm with affection.

He smiled at her with sincere, almost bashful charm. He had dressed with care in honour of this meeting; a dark Armani suit with a snow-white shirt and one of his wildly patterned ties. Sydney felt a swell of pride at his easy grace, his masculinity, his open, honest soul.

"It's a pleasure to meet you at last, Clara. I was sorry to hear that you haven't been well, but I would take it as a favour if you would call on me anytime I can be of assistance." His extraordinary voice rolled through the room like myrrh, its inflections and colours lighting up the face of the older woman.

"Dahlra is a fine doctor, Clara," Sydney explained. "He saved my life."

"Well, I would like to thank you for that, Dahlra. Your Sydney is well-loved here at Ramcat."

Before Dahlra could reply, a man with curly blond hair bounded into the room, a large smile on his handsome face. "Hello everyone! Sorry I'm late. I hope I haven't spoiled tea." His blue eyes were dancing with joy as he turned to Sydney.

"Sydney Chapin! I say, it's lovely to see you—and looking so well." He took her hands in his and kissed them both. "It's been too long, hasn't it?" Still smiling, he released her hands and turned to Dahlra with a formal bow. "And Doctor Gar—it's a pleasure to meet you, truly! Jason Liggon, at your service. Did you have a nice drive over? I think I spotted you coming through the village on your way to Ramcat. That is your Audi in the drive, isn't it? Lovely motor. I'll bet the suspension is like a dream. Is it the model with heated seats?"

As they shook hands, Dahlra glanced at Clara, then back to her submissive, bemused at the steady stream of one-sided conversation.

"Jason, darling, Dahlra and Sydney will be here all weekend. You'll have plenty of opportunities to interrogate him," Clara gently admonished. "My poor, dear boy is practically buried up here with mostly females for company. Any time a bloke comes to visit, he gets to enjoy himself and talk about blokey things for a change."

Jason ducked his head shyly, but his sunny smile never wavered. In his plummy, public school accent, he replied, "Absolutely, my lady, right as always. Let me ring for some more tea. I'm sure it's gone quite cold."

He kissed his wife's hand by way of apology.

As they drank Earl Grey from Spode cups, gold-flecked and delicate as autumn leaves, Clara observed her guests carefully, especially Dahlra. "You'll forgive my impertinence, dear, but you really are quite a beautiful man."

Dahlra coloured slightly, and rewarded Clara with a shy smile. "Thank you."

"Elwess, of course, has told me all about you, but I can see he was being reticent." Her throaty Southern American drawl, overlaid with Home Counties inflection, was pitch perfect for both flirtation and insinuation. "Or, knowing Elwess, merely jealous of your beauty."

"You're the second person to mention Elwess," remarked Sydney. "You *are* talking about Elwess Talbert, aren't you?"

It was Dahlra's turn to look surprised. "You've heard of Elwess?"

"Of course I've heard of him. Who hasn't in this game? How do *you* know Elwess Talbert?"

His blush grew deeper. "Well, I suppose I can't dance around it any longer, can I? Elwess is my oh-so-famous Mentor."

Sydney felt as if someone had dropped a bag of laughing gas on her head. For a few seconds, she was too surprised to do much more than babble. "What- who, um, how did- I mean-"

Dahlra chuckled wryly. "Let's just try finishing one of those sentences, okay?"

"You're telling me that *the* Elwess Talbert works for the Agency's Minder programme?"

"Didn't you know?" Clara was clearly delighted.

"I suppose *you* did. You know everything."

"This is true," Clara replied with a cat-that-got-the-cream smile. "I was asked to consult with the Minder programme during its inception, but I didn't have time. So I suggested Elwess instead. I gather he's done a very good job."

Sydney knew she was gaping at them like a goldfish, but she couldn't help it. While investigating Silverbirch, the name Elwess Talbert had appeared on the radar several times, but Sydney found him one of the most difficult to get a bead on. At Ramcat the submissives spoke of him with a mixture of awe, envy and respect. His credentials were impeccable, and there had never been so much as a whiff of anything dodgy about him. Silverbirch's denizens appeared well aware of him, but in name only; he was never implicated in any of their hunting clubs.

Sydney never managed to be in the right place at the right time to meet him. With that much conflict of interest at stake, it was more than likely he didn't *want* to be met.

"Well, hell." She fixed Dahlra with a hard look. "You certainly kept *that* under a bushel. Why wouldn't you tell me?"

Dahlra shrugged apologetically. "It wasn't as if I was trying to keep anything from you. To tell the truth, I really didn't think it mattered all that much."

Sydney gave him a searching look as he casually placed a chocolate biscuit on his plate. He wasn't lying, exactly, but he certainly wasn't being entirely truthful, either. Knowing Dahlra, he would have his reasons.

In any case, it was neither the time nor the place to call him on it. "Okay. If you say so. But you can't blame me for being just a little blown away by the fact that you were trained by one of, if not *the* most celebrated Dominants in Europe." *Although, on second thought, maybe it doesn't seem farfetched. Not after some of the things you've said and done.*

"Oh, heavens, Dahlra, don't tell Elwess Sydney called him the most celebrated Dominant in Europe! There'll be no living with him."

Dahlra grimaced. "No chance of that, Clara; I'm not very pleased with him at the moment."

He and Sydney related their encounter with Silas to their hosts. Clara and Jason exchanged unreadable glances. "I wouldn't be too harsh with Elwess," Clara said, sipping her tea. "He has a great deal of respect for you, Dahlra. I've known him for ages, and he's always been the soul of discretion—at least, in my presence.

"Silas arranges several play weekends a year with us. That's why he was here today. Knowing *him,* I think it's more a case of overhearing something and using it as a goad."

"Too right, my dear," Jason agreed. "Master Silas is a bit of an odd duck. Type of chap who likes to stir up things and watch them boil over. I shouldn't give much credence to him."

"Indeed." Clara agreed, but something in her eyes made Sydney wonder if Clara was really as dismissive as she appeared.

Jason continued confidently, "Now, Master Elwess—top drawer all round, I say. A better Dominant you'll never meet; present company aside, of course." He looked at Sydney. "Then again, you've always been a good judge of character. How does he strike *you*, Sydney?"

"Never met the man."

Clara and Jason looked at Dahlra in surprise. "He wants to meet Sydney, of course." He looked at her sheepishly. "Truth to tell, I'm a little afraid to introduce you."

"Why on earth would you be afraid for me to meet him?"

Dahlra placed his hand over hers. "I think this might be a discussion for another time."

Sydney met his eyes; they were curiously tense at the corners. She had a sudden flashback to the night they first became lovers. So the mind-blowing move to Maidenvine had been orchestrated by none other than Elwess Talbert, Dungeon Master Extraordinaire.

"Alright, but I'm holding you to it."

"Of course." Dahlra brought her hand to his lips. It felt like an apology, which puzzled her even more.

Clara watched the exchange, then continued smoothly, "Well, pardon the change of subject, but I gathered from Mr Lightoller's call that you wanted to discuss some things having to do with the case you were working on a few years back? That's mainly why you're here, isn't it, Sydney?"

"Mainly, yes. I wanted to pick your brain, Clara. I've heard rumours the old tom-toms are beating again."

Clara looked pensive. "So have we. I've heard mention of some initiations for new members. Someone was looking for a place to meet, someone heard something from a friend of a friend, you know how it is. A lot of people are saying things, but so circumspectly you need an interpreter." A shadow passed over her face. "Nothing concrete, you understand. Just whispers. But they are getting a little louder."

"A lot of time has passed. People think it's all forgotten and they can start again."

"When Mr Lightoller called me earlier, I assured him that nothing would make me happier than to place all our resources at your disposal. Such a lovely man, always inquiring about my health," Clara added with a wink.

"That's Inigo all right. Always putting others first." She replayed the last sentence in her head, and felt her face grow hot. "I'm sorry. That was incredibly insensitive, even for me."

"I'd say it was probably rather accurate, don't you?" Her eyes shone with intelligence and strength. "Men have been underestimating women like us all our lives, Sydney. Calculating your Mr Lightoller may be, but he knows us well enough to realise we're more than capable of taking care of ourselves."

"Hear, hear," Dahlra interjected.

Clara gave Sydney a look of absolute serenity. "If there's one thing this illness has taught me, darling, it's that you really don't know what you're capable of until you're faced with your worst nightmare."

"Quite," Jason added, toasting them with his teacup.

Clara held up her hand. "Now, before we go any further, Jason, my love, will you be so kind as to close the door?" She gave a dismissive wave of her slim fingers. "I trust my staff, but..."

"Of course." He closed the door, and locked it for good measure.

Clara poured more tea, and Sydney began.

"Just over a week ago, a young woman dragged herself into a Police Station in Jersey in the early hours of the morning. She was half-dressed, half-starved. She'd been sexually assaulted multiple times. She was wearing a slave collar, and she told the detective her new 'Master' had sold her to a 'hunting society' as live game."

"Dear Lord." Jason's eyes were wide with alarm.

Clara pressed her lips together in a stern line. "Go on."

"She said she had been curious about the Dominant-submissive lifestyle, and had met a man online whom she called 'master.' They corresponded for about six months, first emails, then phone sex, the classic grooming routine.

"At his insistence, she eventually ran away to be with him. They arranged to meet in a hotel in Guernsey; he overpowered her, and knocked her out. Then he passed her on to a group of three men he referred to as his 'hunting mates.' She was gang-raped repeatedly, then drugged and moved to a different location. According to her statement, her master was given five thousand pounds cash in exchange for her. The men, including her master, kept their faces pretty well hidden.

"But they got sloppy. She managed to escape and found her way to Jersey. Fuck knows how; she was pretty hysterical. We think the men who bought her may have been an 'acquisition' party, going to different places to pick up strays and girls like her who fell victim to online grooming.

"She couldn't provide any physical descriptions, but she recognised all of the men as having Yorkshire accents. DNA testing found no matches in the database, so they might be newcomers to the hunting clubs. Lower rank and file in the organisation, to be sure, and their leaders aren't going to be too happy with them."

Jason nodded. "Five thousand pounds is a lot of money—they won't be popular, having nothing to show for their expenditure."

"Exactly," replied Sydney. "Anyway, the detective at Jersey Nick had a mate at Interpol, and two days ago they contacted the Agency. The facts are too similar from the first investigation to dismiss as coincidence. It looks like the untouchable case might not be such a hot potato anymore." She shrugged. "It's an election year. You know the possibility for a scandal like this is a godsend to the opposing party."

Clara and Jason both looked pensive. While the words 'Operation Silverbirch' had never been uttered beyond the confines of the Agency, Clara had seen her fair share of politicians and public figures embracing the darker pleasures of Ramcat. The estate had a sterling reputation; they knew they were safe there. Anyone involved in less than legal dealings would not be stupid enough to be very vocal about it—at least not around Clara.

But the Fetish and kinkster communities of Britain were close-knit; when they congregated together, they liked to show off more than just their ink and piercings. Eventually the arrogance that had marked the worst of Silverbirch's offenders would make someone careless. They would think they could get away with it again; hell, they had got away with it scot-free once before. Hopefully their boasting would filter back to Ramcat.

"Oh, no doubt the naming and shaming will benefit someone's career. Pity it won't help that poor girl," Clara replied bitterly. "Is she alright?"

"She's in hospital." Dahlra's voice was low and sombre. "Her physical injuries are mostly healed."

Clara sighed. "This just breaks my heart, honey. All my life I've talked about the trust and loyalty of the kinkster life. It infuriates me that people hide behind it as a cover to do such unspeakable things. They're the reason why the fetish lifestyle has grown synonymous with deviance and degeneracy."

Jason's normally placid blue eyes now flashed with indignation. "Do these people have any idea what sort of power they have over another person? Don't they understand the responsibility a Dominant has over a submissive? Don't they realise they literally can destroy another person's life?"

"I don't think they give a shit, Jason," replied Sydney.

"Well, it's up to us to make them. And if we can't, we need to make sure they can never prey on these innocents again."

Grimly, Sydney replied, "You're preaching to the choir, Clara love. Believe me, they won't, if I have my way. This isn't about giving the fetish community at large a bad name. It's about a small offshoot of criminals using it as a cover for something much, much larger. This is just the tip of the woodpile. I'm going to burn them down this time." She glanced at Dahlra. "It's a lot more personal now."

Clara declared, "Of course Jason and I will help in any way we can, my dear. I'd like to think that one of the legacies of Ramcat might be the role it plays in bringing these people to justice. For all of us. I'll make a few phone calls; I know some people who might be in a better position to hear about any increased activities. We'll talk to them tomorrow."

She brightened. "In the meantime, I want you and Dahlra to feel that Ramcat is your home this weekend." She rose, and the two men instantly stood. "This way, you can enjoy your time here and still satisfy Mr Lightoller's request. Scratch two itches with the same hand."

Dahlra chuckled, a deep, sexy rumble that got right into Sydney's marrow. "Thank you for that, Clara," he said. "I live for gems like that."

"Stick around, darling. I've got a million of 'em," Clara replied, her humour restored. "Well, now that we've got our assignments, I think a before-dinner nap is in order, don't you?

"Jason, dear, why don't you and Dahlra see to the bags, and I'll show Sydney up to their rooms." She patted Sydney's cheek affectionately and added conspiratorially, "You two can have a couple of hours to refresh yourselves."

Dahlra and Jason left the room to retrieve their luggage. They were a study in contrasts: the tall, dark-haired man, moving with quiet grace, beside the equally tall, equally handsome blond, gesticulating away as they walked. He was talking a mile a minute, while Dahlra nodded in agreement.

Sydney smiled as she headed for the stairs. Yes, a nap would be a very nice thing; especially if it was preceded with her favourite nap-inducing activity. She somehow doubted Dahlra would be averse. She thought about their earlier encounter with that ponce Silas, and realised with a start that she had been ready to kick his arse just for insulting her lover. It was the equivalent of John Wayne beating up the cattle rustlers to win the love of the school marm.

She found that idea a bit sexy, and wondered if Dahlra had as well. Then she remembered him pulling her back against his chest, and the burgeoning erection pressing against her back as they ended their standoff with Silas.

That would be a yes, then.

CHAPTER SIXTEEN

The Disciplining of Dahlra Gar

Dinner was an enjoyable, not to mention delicious, affair. Sydney had always loved New Orleans cuisine; no one did decent home-style Creole cooking like it anywhere in the UK. They started the meal with an endive and red lettuce salad with grape tomatoes, olives, and shredded carrots. It was followed by Shrimp Etouffee, served on a bed of white rice cooked with coconut milk, petit pois and fresh corn. Chocolate mousse with a vanilla bean caramel sauce finished the meal. Clara's cook came in to accept their compliments, and she promised Dahlra all the recipes.

Clara herself presided at the table with effervescent charm, while Jason kept them entertained. Together they reminded Sydney of a delicate Persian kitten playfully bossing around a large, dopey Golden Retriever. Jason was nearly twenty-five years younger than his wife, but their relationship was beautifully solid. He belonged to her, right down to his manicured nails.

During her visits to Ramcat, Sydney had regarded Jason with a bit of secret envy. He obviously worshipped his wife, and his sweet, absorbing adoration faintly irritated her. She had tried to be dismissive, telling herself that he must be a complete zoom if all he thought about, all he concentrated on, was Clara. That, she now knew, had been her own ignorance talking. Before Dahlra, she had never been the object of that kind of devotion in a man, and had resigned herself to the fact she probably never would.

Now, looking across the table at her Minder, Sydney understood how comforting it was to bask in the regard of a man thoroughly dedicated to her happiness. It made her a great deal more appreciative of Jason Liggon. Posh swot he might be; but beneath the toothy jolly-hockey-sticks exterior beat the heart of a loving, faithful warrior.

When the final plates were removed, Jason took his wife's hand and kissed it; she nodded in return. He rose from the table, setting his linen napkin aside. "If you will excuse me, my friends," he said quietly, and for the first time Sydney had known him, he looked strained; not his usual cheerio-pip-pip self. "I look forward to joining you later." He bowed to Clara, then exited the room.

Dahlra turned to their hostess with a small frown of concern. "Is he alright?"

With a moue of apology, Clara said, "The poor dear worries about me so much." Her eyes dropped to the table for a moment. "Battling an illness isn't done alone, you know. Jason's fought this cancer with me every step of the way. Some days he looks older than I do, the darling."

"So still quite young, then?" Sydney teased.

She was rewarded with one of Clara's husky laughs. "You and your flatterin' ways." Her tone grew wistful. "It interferes with his peace of mind, you see, and his commitment to submission. Not that he is disobedient," she added. "Jason is the perfect submissive; he always has been. And part of what makes him so perfect is his knowledge and understanding of his own needs.

"One of those is discipline. Like so many men, Jason finds the idea of losing control, of losing oneself, quite difficult. Disciplining, as you know, is one of the ways a Dominant can train their submissives into relinquishing that control."

Her serene countenance faded, like a mask slipping, and Sydney could see the true ravages of the illness on her face. Gazing into her wine, she continued, "When Jason and I first came together, I became his sole Dominant. He's never had another. The way we interact, the way we've bonded, is very precious to us both. I've always seen to his disciplining personally, but I'm afraid this illness has left me a bit too weak to give my darling boy what he needs." She smiled at Sydney. "It all comes back down to what we were discussing earlier – trust.

"That's why I would like you to discipline him for me."

Well, if this wasn't a weekend for surprises. Sydney risked a glance at Dahlra, and he gave her a little apologetic shrug. "Jason mentioned it when we were taking the bags upstairs, but he wanted Clara to be the one to ask you. I told him I thought you would give it consideration, but that the choice was ultimately yours."

Sydney turned to Clara. "I don't know what to say. I mean..."

Clara held up her hand; the huge diamond flashed in the candlelight, scattering prisms of light over the table. "I realise this was probably the last thing on your to-do list when you decided to pay us a visit, but please, hear me out."

Her voice trembled with emotion. "You know my Jason. He's a mild, placid soul, as gentle as a lamb, for all of his boisterousness. And he has been a solid rock for me since the day we met, and never more so than during this illness. But he's felt so helpless at times, watching me struggle, and he's bottled up all that anger and tension, because he's had to.

"I've conditioned him through the years to use disciplining as a means to give himself permission to let go of those negative emotions. He knows he needs it. And I want him to accept that he doesn't have to be strong for my sake anymore."

Sydney's' breath left her lips in a huff. "I understand it, I really do. But why me? With all due respect, why didn't you ask that Silas guy to take care of Jason for you? You said yourself he's an experienced Dom, right? I mean, surely his experience and expertise-"

"Yes, my dear one, he is experienced. Quite experienced." Clara chose her words carefully. "I want to explain myself clearly here. Sydney, dear, you've investigated the Fetish community. You know how it works. We don't judge one person's proclivities as being any more deviant than anyone else's.

"Training submissives, or living with them after they are collared to you, it's all the same. In this lifestyle, discipline is about allowing oneself to surrender to one's Dominant with an open, loving spirit. In allowing yourself to submit to any discipline, you are empowering yourself, and at the same time you are allowing your control to be placed in the hands of someone you trust implicitly. It is a symbiotic relationship—or at least it should be."

Sydney nodded, remembering the cane rod whistling through the air, her own triumph at allowing it to happen, Dahlra's pleasure in her trust in him. It was more than kinky foreplay; it had been an exercise in trust and empowerment.

Clara went on, "And in saying that, no Dominant should really enjoy harming a submissive—it's like reprimanding your own child." Clara gave her a Mona Lisa smile. "Unless, of course, your submissive enjoys the pain. Then you must by all means be mindful of their pleasure, even with the administration of the pain. Safe, sane, and consensual. It is our mantra."

Her face darkened. "But Silas is a bit too... selfish for my tastes. He enjoys the process and power of inflicting pain more than I care for."

"Are you trying to tell me-"

"I am not. All I am saying is that Silas understands quite well the S&M mindset, where one partner inflicts the pain the other needs to achieve sexual or emotional gratification. He's very popular. People often seek him out for that very reason. He may not be the most pleasant person I've ever met, but he has never, to my knowledge, broken trust with a submissive or crossed that consensual line.

"But I still won't let him discipline Jason. For one thing, Jason isn't used to being touched by another man, and moreover, he trusts *you*, my dear. And I know you respect him as well."

Clara took Sydney's hand and squeezed it; there was no strength at all in her grip. "Do this for me, honey. He needs this. You see how frantic and frenetic he is. He needs to grieve in the only way he can. And he can't do it alone."

Sydney looked at Dahlra, who returned her gaze with a gentle expression of encouragement. Something in their exchanged looks must have registered with Clara. She sighed.

"Thank you, Sydney. It's a relief to know he's in such good hands."

An hour later, Clara, Sydney and Dahlra descended into a place Sydney had only heard about, but never in all her trips to the estate had gotten up the nerve to visit—Ramcat's famous dungeon, The Catacombs. It was an immense space that ran the entire length of the house, and extended several thousand square feet beneath the manor. Like Maidenvine, it had once held wine cellars and passages to different locations on the estate. Clara had spent untold fortunes to refurbish it fit to purpose. Now it was a rabbit's warren of different areas used for play.

The rooms varied in size, and were themed according to the wishes of those using them. Some were functional, some set the scene for a particular mood or fantasy, and some went over the top and straight into head-fucking territory. All tastes were accommodated at Ramcat.

As they passed each open door, Clara occasionally paused to explain the room's purpose. One of the larger rooms was all marble and chrome, bristling with restraints and weapons and huge black candles that threw ominous shadows on the black walls. As they looked around, it was on the tip of Sydney's tongue to quip, "The Pagan Sacrifice Room, I presume?" But one look at Dahlra's smouldering eyes made Sydney reconsider.

Bookcases ran from floor to ceiling all around a beautiful library, its shelves overflowing with volumes ranging in subject from Shakespeare to Austin to Jung to Erotica. The dense Aubusson rug felt plush and expensive beneath their feet. Seated in the Queen Anne chairs and perched on the green leather sofas placed randomly around the room were a handful of guests. They glanced at the newcomers with mild curiosity, then returned to their books.

This cathedral of reading and contemplation seemed a bit incongruous in a place like Ramcat, but as Clara explained, "Smart is very sexy, darling. Many of our guests are of a scholarly bent, you know. Once you realise that what happens between your legs isn't nearly as important as what's happening between your ears, you open yourself to new worlds of physical pleasure and emotional freedom."

Beside the library was a smaller room. It was pitch black and bare, except for a lone chair, which faced a large, old-fashioned wooden swing, some five feet away. The swing hung from large, vine-wrapped chains suspended from hooks in the ceiling.

Both items were spotlighted from above, giving the room a trippy, Alice in Wonderland vibe. Dahlra solemnly regarded the swing, then looked at Sydney with a gaze full of slow burn. The entire set up seemed at once erotically innocent and outrageously decadent. Sydney pictured herself on the swing, possibly naked, while Dahlra watched from the chair, fully clothed. Now, that was a kink she could definitely get behind. Another room for her Ramcat Bucket list.

Their destination was clinical, almost sterile, in design. The walls were starkly, pristinely white; there was very little furniture beyond a couple of chairs and a large table, cornered with restraining cuffs. A butler's sink and a medicine cabinet stood in the corner. Hooks hung suspended from the ceiling.

Kneeling on the floor in the middle of the room was Jason, his eyes downcast, and his face pale beneath his gardener's tan. There was nothing of Tom-Brown's-Schooldays and-lashings-of-ginger-beer about him now. His hair was damp with perspiration, and his nude body carried a light sheen of sweat. He did not look up as they drew near.

With a final glance at Dahlra, Sydney moved to stand in front of the kneeling man. In a quiet voice, she asked, "Jason, why you are here?"

"I asked for disciplining, Mistress."

"Because your Mistress is still unable to do so, she has asked me to administer this for her. Do you accept that?"

"Yes, Mistress."

"Will you accept my discipline in the spirit in which it is intended?"

Jason answered formally, "It is my privilege to receive discipline from my Beloved Mistress. To be cleaned out of everything but my absolute devotion to her."

"Good." Sydney was grateful she sounded calm; she was anything but. With this kind of disciplining, there was a ritualistic quality to the moment—the formal, stilted phrases, the protocols, the ceremonial aspect of it all. Were all Dommes this freaked out the first time they did this?

Straightening her shoulders, Sydney walked over to the sink that stood in the corner and beckoned to Dahlra. "Will you assist me, please?" He joined her at the sink, and as she had instructed earlier, opened the bottle of rubbing alcohol and poured its contents over her hands, leaving them numbingly cold. After drying them on a white towel, she returned to stand in front of the kneeling submissive. For the first time, Jason looked up into her face. Sydney was shocked at the anxiety and pleading she saw in his eyes.

"You've carried a very heavy load, Jason. You are allowed to drop it from time to time. This is one of those times."

He slumped, breathing heavily. "Thank you, Mistress. I promise to try."

"You will not try. You will do it. Now stand up."

Following Clara's instructions, Dahlra bound Jason's hands with nylon rope and looped the knot onto the overhead hooks, stretching his arms high over his head. Suspended and bound, Jason waited quietly, taut as a bowstring, trembling in anticipation. There was a look of ecstatic relief on his face.

Dahlra gave a nod to Sydney, who took several deep breaths in anticipation. She placed a hand against Jason's torso to still him. His skin twitched under her touch. "Begin to count."

Before he could prepare himself, she struck his buttocks hard; it made a loud cracking noise that echoed in the room. The blond man jerked and said, "Thank you; that was one." Sydney's hand stung immediately, in spite of the chilling alcohol bath. This was going to be a long session.

At "Thank you; that was ten," Sydney realized that she was inadequate for the job. Her hand felt as if it were being held in a fire. To make matters worse, Jason was sporting a huge erection. It was daunting even to Sydney, who was used to Dahlra's impressive hard-on aimed at her on a regular basis. She could feel her face turning the same colour as Jason's firm, rounded arse.

Clara had told her specifically that Jason required an intense disciplining. He needed a physical and emotional release, not the inadequate playacting shit she was laying down. She gritted her teeth in determination. She would have to up her game. *I'm an agent, for fuck's sake. I can do hardcore.*

"Submissive, this is not appropriate." She got right up into his face. "This is not about pleasure. You must control yourself. Master it."

"I'm so sorry, Mistress." Jason's face was stained with embarrassment. "It's been a long time—"

"The fault lies with me. Obviously my method is insufficient. You need something more... impersonal." It was as good a time as any..."Dahlra, may I have your belt, please?"

Dahlra's eyes never left hers as the belt slid from the loops of his trousers. As he held it out to her, their hands touched, and Sydney felt an electric charge between them. She doubled up the belt and ritualistically placed a reverent kiss on the leather. His eyes burned.

She turned back to Jason, who eyed the belt with something like relief. "We'll start again. Yes?"

Jason nodded vigorously. "Yes, Mistress. Thank you."

Sydney waited until everyone in the room was focused, then she struck Jason so hard *she* winced. The sound of leather slapping his bare flesh was like thunder in the room, and Jason yelped.

"Thank you; that was one," he gasped, and blinked as tears pooled in his eyes. He glanced over at his Dominant, and Clara nodded, as if pleased at last.

At twenty lashes, Clara gave a signal to end. Jason was weeping openly now—great, racking sobs of release.

Sydney lowered the belt to her side. She turned to the man she called her Dominant. "Please release him." Dahlra was gentleness itself as he lowered Jason's arms and untied the ropes from his wrists, massaging his shoulders to restore the circulation.

The last of his strength left him, and Jason sagged to his knees. Sydney knelt beside him, crooning softly as she petted and comforted him. It had been difficult, so difficult, to strike this fine example of the perfect submissive twenty hard times.

Even as he wept, there was a calm stealing over him that had not been in evidence since their arrival, and that alone gave Sydney the sense of having done right by him. The wound had been lanced; now the poison would drain away. "You did so well, Jason. As the one who administered your disciplining, I am very pleased."

"Thank you." His voice was thick with tears.

There was one final part to this ritual; she had broken him down, and now she must lift him back up again. Sydney waited until his sobs quieted, then commanded, "Jason, listen to me."

She held up the belt. "Do you see this?" Blinking away his tears, he nodded. "My own dear, precious Dominant gave this to me. He saw you needed something more, and he answered my request without question, because he wanted me to be exactly what you needed.

"But I'm not going to give it back to him. I am giving this belt to your Mistress as a gift, so that Dahlra and I will both remember what perfect submission can be, and what I have to do be worthy of that perfection. After your demonstration, Dahlra will expect no less from me. You set a fine example, once I understood what you needed."

Jason's smile was incandescent. "Thank you, Sydney," he said, his voice trembling with happiness. Silently, Sydney placed the belt in Clara's hand. She smiled proudly at her submissive, her blue eyes glistening with her own unshed tears.

In that moment, Sydney understood a little more what it meant to take pleasure in Dominance as well. It certainly made her acutely aware of the responsibilities Dahlra took upon himself. This wasn't a little slap and tickle, tiesy-upsy game. This was life; this was the kind of thing you sometimes had to do in order to take care of someone who depended on you. It was terrible and beautiful all at once, and while Sydney had done what both Clara *and* Jason had asked of her, she was forced to question her own ability to Dominate anyone other than herself.

Leaving their hosts, Sydney and Dahlra walked back upstairs to their suite, a quietly elegant room, in muted colors of burgundies and cream. Sydney paused at the Louis XIV writing desk.

"I bought you a present for this weekend. After what just happened, I think you might need it." She reached into her bag and retrieved a small, tastefully wrapped package. The elegant engraving on the top of the box read *Gieves & Hawkes, Savile Row.* Dahlra gave her an indefinable look as she placed it in his hands.

"Thank you, Sydney."

"You don't even know what it is."

Solemnly, he stroked her cheek. "It's a gift from you. That's enough."

He carefully untied the black bow and opened the box. It was a new belt, of the finest buttery black leather, perfectly suited to him and his tastes. He looked both pleased and puzzled. "It's great, Sydney. Thank you. But what—"

"It's purely a coincidence. I bought it with other plans in mind, but Jason's disciplining gave me an opportunity to surprise you." She smiled at his look of confusion. "When I realised I needed something heavier than my hand, I knew you wouldn't hesitate when I asked you for your old belt."

"So the whole 'I am giving this belt to your Mistress as a gift'—"

"Well, you can't deny it added a bit of flair to the moment." She grinned. "Besides, the opportunity to shock you with a brand-new belt afterward was just too tempting to pass up."

"Clever girl. Good thing I didn't say no, huh?"

"You wouldn't have, would you?"

Dahlra stroked the leather, his expression thoughtful. "No, I wouldn't have. Not for you."

"I know. Otherwise I would have used this belt to punish *you*. Or isn't a submissive supposed to say such things to their Dominant?"

His eyes did a slow, sexy crawl up her body. "Did you like being the Dominant?" he asked, taking her into his arms. The words slid from his tongue like a whisper of silk, and Sydney felt a delicious splinter of lust slide under her skin.

"Maybe I should discipline you with it anyway." She studied his tie for several heartbeats before she continued. "Pretty intense, isn't it?

Disciplining a sub."

"I think so," he concurred. "It made me very aware of what we do together, how you react to me, and I to you."

"Explain."

"It confirmed to me what I've known all along. That I belong to you." He hesitated, and sighed. "I'm *not* your Dominant; not really. For all that Silas berk said, he was right—I am a Top in name only."

"I don't agree." Sydney looked up into his handsome face. "We may not be Dominant and submissive by his definition, but screw that. We make up our own rules, you and me."

"That's my girl," he purred, stroking her face. "And I love you, top or bottom. But I don't like the idea of another Dominant disciplining you."

"Even if the situation were similar to Jason and Clara?"

He gave a little shrug of consideration. "If I truly trusted the Dominant not to harm you, and you were willing, perhaps. But I would be lying if I said I haven't thought about it."

"What?"

Dahlra stepped back, and retrieved his gift from the box. Wordlessly, he folded it in half, and kissed it reverently. He looked relaxed, yet his body sang with anticipation. She knew what his response would be, as surely as if she had scripted it.

"I want you to discipline me." His voice was low and sensuous, his tone trancelike. "With my gift."

Sydney held out her hand. "Belt." Without hesitation he placed it in her hand. "Take off your coat and tie."

As he unbuttoned his jacket and laid it aside, she felt that sliver of anticipation burrow under her skin a little deeper. The silk tie made a delicate rustling sound as he pulled it from its knot, and he tossed it on top of the coat. He stood in his trousers and white shirt, looking ready for whatever she chose to do with him.

And oh, she was going to do some lovely things to him.

She patted the sofa next to her. "Come and sit beside me, Dahlra." Quietly, he sat down, and looked at her with such a mixture of vulnerability and desire she almost straddled him and begged him to take her then and there. Being a Dominant took a lot of self-control.

"It got your blood up, didn't it? Watching me discipline Jason."

"Yes. But not from watching him."

Sydney gently stroked his earlobe; his eyelids fluttered at her touch. "Then what *did* excite you?" she challenged.

He gave his answer a lot of thought. "It was watching *you*, seeing how detached you can be when doing something you find difficult. You were so patient. I knew it was terribly important to you to do the right thing. I felt like your slave in some sort of erotic ceremony. I *wanted* to be your slave then, pouring alcohol over your hands ..."

"That's an old S&M trick," she replied dismissively. "More for drama than practicality. And we saw how successful *that* was. That's for playing games, Dahlra. Surely you know that's not how I would discipline you."

"With all due respect, I told you long ago that I am happy to take any discipline you feel is necessary. As long as you want me." He spoke rapidly, his voice edgy and vulnerable. "I tore heaven and hell apart to be the center of your world. It's the only place I want to be."

He seized her palm and gave it a searing kiss. "Do whatever you please with me."

"Very well. You have two choices. I can discipline you while you are fully clothed. Afterward, we'll sit and talk about it, or just go to bed. Or... you can undress completely, and allow me to discipline you properly. If you choose that, I will reward you afterward."

He began to unbutton his shirt, his fingers fumbling slightly. She put her hand over his to still his hasty movements and he looked at her, his eyes wide and just a shade tense.

"Don't rush, my love. We have all the time in the world. I want to enjoy this."

He flexed his fingers slightly, as if they had been cramping, and returned to unbuttoning his trousers, his hands steady. With his eyes locked with hers, he continued until he was completely naked. It was odd; she had watched Dahlra undress countless number of times, but now, knowing he was naked for the sole purpose of allowing her to stripe his arse with his own belt—damn, she was pretty sure she'd just won the kink lottery.

"Bend over, and put your hands on the desk."

"Yes, Mistress." He complied perfectly, looking decadent and out of place against the backdrop of the frilly French furniture. His long torso gleamed like fine marble in the soft light.

"Now spread your legs." As he obeyed, Sydney felt an incredible surge of power inside, as if an internal engine was purring beneath her skin.

"Do you feel uncomfortable like this?" She raked her nails over the hard, curve line of his arse. His skin pebbled with goosebumps.

"No. It's like..." He stopped, and lowered his head. "It's like I deserve-"

"Dahlra, you know this has nothing to do with the cell, don't you? It's not punishment. We're far past that."

"I know." He was breathing rapidly. "I know it doesn't. But it's like something I have to do. Something I want to do."

As he turned to face her, Sydney gave the belt a passionate, reverent kiss. She had no intention of hurting him, but he had asked for this, and she wanted him to remember it.

"Start counting." She leaned toward him and gently cupped his balls. They were heavy and tight, and he moaned softly as she gave them a firm stroke.

The first blow was hard, and he gasped and arched his back, but didn't protest. "Thank you; that is one." He relaxed into his stance, like a kitten being held by the scruff.

Sydney's arousal quickly morphed into an addictive surge of power. She hit him again, just to feel it grow.

By the third lash, he was biting back the urge to cry out. By the sixth, he no longer tried to hold back his cries. Sydney timed the blows so that they were uneven in rhythm and force, and never in the same place. By the eleventh, he was as hard as she could ever remember seeing him, and his breathing was ragged. His long lashes sparkled wetly.

By the fifteenth, he was almost on the brink of coming, and tears flowed down his face. He looked rapturous as the belt slapped against him, each blow followed by Sydney's soothing hands against his rosy arse.

By the next blow, Sydney had enough. "Dahlra, look at me."

He obeyed her, looking stunned and distressed and aroused, as if this disciplining had the opposite effect of Jason's. His tear-filled eyes were dark and slightly wild. His erection was so blood gorged the head was almost purple. She brought the belt again to her lips, placing the same tender kiss upon it as before. It was a kiss of acceptance, of finding his submission perfect. Dahlra closed his eyes and sank to his knees, wrapping his arms around her.

He moaned helplessly against her belly. Sydney raked her nails hard through his hair, damp with sweat, and he shuddered and pulled her closer. Sydney knelt with him, kissing his tears away. She tugged at his arm, urging him to stand, and when she made him face the desk again he shot her a worried look.

"Don't worry love. You've had more than enough." She stroked his blistered backside, and he hissed as her hand ghosted over the sensitised flesh. "Stay here."

In the loo, she found a soft white flannel, and moistened it with cold water. When she returned, she found Dahlra still leaning against the desk. He looked calmer, more himself again. She handed him the flannel which he took with a nod of thanks.

There was a pleased look of triumph on his face. Sydney understood that smile all too well; he had presented himself for disciplining and had not been found wanting.

Finally, when he was calm, she took his hand and led him to the bed, pulling the covers back. He winced as his tender, bruised flesh made contact with the mattress. As she stood over him, he shifted restlessly, his body longing for some ease.

Sydney made no move to lie down, but took the opportunity just to enjoy the look of him. Her hands traced lightly up his arms and across his collarbone, brushing his skin with light, feathery strokes. His eyes met hers, and the desire that was burning in him made Sydney feel hot as well.

"Touch yourself." She caressed his cheek. "Show me how and where you like to be touched."

His eyes slid closed as he moved his hand over his chest. He scratched a nail over his left nipple, teasing it. He plucked it, and his breathing hitched slightly. He toyed with his nipples as his right hand copied his left, until both were puckered and stiff.

Once he'd teased them hard, his hand smoothed down his abdomen and onto his waiting cock, and he took himself in hand. His hips rose from the bed and rolled sensuously as he stroked downward. Sydney watched in rapt fascination, her own arousal hot and heavy in her belly. She had watched him bring himself off before, but not at her command, like a queen commanding a slave.

His hands were an education in and of themselves; one deep, and two shallow strokes, massaging the head on the upstroke. He fondled his balls with more pressure. His eyes slid over her body possessively. "Do you like watching me, little girl?" he drawled, heat and lust darkening his voice. "Does it make you wet?"

Sydney' laughter sounded feathery and breathless with excitement. "I love it. I love watching you jerk off for me. I'll bet you love doing it just as much, don't you?"

"Oh yes." He pumped his cock harder. "I want to come for you. I want you to see how much I want you."

Sydney's fingers dipped below his balls to the perineum, and he made a delicious sound as she caressed the silky, sensitive taint. She retrieved a small bottle of lube from the bedside table. Her slick fingers teased at the entrance to his rectum, and his eyes rolled back as she carefully slipped one, then two fingers into the unfurling bud. He whimpered, then bucked, his hips pumping between her hand and his own.

"Oh, *fuck*," he whispered, a look of absolute rapture on his face. His sac tightened, and his motions became less controlled. Sydney pinched his nipple gently.

"Are you going to come for me, Dahlra?" she crooned. "Don't come until I tell you. Do you hear me?" Panting, he nodded tensely. Sydney was totally enthralled. "You want to, don't you? You're so close, aren't you?"

"Yes, oh, God, yes." His breathing turned to gasps, which turned into ragged, incessant moans. "I need to-I can't hold it-"

"Beg for it."

"Please let me—"

"Do it, Dahlra. Do it——"

That was enough to break him, and he came with a harsh cry, his handsome face contorting with ecstasy. Sydney watched him raptly, until her eyes started to burn; she had forgotten to blink.

He relaxed against the bed, limp and sated. Gradually, his eyes lost their wild and drugged look, and he languorously came back to himself. He stretched luxuriously, a cat-like smile of satisfaction on his handsome face.

Before Sydney could react, he grabbed her and swiftly pulled her onto the bed, rolling over her and pinning her down with a deep, sense-stealing kiss. He hungrily feasted on her mouth, as if his mind-blowing orgasm had yet to happen. He slid his thigh between hers, and lewdly rubbed it against her crotch, sending her libido into sound barrier-breaking territory.

"Is my lovely submissive wet from playing her games with me?" The look on his face made her wriggle against his thigh. "Why don't I finger you until you come?" His creamy voice made each word lasciviously dirty.

"You're going to find me very wet," she replied with a gasp. "And I can assure you that I'm open to anything you want to do with me."

"Let's see about that." Dahlra quickly unbuttoned her slacks and drew them from her hips. He pulled her top over her head with a playful yank. "Bra. Off."

He retrieved the belt from the end of the sofa and tied her wrists to the headboard with a suspicious amount of skill. "This position does lovely things for your breasts, my dear." He flicked his tongue against a hard nipple, then rolled it expertly between his teeth. When she moaned deliriously, he gave it a little snapping bite.

With a quick movement that made her squeal in delight, he rose onto his knees and roughly pulled her knickers from her body. Poised to strike, he looked down at her with a slow, devilish smile. "Why don't I make you scream a little for me?"

Their sex was playful and rough, all the more so because they both knew how brief it would be; neither wanted nor needed a slow climb up the hill. Dahlra set a burning, rocking pace, rotating and churning his hips as he pistoned into her.

"Harder," she moaned feverishly, nearly gone. "Make it hard, so hard it hurts... make it hurt—"

He caught her face in his hands. "Never. I'll never hurt you..."

She mewled his name as her orgasm careened down the runway, ready for takeoff. "Don't ever stop," she moaned, her climax igniting, building higher and faster. It blistered down every nerve ending, and sent him over the edge as well.

She lay beneath him, feeling sleepily squashed. She knew she ought to tell him to move, but she was just too comfortable.

Finally, Dahlra rose up on his elbows and untied her wrists, rubbing her arms soothingly. "Well," he chuckled, "I shall always wear this belt with a smile."

"I think I might have to buy you another one. This one's been repurposed."

"Dirty little girl. I'll start to think you're being cheeky just to get spanked." His expression softened. "You know, with your hair scattered over the pillow like that, you look like an angel."

Her silly laughter bubbled up, and he gave her a look of pure bliss. "And when you laugh like that, I think my heart's going to fly right out of my chest."

He gathered her in his arms, and they lay in the dark, holding on to one another. Sydney was almost asleep when Dahlra whispered, "Sydney?"

"Hmm?"

"I will be your Dominant. But I will relinquish my Dominance to you. You only have to ask."

That woke her up. She turned in his arms and faced him. "This is our lives, Dahlra. Who says we can't be both to one another? We're not here to impress anyone, not even Clara or Jason If someone like that dick Silas doesn't approve, fuck him and the horse he rode in on."

"Said a spokesman." He toyed with a strand of her hair. "I don't suppose it matters whether we're a typical Dom or sub, does it? Like my grandfather used to say, 'a tiger doesn't lose sleep over the opinions of sheep'."

"I'll have to remember that." She stroked his smooth, warm skin. "But I'll say one thing for you: you're pretty amazing, Dom or sub."

"I think I like being a sub—on occasion," he mused. Suddenly, she was pushed back against the bed, and he was looming over her, playfully holding her down. He nipped her bottom lip with his teeth, and playfully tugged on her nipple. When she gasped in pleasant surprise, he purred, "On the other hand, pet, I do plan on being your Dominant for quite a long time."

CHAPTER SEVENTEEN

The Tunnel

It was not in Silas Markham's nature to take out his anger on inanimate objects; he preferred by far to take it out on his more-than-willing slaves. After all, that was what they were for. Even so, as he gunned his Merc's engine and spun out of Ramcat's drive, he felt a perverse, hateful pleasure at the gravel spraying against the car's undercarriage.

He was seething as he headed down the A36 toward Sussex. The nerve of that little high-tit bitch, Sydney Chapin! And hiding behind her skirt, that pathetic wannabe, Gar. What the fuck were they doing at Ramcat anyway, swanning around like they owned the place?

And as if that wasn't enough, he'd been given a dressing-down from Mistress-High-And-Mighty Clara afterward. How dare that dried-up old cunt lecture him on protocol? How bloody *dare* she?

It had been bad enough that those two characters had insulted him. He had stormed out of the room in a rage, and nearly run Clara down. She had given him that 'Lady of the Manor' shite, smiling at him like they were old friends. "Heavens, what's the rush, Silas? Are you leaving? I thought you wanted to speak to me about a play weekend—"

"Yes, I came here to discuss a play weekend, as well you know." He ignored her surprised expression. "But I refuse to stay in the same house while you allow those cretins to stand there and insult me."

The old bitch had the temerity to look shocked. "Cretins? I'm sorry, but you have totally lost me, Silas. What sort of insult would I allow you to endure?"

"Those two pretenders in your sitting room. Sydney Chapin, and that doctor of hers with the ridiculous name. They stood there insulting me to my face while you were off fannying about elsewhere. So yes, I hold you responsible." He laughed mirthlessly. "Taking on Elwess' little protégé as a favour? You always did think the sun shone out of his arse. Well, if those two are his idea of how to train submissives, no wonder he's a laughingstock."

"I'd rather you didn't talk about Elwess in such a disrespectful manner in my presence."

"And I'd rather come back when you aren't entertaining posers and amateurs. I'm surprised you'd receive the likes of them at Ramcat. If you don't want the reputation of your business to suffer, I'd advise you vet your guests more carefully."

She never even turned a hair. "Why, Master Silas, that almost sounds like a threat. I'm sure it isn't. I couldn't imagine any situation in which that would be called for."

"Take it any way you like, Clara, but no one treats me like that. Not here. I don't come to Ramcat to be offended by charlatans, pretending to know how to walk the waterfront. You need to have a word with your little friends—" he'd nodded toward the room with a sharp jerk of his head, "and remind them just who I am."

She had listened to his tirade in silence, her eyes growing colder by the second. "I'm important to your continued success, Mrs Liggon. My presence here always ensures you of a very profitable weekend. But I will not tolerate being treated disrespectfully by so-called friends of yours—or anyone's for that matter. You might wish to remember that I have powerful friends, and they will not be pleased—"

"Ah, now that *is* a threat. Something I can work with." Her voice lost its pleasant cadence, and turned to ice. "Silas, perhaps now is the time for me to remind *you* who *I* am. You will leave my house, and you will return when, and only when, I next issue an invitation. I am neither obligated nor inclined to tolerate your childish outburst. And I'll tell you this for nothing."

She leaned forward, her voice dripping with scorn. "The days of your 'powerful friends,' as you call them, are numbered. You see, I have little birds in lots of trees, and I hear what's going on. And don't come the cowboy with me, Sunny Jim, because we both know why Sydney Chapin is here. And if you think she's going to back off this time, injuries or not, you're a lot dumber than you look."

Clara gave him a cold, belittling smile. "And while we're talking about your so-called friends, just remember this: the last time, they were ready to deliver you up as the sacrificial lamb. You're a fool to believe they wouldn't do it again, no matter how important you think you are to them. These are professionals, Silas. Oh, they're happy to let you do all the hard work, but as far as they're concerned, you're really just a shabby little pervert with a fetish they can exploit." She looked him up and down like he was a piece of garbage. "I think this time they may very well get sent down. My advice to you would be to get out of the game, or you'll go down with them."

Silas tried to hide the sick taste of fear that suddenly flooded his mouth. "Why are you telling me all this? There's obviously no love lost on your end. Why the warning?"

To his shock, Clara laughed, a peel of genuine mirth. "Oh, Silas, don't you know the best fox hunts are the ones where the fox knows he's being hunted from the off? I suspect you're going to provide some splendid amusement."

A car approached the front of the house. "Ah, Jason is here. I'd take that as my cue to leave, if I were you, dear." Silas began to splutter, but she cut him off with an upraised hand. "I think you need to take a little drive and cool down. Use this time to think on your sins. Most foxes only get one warning."

He fronted her out for a heartbeat, then spun on his heel and got in his car. He had barely resisted the temptation to run down that grinning baboon, Jason, on his way out. Even as he peeled out of the drive and headed towards Brighton, he was already weighing his options.

Silas padded into his front room, dark dressing gown over his naked body. He had meticulously showered, washing his long hair carefully, conditioning it with the finest products. He only used the best. Even his dressing gown was made of fine silk, with a dull sheen he often stroked approvingly.

None of his slaves saw him like this. To them he was the firm, distant Master, nothing short of god-like. That is how he saw himself: aloof, imperious, beautiful, omnificent—perfect in his Dominance.

He eased into his favourite chair and propped his feet onto a leather ottoman, approving of the way it showcased his pale, slender calves. Reaching for his mobile, he speed-dialed a number. It was almost three o'clock in the morning, but he knew the call would be answered. In Silas' world a slave was there solely for his pleasure and amusement, and he demanded a high degree of obedience as befitting a Master of his calibre. Those he Dominated knew better than to test the boundaries. A slave only had one chance to miss his call, and they would never be called again.

The call was answered on the second ring. A hopeful voice, laden with respect, answered. "Yes, Master?"

"Did you, or did you not, assure me that Silverbirch was a cold case, and not to be reopened?"

"Th-the Senior Principal mentioned it in a meeting a few days ago. But just in passing. There were no plans to pursue it through our channels. He was content to let the Jersey Constabulary handle it—"

"Then what was Sydney Chapin doing sniffing around Ramcat Estate?"

"S-Sydney Chapin? I don't know why. She's on garden leave."

"It seems just a little more than coincidence that you have a meeting mentioning Silverbirch, then days later one of the lead agents in the original investigation has a private meeting with Clara Liggon." Silas dropped his tone. "I would be very disappointed in you, should I find out that you knew the case was being reopened—"

"No, Master! I assure you, I have heard nothing about Silverbirch being re-activated! I've made sure that any possible connections are misfiled or unrecorded." There was a tearful tone in the voice on the other end. "I would never withhold anything from you, Master! You are my world. I'm nothing but shit without you. I am nothing, nobody, a tool, I am—"

"You are a slave who has interrupted me, for which you will be punished. You will not come to me on Friday. You will have a month to contemplate your mistakes."

There was an audible sob. "Oh, please, Master, have mercy! Don't leave me alone for so long. Please don't!"

"Enough, enough. Stop sniveling. I will give you another chance. I'm not, after all, completely heartless."

The sobbing stopped so rapidly, Silas laughed. "Oh, poor slave. You don't know what to do, do you? 'Do I cry, and beg, and plead with Master Silas to have mercy? Or do I calm myself down and do as he says?' Which is the right answer?"

"Master, I—"

"You'll shut up and do as you're told. You already have one punishment waiting on you; do you wish for another?"

"No, Master." Silas took a sip of brandy, and let the silence ring out. It was one of the best weapons for a slave: the unspoken disapproval, the unknown punishment to follow. When the tension had reached the highest vantage point, Silas let it stretch out several more seconds. Softly, he said, "Are you ready to listen to your Master?"

"Yes, sir."

"Good. Your incompetence is the reason Chapin was called back into play. You should have downplayed Silverbirch's involvement with this Jersey business in the first place. You will encourage your senior principal to call off Sydney Chapin. She isn't necessary to the investigation because *there is nothing to investigate*, do I make myself clear?"

"Yes, sir, but I don't know how—"

"I don't *care* how; that's your problem. You're a cunt-hair away from being implicated yourself; I'd think some sort of self-preservation instinct might be in order here."

"Yes, sir. I'll do what I can. I promise."

Now it was time to reward. "Good. Then I will permit you to come on Friday. You will wear the garments I bought you. You will greet me in position four, and I will use my black rod to mete out your punishment."

That implied two things: all was temporarily forgiven, and reclamation was going to hurt enough to warrant needing the weekend to recover.

"Oh, thank you, Master, thank you, thank you—"

"Thank me when I have finished beating you, and allowed you to suck my cock as your reward."

Silas ended the call before the whining could continue. With a little hum of satisfaction, he sat back and finished his brandy. *That went rather well,* he thought. Slaves were so easy to manipulate. Well, the good ones were.

And even better, they were disposable.

His satisfaction soured a little at the thought of Sydney Chapin and Dahlra Gar. They were a minor nuisance; that was all. And yet, when he thought of Chapin's protective, fighting stance, her arrogance and insolence, Silas felt a sudden, vicious rush of arousal. It had been a long time since anyone had really defied him and got away with it. Punishing her would be delightful. She would certainly be fun to break. Then again, so would Gar. Even more so, really.

His good mood returned. His cock stirred as several fantasies spun out in his imagination. Corrupting the innocent, breaking the high-spirited, making the weak cower in fear. He gave his erection a lazy, warm-up stroke as he hummed, "My Favourite Things."

Autumn blew into England with a vengeance, and the mild weather changed almost overnight to cool, grey days and rainy evenings. A few weeks after their visit to Ramcat, Dahlra received an invitation to chair a seminar at the Royal London Hospital, regarding techniques in hypno-narcotic therapy and mnemonic conditioning as alternative methods of pain management. He was to deliver several lectures at the London over the course of a week, so he suggested that, instead of driving back to Maidenvine at the end of every day, Sydney could come with him and they could stay at their old DeVere Gardens flat.

Sydney readily agreed; she planned to use the opportunity to catch up on the agency goss and accept one of Pip Lightoller's invitations to lunch. She and Inigo had both been disappointed over the small amount of new information on Silverbirch, but Sydney was patient. Clara and Jason had put out the feelers; now it was just a matter of seeing what tripped them.

They had not been back to London in months, in spite of Inigo's not-so subtle commands to attend his perennial Ashes party in celebration of something to do with cricket. Sydney had taken full advantage of the driving distance to decline his invitation. She had always hated those damned parties; in her mind they all melded into one dreary, hot afternoon, surrounded by men and women of various degrees of intoxicated toffery sucking down champagne and canapés while she either wilted from sunburn or got drenched in the rain. And all their clever tittering over the baffling, brain-twisting confusion that was cricket scoring generally drove her mental. Besides, Maidenvine was home now, and Sydney honestly didn't miss London much.

Though she didn't see him as often since the move to Windsor, Garnet still called her daily, nattering on about the impending arrival of his own Minder, and filling her in on all the usual suspects at the Agency. Each time he rang off, Sydney asked herself if she missed it. There were times she did, and not even Dahlra could fill that void. At times, when Garnet regaled her with one of his assignments, Sydney would feel restless and guiltily resentful, akin to the frustration kids feel when they've been forced to stay inside nursing a cold while all their friends are out having fun without them.

Perhaps a trip down memory lane to her old cramped and soulless office would be an excellent reminder that, as exciting and rewarding as the job could be, more often than not it was dull, mundane grunt work for months on end.

They arrived at DeVere Gardens in the early afternoon. As they walked into what had been their first home, Sydney felt a sense of déjà vu that she wasn't all that crazy about. All the memories of those early days flooded back, like a low-rent version of PTSD. As homecomings went, it left a bit to be desired.

Dahlra, too, looked discomfited. "Well, as they say, it seemed like a good idea at the time."

"Yeah." When Sydney didn't elaborate, he headed up the stairs, muttering about unpacking before making something to eat.

"I hope this doesn't sound daft, but it feels a little uncomfortable to be here," she remarked, over a rather strained afternoon tea.

Dahlra glanced around the trendy kitchen, so different from the inviting country larder they'd left behind in Maidenvine. "I agree. It's like we've hit the rewind button."

"More like we left parts of ourselves behind, and they want to reattach to us now that we've come back."

"We can always go to a hotel if the place gives you the heebie jeebies." Dahlra's eyes were faintly tinged with remorse. "The last thing I want is for you to feel uncomfortable."

Looking into his face, so grave with concern for her welfare, Sydney was tempted to take him up on his offer; just go to the Dorchester, order room service and forget about DeVere and its ghosts and bizarre vibes. She looked around the bleak flat. In all honesty, it was strangely impersonal, and a little lonely. It was more sad than sinister.

"You know what, Dahlra? Any PTSD shite trying to slip into my head is gonna have to fuck off. It's just a flat. It can't hurt us. I reckon by now we can tackle anything thrown at us, don't you?"

"So that's a vote for just staying here, then?"

"Why not?" She pushed back from the table, and they stood as one.

"What do you say we stick around, and exorcise a few ghosts?" Putting her arms around his neck, she reached up on tiptoe and brushed her lips against the sweet spot on his neck, drawing a soft hiss of pleasure from his lips. "Then, if we still feel wobbly, we'll hit the Dorchester."

She took his hand, and silently led him up the stairs. Once inside her old bedroom, she undressed him, taking her time, enjoying his body. He watched her as she quickly shucked off her clothes, leaving them where they fell.

The big bed wrapped around them like a security blanket, and Sydney took him in her arms and pulled him down to her. "Let's run those demons out of town," she whispered.

He hummed his approval. "The Devil in Miss Chapin," he purred, and slipped deliciously inside her.

At the end of the week, after all his obligations had been fulfilled, Dahlra suggested a walk through St James Park. Knowing London's fickle and capricious weather, Sydney donned a pair of flat-heeled, thigh-high leather boots, weatherproofed and comfortable. A calf-length, gored skirt in RAF Blue and a bronze silk cardi completed her ensemble. As she presented herself to her lover, Dahlra's warm look of appreciation was all the compliment she needed.

Sydney applauded his choices as well: while it was true he rocked a suit like a boss, he still looked fantastic in full Maidenvine mufti mode— lightweight burgundy cashmere jumper, slacks in deep charcoal, and black Chelsea boots.

They stopped at a little café near New Scotland Yard to have lunch and to people-watch. Later, they walked arm in arm toward the Tube Station, planning the evening, strolling in leisurely contrast to those rushing from place to place around them. They met with several approving looks from both sexes.

As they entered the train carriage, Dahlra favoured her with a secret smile, and Sydney felt her face grow warm at the memory of that long-ago day when he stood behind her in the carriage, and whispered his desires and intentions. She still got a thrill thinking about it, and judging from the heated look in his eyes, he did too. *Serves you right*, she thought. She had nearly spontaneously combusted on that bloody train. Having already acted upon quite a few of the suggestions he had made that day, Sydney relaxed and enjoyed the solid, comfortable warmth of his body beside her, without any of the nervy, straining lust she had experienced at the time.

They got off at South Ken, and headed down the long, underground pedestrian tunnel that led to Old Brompton Road. Dahlra suddenly stopped and gently pressed Sydney into one of the recessed alcoves. It shielded them from anyone not walking directly in front of them, and she allowed herself to indulge his attentions. Looking deeply into her eyes, he lowered his head to hers for a long, slow, lingering kiss. His warm, soft lips suckled against hers with languid decadence, as if they were in the privacy of their bedroom and he had all night to explore her.

Then he pulled away, and solemnly took her hand. They continued walking, she following coltishly along after him, until he forced marched her into another recess. This kiss was explosive, plundering, erotically charged, driving a spike of desire into her loins that left her breathless and clinging to him. His hips ground against hers, his bone hard erection backing her into the alcove with proprietary, dominant lust.

The urgency of his attentions, along with the feeling of being so exposed, made her edgy and self-conscious. "As much as I'm enjoying this," she breathed, between his ardent, demanding kisses, "the Old Bill are going to ask us to get a room, you know. Not that I'm complaining."

He raised his head from her neck, gazing down at her with flashing eyes. "You're mine to do with as I want, my girl. If I want to fuck you against this wall, I'll do it, and I promise you'll enjoy it."

"I'm sure I will. Right up until we get arrested and sent to separate detention centres." He laughed with her as he took her hands, and lured her away from the wall. They continued strolling down the tunnel, arm in arm.

As they neared the next recessed wall, Sydney noted that the overhead light above this alcove was burned out, making it a darkened cave virtually invisible to passersby. Dahlra stopped and pushed her against the wall once more.

"Actually, I think I *will* fuck you against this one." His thigh slid between hers, and he nuzzled her ear, murmuring, "Would you like that, pet? Hmm?" His voice was full of rich and dangerous secrets. "Come on, Sydney," he coaxed. "Why not right here, right now?"

What the fuck are you doing? she silently mouthed. He trapped her within the cage of his body, his palms pressed flat on the bricks on either side of her head. "Yes, I'm definitely going to fuck you here, little one."

There was a soft sound of brick rasping against stone. The wall behind her abruptly shifted, making her stagger backward. She jumped in alarm. "What the hell?"

Almost silently, the alcove swung away, revealing a doorway. Beyond that was nothing but an inky, grey-black hole.

As she peered into the impenetrable darkness beyond the opened wall, Dahlra drew closer, until their bodies were touching. She looked up at him in confusion; his eyes were brightly intense. "I want to give you a very special gift tonight," he said. "Do you trust me?"

She nodded silently. He grasped her head in his hands and tilted her face up to his. He looked deadly serious. "You are in a place that requires an answer, my darling girl. Do. You. Trust. Me?"

Sydney studied him carefully. He was practically thrumming with a mixture of excitement and something harder to define. She thought it might even be apprehension, but he was hard to read. "Yes, sir. I trust you. You know I do."

"Then come with me." He took her hand, and quickly pulled her through the door. Once they were inside, the wall swung back into place, leaving them in complete, claustrophobic darkness. A series of overhead lights flickered on with a low, metallic buzz, filling the area with faint, ghostly illumination. One by one, the lights appeared, like phosphorescent moons, gradually revealing a long tunnel before them.

The space was cool, and smelled of damp earth. Sydney could hear the occasional rumble of Tube trains around her. Her eyes adjusted, and the light revealed the rounded walls of an abandoned Underground service tunnel. Peering down its length, she could just make out a pinpoint glow of light, down at the far end.

Dahlra pressed against her back, his arms stealing around her waist. "I have a little surprise for you. One I hope you'll enjoy."

Even with his arms around her, Sydney felt a bit creeped out. The old abandoned Tube lines weren't called 'ghost stations' for nothing. The place was spooky deluxe, and even with the thin, eerie glow of the overheads, she couldn't seem to get her bearings. In the almost-darkness, Dahlra's pale face seemed to float like an apparition. "What is this? Where exactly are we?"

"We're in a place where we can be anything we want to be. We're in a place where all your dirtiest fantasies can come true. Even the ones you keep from yourself." His voice was low and close to her ear, more a vibration than a real sound. He pinned her arms to her sides, and pressed his lips against hers. "And since you've placed your trust in me, you'll be richly rewarded, I promise you."

She smiled in the darkness, her heart tripping merrily in swing time. *Now that's more like it.* He was seducing her with knowledge, feeding her lust for it, and at the same time, teasing her arousal for his Dominance. Nothing got her jacked up like Dahlra's games.

He turned her around. "Do you see the light ahead?" He pointed down toward the end of the long tunnel. "Answer me." He nipped at her earlobe.

She peered into the distance. There was a concentrated light far down the tunnel, but she could not tell if it was one hundred feet or one hundred yards away. "Yes."

The pressure on her earlobe increased; not enough to hurt, but enough to remind her who was in charge. "You called me *Master* at Ramcat. I liked it. That is how you will address me here. Or, if you prefer, *Sir*." The clipped tone in his deep voice, half caress and half spank, made a physical, visceral impact to her body. Sydney felt her heartbeat grow heavy, as if her blood had turned thick and hot in her veins.

"Yes, Master."

"Right answer." He gave her bottom a fond pat and propelled her forward. "Walk toward the light."

Sydney focused on the light at the far end, and walked.

It seemed forever before the bluish-tinted light grew closer, and Sydney increased her pace in anticipation. Immediately, she was grabbed from behind; Dahlra was still right behind her. It was hard to believe he had been that close. Then again, it was hard to hear anything beyond her rapidly beating heart,

"I said slowly. If you won't obey me, you'll have to be punished." His hands slid across her belly and he bent her forward. "Shall I spank you right here, in the darkness?" His touch ignited Sydney's nerve endings, and sweet, erotic excitement juddered through her.

Struggling to think past the hum of adrenaline buzzing in her bloodstream, Sydney pushed against him, and he playfully smacked her arse. He stroked her, caressing her breasts and hips, and she wriggled against him, longing for some sort of friction to scratch that itch. She was stupendously turned on.

His growl of pleasure echoed in the tunnel. "You're making it very easy for me to want to punish you. Now will you be a good girl and do what I command?"

"Yes, Master." She rolled her hips against him once more.

He smacked her bum again, and laughed his deep, sexy chuckle. "Dirty little girl. Now walk, and start undressing. I want you naked by the time I can see you clearly in the light."

As she resumed her walk, she unbuttoned her cardi, removed it, and draped it across her arm.

"Drop it." The garment landed on the hard-packed surface, and Sydney continued her slow march. She unhooked her bra, and slid it from her shoulders. She held the bra out at arm's length for two steps, then dropped it as well. Her nipples grew impossibly tight in the cool, rushing air.

"Now that's more like it, my pet. Oh, yes. Make Master enjoy it." He could not have sounded more teasingly dangerous if he tried.

Sydney felt her world tilt a little as arousal wound an unbroken ribbon of sensation from her tight nipples down into her sex. Three steps later, she unzipped her skirt. As it dropped to the ground, she broke her stride to step out of it. Lastly, she lowered her knickers, bending over, making sure he had a good, long look at her upturned backside. She heard him swear under his breath.

Oh, yeah. If you want a show, Master *Dahlra, I'll give you one.* She straightened her spine, and began to saunter down the long, dark corridor toward the light.

"Very, very nice." The deep, disembodied voice was silky and lasciviously approving. "You look absolutely delicious wearing nothing but those boots, my dear. I think I'll let you leave them on. Keep going. I'll be right behind you."

When Sydney was a little girl, she read the Greek myth of Orpheus, the renowned musician who had gone into the underworld to persuade Hades to allow his dead lover, Eurydice, to return to the land of the living with him. Hades had allowed it—providing Orpheus didn't look back to make sure his lady love was following him. Unfortunately,

Orpheus had been unable to resist the temptation to check over his shoulder, and thus he lost his Eurydice forever. It was a parable of trust, of bargaining with darkness and the devil, of having faith in one's abilities to change the course of life itself.

She had never understood why Orpheus didn't show a little self-discipline, instead of blowing his chance. She appreciated him a little better now. Every fiber of her being begged her to look back, to locate Dahlra, but she resisted. It was one thing to be in this mysterious place, but the idea that he had brought her into this underworld where who knows what awaited her—that he was behind her, watching her—well, it truly was a turn-on of proportions as mythical as Orpheus himself.

Without clothing, Sydney felt incredibly free and feral. There was something about literally shedding her inhibitions in this place that made her throw her head back and enjoy herself. Dahlra's hum of appreciation proved she wasn't the only one.

"My, my, how you do strut, little girl. Perhaps you should walk around naked more often." His tone was a little strained, as if being in control wasn't all it was cracked up to be. Sydney felt a thrill of power; she was exciting him, turning the dial to eleven, and didn't *that* just get her motor greased up and purring?

She reached a mesh-grilled door, and grasped the handle. The door was locked. Something slid over the back of her leg; it was cold, and sharp, like a knife, and it left an icy contrail as it glided over her skin. It traveled around the curve of her hip, then came into her line of sight. It was a large skeleton key, and the cold metal bit snagged on her erect nipple, making it tingle.

"The last time I gave you a key was the night we became lovers. You put on quite a little show then as well, didn't you? You walked halfway up the stairs, then turned around and kissed it. Do you remember?"

"Like it was yesterday," Sydney whispered.

"Mmm, so do I. There are many keys in our world. This is one of them. Another special room for us." He stroked her bare shoulders, then moved the key lower, down her belly. "Do you wish to come through that door with me?"

"Yes, sir."

"I hoped you would." He softly commanded, "Spread your legs."

She moved her feet slightly apart. "Open up," he whispered playfully, and then he did something so sinfully wicked with it that she was brought up on her tip-toes. She grasped the mesh door to keep from staggering. "Oh, *fuuuck*, you're a devil."

With their eyes locked, he licked the key, still wet from her juices. "And you're as sweet as candy..."

He inserted the key into its lock, and slowly turned it. It made a heavy, clanking noise that echoed sharply in the tunnel. The door obligingly swung open; even the squeaking of the hinges sounded menacing. He stepped aside, and placed a warm hand on her shoulder. "You walk in on your own. But I'll be right beside you."

Taking a deep breath, Sydney stepped over the threshold, and into the lair of the devil himself.

Though smaller than Ramcat's Catacombs, it was a large space which left her in no doubt as to its purpose. It was bathed in a low light that pulsed almost imperceptibly, casting sinister shadows over the furniture. "Well, hell," she whispered, awed. She was surrounded by every instrument of every kink known to man.

A highly polished, X-shaped St Andrews cross dominated one end of the room; at the other was a leather-covered rack, bristling with restraints. Candles in every colour stood on a shelf, their sides decorated with long strings of dried wax. To her left was a cupboard with a plethora of toys in differing sizes and implementations; floggers of every kind, including whips, straps, and chains. Clamps, masks, gloves, handcuffs, ropes, blindfolds and gags of every shape and size hung from individual pegs.

There was a strange chair sitting on a raised platform beside the cross; it was low to the floor, with arms that floated independently of the rest of the chair. The bottom was hinged in the middle, so that each half could be swung apart, and it had panels on either side that could be lifted into place, extending the width of the seat. It was also embellished with restraints.

A padded bench with a curved ledge on one end and large leather straps on the other sat low to the ground. Like a set of stocks, it could restrain someone's neck and legs. Smaller leather straps were attached to the foot of the stool to hold wrists in place. There were spreader bars and harnesses of every shape and length and description.

An open-faced cupboard contained boxes of latex gloves, alcohol wipes and sterile needles. Sitting on the shelves were pinwheels, retractors that looked like huge curved forks, straight razors, specula, sounding rods, dental dams and other medical implements. A pristinely white butler's sink sat beneath a cupboard containing instruments which Sydney knew well. Before Dahlra arrived, some had been used on her in the cell.

She took a deep breath, and continued her reccie.

A door to their right showed a bathroom tiled in black and white. A tall metal hook on wheels, like the ones used to hold IV bags, could be seen just inside the door, and for some reason that made Sydney feel both hot and cold at once. Through another door at the far end of the dungeon, Sydney could see the large post of a bed. Anchored around its base were scarves and leather straps. A surprisingly inviting sofa faced the cross and the chair.

Soho sex shops weren't this well-stocked; movie sets weren't this detailed. Hell, even Ramcat's various chambers of depravity weren't this well-appointed. Polished wood, shining chrome, fine leather, soft silk, gleaming needles—they all looked top quality, and they all looked well-used. This place was the real deal.

She became marginally aware of low, hypnotic, almost chanting music. It pulsed in time with the light, seducing the senses and flooding the room with menace. Sydney knew the entire setup was a mind-fuck, carefully constructed to create drama and high tension. This room could inspire either numbing dread, or crippling pleasure, depending on the acting host. Every physical and mental response was catered to and taken into consideration.

Any Dom or sub could lose themselves in here, enjoying experiences they had never previously known themselves to crave. Looking around, taking in every implement, surface and shadow, Sydney felt excitement warring with trepidation. It heightened with the submission the room demanded. The atmosphere itself commanded her surrender.

If she told Dahlra she wanted to leave, he would respect her no less, love her with no less passion. But he had brought her here for the same reason he did everything—to ensure her happiness, to encourage her to open herself to new experiences, to bring her greater pleasure and stretch her imagination.

Sydney knew she was facing another one of those crossroads moments, not only in her relationship with Dahlra, but in her own self-discovery. Choosing to stay meant accepting the part of herself that wanted to go beyond the realm of everything she had managed to steer clear of during her time at Ramcat, everything she had avoided within her own psyche. There would be no hitting the reset button, no pretending she hadn't known what to expect.

It would mean releasing that tiger from its cage, and dealing with its snarling aftermath, if and when it could be restrained again. In this extraordinary room, something extraordinary would happen.

"Good evening, Ms Chapin." Sydney spun in the direction of the unfamiliar voice. From deep within the shadows on the far side of the room, a man approached them. He was dressed entirely in black: black duster coat, black shirt, black tie, black trousers, black shoes. His hair was so black it shone blue in the light. It was tied in a queue at the nape of his neck, and escaping strands hung loose on either side of his still, angular face.

His pale skin and large nose made him look Greek or Black Irish, but Sydney would later discover he was of Romany gypsy stock. No one could have ever accused him of being classically handsome—his face was too long, and his large nose too prominent. His mouth was well-defined, even expressive, but only a step away from cruel. Arresting was the only word that came to mind; for out-and-out charisma, he outdid even Dahlra. He certainly had the proud, arrogant alpha male persona down pat.

There was a powerful, ominous air about him. *If there really is such a thing as a vampire,* Sydney thought, *you would be the perfect prototype.*

He looked down at her from his stunning height with cool eyes as black as his hair. While his posture was relaxed, the very air around him seemed to shimmer. And while he had neither done nor said anything beyond his greeting, Sydney could easily believe he was capable of morphing into one vicious sonuvabitch if properly motivated.

The silent connection between them felt like an electric current. His flat, challenging stare made Sydney itch to say something, do *anything,* to make him react, but hell, she was pinned to the floor by those black, unreadable eyes boring into her with total, focused concentration. She was in his lair, naked, except for a pair of boots, waiting for her lover to tell her what the hell was going on.

Sydney knew only one thing for sure: she was too juiced up not to stick around for this.

As if their host had read her thoughts, a slow smile spread across his face. "Please allow me to introduce myself. I'm Elwess Talbert."

CHAPTER EIGHTEEN

The Mentor

Sydney had always hypothesised that the legends surrounding Elwess Talbert's sexual prowess were so outrageous, they must be the product of a good copy editor—most likely Elwess himself. Nobody could be *that* good. It was said he was the entire package: a physical, mental and verbal Top, and very good at what he did—some said the best. She risked a glance into his dark, intelligent eyes, and wondered if she might have to rethink her theory.

Elwess was very still, but very, very alert. He looked like a man in complete control of every aspect of his environment—including her. Finally, he moved out of the shadows, and Sydney got a little better look at him. He appeared about five years younger and stood at least two inches taller than Dahlra. Their coloring was alike, but there the similarities ended.

Whereas Dahlra was light and shade, porcelain beauty and elegance, Elwess was severe, mysterious, eagle-beautiful. He had the sparse, wiry build of a street fighter, all lean, powerful-looking limbs, large feet and graceful hands. The bridge of his prominent nose had been broken and reset at least twice. He looked like a man grown comfortable in his own skin, and one used to being obeyed.

Elwess' eyes moved over her body with slow deliberation, and his expression was so completely alien Sydney honestly couldn't tell if he liked or disliked what he saw. She made herself relax. She wasn't helpless, though the two men were obviously larger and could potentially overpower her. She wasn't in a dangerous situation, although the atmosphere of the room was calibrated to scream menace. Despite her lack of clothing, and Elwess' BAMF reputation, she knew she was ultimately in control here.

Placing his hands on her shoulders, Dahlra faced their host, who had remained clay-soldier still. "You've both wanted to meet one another. I decided now was the time to introduce you. Elwess is my friend as well as my mentor. Besides you, Sydney, he is the only person I truly trust."

Sydney extended her hand to Elwess. *Never let 'em see you sweat, Syd.*

"I've been looking forward to meeting you, but I can see your reputation doesn't do you justice."

He didn't really react; if anything, he gave her an eyeful of 'I've got your number.' He took her proffered hand as if to shake it; instead, he brought it to his lips and kissed it, making the courtly gesture at once decadent, and strangely formal. His lips lingered just long enough for Sydney to feel the rush of air ghosting against her skin, as he inhaled her scent. Black eyes, snapping with amusement, flicked upward toward hers.

"Shall I take that as a compliment, Ms Chapin?" His voice carried the same deep, purring cadence that made Dahlra's so enticing.

"It was intended as one." Sydney was relieved at how cool she sounded. It would never do to appear flustered in front of a man like Elwess. She had a feeling he liked chewing up little girls for breakfast; in any case, he would do everything in his power to make her think so.

He straightened and released her hand. And then he smiled, a slow, sexy smile that zoomed right into her belly, riding on a wave of dirty thoughts and wicked intentions. It was calculated to make any room he was in feel ten degrees warmer, and guaranteed to make a good woman sin—or at least give it serious thought.

"Then I'll accept it as such. In any case, welcome to my home." He glanced around, still rocking that Smooth Operator vibe. "I call this particular room The Chine."

"Chine? As in Blackgang Chine?"

"Well, it has provided me with a great deal of amusement over the years. And the rides are a little more intense than your average theme park." He spoke in a slow, drawling, flirtatious way that had the feel of an oft-said, carefully rehearsed statement. It didn't take away from the sex factor, though. "And the price of admission is non-negotiable."

"How so?"

"Admission is submission." He tilted his head, a very cryptic smile playing on his lips. "In any case, I've been looking forward to your visit. It's not every day a lowly toiler in the Agency vineyards has a chance to play host to the great Sydney Chapin."

"Oh, I'm just another grape stomper myself. But *you*, now, you're the famous one—I don't think there's a Fet community in the country, maybe even the world, who hasn't heard of you."

Elwess seemed genuinely amused. "The world, you say?" He cocked a dark, well-sculptured brow, and inclined his head in a slight bow. "I'm flattered. But you must admit, your reputation is very impressive. And the Liggons think very highly of you, which is one of the strongest endorsements you could receive, as far as I'm concerned." Without the Big Bad Voodoo Daddy glare, his eyes were surprisingly expressive. "Did you know there is a Japanese sub in residence at Ramcat who calls you *Hayabusa-san*?"

"No, but I hope it means something nice."

"It means 'the Peregrine'."

Abashed, Sydney replied, "Makes me sound like a superhero."

"To her, you are."

"You are to a lot of people," Dahlra added.

Warmed by the regard she heard in his voice, Sydney replied, "While I always enjoy meeting members of the mutual admiration society, I do feel obligated to remind you I'm just a woman, like any other, doing her job."

"*Just* a woman, Ms Chapin? I doubt you could ever be 'just a woman,' especially where Dahlra is concerned." Elwess' gaze warmed to an intensity that was undeniably compelling in its focus. "Your Minder is also my friend. And I have you to thank you for that as well."

"How so?"

"You saved his life."

It was probably the first genuine thing he had said to her since he arrived. It actually made Sydney feel even more naked. It was as if he was trying to read her tells, seeing if she lived up to *her* rep. With that thought came the sudden, certain feeling in her waters that they weren't visiting Elwess Talbert just to inspect this Chine of his. Any lingering traces of doubt were removed with his next words.

"I hope you and I will become friends as well." He stepped closer, those riveting eyes boring into hers.

"I didn't think Dominants and submissives did the 'friend' thing."

"I think it all boils down to the definitions of Dominance and submission, as well as friendship, kitten."

"I suppose that's what I'm here to learn." Almost to herself, she muttered, "I have the feeling tonight's going to be a real education."

He responded with that low, sexy chuckle. "At the risk of sounding patronising, I think I understand why Dahlra Gar loves you so much.

You're really quite remarkable."

"Remarkable is a pretty strong word for someone you just met."

"I like to think of myself as a good judge of character. Besides, it isn't flattery if it's true."

Self-consciously, Sydney crossed her arms protectively over her breasts. Elwess grasped her wrists and pulled her arms down to her sides. In an admonishing tone, he murmured, "Now isn't the time for modesty, kitten. Surely you wouldn't deny us your beauty at this stage."

"I'm a little cold," she protested.

"You won't be, soon enough," replied Dahlra.

Elwess gently tipped Sydney's face toward his. "You're very beautiful, you know. And very desirable. Your pretty face, alight with pleasure... or pain..." He teased Sydney's jaw with his long, slender fingers. "It must be *quite* breathtaking."

'I can assure you, Sir," Dahlra answered softly, with a possessive stroke of her hair. "It most certainly is."

And with that, Elwess changed again. Sydney watched as he transformed from the approachable, if imposing friend, back to the Dominant that she'd heard so much about.

He stepped back, and idly leaned against one of the beams of the St Andrews Cross. "I will find it *most* enjoyable to give you pleasure... *and* pain."

His long fingers tapped idly against the intersection of the beams. The gesture was not lost on Sydney. She really didn't want to give him any more satisfaction of knowing he was geeing her up in the worst way, but in her heart of hearts, she knew she wasn't hiding it very well.

"Safe word?"

After the slightest of hesitations, Dahlra answered, "Inigo Lightoller."

"Naturally. A passion-killer if ever there was one. Let's make sure you don't use your safe word tonight."

"Best not to give me any reason to say it, then, huh?"

"Oh, I can assure you, kitten, you'll have plenty of reasons to say it," Elwess purred, sounding like the biggest cat daddy in the jungle, "and just as many reasons not to. I can't wait to try both."

Sydney could not think of one blessed thing to say in reply to *that*. With his dark insinuations and his dirty smile, he was pushing a lot of buttons she had not even known she was wearing. Elwess may have been Dahlra's mentor, but he had not taught him everything there was to know about being a sexual Dominant. Dahlra's natural instinct for nurture and affection tempered everything he did, up to and including Dominating her. Elwess, of course, had no such agenda. His Dominance over them both was intimidating, to say the least.

She turned away from Elwess, and back to the one man she completely trusted to have her best interests at heart. "I'm not exactly reassured by that."

Dahlra unbuckled his belt and laid it on the table. He looked sexed-up and hungry as he caressed her. "I want to give you something very special tonight. Something that will leave you in no doubt just what your happiness means to me."

Before she could reply, Elwess closed the space between the three of them. He caressed her back, and Sydney could feel his breath gust softly against her skin. "Fear isn't necessarily a bad thing, kitten. A little fear can take you places even lust can't. And so can I."

He put his arms about her waist and pulled her flush against his chest, which only made her more aware of her nudity. His body was lean and hard; he smelled of expensive cologne and testosterone.

Behind her, Elwess enclosed her like a room with no door. Sydney's heart clipped into overdrive as his long fingers slid over the scarred ridges of her back. It was daunting to be surrounded by that much scary maleness, but also strangely empowering as well. Between the two men, she suddenly felt very, very desirable.

She looked into Dahlra's searching eyes, and he seemed to find what he was looking for. He nodded briefly to his friend. Together they looked like two powerful lions eyeing their prey, and it was a dead cert she was the main course.

Elwess spun her around and slowly guided her toward the cross. Sydney winced as her warm back met the cool wood surface, and goosebumps rose over her body. Dahlra mistook her physical reaction for an emotional one. "Sydney, you are safe. Elwess and I would never hurt you—"

"Oh, never say never, Sir." Elwess' eyes raked over her salaciously.

Dahlra gave the younger man a warning look. "That is not why we are here. This is *my* lover, not one of your slaves to humiliate."

Elwess afforded them the most jaded eye roll Sydney had ever witnessed on a man. "Really. Ms Chapin will think I'm planning on cooking her. I'm a Dominant, not a monster."

"And I am *her* Dominant." Dahlra eyes flashed green fire. And in that instant, he took over. There was no other way to describe it. He blazed, incandescent, dimming Elwess' power and Dominance, but Sydney could never say if it was relinquished involuntarily.

"I brought Sydney here to drown in pleasure." Dahlra looked deeply into her eyes. "And that is what you shall do, my girl."

"She will indeed." Far from looking offended, Elwess looked rather pleased. He placed his hand on his heart and gave a slight bow, answering, "I am completely at your service, Sir."

Dahlra imperiously turned away from him. He focused his formidable attention on Sydney; eyes full of power, nostrils flaring, a smile of satisfaction on his lips. "And so are you, *kitten*," he growled slowly.

And then, bloody hell. He *winked* at her.

"Oh, my God." Sydney wasn't sure if she pulled or he pushed, but she was suddenly slammed against the cross, and Dahlra was grinding against her, devouring her with a kiss so blinding everything they had done up to that point felt like a dress rehearsal. She bunched his jumper in her fists, pulling him to her greedily, wanting him more than she had ever wanted anything in her life. Her body was glowing like the Blackpool Illuminations. *Thunderbirds are definitely GO—*

In only the vaguest sense was she aware of Elwess taking up a position behind the cross. She felt his breath ghosting over her neck, and the twin sensations of Dahlra's mouth on hers and Elwess' against her nape tore an impressive noise from her throat.

"I want very badly to bind you." Elwess' strong hands kneaded her shoulders, even as she ground against Dahlra. "If you promise to be a good little girl, I won't do it. But I don't think you can be good enough for me. After all," he chuckled, "I'm just looking for any excuse."

He reached around the arms of the cross, and cupped her breasts in his long, slender hands. Desire rolled over her like a wave of heat, making her gasp.

"Do it, then."

They grasped her wrists, and bound them onto the beams of the cross, their movements swift and efficient. The cuffs were padded, but they gave no room for movement. She sagged back against the cross, feeling her heart beating fast and hard against the surface.

Elwess stepped away, out of her range of vision. When he returned, he was holding a flogger made of long strips of black leather. "Perhaps you'd like a little appetiser before we begin?"

As she stood there, completely at their mercy, Sydney understood and appreciated the little drizzle of fear they had infused into this heady mix of excitement and submission. Her senses were blazing; she could feel every bite of the cuffs, every nick and splinter in the wood against her back.

Dahlra slid his large warm hands down her raised arms and cupped her breasts. As his thumbs stroked her nipples to rock-hard peaks, he leaned in close. "How do you feel, my girl? Naughty? Dirty? Like a little slave for us to play with, hmm?"

"She doesn't have to answer. I can see it. I can smell it," Elwess answered with a sneer of lust.

Dahlra hummed in response. "So can I. And it's delicious. I could eat you up, you delectable girl." With a biting, licking kiss, he stepped away from the cross.

Elwess gave Sydney a smile of pure depravity as he readied the flogger. "Get ready, kitten."

Suddenly, the room seemed to tilt, and the heady, out-of-body arousal state turned to ice in her blood. In her mind, a memory snapped into unnerving, solid-state focus. *She had been bound then as well, and the man was beating her to death.*

"Get ready, doll."

She remembered what happened next. The pain had been inhuman. Her back...

"Oh." Sydney watched the excitement drain from Dahlra's face, as realisation dawned. In slow motion, Sydney saw the flogger dance through the air, and she gritted her teeth and flinched—

"Stop!"

Dahlra caught Elwess' arm on the downswing. Then he was at her side, soothing her, stroking her hair. "Sydney, this is not that moment."

Harsh, unnatural laughter welled up in her throat. "I know it isn't. I did mean to kill the buzz. I'm fine, I'm fine, really, I'm not afraid." She felt angry at her own reaction. "I'm not scared, dammit, I'm not—"

"Say the word, my darling girl. I'll release you. This is supposed to be exciting, not regressive." Behind him, Elwess nodded in agreement.

Sydney took a deep, steadying breath, examining her own headspace. *Great. Talk about a one-woman Morale Suppression Team.* She risked a glance up at Elwess, who was watching her intently, his expression impassive. Sydney felt the slow creep of embarrassment staining her cheeks.

"Yeah, big bad agent. Able to catch speeding bullets with my teeth. Some peregrine I turned out to be."

Dahlra started to speak, but Elwess beat him to it. "I know all about what happened, Sydney. You endured things I couldn't even begin to imagine." His eyes were calm. "Neither of us wants you to revisit that hell, especially not here."

"I couldn't stop it then," Dahlra said. "But I can now."

"I know you couldn't, but you were right. This *isn't* that moment anymore." The panic dissipated as quickly as it had arrived. "I asked for this. And I'm not afraid, because Elwess is right. You would never allow him to hurt me."

"My brave, brave girl." Dahlra took her face in his hands. "Thank you for trusting me. I have never loved you more than I do right now."

"I know," she replied feverishly. "I love you, too."

Dahlra stared at her, stunned. "Say it again."

"I love you," she repeated.

The anxiety left his face. "Again," he commanded.

The anxiety disappeared, replaced by something wonderful. "I love you, Dahlra Gar. And I want you, and I need you, and I know whatever happens here tonight isn't going to change any of those statements one iota." She looked into his handsome face, blown away by her own revelations. "And you won't have to do all the heavy lifting tonight. I want you to enjoy yourself too, because goddammit, I'm going to."

His answer was a swift, explosive kiss that burst her open, feasted on her, replenished itself with her. He moaned ecstatically into her mouth, and she answered his moan with a plea.

With his lips against hers, he whispered playfully, "Now that you've made me very happy, let's recap why you are here tonight, my beautiful submissive."

Elwess had already retrieved the flogger from a nearby table. "And why *are* you here, submissive?"

Suddenly, Sydney understood Elwess' question. He was as protective of Dahlra as Dahlra was of her. And *that* went a long way toward putting him in her good books.

"I'm here to show Dahlra how much I love him."

"No." He looked at her with something like reproach. "You are here to learn exactly how much he loves *you*. And the answer is this."

The flogger sang through the air, and at its final descent, he snapped it back with a skillful flick of his wrist. The very tips of the straps slashed across her belly in a quick, capricious snap. The sting was immediate, breathtaking, and in light of what had transpired, so unexpectedly intense it almost felt like an orgasm. All the breath left her lungs in a gasp of pure exhilaration.

Like everyone else, Sydney had received her share of epiphanies. It was not the first time she'd been shaken by one of those irrevocable, tectonic shifts in the ley-lines of her life, but it was by far one of the most life-changing. Pinned like a butterfly to Elwess Talbert's St Andrews cross, her skin tingling from the first slap of a leather flogger, her words of love still drying its wings in the air, Sydney knew she had just passed from surrender into full-on acceptance. She also knew exactly what Elwess wanted her to do—what she *needed* to do, to make everything right.

"Dahlra."

"I'm here, love."

"I want you to do it." She shot the words like an arrow into the room. "I want you to whip me. Only you."

He never took his eyes from hers, even as Elwess placed the flogger in his hand. Her breasts, her thighs, her belly, all felt the exquisite sting of the flogger. Occasionally, Elwess' voice could be heard, quietly instructing Dahlra in a more efficient wrist movement, a better grip to exert more control, but to Sydney, the only person in the room that mattered was her Minder.

She could feel a thousand little pinpoints of stinging, sweet pain. Her body twisted and jerked when the leather bit hard into too-tender flesh. She saw the faces of the two men, absorbed, totally focused on her.

And just at the point where the endorphins were burning out of her system, and the stinging leather turned fierce and grating, Dahlra tossed the flogger aside and was on her in two strides, his mouth tearing hers open, drawing her tongue hard into his mouth. He ravished her mouth with his own, nipping, licking, sucking her bottom lip into his mouth with a little, teasing bite that turned her hips to sponge, her blood to fire.

She delved between his warm, parted lips with her tongue to explore him. "The next time." She gasped between his suffocating kisses. "The next time, it will be you. It will be you here, and I'll be holding the flogger—"

"Oh, God, yes." He moaned into her mouth, clasping her head in his hands. "Fucking hell, yes, Sydney—"

He stepped back, and another set of hands ghosted over her belly as Elwess stepped into his place. He leaned in, capturing her mouth with his.

It was a kiss like none she'd ever experienced. His surprisingly soft lips suckled her own, nuzzling her with sensual, teasing caresses. It started slow, a dance of ducking, swooping, suckling contact that nearly took the top of her head off. Long, slim fingers slid through her hair, tilting her head, instructing her on how to fully enjoy him. He deepened the kiss, opening her piece by piece, searching for more, his warm, soft tongue easing into her mouth, forcing a moan from her. The saddle between her thighs grew hotter and wetter.

He plundered her, drawing her out of herself until she was straining toward him. He grew more insistent, more demanding. His tongue slid into her mouth and she sucked on it wantonly, her body aching for some other contact. A part of her mind knew these were not the love-fueled kisses of her lover, but the practiced actions of a man well-versed in the art of arousal and abandon, but she didn't give a damn. Hadn't her own Dominant instructed her to enjoy herself? He had stated his objectives; it was obvious Elwess was more than capable of meeting them.

He drew back and licked his lips. He no longer looked the part of the smirking, controlled Dominant. His eyes covetously roamed over her body.

"Fuck me, but I want you, Sydney Chapin." He swiped her bottom lip with his tongue, drawing away when she tried to chase after him. "You have a gorgeous mouth. I'd like to feel those beautiful lips on my cock. Would you, kitten? Would you suck me with that perfect mouth?"

"What do you think, sir?"

"Then show me," he commanded, and slid his thumb between her lips. "Show me how you'd suck me."

She closed her eyes and swirled her tongue around the pad of his thumb, lightly scraping her bottom teeth against his skin. He tasted clean and warm, and she rapturously licked the flesh of his thumb.

"Oh, yes, I'm definitely going to want some of that." He slowly pulled away, and Dahlra stepped in to reclaim his kiss. Sydney eagerly accepted it, growling as he pulled out of reach.

"You always did love tormenting me."

"Oh, we haven't begun to torment you yet. Close your eyes. Unless you'd prefer to be blindfolded."

Obediently, she did as he commanded. She was once again suspended in darkness, drawn taut and edgy against the cross in an ecstasy of expectation. At once, two mouths descended on her hypersensitive nipples, sending a sizzling wire of sensation from her breasts to her core. She cried out, shocked at the exquisite, almost painful pleasure. She opened her eyes and saw two dark heads, close together. Their eyes were closed, long eyelashes beautiful against pale skin. Elwess' tongue curled round her nipple, as Dahlra sucked and nipped at its twin. Both men seemed utterly absorbed, utterly entranced.

She whimpered her lover's name, and Dahlra raised his head. "Tell me, love. Tell me, and I'll make it happen."

"Oh, please, I need..." A sharp nip of teeth shorted out her wiring, garbling her words into something unintelligible.

"I'm afraid you'll have to be a little more specific, my love."

She groaned, banging her head against the cross in frustration. "You know what I want."

He had the audacity to laugh. "Oh, yes, love. I do. But you must tell me what you want. You know I'll give it to you."

She was ready to announce it on BBC4. "Lick me. Make love to me. Fuck me!" The last of her inhibitions burned away. "Please, sir, make me come."

He nuzzled against her cheek. "Master Elwess, would you like to do the honours?"

"Yes, I would." He dropped to his knees, and Sydney felt the warm rush of breath against her belly. "Spread yourself nice and wide for me, kitten." Her thighs parted like water. "Oh, there's a good girl. Such sweet little petals," he slurred thickly, as if made drunk by her. "I've been looking forward to this."

He ran the tip of his tongue over her hypersensitive flesh. Her body arched, as if hit with a taser, and his low, dirty laugh vibrated through her as the mini-orgasm torched her brain like a match to paper.

He laved her gently at first; feathery, fluttery flicks that teased bliss into her nerve endings and bathed her in the promise of more to come. He took his time, allowing the slow buildup of her arousal, reducing her entire vocabulary to 'please,' and 'fuck.'

Suddenly he made a low, dark sound in his throat. He abandoned his slow, sensuous seduction and dove into her with a moan of lust, his lips and tongue enclosing the seat of her pleasure. He suckled it like a nipple, flicking his tongue against the scrap of flesh until she was nearly insensate.

She lost count of how many times he led her to the precipice of orgasm, only to back off and start over. She only knew a coil of pleasure was twisting, tightening inside her.

"It is good, my precious girl? Is he giving you what you need?" Her answer was incoherent as Dahlra grasped her face in his hands, kissing her deeply, savagely, leaving her moaning with ecstasy. His fingers fondled her nipples, milking and tugging them until they were diamond-hard beneath his touch. "Yes, I thought so, my dirty little girl. The higher you ride it, the greater will be the release."

It was impossible to remain silent against the onslaught of the two men. She keened as the tension doubled in intensity, the coil tightening, ratcheting into a wave as deep and intense as the epicentre of an earthquake.

Something snapped loose within, and she nearly sobbed against his warm throat. "Please, D-Dahlra," she rasped, her voice ragged and desperate. "Please, sir, I can't stop it now..."

Dahlra glanced down at Elwess. "Do it. I want them to hear her screaming in Knightsbridge."

Elwess sucked her clitoris into his mouth, flicking his wicked tongue over the sweet spot with the expertise of a virtuoso and the fervor of an acolyte. Her orgasm mounted to a frightening intensity. Elwess answered with a ragged moan that caused her belly to quiver and her hips to surge toward his tormenting mouth. Pleasure and pain narrowed down a molten, searing pinpoint, and there was no stopping the inevitable.

She flew apart, blown like a leaf in a gale through the first peak of that shattering, arching, aching orgasm. Her screams rebounded around the room; her body spasmed over and over, until the pleasure tipped dangerously toward pain.

And still Elwess would not stop. He pushed her through each pulsating crest, sucking, licking until she was driven over the rough road of her second climax. She dragged air into her lungs like a drowning woman, fighting to stay in the moment and not come unglued.

Her senses overloaded, and her over-stimulated body grew slack against the cross. And still they pushed her through another, even more intense and overwhelming release. Her body was on fire, and she couldn't catch her breath. Her vision swam, and the panic she had experienced earlier threatened to return.

"Please, Dahlra, oh, God... make him fucking stop!" Why wouldn't they stop? Why wouldn't they—

"Inigo!" she screeched wildly. "Inigo Lightoller! Inigo fucking—"

Elwess reared back on his haunches, eyes flashing heat, his lips glossy, breathing like a runner. Dahlra pressed against her, calming her, grounding her against his body. "Good girl. Good, good, girl..."

Elwess rose to his feet, and kissed her deeply. "Sweet," he murmured, pulling away. "You taste like candy." He looked down at her with intense want reflected in his eyes. "I could lick your delicious cunt all day. Come on. Up you get."

She watched in a post-orgasmic haze as Elwess loosened the restraints. She sagged drunkenly, and he caught her. Her brain was so fried she could barely think straight. She tried to explain that she was sorry, that in the intensity of the moment, she had forgotten to use her safeword. Hell, in the intensity of the moment, she had forgotten what a safeword *was*. "I'm... I'm tried to—shit, sorry..."

Elwess picked her up like a child, and carried her to the long sofa, where he eased her down onto Dahlra's lap. She was pulled her into a hard, almost painful embrace, which actually calmed her down. In her overstimulated state, a lighter touch would have been anything but soothing.

"It got away from you a little, didn't it, love?" Dahlra murmured, stroking her fondly. She nodded, burying her face against his neck, smelling his cologne and nuzzling the tender, sensitive skin of his throat. He petted and soothed her, his voice crooning his magic into her ear.

"You make it very hard to show any restraint."

"I have to agree." Elwess sat beside the couple. "Nothing is more erotic than watching a strong and passionate submissive lose herself. You're quite an irresistible combination." His long fingers caressed her back. "An amazing woman. What beautiful scars."

With the gallon of endorphins still marinating her brain, Sydney shuddered as he ran his tongue over each ridge, mapping the ruined history of her back. It felt like an act of worship. It was true, Elwess was very skilled, and all kinds of sexy, but in a controlled, held-back manner that made you wonder what might happen if and when he really let himself go. Perhaps that was what made him so alluring; it would be easy to fancy yourself capable of finding that chink in his armour.

Sydney suspected a lot of subs had tried to jimmy that lock. If she was a betting woman, she would say not many had ever succeeded. It was a bit disconcerting to realise she was just as susceptible to his dark glamour as ever other woman.

Nestled between Dahlra's welcoming warmth, and Elwess' pressing weight, Sydney felt a companionship between the three of them that neither threatened Dahlra's place as the Dominant, nor Sydney's as the object of their mutual focus. Gradually, as her head cleared, she wondered if other lovers felt that way with the addition of a third person, or if they were just lucky.

Did Dahlra trust Elwess to keep the boundaries clear? Well, hell, she could take care of that part, at least. She squirmed against Dahlra, and caressed his heavy, hot erection. "I love you. I want you," she whispered, and slid her lips over the sweet spot on his throat.

He shivered, sighing blissfully as she ran her tongue along the column of his neck. "You shall have anything you want. Can you stand?"

Sydney briefly considered lying. It was so comfortable there, sandwiched between the two men. Instead, she struggled to her feet, groaning as her heavy limbs protested the change of scenery. Elwess also stood, and held out his hand to her. "Come with me, kitten. It's time for another lesson in submission."

CHAPTER NINETEEN

Submission From The Inside Out

Sydney took Elwess' proffered hand, and he led her into the large lavatory. It looked like a bathroom the Great Gatsby would have designed; floor-to-ceiling black and white subway tiles gleamed in the bright light. In the centre stood a massive, claw-footed iron bath, enameled white; it would have looked at home in any resort spa. The loo was off to one side, and a large shower stall stood against the opposite wall.

So what the hell was she supposed to be doing in here, alone with Elwess?

To her surprise, he knelt at her feet. It was at once impressive and humbling. Even on his knees he loomed large, as only a wiry, East End thug could. She suppressed an urge to run her finger down the parting in his hair, where his pale skin made a thin, startlingly white line.

He commanded, "Boots off. I want you all sorts of naked for this."

"For what?"

He glanced upward, with only the thinnest hint of impatience. "What's wrong, submissive—not very fond of surprises?"

"Not very. Anyway, I thought we'd already determined I'm not your submissive."

"And I'm not your Dominant. But being a Service Top has its perks, and this is one of them." His hand, warm and strong, slid up the back of her calf, and he gave her leg a playful slap. "Left foot first."

As he deftly slipped the boot over her ankle, he murmured, "You're not a natural submissive, true, but you're the type of submissive I enjoy training. You don't trust blindly, and you're not afraid. That makes your obedience all the sweeter."

"So that's the difference between a submissive and a slave? One chooses, and the other is forced?"

He paused, considering. "It's all semantics, really. But to me, a submissive willingly on her knees is more erotic than a slave forced to hers."

"But the slave is still erotic, you admit?"

"How they got on their knees isn't necessarily important. What happens to them once they get there *is*." His smile was as rich as dark chocolate. "A good submissive is always rewarded. And a bad one often comes to think of her punishment as reward. It's all about teaching her to recognise everything as pleasure. That, my dear, is the key to true enslavement."

He rose to his feet, gesturing to a small wooden chair. "Have a seat. This will only take a moment."

She perched on the edge of the chair, and watched carefully as he turned toward the sink. While water ran, he walked over to the tall IV stand in the corner. A large, rubber bag hung from its metal hook, and a slim rubber tube ran from the bottom and ended in a slightly bulbous tip.

"Fuck me," she swore softly.

Elwess laughed. "In due time, kitten." When she didn't reply, he added, "Feeling a little apprehensive, Ms Chapin? A tad vulnerable? There's no shame in it. In fact, I like to hear a little apprehension in a woman's voice."

"Yeah, well. You should be very pleased then, Master Elwess."

There was a rapid, metallic clink, as the rollers propelled the stand over the tiled floor. The sound was deafening in the small room. He crouched down until he was at eye level with her. "Don't misunderstand me. I don't get off on instilling fear. The Great Sydney Chapin may be at my mercy, but only because she wants to be." He patted her cheek with just the right mixture of playfulness and force. "*That,* little girl, is intoxicating stuff to a man like me."

With seductive decadence on a scale with something she had only ever seen on the better porn channels, Elwess drawled, "Tell me, kitten, do you think you're capable of blind trust?"

Sydney felt her desire pulling her to him like a magnet. With no danger to kill her libido, her initial apprehension quickly morphed into a frisson of the forbidden. "Try me."

"Very good." From his pocket, produced a small vial of clear liquid. "This is Oparim. Ever heard of it?"

"No. No, *sir*." They were, after all, still playing his game.

"It's a mild mood enhancer. Sometimes it's used as a relaxant during demonstrations, needle or wax play, that sort of thing. Helps achieve subspace. That's a term used to describe a special state of mind that a sub enters—"

"I know what it means." She stopped herself. "Yes, questioning a Dominant and interrupting him isn't exactly subspace, but..."

"Baby steps. As I was saying, Oparim is safe, non-habit-forming, and its effects are very subtle. You can examine your inhibitions and decide whether or not you need them."

She must have looked a little wary. He flicked his eyes toward the other room, where Dahlra waited for them. "We've already discussed this. He has assured me it would be perfectly safe for you to take. I wouldn't give you anything that he hadn't personally sanctioned. It's more than my job's worth."

"More like your life's worth." She cleared her throat. "Sorry. Peregrine talking. And I'll remember everything?"

"Believe me, love: Oparim or not, you're not going to forget tonight."

"Bottoms up, then." Sydney reached for the small vial, but he teasingly pulled it out of reach.

"Stand down, agent. A little finesse, if you please."

To Sydney's confusion, he poured the contents into his own mouth. Then he brought his lips to hers in a kiss. The moment their mouths touched, he forced hers apart, and the liquid poured onto her tongue. It tasted like peppermint schnapps, sharp and alcoholic and bracing. He released her, licking his lips. "Swallow."

Sydney did as she was told, then waited, her senses alert for any change. "No seismic shift in consciousness, no sudden compulsion to start tearing at my clothing. Pity," he drawled. Pointing to the bath, he instructed, "Lean over the edge." He removed his coat, and placed a large, thick towel on the side of the tub. "Rest against this."

Too curious to refuse, Sydney obeyed, wondering if and when she would feel the effects of the drug. For several minutes she waited, licking the minty taste from her lips. Then she heard the snap of latex gloves, and her entire body flushed pleasurably. The thought of Elwess touching her, wearing those impersonal gloves, made her shift restlessly. *Oh, it must be this Rhohypnol Lite—Oparim, or whatever it's called. It must be kicking in—*

She jumped as a gloved hand caressed her ribs. "Easy. Have you ever been given an enema, Ms Chapin?"

"What?"

"Enema. It's a procedure in which liquid is injected into the rectum, to expel its contents."

"I know what it is-"

"Then just answer the bloody question."

"Well, hell. No. I mean, not that I'm aware. I've always preferred being an, um, exit-only kinda gal, if you catch my meaning.

"Nice turn of phrase. I'll have to remember that. But many find it quite a pleasant experience, even relaxing." His voice took on a more ironic tone. "Consider yourself in very capable hands."

She glanced over her shoulder. "If I didn't, I wouldn't let you kiss drugs into me."

He stared at her for a moment. Then he rewarded her with a delicious, no-holds-barred laugh that was pure sex. It was a deep, dirty bark of mirth that made the years drop from his face, and he became almost handsome. And Dahlra said *she* had a sexy laugh.

Okay, Bad Boy, you got me there. I can totally see where you could make a good girl get dirty in a hurry. Who needs WMDs when you have that kind of ordnance?

"I must congratulate Dahlra. He's done very well with you." His laughter subsided, easing into a tantilising grin as crooked as he no doubt was. "You know, I've had a lot of women in my time. Some were stunning, and a few had power and charisma. One or two even intrigued me. But I can't remember the last time I've enjoyed talking to a woman this much." He knelt down behind her, still chuckling. "No, you're not a natural, but you do submit with great style. Now relax, kitten. This is going to feel very, very good."

Air gusted from her lungs as long fingers tenderly opened and probed her. He hummed appreciatively, and she fought the urge to squirm. Holy shit, this was... this was intense.

His hands stilled. "You have more scarring than I'd anticipated," he said quietly. "Is this all from... from your incarceration?"

She nodded once. "It wasn't... at the time I couldn't..." The pressure of his hands changed ever so slightly. It wasn't something she could define, but it was there, and it was kind.

"It's alright. Don't be afraid. I'm not going to hurt you." Elwess' tone was *everything* but reassuring. "Now, you'll feel pressure—not unpleasant, but I must insist you tell me if you start to cramp."

Sydney heard the snap of a cap, then his experienced fingers were smearing cool lubricant around the edges of her entrance. As he introduced the tip of the enema nozzle, he murmured, "Breathe. Slowly. Relax."

It was a very strange sensation—warmth and pressure and a slight pinching where the nozzle pressed past the opening. True, it wasn't unpleasant, but it wasn't the relaxation station, either. Sydney was grateful for the solid tub supporting her.

"Hold it in until I tell you to release it," he intoned. He reached around and gently massaged her abdomen until Sydney gasped, breathing through her mouth.

"Are you in pain?"

"No—sir. But, I don't..." The question could no longer contain itself. "What is the exact purpose of this? Sir?"

Leaning very close to her ear, he purred, "Why, little girl, I'm going to fuck your perfect, heart-shaped arse, and I want you to be ready for me."

Dahlra had spent a lot of time in The Chine during his Minder training, but until tonight, he'd always been a spectator, never a participant. He could hear Elwess and Sydney through the open door, their voices soft and intimate, and he felt a little tension ease from his heart. Sydney's 'I love you' still reverberated in his head, and he closed his eyes, savouring it.

He told himself that he was doing the right thing, but in the back of his mind he wondered what it said about him that he was basically okay with another man having sex with the woman he loved. *This isn't just another man, though; it's Elwess,* he thought wryly. For one thing, this was just sex. *Think of me as nothing more important than a good vibrator,* Elwess had told him. *I'm just a sex toy, Dahlra.*

But that wasn't exactly true, was it? If Sydney was an exceptional woman, then Elwess was the male equivalent. Amongst those in kinkster lifestyles, his name was spoken with respect by both Doms and subs. He was, by all accounts, one of the most credible and legit of his kind in the world. The most jaded subs swooned at the mention of his name, as enthralled by him as they were frightened by his reputation.

They all clamoured for the chance to play his wicked games, even though they knew he would always win. His Dominance was real, his particular proclivities for keeps. Elwess never considered another man his competition; as far as he was concerned, he was in a class by himself. He had no hidden agenda when it came to women, either.

It had been fascinating to watch him in the early days. The first time Elwess had brought him to the Chine, Dahlra suspected he was merely showing off. Dahlra had been given the instruction to "pay attention, and if you want to dive in, just do it. The sub knows what's expected of her; you need to know what's expected of you as a Dom."

It had been a night he had never forgotten, like Dante's Inferno, Heaven and Hell and a Scandinavian Death Metal concert all rolled into one. Elwess had been terrifying that night; powerful, demanding, cruelly compelling. The sub, a stunning blonde Amazon named Marie, had been like putty in Elwess' strong hands. Instead of coaxing her body to respond, he had ruthlessly taken what he wanted, dragging her down into an abyss of such sinister pleasure that she was soon reduced to crawling to him like an animal, begging to enjoy his attentions again.

He had taunted her, made her scream and cry and plead—and she had kissed the tops of his shoes in sobbing gratitude. Even as he spanked her arse raw, she thanked him, before he made her orgasm into unconsciousness. And all the while, Dahlra had stood transfixed in the shadows, so blown away by what he had witnessed he could barely sleep that night.

Watching Elwess in his element, Dahlra gradually came to understand the nature of a true, natural sexual Dominant—and with it came the longing, obsessive desire to put observation into practice with Sydney. He learned how to stir up that compelling/repellent kink of hers on a regular basis, and their relationship grew more exciting and grounded with every passing day.

He had brought her here as proof he was fearless in the pursuit of her pleasure. But was he, really? He had seen an expression on Elwess' face tonight he had never seen before in any session, any disciplining, any sexual act he had witnessed. When a submissive came to Elwess for training or discipline, he did not disappoint. But he always placed boundaries, set and honoured limits, and treated them all with the same aloof, dismissive calm. It was Elwess who set the rules, Elwess who decided how far and how deep a sub would go. There was always a wall of self-control, and never once had he lowered it.

Until tonight.

Dahlra had watched beautiful women walk through this room and barely cause a ripple. A part of him glowed with pride that his girl could rattle the cage of a man like Elwess. Another part of him was worried; when Elwess decided to possess a woman, he could prove just as addictive, consuming, and destructive as heroin.

And Elwess had seen something in Sydney he wanted.

Dahlra hadn't realised the extent of it, until the three of them were sprawled across the sofa. As he held Sydney, Elwess had kissed Sydney's scarred back with a tenderness akin to veneration. The look on his face had shaken Dahlra.

And it's not just that, is it? A darkly taunting voice accused. *You've never done that. You've never felt worthy of the gesture. You've denied her that same reverence, because your guilt has always come between you and her.*

No more. Tonight, he had put guilt and pride behind him. He had done it for Sydney, always for Sydney.

The rules of the game, it seemed, had changed—for all of them.

"You're doing very well."

"I'm starting to cramp." Gritting her teeth, Sydney calmed herself with her old mnemonic number string, and soon the cramps did ease. She relaxed, feeling absurdly proud of herself, like she'd won some sort of Enema Award. The Golden Shit, or the BATHTA, or something equally ridiculous...

Elwess stroked her long hair soothingly. "Alright, I think five minutes is enough."

Five minutes? It had seemed like five hours. Sydney tried to push herself upright, but she was unable to completely straighten. Elwess placed a patient arm around her waist, and led her to the toilet. She sat down heavily, her face burning.

"Go ahead."

"Go ahead, what, exactly?"

"Let go."

"Yeah, right." When he didn't move, she huffed, "You *are* joking, aren't you?"

He crossed his arms and raised a single eyebrow.

"I... I can't with you..." She stopped, feeling queasily mortified. "This is a very private thing for me. Even Dahlra doesn't make me-"

"My dungeon, my rules. I say let go now."

It became a contest of wills Sydney knew she could not win, but she grimly held on. Sweat popped out on her forehead, clammy and offensive. She was cramping in earnest now. Elwess watched her with dispassionate patience, until she began to rock back and forth in pain.

With a sigh, he knelt beside her, and massaged her abdomen. The pressure became more than she could stand, and her body let go with a shudder. She turned her face away from him.

"Why should you feel ashamed?" His voice sounded mildly surprised. "It's a natural function. And it was just the two of us. If I don't care, why should you? Did I deride you? Laugh at you? Harm you?"

"No."

"Then no more sulks." He took her hand, and steered her back to the edge of the tub. "Now, one more should do it."

"What?" she screeched.

"Twice is the usual practice. Three times is better, but I'm not that patient," he explained, with a jackal smile.

After he finished the entire procedure to his satisfaction, Elwess cleaned her meticulously, and with gentle care. Sydney stood, expecting to feel shaky and unstable. To her surprise, she was alert, relaxed and euphoric.

When she confessed as much, he was unsurprised. "Submission is not always about what you want to accept, kitten, but it is always about what you are capable of receiving. From now on, when you see the enema bag, you will associate it with pleasure."

She raised a skeptical eyebrow. "You think?"

"I think you'll be surprised just how far you'll be willing to take everything in future, Sydney. This was a gesture of trust. You honoured me with it."

"Some honour. Watching me evac isn't exactly honourable."

"The gesture is inconsequential. All trust is honourable. Dahlra has honoured you by bringing you here."

"What do you mean?"

He looked at her levelly. "Don't be dense. The man loves you more than is probably legal. Tonight is a risk for him. But nothing is too good for you, in his eyes." He headed for the door. "Take all the time you need to compose yourself. But not too long. We'll be waiting."

Dahlra and Elwess were lounging on the sofa, drinks in hand, when Sydney returned to the Chine's main room. Placing his Jameson's on the end table, Dahlra rose to his feet and held his arms out to her. Sydney rushed into them.

"Are you alright?" His voice was quiet and calm, but his eyes held some tension. She gave him a smile that felt silly on her lips. With this Oparim or whatever it was called singing in her veins, she felt calm and clearheaded, yet her arousal skipped and skittered through her bloodstream.

He stroked her cheek with the tips of his fingers, and she felt a hundred pinpricks of longing and desire tickling beneath his hands. He was sexy as sin when she was fully sober; now, remembering every wicked thing he'd ever done and promised to do, he was nothing short of enthralling.

Over his shoulder, Sydney could see Elwess watching them intently. He was waiting for her to do *something*. Realisation dawned. *I want to do this. I want him to know that I'm ready to do this.*

Going on pure instinct, she knelt at Dahlra's feet, and leaned forward, touching her lips to the tops of his shoes. She was dimly aware of Elwess approaching. He brusquely nudged her knees further apart with a careless boot. "Very impressive, submissive. Most slaves have to be ordered to debase themselves so beautifully."

Dahlra's voice rolled over her like a warm breeze. "I would never require her to debase herself for me."

"Nor should you. Your submissive is simply better versed than most."

A hand appeared in her line of vision. "Stand." Elwess helped her to her feet. "Undress your Master like a good girl. Then you may undress me."

Sydney couldn't move quickly enough. Still feeling high and off-balance, she gracelessly pulled Dahlra's jumper over his head and fumbled his trousers off. After kneeling once again to remove his shoes and his briefs, she rose and put her arms around his waist, and they both shivered at the sensation of skin against cool skin.

Strong fingers pinched her earlobe. "Stay on task, submissive." Elwess pulled her from Dahlra's arms. He loomed over them, glowering impatiently with thinly veiled lust. "Disobey again, and it will be clamps on your nipples."

Sydney turned to him uncertainly, and undressed him, her fingers clumsy with his unfamiliar clothing. He stood very still, his breathing slow and calm, a complete contrast to her heavy, open-mouthed panting. He was leaner, wirier than Dahlra, his skin tone duskier. His body carried a cruelly austere beauty.

A dark, circular tattoo on his right hip stood out in stark contrast to his pale flesh; a compass, drawn like the elaborately engraved antiques in maritime museums. It was tilted, so that true north pointed toward his heart. Surrounding the edges was a banner which wove in and around the compass itself. In a florid script, it read, *Desire shall not preclude Dominance*. His cock, cradled in a bed of black, coarse pubic hair, was heavy and uncircumcised and showing the signs of becoming a very impressive erection.

As Sydney finished removing the last of Elwess' clothing, Dahlra crossed to the strange chair on the other side of the room. He raised the padded sides of the seat to widen it, giving her a glimpse of his tight, rounded arse and powerful thighs. He turned and sat down, gripping the curved arms of the chair, and Sydney drank in his long, lean body, lounging elegantly on the leather seat.

From behind, Elwess slid his hands over her breasts; his long fingers alternately tweaked and soothed her sensitive nipples. "Do you like what you see, kitten?"

"Yes." A finger slipped inside her, flicking against the swollen nub within, turning her body into fire.

Elwess called out, "Feeling left out, Master Dahlra?"

"Not at all." He opened his thighs invitingly; his large hand closed over his exquisitely hard cock, stroking lightly in time with her breathing. His balls rested heavy against the seat.

"I want to suck him." Sydney's voice sounded throaty and drunk to her own ears.

"I think it's unlikely he'll refuse you. Go. Worship his cock like a good little girl."

Sydney took a step forward, but Elwess caught her by her hair and pulled her back. "If you want him that much, prove it. Crawl to him. On your knees."

Dahlra watched intently as she crawled on her hands and knees to him, like an animal. When she reached his slender, pale feet, he invitingly spread his thighs wider to accept her.

Sydney leaned in, licking from his taint line up the underside of the stone-hard shaft. He braided his fingers through her hair while she swirled her tongue over the tip of his cock, then allowed him to part her lips with the blunt, smooth head. She took him down to the root, humming as her nose brushed against his crotch. Dahlra growled rapturously, his hips rising from the chair to penetrate her eager mouth.

Sydney cupped his sac with one hand, and encircled the base of his cock with the other, sucking hard. Dahlra moaned feverishly, lost to the pleasure of her mouth. Sydney surged forward, wanting to take him deeper down her throat, wanting to feel him, wanting to taste his release. She loved making him come this way, loved the power of orchestrating his abandon. He was close; it would only take a few more strokes...

"Not yet." Elwess calmly grasped her shoulders and pulled her away. "Come here."

Dahlra caught her before Elwess could gain control. "She's mine, and I say come *here*," he growled. He roughly pulled her onto his lap, until she was straddling him.

Sydney whimpered, grinding against his hot erection, too far gone to care that another man was in the room, waiting, watching.

Elwess swore under his breath. "Fuck, Dahlra. If she was my little girl I'd never let her out of this dungeon."

"There are times I want to build one for just that reason." Dahlra pulled her closer to toy with her tight nipples. "Lock you away and tie you down at every opportunity." His smile faded, replaced by a look of intense, intoxicating lust. "Enough. You know what I want. Ride my cock."

Sydney tried to comply, but her legs were doing the new-born colt wobble. As she knelt, poised over him, his arms encircled her waist in a crushing grip. His body was burning hot, and seared her like a brand.

"I'm going to fuck you until the devils blush."

He impaled her in one sharp stroke. Her body was too primed and ready to put up much resistance, but he was so big and rock hard it still took her breath away. He set a slow, rocking pace, hitting every sweet part of her. She kissed him wildly, thrusting her tongue into his waiting mouth, in rhythm to their slow, deep strokes.

Behind her, Elwess placed a trail of hot, wet kisses down her back, lower and lower until his warm breath ghosted against her entrance. Surely he wouldn't... Every part of her brain was screaming taboo, telling her this was wrong, unhygienic, degenerate.

Then his warm, pointed tongue slid into her.

She froze and instinctively pulled away, only to be pushed back in place by two sets of hands. "Ohhh...*that's so...*" She wasn't even aware she had actually made the naked sound ringing out in the room.

"Come now, kitten." Elwess' nails scored delicious ribbons of sensation over her arse. "Tell me you don't like it."

In that moment, Sydney was incapable of telling him anything. Elwess' warm, velvety tongue teased and explored and invaded her, ramping her body higher with each wicked lick.

In the midst of this carnage of sensation, Sydney felt a long, slickly lubricated finger questing at her entrance. Elwess was patience itself as he teased her opening with his long fingers, his movements slow and unhurried, in rhythm with Dahlra's deep thrusts. "It's alright, kitten," he soothed. "We have all the time in the world."

A second finger joined the first, scissoring her open, making her ready for him. Dahlra gentled her as only he could. "Relax, Sydney. Breathe deeply, and bear down." Elwess placed a steadying hand on her back, and firmly pushed her into Dahlra's arms.

"Good girl. Relax and lean forward. That's it." His voice was hypnotic. "Pant for me, kitten. That's my girl. Pant for me."

Elwess slowly introduced his cock into her opening, and he held her hips, steadily pushing, pushing.

"Pant, Sydney. Breathe, my love. Good girl. Such a good girl." In one long, time-stopping slow movement, Elwess penetrated her anally, burying himself to the hilt.

The room was silent except for their harsh breathing. Sydney was completely overwhelmed at being filled with these two men at once. It was beautiful and painful and glorious, and she shuddered helplessly. Elwess rolled his hips, screwing into her, ignoring her hiss of pain.

He sounded breathless, and dangerous. "Oh, yeah. You can take it, kitten. Next time, you're gonna beg me for it. You're gonna need it like a drug." He drew back, like pulling an arrow on a bowstring. "Let's see what makes you really scream," he rasped, then released the arrow with a roar of triumph.

Sydney's eyes flew open wide as she was pierced, pinned between the two men. It hurt, in the way long-denied pleasure can bring its own brand of suffering. Within, an incredible combination of burning pain and unspeakable pleasure was engaged in its own power struggle. She scrabbled for Dahlra's shoulders and rose off his cock. "Please, please move!" she wailed, and rocked between them.

"So hot... so smooth... my cock was made for your sweet arse..." Elwess moaned deliriously, his thrusts lightning fast, setting the speed for them all. "I told you it would feel good, didn't I, kitten? Ah, fuck, I can feel you both against my cock..." He abandoned all pretense of control or seduction. He wrapped his arms around her waist and began to drive into her.

They fucked her mercilessly, wringing every ounce of brutal ecstasy from her body. The penetration of her fundament played an overwhelming counterpoint with the sweet pleasure of Dahlra's cock sheathed within her sex. She rode between them, unmindful of anything but being filled, emptied, and filled again with their solid, smooth thrusts. Dahlra's hips surged against hers, and the hard, invasion of Elwess' cock answered, corkscrewing into her as deeply as he could. It was a duel, and her body their weapon of choice.

The room pulsed and throbbed with their moans of lust, the feral growls of the men, the cry of the woman they pleasured. Their thrusts grew harder, faster, pumping into her until she was lost to herself, reduced to nothing more than an instrument for their purpose. The decadent, pervasive presence of the forbidden seeped into what little was left of rational consciousness, and she drowned in the depths of it.

Dahlra wrapped his arms around her, and she grasped his shoulders, riding him mercilessly as her hips jerked out of rhythm. As he surrendered to his release, his eyes locked with hers, his face a mask of pained, intense ecstasy.

The last foundations of control fell from beneath her, disintegrated by voracious and uncontrollable pleasure, and she came in a great, rushing cry which seemed to sear the air around them. She wailed her lover's name, holding onto his hands, blinded by the tremours that raged through her like an earthquake, and all she could do was hold on for dear life.

Elwess tightened the grip on her waist to bruising intensity. He came with a bellow of ecstasy, his cock a jack hammer inside her, each deep, blazing thrust tearing a howl from her lips. He staggered back, releasing her from his crushing embrace.

Sydney slipped out of Dahlra's arms, too shaken and overwhelmed to keep her balance. Elwess sank to his knees, and caught her as she fell back. Groggily, Sydney looked into the bottomless depths of his large, dark eyes. Panting like a runner, his face beaded with sweat, Elwess was completely open, more naked than any lack of clothing could produce.

With something like wonder shading his bruised voice, he marveled softly, "You are an incredible woman." He brushed her tangled and sweaty hair from her forehead with more gentleness that she would have thought him capable of.

Dahlra leaned forward and stroked her belly. "Are you alright, love?" He pulled her upright and into his arms.

"That was..." She faded, too sex-stoned for eloquence. "Perfect." She kissed him with all the tenderness she possessed. "Oh, Dahlra, I'd pull this world down for you..."

His held her so tightly she couldn't breathe, but she didn't mind. She couldn't get close enough either. The spaced-out high of the drug deflated, replaced by exhausted affection.

Behind them, Elwess rose, and placed a careless kiss on the top of her head. "Back in two ticks." Shortly he returned, a washing flannel in one hand and a large, opaque jar in the other. "You're going to be sore tomorrow," he explained, kneeling at Dahlra's feet. "This will help."

Sydney remained still as he cleaned her, then she heard a metallic skirl as he unscrewed the lid from the jar. He gently coated the area around her sensitive, sore opening with ointment. It felt cool and numbing, and she didn't protest when Elwess' long finger slid into her passage, slow and deep, unable to resist one last gentle probe. His finger rotated, shocking the breath from her lungs.

He was still sexed up, and even in his post-coital state, his supreme confidence and control were firmly in place, like a garment he could put on and remove at will. "Dahlra, I cannot believe you've never fucked this exquisite arse. When you visit me again I would be happy to switch places with you."

"I'm sure you would." Dahlra sounded logy and indolent, but there was an underlying tension that Sydney couldn't quite get her sex-fogged head around. Before she could question it, Elwess gave her a tender, almost loving kiss. When he pulled away, it was with undisguised reluctance.

Sydney looked into his black, black eyes, and thought, *I'd love to know exactly what you're thinking right now, Big Daddy.* The possibilities made her shiver.

"Cold, my love?" Dahlra rubbed her limbs to warm her.

She shook her head. "No. I think I'm still tripping on this Oparim stuff. Are you sure it's not habit-forming?"

Elwess laughed. "Oh, kitten, you're running on nothing more than endorphins and oxygen now. The Oparim wore off about thirty minutes ago. It's a very short term buzz; it usually only lasts long enough to allow you to initially relax." He stroked her back, his long fingers tracing patterns over her scars, as if to memorise them. "The only thing that's addictive here is pleasure."

His words burned out the last of the afterglow fog. It was one thing for Sydney to acknowledge that everything he did was designed to seduce and enthrall, but it was quite another to be find herself staring down the business end of it. She had a feeling that he could quickly become a destructive habit she could live without. But didn't all addicts say the same thing, even as they were plunging the needle into a fresh vein?

Dahlra kissed her softly, bringing her headspace back in line. "So you enjoyed yourself, my girl?"

"I enjoyed you." A swift, sweet emotion for him carved into Sydney's heart, blowing all her thoughts of addictions and habits and unbroken veins. She returned his kiss, her unspoken vow hidden behind this silent tribute of lips and tongues.

Not to be outdone, Elwess gave her a lazy smack on her bottom. "Come on, you two. Bed."

Dahlra swung Sydney up into his arms, and followed Elwess to the massive bed in the antechamber of the Chine. He laid her in the middle of the huge expanse of crisp, white cotton, then joined her. Sydney curled up against Dahlra's side, his shoulder her pillow, his arms her blanket. Elwess nestled behind her, spooning against her back. Blanketed between the two men, their arms entwined around her, Sydney felt blissfully warm and light. It felt comfortable, even familiar. The three lovers gradually grew still and quiet, and Sydney tumbled into a sleep so deep she neither dreamed nor moved.

She was awakened sometime later by the sound of quiet voices in discussion. Blearily, she opened her eyes and spotted Elwess standing beside the bed, clad in a dark dressing gown.

"I hoped you'd wake up before I left. I wanted to say goodnight." He spoke as if addressing them both, but the look in his eyes was obviously meant for Sydney alone. He tightened the belt of his robe. "I very much enjoyed playing with you. I hope that, should the two of you desire my company again..."

His eyes met Dahlra's. "Oh. I almost forgot. Seeing as these were left behind, I couldn't bear to see them go to waste."

From the pocket of his robe, he produced the knickers Sydney had discarded in her long walk to the Chine. God, had that only been a few hours before? She would not be surprised to walk back out of that long tunnel to find the season had changed.

"One of my submissives gathered your things and brought them to my flat," he was saying. "I'll have them washed and returned to you in the morning. But I'm sure you won't begrudge me keeping these as a memento of the evening." He returned her knickers to his robe pocket.

Sydney turned to Dahlra, who nodded with an uncharacteristic air of noblesse oblige. "Be my guest."

"Lovely." Just as he approached the door, he turned. "One more thing, kitten." The pleasant, friendly expression dropped, and he seemed to grow at once taller and darker.

In a voice that was hard and cutting in its East End rasp, he said, "Your Minder is my friend. He moved heaven and earth to save you. He's a good man."

"Elwess—"

"Hang on, Dahlra. I will have my say."

"Say it, then." Sydney returned Elwess' thousand-yard stare with a long road of her own. Dahlra's soothing hand on her thigh could not dispel the tension.

The temperature of the room seem to drop by about twenty degrees, and in that instant Sydney saw the man so many feared, envied and coveted. "I will tell you without conceit that I'm the real deal. I'm a hard bastard, and I enjoy making subs cry as much as I love getting them off.

"But I know love when I see it. Dahlra Gar loves you. If you meant what you said earlier, if you truly love him, I'm your friend for life, no matter what.

"But if you're just playing him, if you think he's some toy to use and then discard when you get bored, then there's nothing I won't do to make your life a misery. And if you break his heart, I swear I'll find a way to make you disappear."

A cool ball of ice settled in the pit of her solar plexus. It wasn't the first time she had felt the sting of being underestimated on behalf of Dahlra Gar, but it was the nastiest. She hopped out of bed and stepped up into Elwess' grill, nose to nose. He did not move or flinch, nor did she expect him to. She raised her chin and met his uncompromising stare with her own, one hardcase to another.

"You sound the part, I'll give you that. Let me tell you a little something about threats. They show too many weaknesses, and they give too much away.

"If you ever plan on making me disappear, you'd better not let me see you coming. And I'll tell you something else for free. I don't lie to people I love. As for anyone who so much as touches one hair on Dahlra Gar's head, I can assure you they *will* disappear, and they won't see *me* coming."

Behind her, she heard Dahlra quietly slip out of bed. He put his arms around her waist, and pressed his face against her neck. Leaning against his solid, dependable body, she added, "Say what you like, *Master* Elwess, but if anyone, including you, hurts my boy, I'll hurt them back."

Elwess held her stare for perhaps five more seconds, then held out his hand. Just like that, they were on equal footing again. "I'm protective of my Minders, Agent. I'm even more protective of my friends."

Sydney shook his hand and told her racing heart to stand down. "You've been watching too many Bond films, Elwess."

"You can't blame me for making sure my friend is well taken care of, can you?"

Sydney felt Dahlra relax against her back, and felt a pang of conscience. He was finer made than this. She turned and took him in her arms. "It's alright, love. We're just two hard bastards, talking trash." She rose on tiptoe and pressed her lips against the faint line between his fine brows. "But I meant every word I said."

Dahlra smiled bleakly. "Just don't beat him up. The paperwork alone is a mess, and he's such a drama queen he'll make it look twice as bad as it actually is."

She stroked his face apologetically. "Honestly, love, we're just playing 'my dad's bigger than your dad.' I promise you, Mr Bad Guy is perfectly safe. And so am I. Didn't you make sure of that?"

"Of course he did. That's his job. He's the perfect Minder." Elwess placed a brotherly hand on Dahlra's shoulder. "Well, I think that's my cue to leave you for the evening. Enjoy the room, mate. And call me before you return to your stately pile. Let's all get together for a drink sometime, yeah?"

He smiled down at her, the Dominant Master persona firmly locked back into place. "Tonight has truly been a revelation. Until we meet again, kitten." He pinched her cheek playfully, then turned and left.

For a moment, they were still, letting the room catch its breath. Finally, Sydney turned back to Dahlra, and gave him a gesture of 'what the fuck was all *that*?'

"I'm not sure what that little pissing contest was all about, but I think you won." Dahlra put his arm around her and added wryly, "Elwess wouldn't agree, of course. As far as he's concerned, he always wins."

The decadent, tawdry glamour of the night's activities faded; in spite of her state of numbed-out bliss, Sydney couldn't fail to hear uncertainty, perhaps even insecurity in his tone, as much as he tried to hide it. She knew she had to do something to fix this. "Hey, you."

"Yes, my girl?"

She kissed him lightly. "There are three things you really need to know, and I mean them sincerely.

"Go on." He was smiling, but there was still some uncertainty in his eyes. He had brought her here as a gift; but he was going to leave a worried man unless she clued him in on a few home truths.

"Number one," she began, "I think you're the most beautiful man I've ever known, and I'm even more excited by you today than I was the first time you took me to bed, and that's fucking well saying something." Dahlra ducked his head shyly, but a little more confidence seeped into his bearing.

"Two, as beautiful as you are to me naked, I find you every bit as fascinating fully clothed, and when women, and men for that matter, look at you, I have to bite my tongue to keep from shouting, 'back off, bitches, this man is mahn.'"

That earned her a laugh. "And three, this was all great fun, but it's nothing compared to how I feel when it's just you and me at home alone, reading aloud, or playing Scrabble, not that I'll ever win." She put her arms around his waist and they held on to one another. "I happen to think that muscle between your ears is just as sexy as the one between your legs."

She sighed happily. This reassuring stuff was catching. "Hell, Dahlra, don't you know you thrill me just by walking into the room?"

He held her tighter. "After all that's happened, it's more than I could wish for."

"Those two people are gone, remember? We let them go, and I'm glad, because you're the only one I need. The only one I want. The only one I love. Now, be a good boy, and tell me you love me."

Dahlra took her hand, and solemnly placed it on his chest. "Sydney Chapin," he declared, "the day I stop loving you, is the day this stops beating."

He lowered his face to hers and covered her lips in a kiss that was beautifully, achingly tender. He placed soft kisses against her forehead, her cheekbones, even the tip of her nose. Finally, he drew her back into bed, and as they snuggled together, he chuckled softly.

"I must say, you look like the cat whut got the cream."

"Me?"

"Yeah, you."

He stretched, and tucked his free hand behind his head. "My girl just cowed the biggest, baddest Dom in the free world. I think I'm entitled to feel a little smug." Dahlra gave her his thousand-watt smile. "I like the way you fight for me. It's dead sexy."

She laughed. "Well, he was being a bit of a bully."

"You should've seen him during training. Bullying was one of his charms."

"Acting as if I didn't know how lucky I am," she scoffed.

For a time the silence stretched on, comfortable and easy. In the dark, he enquired, "You don't regret this, do you?"

"No, of course not. Do you?"

"Not when it made you scream like that." It took several heartbeats before he asked, "Would you want to do this again?"

She heard the faintest trace of insecurity in his voice, and thought again of the needle and the vein. "Maybe, but not anytime soon." Pulling him so close she couldn't tell when he began and she ended, she added, "Besides, I've decided I don't like sharing you."

"'Back off, bitches, this girl is mahn.'" He tried the words on for size, drawing them out in an uncanny imitation of Sydney's southern American accent. "Oh, you *are* mine," he repeated, his voice soft with wonder, as if the truth of it had finally come home.

Sydney smiled against his chest; he could be so fucking adorable. "I suppose there'll be no living with you after this," she teased.

"I'm actually hoping there'll be no living *without* me after this. Wait a minute..." he said, turning her to face him. "Is that a proposal?"

Sydney told herself that her heart was most emphatically *not* doing barrel flips. "Well, I can't have you meeting Elwess here with anyone else, can I? Not even test dummies—"

She had expected him to laugh, but instead he crushed her to his chest so tightly it almost hurt. She looked into his face, and saw love and devotion smolder into something less easy to tame with soft words and kisses, and met it with her own tough passion.

From his vantage point upstairs, Elwess Talbert sat at his desk and took another deep hit from his joint, squinting through the blue-grey smoke at his CCTV monitor. He was not one to indulge in cannabis on a regular basis, but tonight's session had promised to be good, so he arranged to have some waiting for him afterward. He found a fat, quality spliff the perfect accompaniment to an evening of autoerotic voyeurism.

The Chine contained four motion-activated cameras; nothing happened there without video evidence. For all his perversions, Elwess Talbert was very careful, and knew how to armour-plate his arse. And in the instance of an evening such as this, the cameras also provided him with a nice little souvenir.

He backed up the recording to the moment he started rimming Sydney, smiling at that first juicy curse of surprise. She had been so naturally responsive – not like so many jaded, fucked-out birds who tried to fake it, warbling and screeching the entire time to prove how great he made them feel.

Elwess took another long, tall hit of the blunt and held it in as Sydney climaxed, pressed tightly between her two lovers. She was like Venus rising from the ocean, beautiful and strong and exultant.

He knew the exact moment he'd made her come just by the look of ecstasy on her face. It was not the ersatz shit he often saw on the faces of women tied to his cross, or writhing in pretended fear and rapture on a stranger's rack. *This one is definitely a keeper.*

Normally after a session with another Dom and his sub, he felt energised, recharged and smugly satisfied. He got off on the power of it all; the formal Dom-speak he used to get a sub all hot and groveling at his feet, getting what they needed from his whips.

He took another toke and fingered the peach-coloured knickers he had purloined. He gave them a delicate sniff. She had been sexed up and wet before she removed them; the nostrils of his large, sensitive nose flared at the sweet, clean scent of her. His mouth watered, and his erection eased from the opening of his robe.

As he replayed the moment he buried his face between her creamy thighs, he slipped the silky material around his cock, and gave it a hard, satisfying tug. He whispered her name, trying it on for size, and decided he liked the way it sparked on his tongue. The fabric slithered over his prick, embedding little spurs of pleasure in his balls. He thought of Sydney's lovely mouth, warm and softer than the silk, wrapped around his cock. Oh, yeah. Next time he would have those sweet DSLs all over his dick. *I will most definitely want some of that.*

He cupped his balls in his hand, stroking them firmly. He would show her how he wanted it; yeah, he would teach her how to do him proper. He pictured her on her knees between his thighs, looking up at him with those fascinating eyes; sucking him, obeying his commands, growing wet as he urged her on with his filthy promises...

Between the fantasy, the pot, the knickers, and his own sure strokes, he did not last long. He gasped out her name, his release spurting into the fabric, as if it he was spilling into her. He leaned back in his chair, eyes closed, breathing in the smell of his spunk, mingling with the musk of her sex. It was a few moments before he was compos mentis enough to move.

After polishing off the roach, he burned a recording of the night's activities onto a DVD and carefully marked it, using a shorthand of his own devising. He placed it, along with Sydney's knickers, in a small box, and locked it away in his desk drawer.

He poured himself a glass of his favourite Neisson Rhum, turned on his stereo, and flopped onto his large sofa. Rosemary Clooney's teasing, innocently lascivious voice skipped from the Bose speakers: *Come on-a my house, my house, I'm gonna give-a you candy, Come on-a my house, my house, I'm gonna give-a you everything...*

Balancing the drink on his chest, Elwess allowed his cannabis-baked thoughts to drift down to the two people in his bed. There was something about them that affected him more than he was prepared to admit. Sydney Chapin was an intelligent, beautiful woman. She had personal integrity and inner power. And yet, there was vulnerability that made him feel absurdly protective. In his mind's eye, he pictured the incredible scars she carried on her back like a banner. To a man like Elwess, it was one irresistible, sexy-as-fuck combination.

He took a long pull of his rum to quell the almost overwhelming desire to go back downstairs and join them again. The only thing keeping him topside was the realisation that he didn't really want any more sex. He wouldn't be averse to watching the two of them, but the scary bloody truth of it was he just wanted to lie beside them. Christ, what a pussy thing to admit, even to himself. The pleasure of wanking to his home-made porn faded. Now, he felt empty, yearning – left out.

And it wasn't just the fact that he wanted to possess her, though there was plenty of that. When she had made that little quip about watching too many James Bond films, he had wanted to remind her that she was not that far off from 007 herself. She had always loomed larger than life in the little planet that was The Agency; the quintessential agent who killed without hesitation, interrogated without mercy, did whatever it took to break, to decipher, to destroy, to protect.

She might have taken her sweet time warming up to Dahlra Gar, but she wasn't going to let anything come between them, either. Was that the difference? He didn't think so. He had never coveted any woman enough to try and take her away from another man, especially a friend.

He freely admitted to sharing quality time with the majority of the seven deadly sins, but envy was not one of his bedfellows. He hadn't been jealous of a bloke since he lost his virginity.

So, what set her apart? And why was it so important to analyse this?

He had known a lot of different women in a myriad of situations. He had always been able to *get* any woman he truly wanted; it was just a matter of tripping the right switches, twisting the proper dials, saying the right, or the wrong words. He knew how to make fantasies come true.

He had enjoyed mind-blowing sex with several of the most heart-stopping, beautiful women in the world—sometimes several at once. He had trained more obedient and disciplined submissives. He tied them up and taunted them, making it hurt if they asked for it, making them scream for a different reason altogether when they pleased him.

He had known women who were just as clever, just as tough, just as ruthless. He had reduced them all to crawling, groveling slaves, ready to walk through fire just to feel the bite of his tawse on their desperate flesh one more time.

And if any of them pulled any kind of jealousy or possessive or entitlement bollocks, he tore up their contracts, took away their access to The Chine and broke contact faster than you could say 'BDSMblem.' None of them, *none,* were as important to him as the next one in line.

Desire shall not preclude Dominance.

So why was he still thinking about his best friend's lover?

Perhaps it was as simple as the thrill of binding her slender wrists in his restraints at her request. The very idea of it made his head spin. *I had Sydney Chapin shackled to my cross. I made her scream her safe word.*

She was the kind of woman he loved to break, simply because of the skill involved. Knowing the pressure points, sensing the perfect moment of surrender. Having the skills to make her beg for the pain. And what then? While you were taking the victory lap, she just might have you doing a little begging of your own. It was certainly something to consider.

Tonight had given him the most pleasure he'd had in, well, he couldn't remember when. He was as straight as an arrow, but he liked Dahlra. Hell, he liked Sydney. Perhaps that was the problem. Sex wasn't about 'like'. He had not given a shit whether or not 'like' was part of a relationship for longer than he cared to think about. 'Like' was vanilla;

'like' was normal, and normal was the last thing he wanted to be.

No one else treated him like a normal bloke anymore. If he was going to indulge in some honesty, he would have to admit how much he had enjoyed just sitting and having a drink with Dahlra as they waited for Sydney. He was good company; during his days as Dahlra's mentor and trainer, they would always spend at least one evening a week putting the world to rights over a pint or three. Perhaps Dahlra and Sydney had given him the first dose of real he'd had in what felt like years.

Elwess groaned aloud. He was so fucked. He drained the contents of his glass, grimacing as the Neisson's burned all the way down. He sat the glass down on the table and fell back against the sofa with a frustrated growl. "Time to get unfucked," he muttered under his breath, and reached for his mobile.

He thumbed through several numbers, until he found the one he sought. This one was talented, and grateful, and had long auburn hair and blue eyes. She would be pliant and cringingly obedient, and do everything he said without question or imagination. He would probably make her cry. But at least she didn't look or sound or smell or act in any way, shape or form like the woman he had just kissed goodnight.

As he waited for her to answer, Elwess had a sudden, sinking feeling he might have just tossed his dark, jaded heart to Sydney Chapin for a laugh, only to find she had deftly caught it in her strong, tiny palm. He was so fucked.

CHAPTER TWENTY

Christmas

The doorbell rang, and Sydney glanced at her watch. Five forty-five. Flippineck, his flight must have landed early—an hour early, to be exact. Well, better than last time, when he was two hours late.

"Dahlra, Elwess is here," she called up the stairs.

From above, she heard the huff of exasperation. "Already? Oh, arse! I'll be down as quickly as I can."

Sydney laughed aloud as she padded to the door. She had already had three hot toddies and was quickly approaching comfortably numb. Well hell, if you couldn't get a bit twatted on Christmas Eve, when could you?

Elwess was looking downward, as if inspecting his shoes. He looked up as the door swung open, and took in the sight of Sydney, in a bathrobe that had seen better days, fiddling with an earring while trying to wrestle the door open with her foot.

"Have the party games already started?" He pushed the door open. "If they have, I don't want to be on your team. You're rubbish at this one."

"Prat." She accepted his kisses on both cheeks and returned them. "Happy Christmas Eve. Dear me, you're early, what a surprise."

"Cheeky. I got an early flight back."

Elwess had been a somewhat unusual addition to their lives after that first, mind-bending night in the Chine. Later that month, he invited them to his flat for dinner; he sent them tickets to join him at the Royal Albert Hall for a Bonnie Raitt gig. He would show up unexpectedly at Maidenvine, Harrod's hamper in hand. They set aside one of the bedrooms for his use, and they were always glad to see his car pull up in the drive.

As the weeks passed, the Big Bad Dungeon Master persona gradually faded, revealing the man behind the whips and chains. Sometimes, when the three of them were sitting around laughing or sharing a bottle of wine, it felt as if they had been together for years. At the end of the evening, after kissing him goodnight, and watching the two men give one another a very manly, British sort of hug, Sydney would recall that moment when the three of them were nestled together in the Chine's massive bed, resting against Dahlra like spoons in a drawer. It felt like a triangle which managed to stay perfectly balanced on point, no matter how hard or how many times Elwess tilted against it.

"Make yourself at home." Sydney perched on the arm of the sofa. "Dahlra is still dressing. So, how was Portugal?"

Elwess carelessly draped himself on the sofa, stretching his long legs and crossing them at the ankle. "How's Maidenvine? Ready for Christmas in London, I see." He nodded toward the sparsely decorated tree in the corner, surrounded by presents and little else. His voice echoed emptily against the bare walls.

"Yeah. We knew you'd get back in the country late, and we thought we might as well stay in town for the Lightoller's party, so DeVere seemed the best option. We'll all go to Maidenvine on New Year's Day, though. It's decorated to the nines up there, but we thought we'd at least make an effort here, since we were going to be around for the week."

He looked around their old flat. "It's hard to remember how nice it used to look. I'm certainly not feeling any 'Home Sweet Home' vibe now."

Sydney glanced around the massive space, wrinkling her nose. "Pretty soulless, huh? Dahlra calls it the Island of Misfit Furniture." Beside the tree, all that remained in the large room was the sofa, an armchair, and a small television. Those items, along with the refrigerator, a few kitchen utensils and the two beds upstairs, constituted the entire list of belongings left in DeVere Gardens. Everything else was either in storage or at Maidenvine. The Christmas carols playing on Sydney's iPhone did little to mask the emptiness.

Elwess stared at the tree, his brow furrowed in thought. "You could have stayed at my place."

"You've been out of town."

"I have house sitters when I'm out of town." A shadow passed over his face. "You could have earned your keep."

Sensing his change of mood, but not truly understanding it, Sydney teased, "Would you have allowed me decorate it while we were there?"

"What, you mean a Christmas tree and all the trimmings? Just how much *have* you been drinking?"

"Aw, c'mon. I'd trim your tree with chains and nipple clamps and wrap the pressies in black leather. Crimbo, S&M Styl-ee. Are you saying you didn't decorate at all?"

Elwess rewarded her with one of his deep, sexy laughs. "I should coco."

She playfully patted his thigh. "*You're* a mean one, Mr Grinch."

He gave her a look that was two parts cool, one part badass. "Careful, submissive. That attitude will get you into a lot of trouble. I happen to have the ear of your Dominant, you know."

Sydney resisted poking out her tongue at him. "And I happen to have the rest of him, *Master* Elwess." She smiled and tried again. "Portugal? How was it?"

No one could roll their eyes like Elwess Talbert. "Oh, Christ. Portugal is hot, expensive and boring in equal measures. It's not until you get there you remember these Fet Expos are only fun for about the first two hours. After that, I was bored out of my skull. That's why I came back early." His expression darkened. "Good thing, actually, because my house sitter—"

"Elwess, welcome home." Dahlra entered the room, a bottle of wine in one hand, and three glasses in the other. "How was Lisbon? Took full advantage of the Portuguese sunshine, I see."

"Ha bloody ha. I've done the sun thing; I looked like a Spanish ice cream salesman. Not very intimidating."

Sydney smirked. "Especially not for England's pre-eminent sexual Deviant—sorry, Dominant."

He smiled tightly; there was something automatic about it, as if his thoughts were elsewhere. He reached for her hand. "At any rate, thank you for letting a jaded, covetous sinner share Christmas with you two. For the first time in a long time I won't be alone during the holidays."

Sydney twined his long fingers with hers and gave them an affectionate squeeze. "No one should be alone at Christmas. *Especially* jaded, covetous sinners. No telling what mischief you'd get up to on your own."

"Now that's a thought. What *do* you usually do over the holidays?" Dahlra settled into the armchair, wine glass in hand.

"Well, submissives don't want the likes of me around this time of year, do they?"

"I'm probably going to regret asking, but why not?" asked Sydney. "What does the time of year have to do with it?"

Elwess made a dismissive gesture with his hands. "Well, it's the guilt thing, innit? These quasi-religious martyr types always gravitate toward S&M. To them it's one step away from self-flagellation."

"Elwess!"

"It's true. But Christmas gets them all warm and fuzzy with the virgin birth and the Father Christmas, 'he sees you when you're sleeping, he knows when you're awake' crap. Now, if you want to talk about a voyeur-

"Well, they feel they ought to 'shun the fruits of the flesh' during the holidays, and I'm the devil incarnate, leading them down the road to perdition. So, between Christmas and the middle of January, I do spring cleaning and taxes."

His dark eyes took on a hard gleam. "Yeah, mid-January. That's about the time all the self-improvement resolutions go out the window. The old itch starts begging to be scratched, and suddenly they remember why they don't have husbands or regular boyfriends. Then they remember that *I'm* the only one who truly understands what they need, and nobody else can take them there. Or so they believe."

Sydney shot Dahlra a quizzical look, but he could only shrug, equally nonplussed. Breezily, Elwess continued. "Oh, make no mistake, by the end of January the Chine is a cattle market. All that pious abstinence gives way to base corruption and the utter abandonment of their dearly held principles. They become complete pain whores for at least a month. I'm up to my nipple clamps in it through Lent." He sneered. "That's when the next wave of guilt-propelled abstinence hits. By then, I'm ready for a holiday myself."

He looked from Dahlra back to Sydney, then rose to his feet, laughing. "Blimey, your faces. There are times when I really wish I had a camera." He pulled them both into his long-armed embrace. "I think my Christmas present just came early." He rewarded Sydney with a hard, smacking kiss, then pressed the two of them close to his chest. He held them a long time, as if he'd been waiting for the opportunity, and didn't want to waste his chance.

For all they were happy to be together, it was a bit of a strained evening. Elwess seemed both moody and tense, but when questioned, he shrugged indifferently. "Travel worn, mostly. Here, let me top up your wine." Sydney and Dahlra tried the circumspect route, but their queries met a stone wall of evasion and sleight-of-hand distraction. Any attempts at serious conversation were answered with more wine, extra brandy, another hot toddy.

By two in the morning, Sydney was none the wiser as to his mood, decidedly two, if not three sheets to the wind, and had run out of shit to give. Dahlra finally looked at his watch and yawned so hard his jaw cracked.

"That's me done, kids. I've got a Christmas dinner to make tomorrow." The three of them stood, making bed-going noises. Sydney found herself leaning a bit more on Dahlra than usual; she could fake it sitting down, but standing up revealed just how rat-arsed she was. At the landing Dahlra gave Elwess a brotherly hug, and she kissed him goodnight.

As she turned to close the bedroom door, their eyes met in a silent, intense connection. The preoccupied look was gone, and in its place a look of longing, bordering on hunger, flashed across his face. He took in her slightly swaying form, and the yearning disappeared behind a slight, wistful quirk of his lips.

"You're going to need some paracetamol in the morning, kitten," he said. "Goodnight, you two. Watch out for Father Christmas."

Elwess opened his eyes, looking blindly around in the darkness. Something had awoken him, but he didn't know if it was a dream, or just some random sound in the unfamiliar flat. He rolled over, and looked at his watch. The luminous hands told him it was 3:57.

He heard a low, muffled moan, and smiled. Dahlra must be giving Sydney her Christmas gift early. Since their first night together, they had not invited him to share their bed; Elwess had been hoping that a little Yuletide bonhomie and cheap liquor might persuade them. *Perhaps I could just slip in, and if they' amenable —*

A sudden, keening wail ripped through the air; an eerie, chilling sound that made his heart kick hard in his chest, bringing him fully awake and breathing hard in an instant. It was Sydney's voice, and the scream slicing through the air had nothing to do with pleasure. It was the shriek of a pain and fear. He was on his feet and at the door before his mind even registered he was vertical.

Another cry tore a jagged hole into the air like something in a horror film. What the hell? He stepped into the hall, when a choked moan hit him like a punch in the gut. It was Sydney's anguished voice, low-pitched and mad with terror.

"Please, please don't... it hurts..."

Another desperate cry for help made him forget niceties like knocking, and he burst into the room, his heart in his throat. It was dark except for the dying remnants of a fire in the tiny grate. Beyond the bed, harsh white light from the open bathroom bisected the room, cutting a path across the bed.

Sydney was thrashing wildly, twisting the covers around her body. Her legs scissored back and forth, tangling the bed sheets around her. "Please, stop...I can't stand it... Don't, please!"

Dahlra emerged from the bathroom, a glass of water in his hand. In the harsh light, his expression was tense and grim. He sat on the edge of the bed and gathered Sydney in his arms. She took in a gulping breath and choked out, "Please don't hurt me anymore! It's too much! I won't tell—" She fought and pushed against him, but she had no more strength than a child.

"Listen to me, Sydney." Dahlra shook her gently but urgently. "My darling, girl, it's another dream."

She coughed harshly as her body snapped into wakefulness, her cries dying in her throat. For a small eternity, she peered searchingly into his face.

"Tell me what you see," Dahlra commanded softly, looking deeply into her eyes. "Tell me who is holding you. Tell me."

For a moment, she was quiet, then she whispered, "Dark hair. Green eyes." She touched his face almost tentatively. "Dahlra?"

"Yes, my little one. It's Dahlra. I'm here."

Sydney's whimper of relief made the hairs on Elwess' arms stand on end. "I thought she was over her nightmares."

Dahlra glanced up, noticing Elwess for the first time. He nodded toward the loo. "Would you fetch me a cool, wet flannel?"

"Of course." Elwess crossed the room and plucked a white flannel from a stack on one of the shelves. He ran it under the tap, gave it a squeeze, and quickly returned to their bedside. "You said cool, but the water's—"

He stilled, mesmerized by the sight before him.

Sydney was clinging to Dahlra as if he was her lifeline. She was shaking so hard Elwess could hear her teeth chatter. As he gently bathed Sydney's flushed face and neck, he never ceased his rocking, or his soft, loving words of endearment.

He glanced over at Dahlra, and saw a tear roll down his handsome face. Love, concern, regret, guilt; they were all there in that single tear. Elwess swallowed, feeling his black heart threatening to break apart. It was both beautiful and horrible, he realised, to love someone this much.

Elwess gingerly sat on the other side of the bed, feeling as helpless and stupid as a green kid. This was an intimacy he had no right to share. God, what was he even doing here? He should get out; out of this room, out of this flat, out of their lives. In the morning, he would give them some lame excuse, and leave, Christmas or no Christmas.

Unsure of what else to do, he stroked Sydney's bare, vulnerable-looking calf. He could feel it trembling beneath his hand. "What is she dreaming about? Are these nightmares about..."

"She's pleading for me to stop them. When she was captured, I...well, you know what I had to do to keep her alive..." He buried his face against her shoulder. "Christ, I hate these fucking nightmares."

Elwess rubbed his back consolingly. "Jesus, mate. I'm sorry."

Dahlra straightened. He sniffed. "To tell the truth, this one wasn't as bad. At one point, she didn't have true, deep uninterrupted sleep for almost a month." He sighed harshly. "The dreams finally slacked off almost a year ago. Since then, she hardly ever has the really bad ones, thank God. It wasn't nice, but it could have been worse."

"Don't talk about me like I'm not here." The two men looked at the owner of the groggy voice. Sydney was lying limp against her Minder, her eyes closed.

Dahlra smiled tenderly. "I'm sorry, my love. I brought you a glass of water. Are you thirsty? Why don't you take a drink... that's a good girl."

She sleepily gulped at the water until the glass was emptied. Elwess took the glass from her hand, and Dahlra held her to him like a man clasping the world to his breast. Gradually, she drifted off. He laid her back down on the bed, and Elwess helped him straighten the bedclothes until she was tucked in again.

"She probably won't remember most of this. That's one good thing, at least. She hardly ever does anymore," Dahlra explained.

Elwess looked down at Sydney. She looked as peaceful as if she'd been dreaming of nothing more taxing than what to wear on Christmas day. "I had no idea, Dahlra. I thought after all this time, she would have worked this out in her head. She's always so strong."

"She's not weak," he said defiantly. "She's as tough and bolshy as anyone you'll ever meet. She's worked hard to deal with what happened to her. And she's succeeded." His voice turned bitter. "Her subconscious, though, sometimes likes to muscle her around a bit."

Sydney made a soft, inarticulate sound, and he gently stroked her cheek. "It's alright, darling girl. Shh. I'm here. Dahlra's here," he crooned, and she nuzzled his palm as she eased back into sleep.

"She only really has the bad ones if she's overdone the alcohol, like tonight, or sometimes during her period. That's due next week. If I can catch the beginning of the dream cycle before it kicks in, I can pretty much stop them before they snag in. I try to stay awake on the nights I think they might happen, but I had a little too much brandy myself this evening." Dahlra's voice stained with remorse.

Elwess flinched. Dahlra was too polite to say it, but they both knew he had been the one topping up Sydney's glass all night. This was his fault. And only minutes ago, he had been planning on leaving them like this? How could he? Even *he* was not that big of a bastard.

"I'll help," he blurted, desperate to say something, anything that might give his friend some peace of mind. "From now on, if I'm around, and you think it might be a bad night, I'll stay, and keep awake, just in case. I promise."

Dahlra looked at him uncertainly. "You'd really do that? You'd be there for me? For us?"

"Always, mate," said Elwess fervently. Looking into the anguished, love-gilded face of his friend, his throat tightened. "Anything I can do to help. Just name it." He stroked her tangled hair. "Whoever did this should roast in hell."

"I did this." Dahlra looked like a condemned man. The shame in his eyes nearly made Elwess look away. Another tear rolled down Dahlra's cheek. "When all is said and done, I caused this, and I'll live with it every day for the rest of my life."

Before guilt and alcohol had the chance to turn the situation into something he wasn't prepared to deal with, Elwess took Dahlra's arm and frog-marched him into the hall. Shutting the door behind them, he switched on the hall light. Both men winced at the brightness.

"Now listen to me, Dahlra Gar," he hissed. "We've been through this over and over, you and me. You will stop beating yourself up about this. Sydney doesn't blame you, and you know it. Not anymore."

"It's just that-"

"If you'll recall, I was the one pouring booze down her throat all night. If anyone's to blame for this, it's me, so don't—"

"Dahlra?"

The soft voice in the other room was like a siren's call to them both. Dahlra hastily wiped his eyes, and switched off the light. Together they walked back into the bedroom.

Half awake, Sydney looked from one man to the other and smiled weakly. "Was I dreaming?" Dahlra nodded, too emotional to trust his voice.

Her face crumpled with remorse. "Oh, sweetie, it's alright. I'm fine. I'm fine..." She pulled him back down on the bed, and took him in her arms. When she kissed his cheek, she licked the salt tear on her lips, and pressed his head against her shoulder. Dahlra nuzzled her closer, as she comforted him in his turn.

Elwess watched this tiny drama unfold, overwhelmed with conflicting feelings. How many nights had they spent this way, stubbornly chasing away one another's demons?

He touched Dahlra's shoulder. "If everything's okay, I'll just head to back my room. Give you two a few more hours' sleep." He made to rise from the bed, but to his surprise, Dahlra caught him by the wrist.

"Stay, Elwess. If you want to be part of my family, stay and help me take care of my girl."

He watched Dahlra slip into bed beside Sydney, and enfolded her in his arms. She turned to Elwess, and held out her hand to him, her voice furry with sleep. "Come on. Get in."

His heart pounding, Elwess pulled back the covers, and spooned against Sydney's silk-covered back. His body responded instantly to her lush, soft flesh. She smelled warm and milky; her lovely bottom nestled perfectly in the bowl of his hips, and he melted against her. Warning his cock and balls he would chop them off and toss them in the disposal should they betray him, he willed his body to chill the fuck down as the three of them shifted until they were comfortable.

Elwess planted a chaste kiss on her shoulder, and slipped a tentative arm around her waist. To his surprise, she threaded her fingers with his, and drew their hands around Dahlra's waist. Dahlra gave Elwess' hair a soothing, almost fatherly stroke, before resting his hand against his lover's head.

"Good night. See you in a few hours." Elwess was relieved he managed to sound sleepy; he felt anything but.

"Good night," both voices answered in unison, like a lullaby sung in duet. Sydney relaxed against him, and gradually her breathing slowed until she was asleep again. Dahlra followed her shortly, his warm, firm torso rising and falling beneath their clasped hands.

In the dark, inhaling the air they exhaled, Elwess tried to work out how he had gone from planning on skipping out at first light, to curling up in bed against Sydney's gorgeous back. Perhaps he should have seen this coming, but there were too many variables, too many anomalies he had not factored. Nothing about this night had gone to plan. Nothing.

It was a long time before Elwess fell asleep.

Gloriously sunny light streamed in through the windows; it was as perfect a Christmas morning as London could offer. Sydney stretched herself awake, enjoying the snap, crackle, pop of her joints as oxygen flooded her system. She felt surprisingly refreshed; aside from the driest mouth this side of the Dead Sea, she didn't even feel hungover. A true Christmas Miracle.

Beneath her, Dahlra's chest rose and fell in a slow gentle rhythm; he was sleeping like a baby. Sometime during the night, Elwess had rolled onto his back and was snoring softly, his mouth open, his hair a wild black tangle over his pillow. One hand was flung out over the edge of the bed; the other was tucked behind his head, revealing a tuft of jet black armpit hair. His impressive morning wood tented beneath the sheet. Big Bad Dom in all his glory. Sydney nearly laughed out loud.

A glance at the clock showed it was just almost ten o'clock. *Oh, this won't do at all.*

She rose quietly, careful not to jolt them, then jumped to her feet and started bouncing up and down on the bed as hard as she could, shouting at the top of her lungs. "Rise and shine, you lazy sods!"

The effect was immediate and hilarious. Both men bolted awake, squawking in surprise and protest. They tried bombing her with pillows, but when that didn't shut her up, they curled up like pillbugs, protecting their delicate bits.

"Wake up, sleepyheads!" she crowed "Tis Christmas Day, Mr Scrooge! Time to buy the biggest turkey in the window and save Tiny Tim and open presents! Get up, get up!"

Dahlra was the first to recover; he pulled her down on the bed between Elwess and himself, and they exacted revenge by tickling her mercilessly. Breathless with laughter, she put up a token resistance, but she was soon screaming, "Inigo Lightoller! Some people just can't take a joke! Inigo!"

Elwess smacked her arse sharply, and rolled out of bed. As he stalked out of the room, he growled over his shoulder, "You'll pay for that, come the revolution! Wicked girls get coal in their stockings for less!"

Still lying in bed laughing, Dahlra pulled Sydney into his arms and kissed her passionately. Still breathless from her 'punishment,' she returned his kiss, looking up into his face. It was darkly stubbled, and his hair was spiked in every direction on his head. One eye was slightly matted with sleep, and he had morning-after-the-night-before breath.

Bloody hell, he was gorgeous. "You look like all I've ever wanted for Christmas," she declared, falling in love with him all over again.

A contented rumble sounded deep in his chest. "Happy Christmas, love."

Sydney snuggled against his chest. Now that her burst of morning energy had ebbed, she started to shiver. "I wonder if we can build a fire without actually having to get out of bed."

He waved a lazy hand toward the fireplace. "Alas. My superpowers must be on the blink."

"Maybe you should wave your magic wand."

His deep laughter vibrated in her ear. "I'm not waving any wand around while Elwess is about, my girl—"

He stopped abruptly. From the floor above them, they heard a strange noise, like something heavy being dragged across the floor. A *thump-thump-thump* sound moved down the stairs, then the dragging commenced toward their room.

As they looked at one another in puzzlement, Elwess appeared in the doorway, wearing nothing but a black velvet Santa hat and a glorious smirk. Behind him he dragged a huge, black velveteen bag bulging angularly with gifts.

"Well, at least he's wearing the Santa hat on his *head*," Dahlra muttered.

Elwess jumped onto the end of the bed, pulling the heaving bag with him. Towering over them, he drawled in a commanding, arrogant tone of pure smug, "All right, you tarts; enough of this sentimental shite." He upturned the bag on them. "Let's get on with the true meaning of Christmas. Bring me my presents!"

They were pelted with gifts, each tastefully and meticulously wrapped with black and white paper and trimmed with black velvet ribbons and bows. They pulled the bed covers over their heads as the boxes rained down on them, and all the while Elwess laughed like some demented horror movie Father Christmas.

Dahlra cursed as the pointed corner of the last box landed on his head. Digging his way out of the gift mountain, he threw on a robe and headed for the door. "As long as we're having Christmas in bed, I'll go and get the rest." Elwess removed his Santa hat and plopped it on Dahlra's head as he passed.

Sydney peeked out of the covers, stunned at the sheer number of presents. "And to think, you've been acting like the biggest humbug on the planet! Who would've thought?" She picked up one of the large boxes and admired it. "The wrapping is stunning," she added, looking at him slyly. "Don't tell me you did it yourself, Elwess."

His derisory snort was the audible equivalent of his famous eye roll. "What good is being surrounded by lovely sex slaves if you can't get them to wrap your pressies for you? The fun part is punishing them if they don't do a good job. You'd be amazed how crap some of them are at gift wrapping when they're properly motivated."

Dahlra returned, arms full of presents. "Bloody hell, Elwess. There's a child's bicycle out on the street two blocks away. Show some respect and put on some pants, man."

It took almost two hours to open every present, due in part to Dahlra's insistence that no presents would be opened until Elwess dressed. Sydney also insisted they all open one gift at a time so they could all admire and enjoy them, a tradition Elwess pronounced 'too American' for his tastes. Nevertheless, it was nice to see him laughing, relaxed and pleased as he watched them open their gifts. It was obvious he had chosen their presents with care and attention.

Dahlra was precise and methodical; he removed the bows, slit open the tape, and tossed the wrapping paper aside. Among his plethora of presents were jumpers, silk neckties, cologne, books, several bottles of Jameson's Special Reserve Irish Whisky, and a new smartphone.

Elwess was, predictably, very messy and careless, ripping paper all to hell, throwing the bows over his shoulder and exclaiming over his gift before greedily reaching for another. His gifts included a cashmere jumper (black, of course), a lethal-looking leather tawse, for which Sydney received a lecherous look of anticipation, several CDs, a book on BDSM Poetry, a case of his favourite rum from Martinique, and several gift cards from various online stores specialising in 'adult materials.'

As far as unwrapping gifts, Sydney was somewhere in between. While she wasn't anal enough to save the paper or recycle bows, Elwess' were quite beautiful, so she laid one aside as a memento of the day. She received an ultra-fancy, all-singing-all-dancing e-reader, several real books, DVDs, jewelry, her favourite Jo Malone perfume, various sex toys (from Elwess, who offered to demonstrate each one in turn), and a gorgeous pair of the sexiest, buttery soft, sage-green silk pajamas she had ever seen.

Later, Dahlra made a roast turkey dinner, complete with all the trimmings, and bade Sydney sit in his lap as he fed her the choicest pieces. Both men seemed to enjoy watching her eat. Dessert was Christmas pudding served in a haze of blue alcoholic flame, which they blew out after Elwess suggested they all make a wish. "I thought that was only for birthday candles," Dahlra remarked.

"It's Christmas," said Elwess. "My Baba always said Christmas wishes come true."

The three of them spent the afternoon lounging around the front room, enjoying the excellent goodies from an enormous Harrods food hamper, a gift from the Lightollers. They roamed in and out of the kitchen, noshing at their own rate, sampling the wine and port gifted by various friends and colleagues, and did what all British subjects did on Christmas Day: watched the Queen's speech and the day's telly offerings.

Later, at Sydney's insistence that she needed to clear her head, they all took a walk around the neighbourhood. As usual, DeVere Gardens was a silent, empty row of houses and cars. The three of them roamed the deserted streets, the two men flanking Sydney on either side. Dahlra's stride was relaxed and graceful, and they strolled side by side.

Elwess' gait was stronger, and he glanced around often, as if on guard. His long legs ate up the distance; periodically he would glance behind, stop, and wait for them to catch him up. Both men were dressed in black coats, gloves and scarves, and with their coloring in the gloomy-white weather, the world looked rendered in grayscale. Even the cars on the street were mostly white, black and silver. Sydney's bright red coat was the only splash of colour.

Feeling marvelously replete, Sydney threaded her arm through Dahlra's and leaned her head against his shoulder as they walked. It was a lovely, comfortable silence; the two men walking with her were solid and alive and she felt damn good, as if she was exactly where she was supposed to be.

My two champions, she thought, and rolled her eyes. In no time at all she had morphed from special agent Secret Squirrel to Perilous Pauline. She had a sudden image of Elwess tying her to train tracks, and hid her laughter behind a cough.

"Alright, love?" Dahlra murmured, kissing her hair.

"Never better." It was one of the truest statements she had ever uttered.

Dahlra's gloved hand folded over hers in the crook of his arm. She recognised them as the same gloves he had worn the first day he caned her at Maidenvine. She looked from his hand to his handsome face, and his lips curved upward in a knowing smile. *Love you*, he mouthed, and she put her arm about his waist and held him close.

The day had started bright and very cold; in the encroaching twilight, it looked as if it might snow. They talked desultorily about what they would do on Boxing Day if it did, and on cue, the first fat flakes started to fall. *A white Christmas. We must be living in a Harlequin Romance*, Sydney thought.

It was dark when they returned to the flat, numb with cold, their hair and shoulders dusted with snow. Elwess built a fire, and the three of them settled in the front room, watching the fairy lights winking on the tree. The roaring fire lulled them, and the Irish coffee, which Sydney liberally laced with Jamesons, warmed and mellowed them. They listened to Christmas carols on the telly as the snow blanketed Kensington, enveloping them in a silent cocoon.

With a grunt of effort, Elwess sat up. "I have one more gift." He dug into his pocket. "It's for you both."

"I can't imagine what it could possibly be. I don't think there's anything left in the shops."

"Hush, Sydney. I'm serious. Hold out your hand." Elwess placed his hand over Dahlra's, then took it away, leaving behind a single house key. "It's to my place," He explained. "I've been thinking about this flat. You said yourself it's so empty you feel like squatters when you stay here.

"And here I am with this massive home five minutes away in Pelham Street, with two empty bedrooms, and two en-suites. I propose you sell this place and stay with me whenever you're here in the city."

Sydney glanced at Dahlra. "This is quite generous of you, Elwess, but wouldn't we be in the way?"

"Not if I say so. You know how I feel about you both. Any chance to get you into my flat means a sporting chance I'll get you down to the Chine for more fun and games. And I have an ulterior motive as well."

"Why am I not surprised?" Dahlra asked. "Let's hear it."

For some reason, Elwess could not quite meet Dahlra's scrutinous gaze. "Here's the thing. Dominants often ask if they can use my dungeon for private sessions." He made a conciliatory gesture. "They 'rent' the Chine for special occasions. It's not a problem when I'm at home, but I don't like leaving my house unattended if people are downstairs. When I go out of town, I normally arrange for a house sitter; it's usually another Dominant I know—Brian Collins."

"I know him. Nice chap."

"Yes, well, because of the holidays, he wasn't available, and I had spot of bother with the bloke who depped for him. It got me to thinking, who better to make sure no one was misbehaving in my gaff while I'm away than you?"

The mystery of Elwess' behaviour the night before suddenly made sense. "So, Elwess," said Sydney, "who *did* you get to housesit this time?"

Elwess' expression grew shuttered. "Silas Markham."

She wrinkled her nose. "As in, tall, blond, 'too-creepy-for-words,' Silas?"

"The same," he said, and a dark look came over his angular face. With a shrug, he continued, "I wasn't all that keen on having him there, but he wanted to use the Chine, and he was willing to pay, so I agreed to it. When I came home early, I wasn't too happy with some of the things I found him doing, so I asked him to leave.

"Nothing illegal, mind," he added hastily, at their concerned expressions. "But yes, it's nice to know I don't have to deal with the likes of him again." He tried to sound flippant, but there was a strained edge to his voice. "So what do you say? Why don't you offload this white elephant and come and stay with me from now on?"

"It does make good sense," Sydney offered.

Dahlra rolled the key over and over in his large hand, studying it thoughtfully. Then he looked up, as if he had made a decision. "All the sense in the world, love," he replied, and placed the key in her hand. "Thank you, Elwess. It's a very generous gift, and we accept."

It was amazing how Elwess could go from Mr Bad Guy to Kid-In-A-Sweet-Shop in a heartbeat. "Excellent! Next week I'll email you the name of an estate agent friend of mine. She's the best in town. You won't have to worry about a thing."

"And you won't have to worry about Silas anymore."

"A definite bonus," Elwess replied, toasting them with his Irish coffee. "Here's to never having to deal with that blond cunt ever again."

Dahlra was fond of saying, "Let my words be soft and juicy, for one day I may have to eat them." If she had known how bitter Elwess' words would eventually taste, Sydney would never have accepted his offer.

CHAPTER TWENTY-ONE

New Year's Confidential

The dead days of December were spent shuttling the last of their belongings from DeVere Gardens to Pelham Street, and emptying the remainder of furniture from the flat. By the time December 31st rolled around, the three of them were more than ready to don a bit of swag and enjoy Inigo and Philippa Lightoller's annual New Year's Eve party.

It was *the* no-miss event for agents and associates in his charge—in other words, if you worked for Inigo, you attended his wife's party. Phillipa, or 'Pip' as she was known to friends and family, was a warm-hearted woman who loved her husband very much. She also adored entertaining; she spent months, not to mention a fuckton of Inigo's dosh, planning and preparing her parties.

In the past, Sydney's tolerance for these affairs typically faded around the moment she found herself pinned in a corner, fending off some long-winded and usually drunk former MP who wittered on about the long-reaching ramifications of the increasing tensions in Syria or the political machinations of Downing Street. She had cried off the previous year, mainly because she and Dahlra had just become lovers and couldn't drag themselves out of bed long enough to dress.

This year she promised herself she would go, and enjoy it. And while she would never think of Dahlra as pure eye candy, or some sort of trophy, one of the main reasons she was looking forward to it had to do with showing him off a little. Besides, the last time she had properly shopped for a party frock was the night she and Dahlra became lovers-she was due.

She was sitting on the sofa reading when Elwess appeared in the front room. He was dressed in a smartly tailored suit—black, of course—right down to his silk shirt and tie. Even his cologne was dark, with traces of patchouli and vetiver notes that managed to be both subtle and mysterious. His Chelsea boots were identical to Dahlra's Hermes'; Elwess had remarked on them during a previous visit. An elegantly understated platinum tie pin completed the ensemble. His raven's wing hair was pulled back in a ponytail. It was a hairstyle that would have looked naff on anyone else, but on Elwess it managed to look rakish. Loose strands framed his long, angular face. He was intimidatingly, intensely masculine, and he played it for all it was worth.

As Dahlra descended the stairs, adjusting his cuffs, Sydney felt a huge smile spreading over her face. Seeing Dahlra Gar in full livery was definitely worth the price of admission. He was wearing a Gieves and Hawkes charcoal suit with a wide pinstripe in the faintest silvery pink. A snowy, collarless shirt peeked from underneath.

He caught Sydney's eye and raised an eyebrow in question: *Does this meet with your approval?*

Oh, hell yes, Sydney thought. *I might just have to rethink that whole 'he's not eye candy' thing.* As she rose to her feet, she gave his lapel a little possessive pat. "You look marvelous. Very GQ."

Dahlra smiled, but his eyes looked faintly puzzled. "And you're still in your bathrobe."

She shook her head. "I told you: if Pip says the party starts at six, what she actually means is to show up at eight."

"That makes no sense."

"Not my circus, not my monkey, darling. The one and only year I showed up at the time written on the invitation, the door was locked and I had to go in the tradesman's entrance. I ended up replenishing snacks most of the night."

"Did they make you wear the little French maid's outfit?"

"Oh, stop twirling your moustache, Elwess."

Dahlra looked both puzzled and dismayed. He was hard-wired for punctuality; Pip's concept of time was obviously short-circuiting his brain. "So...when exactly are we leaving?"

"Right after I shower and dress. Back in two ticks."

As Sydney lightly ran up the stairs, it occurred to her that the men were much too quiet. She looked over her shoulder in time to witness both of them gazing at her backside with identical expressions of rapt appreciation. Feeling mischievous, she put a little more sass in the sway of her hips as she ascended. Elwess swore softly. "Cocktease."

"Indeed. Stop enticing us, you wicked girl," Dahlra added.

"Yes, sir," she replied with mock contrition.

As she continued upward, she heard Dahlra clear his throat. "Well, now that we're two hours early instead of an hour late, I'd say this calls for a little liquid fortification. I can tolerate Inigo alright, and his wife's lovely, but these parties of his..." His voice faded as Sydney headed into the bedroom, shucked off her ratty old bathrobe and jumped into the shower.

She took more than a little extra time with her hair and makeup, then took her dress from its padded hanger. She had probably logged more hours looking for the perfect outfit to wear to this damn party than she had working on her Master's degree, and ended up spending more than the national debt, but it was definitely worth it.

The shopkeeper, a dainty, handsome woman who reminded her of Clara, had smiled as she entered. In a surprisingly thick South London accent, she said, "Hello, dearie! What can we do for you today?"

"I need the perfect dress for a work do." She ticked off the criteria. "It should be gorgeous but not ostentatious, sexy but not sleazy. I need for it to say, 'I'm all yours,' but not in a tarty way, and it should be comfortable and pretty and have my man on his knees in five minutes begging me for the privilege of licking the dirt from my shoes."

The shopkeeper never batted an eye. She pointed to the changing room. "You, in there. Leave it to me."

Fifteen minutes later, Sydney was in the dress of her dreams-a sexy, vintage, tea-length gown in deep blue velvet. Intricate beadwork covered the cap sleeves, ending in a point at the bottom of a dropped waistline, emphasising her slender curves. A sweetheart neckline enhanced her long neck and shoulders, and the colour made her skin glow. A sapphire-blue silk suspender belt with matching bra and the tiniest silk knickers she'd ever worn completed the ensemble.

As she stared at herself in the mirror, the owner had caught her eye and beamed. "Let's hope your man speaks fluent 'Sin,' dearie, because you and that dress are from the Mother Country."

Sydney finished the look with a teardrop-shaped sapphire pendant on a spider-web-thin silver chain, and a pair of pointed, ridiculously high-heeled beaded satin stilettos.

After ten minutes of flexing her elbows and contorting her limbs in a fruitless gesture to do up the dress, she headed down the stairs, calling, "Dahlra, would you—"

The two men were standing apart, their voices low and careless. At the sound of her voice, their conversation ended abruptly, and their eyes shot toward the stairs. "Yes, love?"

"I was hoping you'd help me with my zip."

"Of course."

She turned around, holding her long hair back as Dahlra zipped those last few elusive inches. "It seems such a shame to zip this dress, when all I really want to do is get you out of it," he whispered. He gently blew on the back of her neck, and she shivered pleasantly.

She looked over her shoulder and gave him what she hoped was a flirtatious look. "I can hardly go to the party without it, can I?"

He pressed against her, and slipped his arms around her waist. "I don't want to go to the party at all. I'd rather stay home and make you undress slowly for me." He placed a line of soft kisses down the column of her neck, and she bit back a moan of pleasure.

"Then what?"

"Oh, fuck's sake," Elwess grumbled. "I *can* hear, you know. Stop talking dirty to one another."

"Dear me, Dahlra, Elwess is feeling left out."

"Again?"

"Oi, you two. A little respect, if you please." He made a stirring motion with one finger. "If you're not going to behave, kitten, at least give us a twirl."

Obligingly, Sydney turned in a slow circle. Elwess studied her solemnly. "You know, I've only just noticed how your eye colour changes. Sometimes they look green, but that colour makes them look hazel, almost brown." He nodded. "You look very nice."

Sydney smiled her thanks. She felt good. And more than that, she felt relaxed and confident again. It didn't hurt that Dahlra was looking at her in a way that was making her heart do the rhumba. There was a whisper of sensuality in his smile, and he murmured appreciatively, "Tell me I don't have the most beautiful girl in the world, Elwess."

Elwess sighed and crossed his arms. "Now you're just being cruel. I'm only human, you know."

Sydney accepted a glass of wine from Dahlra, as she joined Elwess on the sofa. "Cheer up, Elwess! We're going to a very lovely party with lots of eligible girls in spangly tops and little black dresses, all eager for a New Year's pull. You're going to be the hottest thing on the menu."

"Be still my beating heart. A room full of Croydon secretaries at an Agency party, whose idea of adventurous sex is 'doing it' with the lights on. Believe me, kitten, I'm not going to this 'do' to get lucky." He sighed wistfully, and reached for the bottle. "Come on, Dr and Ms Truly Madly Deeply. Let's have another drink, then go to this New Year's Eve party and chat up secretaries."

As they rode in the taxi over to the Lightollers' massive home in Mayfair, Dahlra shyly confessed he had gate-crashed one of the previous parties, solely in hopes of seeing Sydney. It was embarrassing, actually; she had not noticed him. He dismissed her self-recriminations with a wave of his hand. "Oh, I stayed in the shadows a lot," he smiled. "I wasn't supposed to be there, you know."

"Bloody stalker, more like," Elwess muttered. "I tried to get him to stay away, you know. I knew if he got caught, it would be *my* arse. But no, he had to get a glimpse of you. Had to get his fix," he smirked, not without affection. "I don't think I've ever known someone as stone in love as Doctor Dahlra Gar."

Sydney slipped her hand into her Minder's and felt his long fingers close around hers. "Oh, I don't know."

As Elwess paid the cabbie, Dahlra pulled her close in the frosty night air, and tucked her hand in the crook of his elbow. He smiled down at her. "I'll be the envy of every man here tonight." He pulled her closer. "I want you tonight, in this house, and I'm going to have you."

In spite of the cold, she felt a hot kernel of lust take root in her solar plexus. Even now, a year after they had first become lovers, he could still have her head buzzing with a few softly-spoken words. Of course, over that year, she had learned how to get him on his knees with a heated look and the right pair of knickers.

Tonight, she decided, that was *exactly* what she was going to do. A frisson of anticipation made her blush rise, and Dahlra read it as accurately as if she'd downloaded her intentions directly into his mind. His warm hand caressed her bottom, and gave it a proprietary squeeze.

"If you're thinking what I'm thinking," he purred, "seek me out. Later."

"Come on, you two." Elwess' scowl was firmly back in place. "God, I hope I get lucky tonight and chat up a cute brunette with a penchant for being tied up and abused. I'm going to be feckin' cockblocked otherwise."

The party was just hotting up as they entered the massive foyer. As Dahlra took their coats, Sydney watched in amusement as Elwess made his entrance. As promised, the room was full of females dressed in all manner of evening and party wear. Almost to a woman, they turned to watch him, his stride graceful and studied, his angular face arresting and predatory with only the slightest trace of arrogance. He moved with deliberate nonchalance, and yet, those he *wanted* to notice were transfixed by him immediately, as if he exuded a magnetic pull solely for their benefit. Every move carried a masculine, sinister air of menace. He was a walking personification of sex.

There was an almost instantaneous change in the atmosphere. Fingers fluffed and adjusted already perfectly coiffed hair. Conversation and laughter increased in volume and animation. His eyes casually swept over a group of women, who gaped up at him as if beholding Zeus. He favoured them with a slow blink, and the tiniest quirk of a smile. Each woman reacted as if he was looking at her and her alone.

"Christ, you can almost *see* the estrogen levels rising, can't you?" Sydney whispered.

Dahlra nodded. "You have to admit, what he lacks in movie-star looks, he more than makes up in sheer chutzpah."

Sydney smothered a laugh. There was nothing pretty about Elwess, but he was the real deal. His cat-amongst-the-pigeons routine was going to be more entertaining than any turn the Lightollers hired for the evening. His phone would be full of names and numbers by the end of the night.

Inigo and Pip stood by the entrance to the large front room, greeting their guests. With a loud squeak of excitement, Pip almost knocked Sydney off her feet with her hug of welcome.

"Sydney, Darling! Happy New Year!" Her smile lit up her cherubic face. "You look absolutely stunning in that lovely dress!" Another hug engulfed her. "And Dahlra, welcome to our home at last. I hope you'll enjoy your first party with us."

Dahlra kissed her hand, European style, and turned to their host, whose smirk made it plain he was quite aware this was not Dahlra's first attendance. "Enjoy yourself, Doctor," Inigo said, with his politician's smile.

The party was typical Lightoller chic, with astounding amounts of nibbles, drinks and entertainment. A four-piece band provided the soundtrack, playing renditions of holiday music, ranging from jazzy to cheesy. The mood was festive, but it was still early enough in the evening to maintain propriety.

Being at one of Pip Lightoller's parties felt a lot like being in a film, though few cinematic productions were organised with such precision. Nothing was left to chance. Though the booze flowed freely, nobody misbehaved; people never got bored, or vomited in the potted plants, or jumped up onto the piano and started a drunken striptease, or picked a fight. It simply wasn't in the script.

Sydney wasted no time wading in, mingling her way through the groups of people, waving at this acquaintance, chatting with another. She spotted Garnet Pinkerton, but before she could head in his direction, she was intercepted by a young woman with gorgeous red hair and a face that could only be grown in Ireland.

"Wotcha, Sydney!" she exclaimed, giving Sydney a quick hug.

"Mel! It's great to see you." Melissa Morrin had briefly worked under Sydney when she first arrived at the Agency, and she had instantly taken a liking to the hard working, intelligent young woman. Mel was also gorgeous: a petite, angelic-faced girl with rich auburn curls, a smattering of freckles across a button nose, and large, cornflower-blue eyes. The young bucks in the Agency swarmed around her like bees to a hive. Beside her, Sydney always felt a bit like mutton dressed as lamb.

"Ah, you're looking grand! Garden leave must suit you," Melissa proclaimed, her lilting Limerick accent soft and musical. She bit her lip, and leaned in conspiratorially. "Now, you have to tell me. Who's that tall, dark and handsome man you came in with?"

Sydney felt a swell of pride. "That's my um... my partner, Dahlra Gar. I'd love for you to meet—"

"No, Syd, not him! I mean, he's lovely, of course, but," Mel nodded toward Elwess, who was standing by the fireplace, talking to a woman Sydney didn't recognise. "I mean *that* one. I've never seen a man so, so..." Mel threw her hands in the air, as if unable to express herself.

"Yes, he does seem to have that effect on people," Sydney replied dryly.

"Gawd! He's feckin' gorgeous. I mean, a *real* man. D'you think you could introduce me?"

"Umm..."

Mel face fell. "Oh, don't tell me—he's married! I always zero in on the married ones."

Sydney shook her head, grasping uselessly for an explanation. "No, it's not that. He's just, umm..."

"Oh, Jaysus, he's gay, isn't he? I should've known. Why are all the really interesting ones only interested in-"

"He's not gay, Mel, I can assure you! And he's not married, either." She sighed. "Oh, hell, how do I explain this? He's a decent guy, and a good friend, but well, Elwess is a bit, um, different, I guess you'd say."

Mel froze, her mouth gaping open. "Elwess? Oh, you don't mean that's Elwess Talbert? *THE* Elwess Talbert?" She craned her neck to get a closer look. "Oh, fackinell, I've heard about him." She looked at Sydney with eyes as huge as saucers. "Is it true what they say about him? That he's—" she leaned in closer, and whispered, "He's a real Master, as in 'Master-stroke-slave Master'?"

"Well, yes, but—"

"Saints and apostles!" Mel gasped. She turned the full battery of her large blue eyes up at Sydney. "Oh, please, Syd, would you introduce me?"

Sydney mentally shrugged. Mel was a big girl, and one more addition to Elwess' harem would hardly make a difference. She took Mel's hand and let her toward her fate.

"Elwess, excuse me, but I'd like you to meet a friend of mine. Agent Melissa Morrin, Elwess Talbert."

Elwess took Mel's hand in his, and brought it to his lips. His dark eyes flashed over her. "A pleasure, Miss Morrin," he replied. "Any friend of Agent Chapin's is a friend of mine." Melissa blushed, and Elwess hummed approvingly. "Charming."

Sydney bit back a laugh. He could be such a lech at times. "Well, I'll just leave you two to get acquainted. Behave yourselves."

He gave her a look she could feel between her breasts. "I could say the same for you, kitten."

Without blinking, she turned away and began to search for Dahlra. The little pantomime she and Elwess had just played, not to mention the general crush of the room, was making her antsy as hell.

Yeah, right. The noise and the heat had little to do with her restlessness. By ten o'clock she was as randy as a teenager and ready to drag Dahlra into a cupboard if necessary. Looking around, she spotted him speaking to a short gentleman with the tweedy look of a scholar or teacher. She stared until she finally caught his eye. He smiled knowingly, and mouthed *later*. As he nodded to his conversation companion, Sydney decided that *later* wasn't sodding cutting it. She wanted *now*.

She placed her champagne flute on a passing waiter's tray and made her approach. Out of the corner of his eye, Dahlra tracked her movements, and as she passed behind him, his words faded to a distracted halt. Sydney trailed her hand across his lower back, and kept moving toward the back part of the house. A quick glance behind confirmed he was following her. No one paid them any notice—except the man standing by the mantle.

Sydney ran quickly up the back stairs and turned right. She ducked into a tiny loo. A candle floated in a glass bowl on the side of the vanity, its soft glow suffusing the room with dreamy light. She quietly closed the door, and listened for approaching footsteps.

She did not have to wait long. The footsteps slowed, then paused on the other side of the closed door. The handle slowly turned, and unable to wait, Sydney yanked opened the door, grabbed a handful of coat and dragged him in.

As she closed and locked the door behind him, Dahlra laughed at her impatience. He looked down at her, his handsome face glowing in the candlelight. A ghost of a smile played across his lips. "Why, hello there. I'm Dahlra Gar. Have we met?"

Looking up into his large eyes, arousal-drenched and glowing, Sydney felt giddy. She might be rounding the corner on forty, but that didn't mean she had lost her taste for playing 'let's pretend'. "I don't think so. My name is Sydney," she replied breathlessly. She placed her hands on his chest, and felt his heart beating, steady and strong. "I'm sorry to be so forward, but I saw you earlier, and I couldn't take my eyes off you. You must hear that all the time."

His hands stole around her waist, and he pulled her against his body with all the flirtatious flair of a player. "What a coincidence. I've been watching you as well," he replied, his voice as smooth and cool as chilled liqueur.

"Have you? Why?"

"Why?" He caught her wrists in his hands, shackling her within his grip. "Because you're mine."

His kiss was a full-on assault of masculine lust that scorched her to cinders and caused her core to pulsate. He kissed her like a lover long denied; a wild tangle of lips and tongues and moans of lust. They ground against one another as if they'd not touched for weeks. Dahlra bent her back over his arm and clasped the back of her head, draining her mouth demandingly, rushing all her blood and heat down to a sharp pleasure ache between her legs.

His tongue slid against hers, and he suckled at her lips until she was gasping for air, and still he kissed her. As she sucked his tongue into her mouth, he made a soft mewling sound that nearly drove her to her knees. Her hands scrabbled at his shoulders, pulling him closer.

He finally slowed, leaving them both panting. Sydney cupped his raging erection, and he smiled, his kiss-swollen mouth lush and parted. "You're a dirty little girl, luring me here..."

She unbuckled his belt and unbuttoned his trousers as if she were being timed. He closed his eyes, and a ragged sigh stuttered from his lips. "Get on your knees... take me out."

She knelt, opening his clothing and releasing his heavy, straining cock to the cool air. It was as hard as bone, and so hot it burned her hand.

She grasped the base of his cock, and he rasped, "All those years of watching you... I fantasised about you... you know what I want, Sydney... oh, God, yes—" He staggered against the door as she engulfed the entire length of him. Swirling her tongue around the head of his erection, she pleasured him with a relentless twirling motion that reduced his vocabulary to soft, inarticulate moans of pleasure.

She fucked him with her mouth, stroking him hard with each upward, sucking pull. He gasped and shuddered as she milked him thoroughly, his soft, sweet noises unbearably exciting to her. His balls grew heavy and tight in her hand, until he grasped the back of her head roughly. "Take it all," he growled, pumping harder, faster into her mouth.

Sydney relaxed her throat until she was taking him as deep as possible, moving with his driving hips, feeling him rushing to his climax. He was holding her hair tightly, but she didn't care; she wanted to taste him, to grow drunk on the thrill of bringing him off while he shook and shivered and spilled into her.

He made a sudden sound that was equal parts pleasure and shock, and he grasped her hair painfully. "I'm coming, oh, fuck, make me come, make me come—"

His climax sprayed down her throat, hot and salty sweet, and he snarled and kicked back against the door. "Jesus," he breathed, as each thrust grew slower and looser.

When she at last released him, he took a deep calming breath, and slowly pulled up his trousers. For a long, slow moment, they stared at one another. He reached for her, but she stopped him.

"No."

He looked startled at first, but something in her expression made him smile. "No?"

She eased into his arms. "Right now, if you touch me, I'm going to come, and I'll scream the house down."

"You make that sound like a bad thing."

"It will be if everyone comes running to see who's getting murdered. There are folks out there packin' heat, you know."

"There is that." He kissed her slowly, deeply, until her head was swimming. "Later, then," he whispered against her lips.

Sydney moaned in frustration. This self-discipline shit was for the birds. "God, yes. Later. Promise?"

"I'm all yours."

With as much dignity and decorum as they could muster, they restored their clothing to order and Sydney retouched her makeup. When she was presentable, Dahlra quietly opened the door.

A very aggrieved Elwess was leaning against the frame, arms crossed. His sensitive nostrils flared at the whiff of sex musk emanating from the small room.

"Blimey, I should've known. What a couple of tarts. The other loos were full, so Lightoller sent me to this one. Good thing it *was* me. It sounded like you two were mauling one another in there."

Sydney glanced at Dahlra, who returned Elwess' scowl with bland inscrutability. Sighing, Elwess checked the hall, found the coast clear, and beckoned them out of the room with a jerk of his head. "C'mon, you two." As they traded places, he gave them a warning look. "You can wait on me this time."

Moments later, the three of them fell in step down the hall. Sydney cleared her throat. "Actually, I didn't think you'd miss us too much."

Dahlra nodded in agreement. "When I last saw you, you were up to your parts in female company."

"Not to mention the lovely Melissa. It looked like you two were getting along alright," Sydney added.

Elwess grunted. "Yes, well, Melissa—that remains to be seen," he replied cryptically. "As for the rest, do spare me; a roomful of vapid waitresses who talked about clothes, the latest Britain's Got Talent winner and getting pissed down at their local. At least with you two I can enjoy a decent conversation about things that hold some interest for me—when I can catch you between bouts of bodily assault, that is."

"Forgive us, dear." Sydney patted his cheek indulgently. "We'll try to contain ourselves long enough to supply you with some entertainment."

"You could have at least invited me to watch," he pouted.

Before they returned to the front room, Dahlra excused himself and made his way to the crowded bar to refresh their drinks. As Sydney waited, someone bumped into her from behind, nearly knocking her glass from her hand.

"Oops, sorry—Oi, Sydney! Hiya."

"Oh! Hiya, Ross. You doing ok?"

Pink was fond of saying the only reason Ross Bullard became an agent was that he had accidentally shot himself in the foot with what was supposed to be an unloaded gun, and they gave him the job for spotting the difference. He was one of those colleagues you couldn't quite respect enough to like, but was a bit too dull to provoke actual aversion. He was certainly the most accident-prone bugger she had ever met.

He was a handsome enough guy, but he always dressed like a man who doused himself with super glue every morning, ran through his wardrobe, and wore whatever stuck to him on the trip. Even in party togs he looked disheveled and feckless. Scuffed brown loafers accompanied his slightly crumpled black suit; his shirt tail sagged from his waistband. His sandy brown hair was mussed and looked as if it could use a wash.

He swayed slightly, his pale blue eyes watery and slightly out of focus. With inebriated sincerity, he placed a liquor-wet kiss on her cheek. "So lovely to see you, Sydney. How've you been?"

"I'm great Ross, thanks." Sydney dutifully returned the kiss. His cheek was warm and clammy; there was a lipstick smear from some other woman's kisses.

He beamed the happy smile of the comfortably pissed. "It's been bloody *ages*! Where are you living now?" The music swelled around them, and the volume of the band soon reduced their conversation to hand signals of the 'I'll call you' variety. With a vague, drunken wave, Ross moved on, tripping over the corner of a rug as he hallooed someone else.

A familiar voice sounded in her ear. "Oh, I see, darlin'. Our Syd's got time for ol' Rusty Bollard here, but none for her old mates."

With a smile, Sydney turned and was immediately engulfed in Garnet Pinkerton's suffocating bear hug. "I was trying to make my way over, but I kept getting interrupted. How are you, mate?"

Garnet leaned down to make himself heard. "Not so dusty. What about you and the good doctor? I'm sorry I haven't been up for ages, but I've been a little busy." He turned to the diminutive blonde at his side. "Sydney Chapin, this is Celia White, my, um, my Minder," he finished proudly.

Celia held out her hand to Sydney. "You need no introduction, Ms Chapin. I'm quite a fan of both you and Dr Gar." She had a soft Lancastrian accent, and she looked up at Pink with open affection. "Garnet has told me a few war stories, of course."

"Oh, I wouldn't put too much credence to them, Celia. Pink's a pork pie salesman."

Celia laughed. "Don't I know it!"

"Oi, you two! I *am* right here." Sydney looked up at him in mock surprise.

"Why yes, you are. What was your name again?"

Celia laughed. "I'll leave you two to re-introduce yourselves while I go to the loo. Be back shortly." Celia kissed the tip of her finger and placed it on Garnet's lips, then slipped through the crowd.

Sydney watched Garnet watching Celia disappear into the sea of party-goers. Wryly, she asked, "So, happy with your Minder much?"

"She's a fine gel, mate. I'm damn lucky." He turned back, a look of contentment on his long, bony face. "Been nice having someone to come home to. And she treats me like a king. Well, I feel like one, nutmeen?"

She patted his arm. "I'm glad, Pink. You deserve it. Really."

"Dunno about that, but I'm enjoying it until she comes to her senses."

It hit Sydney with a jolt that, as long and as closely as they had worked together, as much as they had joked about James Bond getting more grind in a single film than they had got since graduation, they never seriously discussed their sex lives with one another.

By tacit agreement, they had never gathered round the tomb of the forbidden subject to swap one particular kind of war stories. She did not know why, exactly, but it just seemed wrong, like brothers and sisters telling one another about their love lives. And yet, if anyone had asked, Sydney would have stated unequivocally that she and Garnet knew one another as well or better than anyone else on earth.

At least, professionally.

"Hey, did you get a chance to use those Chelsea tickets?"

"Actually, Dahlra went with his friend Elwess. I knew he'd enjoy it more with the added testosterone."

Garnet's smile faltered. "Elwess... Talbert? He's not one of Dahlra's mates, is he?"

"Yes, well, actually, Elwess was Dahlra's mentor and trainer in the Minder program. Why?"

He gave her a narrow-eyed, pensive look. "Probably nothing, but seeing he's the Top Dog in the fetish scene here in London..."

"He's clean. I've practically scoured him with bleach—"

"That as may be, Syd, but the Fet community here in England is tight. Everyone knows everyone else. You know that. They look after their own."

"What are you trying to say, Pink?"

Garnet glanced around, scoping the room to see if anyone was paying any undue attention.

"Ol' Basil won't thank me for letting the cat out of the bag, but Silverbirch is more active than we've been letting on. Something has changed in the past couple of months. We're hearing things that, well, they ain't good. People are disappearing. Trafficking on a global scale, infiltrating the clubs, passing round dodgy gear."

Garnet made a show of swirling the ice in his drink. "Not to cast a pall on the festivities, but I can tell you we're hearing things that make the Ripper murders look like a bit of slap and tickle. Lightoller was all set to ramp the case back up after the holidays."

"Was?"

"Our own intelligence keeps pinging back."

"You think it's an inside job?"

He drained his glass, using the lifting motion to look around again. "I dunno, and neither does Lightoller. But every time we receive intel, they're always one step ahead of us."

She glanced over to where Elwess was standing. He and Mel were chatting again, and he was leaning down solicitously, as if to catch her words. Whatever she was saying had a sobering effect on him; his reply seemed quite solemn. Mel, too, looked serious, and she nodded in a way that could have almost been construed as a bow.

"I would have a hard time believing Elwess Talbert would align himself with Silverbirch. I think I'd know."

Garnet scoffed, as if she'd said something witty. Quietly he replied, "You might, and you might not. Just be careful, that's all I'm saying, Syd. Word is Silverbirch has a new broom, and he wants to prove himself. Smarter, better informed, better-connected. From what little we've heard, they want to run with the big dogs now. No more two-bit stag nights with live bait. We're talking grand scale—drugs, trafficking.

"Basil's not messing this time. The ones that go down will go down hard. If your friend's involved, he'll be found out. And if he's not, he's got a high enough profile in the Fet world to call attention to himself. He may be targeted or blackmailed. I just wanted to give you the head's up. We flushed out the first mole. Lightoller will want you involved so we can nick this one."

"You got an ETA on that?"

"Blimey, what a queue for the ladies! I was getting a little worried for a moment. There was a large plant pot in the hallway that was starting to look tempting."

Both Sydney and Garnet returned their expressions to casual mode as Celia returned to Garnet's side. He gave Sydney a look that any long-term partner would recognise. *We'll talk later.* He put his arm around Celia and gave Sydney a nod. "Well mate, my ice cubes are dry. I think we'll head over to the bar and gis a top up."

"If you see Dahlra, make sure he has provisions," said Sydney. "I think the queue for the bar must reach all the way to Epiphany."

"Will do. Here, let's plan on getting together sometime this month, yeah? Celia bakes a mean lasagna." He patted her arm. "Give us time to catch up."

"Sounds like a plan."

Celia gave her a warm look. "It was great meeting you at last, Sydney. The next time you're in London, please let us know."

"We'll be in touch."

As midnight approached, the volume of the room increased with the blood alcohol levels, making Sydney feel trapped and wondering where the hell Dahlra was. Finally, she spotted him in a far corner, talking to Inigo. Their faces were closed and surreptitious, and Sydney wondered if their conversation was in any way similar to the one she had shared with Garnet.

It was a brave, new year; Garnet had seemed to hint that Silverbirch was going to be the Agency's top priority. That both worried and excited her. Silverbirch had been her cross to bear; after what had happened to her, most agents would want to get as far away from it as possible. She had been out of the game for going on two years, and yet, when Inigo called, she jumped at the chance to visit Ramcat on the slimmest chance she could dig up some more evidence.

But it's not just you anymore. You have to think about Dahlra now. Do you really want to drag him into the big top of that sleazy circus?

Across the room, Sydney observed Elwess, holding court against the fireplace mantle, as not one but three ladies, including Mel, were hanging on his every word. Elwess wasn't beyond a little predatory shit when on the prowl, but those women, Mel included, were of age; they didn't need Sydney playing lion tamer.

The more she thought about what Pink had said, the less she could picture Elwess batting for Silverbirch. His position in the Agency was too exposed; he could never go deep enough to cover something of that magnitude. Sydney bit her lip thoughtfully. Moreover, the real truth is she didn't *want* to believe it of him; she couldn't see him using her, using *Dahlra,* that way. If there was indeed a mole, it wasn't Elwess. She felt it in her waters. Huh-uh. No way.

As if he could sense her thoughts, Elwess stopped talking, and looked directly at her. He raised an arched and elegant eyebrow questioningly, and as she watched, his dark eyes began to smolder. Like a torch to gasoline, they sparked a sharp heat in the pit of her belly. As he held her captive with that hungry, sardonic gaze, she could almost hear his voice: *You know what I want, kitten. And one day, very soon, you and Dahlra will give it to me. Both of you.*

And you'll like it.

Dahlra and Sydney took to the dance floor for several slow tunes. He led with a light, easy touch, and she relaxed in the safety of his sure embrace. She was tired, and feeling curiously emotional. Holiday music would ever remind her of that magical concert at the Albert Hall, and the life-changing evening that followed. That, coupled with Garnet's disturbing and cryptic mention of Silverbirch, seemed portent.

Inigo begged a duty dance as Dahlra charmingly took Pip for a spin, but the moment she mentioned speaking with Garnet, Inigo barraged her with a series of pointless questions about nothing at all, so she let the matter drop. They danced the rest of the song in uncomfortable silence.

When the band struck up the opening bars of a rather suave rendition of 'Baby It's Cold Outside', she gratefully accepted Elwess' request to cut in. He was, unsurprisingly, more assertive in his leading; a man used to telling a woman what to do and having it obeyed without question. As they moved in time with the music, Elwess said, "Thank you."

She looked up in surprise. His severe features looked even more arresting in the candlelight. "Whatever for?"

He did not reply at once. Instead, he cleared his throat, his eyes focusing somewhere around the vicinity of her right ear. When not in full Dominant Nasty Bastard mode, Elwess could appear as vulnerable as a teenage boy with poor self-esteem.

"For inviting me to share the holidays with you and Dahlra."

"You've already thanked me for that."

"I don't really have that many friends. I have acquaintances, and several who call me names of respect." He spoke the last words with clipped formality, as if they were rehearsed. "I would like, I would *hope,* that you think of me as a friend."

She bit her lip; she had to proceed carefully. "Elwess, I don't understand why you haven't found a nice little sub and settled down and had lots of black-haired babies. You have money. You're smart, you're sexy; you're a great lover. You don't strike me as a man who looks for trouble. A lot of beautiful women would kill to be with you."

He studied her face intently, but didn't answer. Unable to stand this much unasked-for scrutiny, Sydney looked away, silently cursing her lack of finesse. She spotted Dahlra, talking to Garnet. Elwess followed her line of sight, and sighed.

"I know who I am. Do you know who you are? I'm holding that 'once in a lifetime' woman in my arms, Sydney. Why would I even want settle for anything less? The women who come to me are addicted to pleasure and pain. That's why I can control them; I provide what they want at my whim. That's my addiction: power."

He looked down on her with the same thrilling intensity as before. "But you're not like them. You aren't enslaved by anything, except perhaps Dahlra. A Dominant like me finds a sub like you only once or twice in his lifetime."

"And what kind of Dominant does that make you?"

"The kind of Dominant who would never try to come between you and Dahlra. The kind of Dominant who'll take whatever the two of you are willing to share." He pulled her closer and growled softly in her ear, "The kind of Dominant who would get on my knees, and allow you to Dominate *me*."

The music ended, and he caressed her cheek with the back of his hand. Some of the animal, angry passion had cooled. "I want you. During the times I can't be with you and Dahlra, I'll play—I'll give the pleasure-slaves and the pain-whores what they need. And I'll enjoy the power that comes with it. But you and Dahlra are the only ones I want."

"As my Dom, or his sub?"

"Perhaps as your lover, and his friend."

Sydney felt Dahlra's familiar hand on her shoulder, and nearly sagged in relief. This was getting too heavy to deal with at a fricckin' party. His cool, unreadable mask firmly back in place, Elwess formally released her to Dahlra, then walked away in the direction of Melissa Morrin, who smiled shyly and offered him a glass of champagne.

Dahlra took her in his arms, and they moved gracefully to the music. "Did I miss something?" he asked, watching Elwess with puzzled curiosity.

"And how."

As they danced, Sydney told him everything. On one side of the equation was Elwess' passionate declaration of his intentions. Bookending the other was Garnet's suspicion and distrust. And caught in the centre, her Minder and herself.

"Garnet said as much to me a few moments ago. I told him for what it's worth, I've known Elwess for over five years now. I don't think he's any more involved with Silverbirch than you are."

"My words as well."

Sydney nestled against Dahlra's shoulder as he led her. "Elwess has never struck me as the type to obsess over something, even us. I don't think it's anything to be concerned over. Circumstances have fostered the relationship in a very unique way, and he's opportunistic enough to exploit that."

Sydney laughed silently. "You have the most marvelous gift for understatement, Dr Gar."

"I also know for a fact he would never hurt either of us. I trust him in ways I would never trust anyone other than you, dear one. He's in love with you."

Sydney stopped moving. "What?"

Dahlra looked no more concerned than if he'd been told he had a piece of cotton on his shoulder. "It's as plain as the nose on his face. As the nose on *my* face."

"Enough of that-"

"He adores you, Sydney."

She let that sink in. Geez, you think you're just going to a party, when out of an orange coloured sky..."Does that bother you?"

Dahlra shook his head. "No. He would never try to come between us. He loves me as well. Well, not *quite* in the same way. To my knowledge, he isn't into men, and I most certainly am not."

"Thank fuck for that," she said, and felt his laughter stirring her hair.

"He tries not to show it, but I think he's lonely. All his people are dead or scattered to the four winds. I think he's realised it's something he needs, and he wants to keep it." He took her back into his arms as the music started again. "Elwess is a man who sees love and sex very differently than you and me. He would never come between us. It's the *us* part that attracts him. Does *that* bother *you*?"

Sydney dug deep. Her feelings for Elwess never seemed to stand still long enough for her to draw a bead on them. For someone who wasn't into the introspective head-shrinking stuff, Sydney found Elwess a hard man to feel ambivalent about. It was strange; she loved Dahlra completely and unquestioningly, and her love for him grew with every passing day. But she could and did feel sexual desire for Elwess, and she was able to acknowledge that fact without feeling like she was being unfaithful. It was both familial and sexual and those two reactions struck her as being mutually exclusive.

"Actually, no, it doesn't bother me. Like you and me feels right; you, me, and Elwess has its own 'feel-right' factor as well."

"I agree. I never thought I'd feel that way about another man, but I do. It's comforting, knowing he cares so much for you."

The music stopped. "Let's go someplace quiet. I want to tell you something." He drew her into a quiet alcove.

He looked down at her with quiet, mellow affection. "Sydney, do you know why I'm so good at Scrabble?"

Sydney was so surprised she burst out laughing. "Because you're a swot and swallowed a dictionary?"

He gave her one of his easy grins. "Think again."

Stumped, Sydney threw up her hands, like a straight man in a vaudeville show. "I give up. Why are you so good at Scrabble, Dahlra?"

"Because I don't play to win. Even if I don't win, I still win."

She studied him for a long time, trying to parse exactly what that meant. Dahlra *was* good at the game—a fact that was unassailable. He was patient, took risks, he wasn't afraid to hold onto difficult letters until the perfect opportunity, he didn't miss obscure words or plurals. He wasn't afraid to play the long game.

Those were also unassailable facts, but she could say the same thing about her own talents.

Dahlra was a driven person. When he played, he played with his entire being, his entire formidable focus pinpointed on that moment. When something interested him, he studied it, he researched it and learned everything he could about it. She was living proof of that.

But was that the answer?

He never cheated, he won with modesty and grace. Dahlra Gar was not a ball-spiking, dance in the end zone type of winner. And on those rare occasions when he did lose, he was no less gracious. No drama, no petulance, no insistence they play again just to recoup his ego. He played for no other agenda than to simply play.

He was good at it because he loved it, and played in a way that made her want to play *with* him, over and over. If she considered it that way, he never lost, even if he didn't actually win the game. "I think I understand," she said slowly. Dahlra took her face in his hands, and looked at her in that way that made her want to find an empty bedroom, throw him on his back and ride him until he lost his mind.

"Elwess was a good friend to me before you and I got together, and unless he gives me cause to think otherwise, he'll be a good friend to you as well. And I believe if we take this relationship further, he will push us both in directions we might not go on our own. Directions we may find very pleasurable, with the proper guidance. As long as he loves you, I'll welcome him into our lives As long as you want him. As long as *you* come first."

Sydney drew him closer, her heart beating hard. "Let's get one thing straight, Scrabble Boy. You're all I need. You're decent, you're sexy, you're kind, you're nice—"

"They say nice guys finish last, don't they?" He was smiling, nevertheless.

If it's the last thing I ever do, she vowed, *I'm going to prove you don't have to do anything beyond breathing to ensure my devotion.* "But they *do* finish, Dahlra. And you will never finish last with me."

With a flourish, the band stopped mid-song. Inigo stood and tapped his spoon against his crystal champagne flute. "If I may have everyone's attention, please." He waited until the room grew quiet. He raised his glass, and caught Sydney's eye. "It's lovely to have you all here to share the season with us. It's been a good year; a year in which we've come through safe and sound, and that is my perennial wish for us all.

"Now, remember, there are enough comestibles to see us through a nuclear winter, and the band has been instructed to play as long as anyone is still on their feet. Indulge yourself all you want, only do not drink and drive. I have a fleet of cabs lined up for party's end, so if anyone needs one, be a good chap and take their keys."

He paused for emphasis. "And now, to the real reason we are here..." He made a show of checking his watch. "I'm synchronised with Big Ben, and the countdown is about to commence!"

Sydney smiled to herself as the guests rose to their feet, glasses in hand. Inigo always loved this little bit of drama. "Here we go, in ten..."

The room was filled with voices counting down the seconds until midnight. Beside her, Dahlra and Elwess counted with her: "Nine eight, seven..."

She could feel the energy of the room rise with each second, and she allowed herself to be caught up in the excitement as well. "Six, five, four..."

Dahlra caught her hand in his. "Three, two, one..."

"Happy New Year!" the roar of the crowd rattled the doors, and the band swung into "Auld Lang Syne." Amidst the clinking of glasses and drunken singing, Dahlra spun her into his arms, pulling her off her feet, and kissed her fiercely. There was a sweet, possessive edge to his kiss, and Sydney returned it with a ferocity of her own. When they parted, she found herself face to face, eye to eye with him, and the look on his handsome face told her she was the only woman in the room, and that she always would be.

"Happy New Year," he whispered, and slowly released her. Her feet touched the floor, and she reluctantly let him go.

By three a.m., Sydney had about as much corporate revelry as she was prepared to endure, and the trio returned to Pelham Street. As the Asian cabbie drove them through the almost deserted streets of London, talk turned to Elwess' favourite subject, sex. More to the point, the pursuit of the ultimate sexual experience, using his own formidable skills, his collection of sexual weaponry and the atmosphere generated in the Chine.

While at the Lisbon *Sexpo*, Europe's annual trade show for 'adult entertainment,' Elwess had met a Pilates equipment builder from the States, and commissioned him to build a new St. Andrews Cross based on his own design. The apparatus, he explained, would pivot backward and forward, and rotate. The individual arms could also be moved closer together or farther apart, effectively making it part cross, part wheel, and part rack.

"This geezer, Allan Teredo, builds bespoke exercise equipment, so when I told him what I wanted, he was hooked." Elwess sounded like a kid getting a new bike for Christmas. "It's due to be delivered just in time for Valentine's Day." He gave Sydney a cool, confident look of invitation. "Would you two care to launch its maiden voyage?"

Sydney and Dahlra exchanged glances. She considered the idea of being manipulated on that cross, and found it quite appealing. She then considered the idea of placing Dahlra on that cross—oh, that was definitely worth thinking about.

From the Chine, talk moved to the subject of Ramcat. Sydney recounted the disciplining of Clara's submissive Jason and the belt Dahlra had sacrificed to achieve it. As Dahlra looked on indulgently, Elwess gave her an 'I'm impressed' look. "That was a very elegant display of Dominance. I especially liked the use of alcohol to chill your hands. Very old trick; I learned that one in Amsterdam. Well done, *Mistress*."

Once home, they changed from their party togs into something comfortable. Dahlra, in an old burgundy jumper and black tracksuit trousers, managed to get the flue drawing and a fire in the grate while Elwess poured brandies to warm them. Sydney donned a pair of yoga pants that had seen better days, and a jumper she had purloined from Dahlra's wardrobe; it was the same blue as her dress, and made of cashmere so soft it was like wearing a cloud. She cuddled against Dahlra at one end of the sofa, and Elwess lounged at the other, clad in black trackies and a black t-shirt.

As he studied the liquor swirling in his glass, he asked, "Sydney, why, may I ask, do you not like the term *Mistress*?"

"Who said I didn't?"

"No one. It's just that I called you that in the cab, and you didn't look pleased."

"Um, I don't know, really." She paused for a moment, and mentally replaced any possible references to Silverbirch with something more generic. "I once had to go undercover at a nightclub. The whole 'leather corset and boots' outfit made me look stupid and awkward as hell."

That much had been true. She had clumped around in that club looking so out of place, it was no wonder any potential sources avoided her like the plague. She left feeling like the Prat of the Year.

Both men looked at her incredulously. "What? I was really self-conscious and uncomfortable. Much like right now," she added ruefully. "And besides, to me, 'Mistress' just sounds like someone your husband is having an affair with."

Elwess took a thoughtful sip of brandy. "Well, confidence does make a difference, I'll grant you." His black eyes slid over her with cool appraisal. "You know, I've had a little experience in dressing females."

"Do tell."

"Watch your cheek. I'm only saying if I were to dress you properly, I guarantee you would feel and look anything but stupid. And I'm sure your Minder would be very appreciative."

Sydney peered up into Dahlra's face. "*Would* you be appreciative?" she asked slowly, wondering exactly what she might be letting herself in for. It was one thing strutting down the catwalk tunnel between Brompton Road and the Chine with "I'm Too Sexy" playing in her head. It was quite another thing to do it in the company of strangers.

Dahlra smiled sleepily and stroked her thigh. He had, by his own admission, more to drink than usual, and he looked relaxed and a little flushed. She wasn't fooled; he might appear so laid back as to be horizontal, but there was definitely a spark of interest.

"My dear, you are a beautiful woman. I can positively assure you of my appreciation. I want you to have every opportunity available to explore your sexual freedom, as well as your limits. But, because I am also a man who loves you very much," he added, "I would leave that decision to you."

Sydney laughed, feeling partly nonplussed – and partly turned on. "You'd honestly like to do the whole 'Dom-whip-me-beat-me-make-me-write-bad-cheques' thing in public?"

Dahlra snorted into his brandy snifter, and Elwess gave her a hard look. He retorted loftily, "I assure you, kitten, I'm being quite serious. If you want a true Dominant, you have to take his Dominance seriously."

It was amazing how Elwess could launch from zero to BAMF in a matter of nanoseconds. "I'm sorry," she began contritely. "Look, I truly didn't mean to insult—"

"And you will be disciplined for it, I'm sure, but you're changing the subject. Now, if you truly want to take this to a higher level, I will work with you. On one condition."

There was no mistaking the gravity of his words. "And what would that condition be?" she asked warily.

Elwess shot a quick glance to Dahlra, then turned his dark gaze on her. Quietly, he answered, "I want in. I want to be the third person."

She could feel Dahlra shift against her. "Meaning what?" he asked.

"I want to watch. I want to play." His obsidian eyes flashed over her body possessively. Like the flip of a switch, everything about Elwess transformed in that moment. It was subtle, and had the evening been spent anywhere else but a very upbeat, distinctly vanilla party, she and Dahlra probably wouldn't have noticed the contrast so much. This was the man who had declared his intentions on the dance floor; there was no friendly 'I want to get to know you better' fluffy stuff.

Still, it was exciting, knowing she could get a man like Elwess this fired up. It was like pulling the pin on a grenade and seeing how long you could hold your nerve before you threw it. She turned to Dahlra. "You're being very quiet about all this." She reached for his hand and squeezed it. "Please, tell me what you are thinking."

Dahlra hesitated for a few seconds before answering. "As your Minder, my job is to see to your every need, and I love doing that. As your lover, I want to please you in every way possible.

"But I would be lying if I said I didn't want to experiment further with my Dominant side. What we've experienced so far was extremely exciting to me. And I've observed Elwess training submissives; it's highly erotic. I can only imagine how arousing it would be watching you."

Sydney regarded him thoughtfully. After months of living with Dahlra Gar, Sydney knew everything there was to know about the man. He was as open as a book; hell, he was about two inches shy of bashful. And yet, he still had the ability to excite her as if he were some mysterious lover she'd only just met. He could walk into a room and her body went into warp drive, both in the happy and arousal states. Thinking about him watching Elwess train other submissives, thinking about him watching Elwess train *her,* was pretty high up there on the old thrill-o-meter.

"Only if you would truly enjoy yourself."

"Oh, he'd enjoy it," Elwess drawled.

Dahlra held up a hand. "But I want to very specific on how you interact with us, Elwess."

Their eyes met, and Elwess instantly morphed from the proverbial serpent in the Garden of Eden to the cool, imperious Dominant. "Of course. I am perfectly happy to discuss guidelines on this, sir." He slipped effortlessly into the more formalised style of Dom Speak.

"I am first and foremost a sexual Dominant, but I'm also a voyeur. I would be content to watch, but I would also welcome the idea of play with Sydney. I'm not a man who enjoys sex with men, so I wouldn't ask to engage you sexually."

Dahlra caught Sydney's eye, and she knew exactly what he was thinking. "Sydney and I will discuss it."

"Very good. And if you do decide to seriously engage in Dom-sub play, let's plan for Valentine's Day. That gives me time to get you measured and engage my tailor—"

"Get measured for what?"

"A corset, obviously."

"Why?"

Elwess cocked a dark eye at her. "If you wish to continue with this, you won't question me on every point."

It was on the tip of Sydney's tongue tell him to stuff it, but Dahlra's fingers trailed across the back of her neck. The gesture was not lost on Elwess.

"If you want me to train you, you'll wear what I command, and therefore I will provide it. And for you, it has to be a corset and it has to be leather. All leatherwear should be created bespoke. It should fit like a second skin. Didn't you get fitted when you did your undercover work?"

"No, I just went to Ann Summers and picked out something."

Elwess could sweat disdain with the best of them. "No wonder you felt silly. I promise the clothing I give you will make you feel like a queen. A queen wearing a crown of thorns." His eyes raked over her as if she were already decked out in black leather, instead of ratty old yoga pants and a hand-me-down jumper. "Consider it an early Valentine's Day gift for you both.

"Now, next point: Location. Just dressing up and parading around in your bedroom's no good. There must be a sense of occasion, not to mention drama."

"How about Ramcat?" suggested Dahlra.

Elwess shook his head. "Too formal. And too intimate. They do their Valentine play weekend every year, and it's a very proper, staid affair. It's about as titillating as afternoon tea. No, I had something a little edgier in mind. I want to take you to The Library."

Sydney whistled, impressed. The Library was an exclusive private club in Soho, catering to the most hardcore, committed kinkster lifestyles. It was considered *the* ultimate location for public dungeon play. Membership was highly sought after, sparingly granted, and jealously guarded.

"Have you been there before?" she asked Dahlra.

"Only as a spectator. Elwess used to drag me there to watch him ply his trade. I had no desire to participate."

A little pilot light sparked pleasantly in her solar plexus. "And what about now?"

"Oh, I think I could be persuaded to lie back and think of England."

"Oh, fuck's sake, don't be coy. You're dying to get in there and grab a flail," Elwess replied, his humour restored. "Good, that's settled, then. Leave everything to me."

Dahlra felt more than saw Sydney stifle a yawn. He and Elwess stood as she rose to her feet. "I'm going to take a quick shower. Scrub off the war paint. I'll be back down in a bit."

The two men sat, gazing into the fire, nursing their respective Christmas presents. Elwess stared thoughtfully into his Neisson's. "I was watching the three of us tonight. We actually look a bit alike, you and I. Like brothers, maybe."

"Sydney says that all the time. Same father, different moods, is how she put it."

"What is it about her, Dahlra? I know agents like her could probably chew me up for breakfast, but hell, after Christmas Eve..."

Dahlra nodded, watching the hypnotic flames. By some unspoken rule, they had not mentioned Sydney's nightmare. "I suppose it's because she doesn't ask for it. What's more, she doesn't need it. She's nobody's snowflake."

He tilted his head back and closed his eyes, watching her in his mind's eye, moving through his life with grace and purpose. "I would love to wrap her in cotton wool and baby her for the rest of my life." His eyes grew wide. "But I have to let her live *her* life."

The silence stretched between them. A burning log popped, a comforting sound. "It was good of you to make the offer to let us stay here. Christmas Eve only served to remind me just how much I'd grown to hate DeVere."

Elwess nodded. "I get the feeling it's worse for you than for Sydney."

Dahlra took a long drink, and allowed the Jameson's to burn the last vestiges of his uncertainty away. It was now or never, for better or worse. Quietly, he began, "The day after we moved in, she kept insisting she wanted to see her back. I wouldn't let her near a mirror in the hospital. I didn't want her to see it until it had a chance to heal properly..."

He stopped. Even now the memory had the power to break something in him.

Two days after they left hospital, Dahlra heard a strange sound coming from Sydney's room. He stopped at her opened door, listening carefully. It was a muffled, hiccoughing sound; Sydney was crying.

Alarmed at her obvious distress, Dahlra rushed in without knocking or announcing himself. "Sydney! What's wrong—"

She looked up, and her streaming eyes met his. She was standing with her back to the bathroom mirror, naked from the waist up. In her trembling hand she held a smaller mirror.

"Oh, Sydney." His heart flooded with the same, sick shame he had felt the day Nurse Madgerton ripped off her bandages in the hospital. Sydney had split his lip and bloodied his nose and blackened his eye that day, and he would happily take that beating again, rather than bear witness to her palpable, un-asked-for misery.

Even months after all the painstaking work to heal it and escape the possibility of infection, her back had remained a hideous reminder of her last day in hell. And she was getting her first, full-length view of it.

When Dahlra closed his eyes he could still see her suspended from that hook like a side of beef. He could still smell the sickly-sweet smell of bloodlust in the air; he could see the bloodied teeth lying on the table. He could even recall the brand name of the pliers lying beside them; he kept a similar pair in his toolbox.

Worst of all, the one memory that still kept him awake at night, was the empty, vacant look in her eyes, so insensate with agony there was nothing left of Sydney in them. He knew, given time and luck and the best of care, her back would heal; he had not known at the time if he would ever find Sydney in those staring, terror-blanked eyes again.

The deepest, longest lacerations crisscrossed over her spine in long arcing trenches, starting at her left shoulder and ending at her right hip. Some wounds, reopened during her tussle with that malodorous cunt, Madgerton, left puckered and ragged scars, like a garment clumsily sewn together by an incompetent tailor. Shallower gashes and contusions dotted the landscape like some grisly connect-the-dots game. They were almost healed, and already itching terribly.

They both knew her back would never be as it had been, pale and smooth and flawless. It would remain the last tangible proof of their first, bitter communion. Sydney would move on, live the rest of her life as she chose, but those scars would always be the road map, that lead her right back to the cell.

As Dahlra stood there, trying to breathe, trying to think, she wiped the tears and snot from her face with the back of her hand, and to his utter astonishment, she laughed. It was a harsh, bitter, unnatural sound—could it have possibly come from the same throat that had gifted him with that sweet, bubbly laughter the day before?

"Well, you did warn me," she said bleakly, with another croaking laugh. It quickly turned into a sob so pitiful and hopeless it nearly drove him to his knees. The hand mirror slipped through her fingers, shattering on the bathroom floor. She buried her face in her hands. "Oh, God, I look like Frankenstein. I'm a fucking monster."

He could have done the right thing, but he automatically pulled the male card and dealt with the solution instead of the problem. Instead of taking her in his arms, he grabbed her bathrobe from its hook and wrapped it around her, as if hiding the evidence would make it disappear.

Instead of telling her it would be alright, when in his heart he knew it wouldn't, he gingerly picked her up, and unceremoniously hauled her out of the room so she wouldn't cut her bare feet. Instead of encouraging her to talk about it, he spent the next fifteen minutes sweeping, then hoovering the floor to rid it of the broken glass.

And when he was done, instead of turning to him for comfort, Sydney listlessly asked him to leave. He acquiesced, because he didn't know what else to do.

Later that evening, she came downstairs for dinner. Compared to the pleasant, comfortable meal they had shared the evening before, they listlessly picked at their food in stilted, uncomfortable silence. Sydney, stunned and defeated; Dahlra, frozen, desperate to say or do the right thing, if he only had the first idea what that would be. Every mouthful tasted like ash.

Finally, he heard himself say, "Sydney, I realise it was a bit of a shock, but you must understand that some of that will fade in time."

She stared at him in disbelief. "A bit of a shock? Is that all you think it is?"

"Of course not! Why do you think I didn't want you to see it?" Her eyes grew angry and accusing. He pushed his plate away and sighed. "I'm sorry. I should have prepared you better. You're still beautiful to me," he added, knowing how groveling he sounded and hating it. Jesus, why did this have to be so hard?

She had snorted at him, an ugly, scornful sound. "Oh, well, that makes it all better, doesn't it? Happy ending, here I come."

He tried to explain himself, but she cut him off. "I can just about stomach the patronising, Doctor Gar. But the pity I can definitely do without."

She rose from the table, and headed up the stairs. When he followed and tried to reason with her, she shut her bedroom door in his face. He stared at that locked door, as pitiless and unforgiving as her scarred back, then went downstairs to clean up.

He was pissed off and humiliated, and wondered if Sydney would ever speak to him again. He figured it would probably be the last night they would spend together. His career as a Minder was quickly shaping up to be the shortest in Agency history.

Of course, they eventually resumed speaking terms; Sydney was too honest not to own her part in the debacle. During one of those long, sleepless nights after her illness, she had actually apologised to him, and of course, he had accepted her apology. In time, she was even able to laugh about it, but Dahlra had never forgotten the aching sadness in her eyes, as the last vestiges of her pride shattered on the floor, along with that broken mirror.

"So...you didn't want her to see it. And..."

Dahlra came back to the present with a start. Elwess was looking at him curiously, eyebrows raised, waiting for him to continue.

"Right. Well..." Dahlra knew what he was about to say would in all likelihood change everything. It would certainly give Elwess an advantage; whether he would use it against Dahlra or not, only time would tell. He only knew that it was the right time to say it, not only for Sydney, but for himself, and for Elwess.

His conversation with Garnet had troubled him more than he wanted to admit. Lightoller wanted Silverbirch, by any means necessary, and he would not spare the rod to get it. Dahlra had been forced to watch the woman he loved take the beating for The Agency; he would not stand by and let Lightoller make Elwess the whipping boy for Silverbirch if he could do something about it.

He turned back to the flames; it was easier to talk to them. "Do you remember the three of us sitting together on your sofa, that first night?"

"Of course I do. Look, Dahlra, if this is too hard to talk about, don't—"

"She looked in the mirror and saw something ugly, and nothing I said or did changed that. I told her over and over how beautiful she was, but all she could hear was my guilt talking. She thought it blinded me to what she really was. Do you understand?"

"I'm not sure."

"That night, you and I, we made her feel like the most beautiful, most desired woman in the world. 'Like a goddess being worshipped' was the way she put it. I had tried time and again to convince her the scars didn't matter; you confirmed they did. And she was beautiful *because* they mattered. And because she believed you, she knew she could believe me. It changed the way she thought about herself. And it changed the way she thought about how *I* thought about her."

He took a deep breath, and played his hand. "I suppose what I'm trying to say is this: That night, you gave her something I couldn't. And that gave me all I ever wanted. Elwess, if you truly want to be part of our lives, you have my blessing. But it's the three of us together, or nothing."

Elwess stared at his friend so long Dahlra started to look uncomfortable. He didn't have to be Einstein to know what it cost Dahlra to sign that blank cheque. His first thought was that Dahlra had given him something beyond price. The gypsy in him—the *Dominant* in him, demanded he must give something back in return.

"Look mate, you know I've been a Dom almost as long as I've known what a Dom was. That's how I was trained, and that's how I trained you." He put his hand on Dahlra's shoulder, and was surprised that the older man flinched a little.

Elwess sat his glass on the table, and formally knelt beside Dahlra's feet. "I'll give that all to you. I will submit to you."

Dahlra could not have looked more flummoxed if Elwess had started undressing him. "You don't switch, Elwess. I'm not asking for that."

"No, I don't switch," he replied. He looked up into Dahlra's handsome face and thought, *but I would for you.* "And I wouldn't submit to anyone else. I'm telling you this so you'll know my submission is true. If you two want me, you can have me. Your Dominance, your rules. But only if you truly want this, and only if Sydney agrees to it."

Dahlra tried to speak, but Elwess held up his hand. "With all due respect, sir, let me finish. I'm not doing this because you somehow owe me. I won't accept your offer out of a sense of misplaced debt. Remember how Sydney felt when she thought you were doing that to her?"

Finally, Dahlra nodded. "That's fair enough. Your 'offer' just took me by surprise. I'm not going to lie. I'm not sure I understand all the BDSM formalities, but—"

His words drifted off as Elwess gave him a real Paddington stare. Finally Dahlra laughed. "Every time I think I know you, you knock me for six."

"Pot, kettle, mate."

Dahlra took another drink. He was clearly at a loss as to how to proceed. Finally, Elwess took pity on him. "May I resume my place on the sofa?"

"Jesus! Sorry, Elwess. Of course, please," he replied, looking abashed and a little embarrassed. "I suppose I'll need to learn a whole new protocol as your Dominant, won't I?"

Elwess pushed himself back up onto the sofa and picked up his drink. "The fetish communities have their rules and regs like everything else. And when I interact with them, I abide by them. I don't deviate from that—everyone knows what's expected of them, and nobody gets hurt.

"But when it comes to you and Sydney, well, let's just say we're off the map here, Dahlra." He laughed. That was the bloody understatement of the century. "Hell, I've been off the map since the day you waltzed into my office and told me you were going to be Sydney Chapin's Minder, come hell or high water."

"I was rather idealistic, wasn't I?"

"You made a believer out of me. Now it's my turn."

"I understand the significance of what you're offering, and I want you to know I don't take it lightly. I won't force my Dominance upon you, but I will command you with regards to Sydney." He looked at Elwess expectantly. "Happy now?"

"Happy about what?"

Dahlra looked up to see Sydney standing before them, a quizzical smile on her face. She had bathed and changed into her new silk pajamas. Her hair was piled high on her head and wrapped in a messy bun. Damp tendrils escaped and framed her lovely oval face in curling chestnut ribbons. She looked relaxed and content and so beautiful Dahlra silently cursed that they were not alone. Even after his dramatic offer and Elwess' equally magnanimous declaration, Dahlra greedily wanted her all to himself.

She was looking from one man to the other, her eyebrows raised in question. "Do you two have something you want to share with me?"

"Oh, I've definitely got something I'd love to share with you, kitten." Elwess graced her with a rapacious grin. "Come on then, you know the drill; give us a twirl."

As she obligingly performed a model turn, both men made the same sound of masculine approval. The trousers sat low on her hips and fitted perfectly, and the camisole top cupped her breasts sweetly, the brushed silk teasing her nipples to pertness.

She gave Dahlra a mischievous wink. He sat his drink on the table, and gestured for her. A man could only be so strong, after all.

"Come here, you wicked girl. You look good enough to eat." She settled into the crook of his arm with a happy sigh.

"Do you like you gift?" she whispered. She smelled of Jo Malone soap and her skin glowed in the firelight.

"I like it very much."

"I'll like it even better when you take it off. With your teeth." Dahlra buried his nose in her fragrant hair, and gave her an approving growl.

"You just can't stand to see me happy, can you?" Elwess groused, looking petulant and left out. Sydney took his angular face in her hands and kissed him. His eyes widened in surprise, but never let it be said that Elwess Talbert failed to take advantage of an opportunity. His mouth moved against hers, skilled, knowing and practiced, but he permitted her to lead the kiss, and released her when she ended it.

"I love seeing you happy, Elwess." From her perch on Dahlra's lap, Sydney gave Elwess a questioning look. "And what exactly are you happy about?"

"You in that silk top, for a start."

"Pull the other one. Dahlra asked the question before you even saw me. And it sounded important. Happy. About. What?" she repeated.

"Nosey girl." He tilted his head and regarded her pensively. With a glance at Dahlra, he replied formally, "I've just asked your Dominant to accept my submission. From now on, until he tells me otherwise, in this relationship," he added, gesturing with his arm to include the three of them, "Dahlra is my Dominant."

Sydney looked from Elwess to Dahlra, who appeared completely cool about this strange and mystifying announcement. "I'm not sure I understand," she said. "Are you saying you're a submissive now?"

"Only with Dahlra."

"So, you're still Mister Big Bad Dungeon Master, just not around us?"

"Of course I am," he said, with the first tones of exasperation. "Think of me as a Service Bottom, if you will. If the two of you are agreeable to play, then you and I would be submissive to Dahlra. I have chosen this. I have relinquished this. Just for you and Dahlra. I'd never do it for anyone else."

"Okaaay. Remind me to look all this up on Wikipedia. I obviously need to brush up on my BDSM terminology."

"We're making up our own lifestyle here, love. You won't find in online." Elwess glanced at Dahlra. His eyes were so blackly opaque Dahlra could actually see his reflection in them. It was like looking into a fire, full of heat and the potential for destruction.

Sydney smiled. "All right, then. I don't really understand everything, but I think you've just paid me a great honour. I hope I'm worthy of it."

And while it was to Elwess that Sydney spoke, it was Dahlra who answered. "Oh, you are, my love. Believe me, you are."

She leaned against him, and Dahlra enfolded her protectively in his arms. She was a beautiful weight, a privilege for him to hold. A Dominant could not dominate unless a submissive allowed it.

A person could not accept love unless they allowed themselves to be loved.

A lifetime ago, Sydney had killed a stranger to save his life. That one defining moment had charted their course, and taken them on a voyage neither could have ever truly predicted. The only thing Dahlra had known was the discovery of his own heart, his own desire to love her and take care of her. And once Sydney had accepted that love, and cultivated it, she had given it back to him with interest.

Dominant, submissive, Daddy, little girl, man, woman, companion, lover, partner: all the exotic concepts of trust and belief and protection and loyalty. They were part of his DNA now because she *sang* in his very bloodstream. Everything he had become was because of her. Dahlra felt elated, ferocious pride, not just in Sydney and her own journey from who she had been to who she had become, but in himself as well.

Now it seemed they were destined to embark on a new leg of the journey, with Elwess at their side. It would no doubt be one of decadence and pleasure and hedonism, but to Dahlra, that was only the window dressing. His offer of submission was Dahlra's burden to carry now, his watch to keep, but he doubted it would ever rest easy on his shoulders. Elwess was another to protect, another to defend, another to love.

He was wily, and manipulative, and he would always test the boundaries, strain at the lead. He belonged to no one, and would never completely give up his Dominance, not even for Sydney. It would be like a priest giving up his religion.

Dahlra would have to be vigilant; he would have to be powerful. But, he reminded himself, he also had good teachers. And now, he had taken his first step to becoming the man both Sydney and Elwess would one day call their true Master.

This time, he had played to win, and won it all.

The Yorkshire Moors

Lorcan's phone rang as he poured a tumbler of scotch. For a moment, he considered not answering. It was late, and whoever was on the other line would be calling with unpleasant news.

He paused, then decided *what the hell?* and picked it up.

"Yes."

"Master? Is it you-"

"Must I remind you of all people we are *not* on a secure line?"

He could hear the fool breathing heavily. "What is so important that you call me at-" He glanced at his watch. "Three thirty in the morning? I hope it's not just to wish me a Happy New Year."

He listened in silence for almost fifteen minutes, interrupting only to clarify a statement here and there. When he had gleaned all he could, he said, "And she was there?"

"Where?"

"At the party, you fool! Was Sydney Chapin there?"

"Oh, oh yes! I spoke with her myself. She and her Minder and the other one."

"Never mind him. Did she mention returning to the Agency?"

"Well, no, but-"

"Find out if and when she's going to be reassigned to the Silverbirch investigation."

There was the minutest of pauses. "I-I'm not cleared for that information."

"Then I suggest you find a way to clear yourself."

"I'll try sir, but-"

"Do I have to remind you of the consequences of failure, dear?"

There was a spark of panic in the voice. "No sir! I'll find a way. I'll do whatever it takes to please you. I promise!"

"Good." He sat back and took a sip of his scotch. Smooth stuff, that. A smooth drink to herald a smooth year. "Come to the lodge sometime in the next week or so. Perhaps we can find a way to reward you."

He could almost see the silly fool's eyes rolling in rapture. "Yes, oh, thank you, Master. You won't be disappointed."

I sincerely doubt that, he thought. He answered with his softest, most beguiling tone. "I have absolute faith in you."

The pleading, fawning voice was silenced mid-sentence as he ended the call. Good help was so hard to find. It would probably be a good idea for this new mole to suffer an accident soon. He would need to have a word with Silas; now *that* was a man who didn't mind getting his hands dirty for a good cause.

He took another drink, admiring how the liquor danced in the swirls and eddies of the melting ice, and thought of Sydney Chapin. His idiot predecessors had let her slip through their fingers once, her and that doctor with the ridiculous name. He would not allow that to happen again. Not on his watch. They had much more to lose this time round.

To the fiery liquid, he mused, "It seems you have forgotten your time in the cell, Ms Chapin. Perhaps you need a reminder the stakes are much higher now."

ABOUT THE AUTHOR

Teddy Raye wrote her first novel at sixteen, and her first book of short stories in her early twenties. She was too shy to read them to anyone, but with encouragement of friends, she started writing fanfiction, resulting in over 250 essays, short stories and novel-length pieces. Though her first love was erotic romance, her stories grew in scope and depth, ranging from humor to horror. It was only a matter of time before the lure of writing her own characters became too strong to resist.

The evolution of the *Her Minder* series began on a Tube ride into Central London, and grew over the years from a simple story of an erotic encounter into a trilogy of suspense, intrigue and lush romance. Book Two, The Chine, was released in 2020, and Book Three, *Silverbirch*, is in the works. She is also currently working on a Steampulp Murder Mystery entitled *Oubliette*.

Teddy lives in South Carolina with her two cats, Sevvy and Bello.

Dahlra's Crème Brûlée

4 cups heavy cream
2/3 cup granulated sugar
1 pinch salt
1 Vanilla bean – a real one – don't skimp!
10 Large egg yolks
1/4 cup turbinado sugar (i.e. sugar in the raw)

Directions

Adjust oven rack to the lower middle position and preheat oven to 350°F. Cover the bottom of a roasting pan with dish towel. Arrange eight 6oz ramekins in the pan making sure they don't touch.

Bring kettle of water to a boil.

Combine 2 cups of cream, granulated sugar and salt in a medium saucepan. Scrape the seeds from the vanilla bean and add it to the pan along with the pod. Bring the mixture to a boil over medium heat, stirring to dissolve the sugar.

Remove from heat, cover and let steep for 15 minutes.

Place egg yolks in a large bowl and whisk.

Stir the remaining 2 cups of cream into the hot mixture.

Slowly add in 1 cup of the cream mixture whisking constantly until smooth. Whisk in the remaining cream until thoroughly combined.

Strain through a fine mesh strainer into a large measuring cup or pitcher. Pour the custard evenly into the ramekins. Put pan in the oven and pour boiling water to 2/3 up the sides of the ramekins.

Bake until the custards are barely set and are no longer sloshy (30-35 minutes or 25-30 for shallow or fluted dishes).

Transfer the ramekins to a wire rack and allow to cool for 2 hours.

Set on baking sheet, cover with plastic wrap & refrigerate for at least 4 hours.

Before serving uncover the ramekin and blot the top dry with a paper towel. Sprinkle the top with turbinado or demerara sugar and shake to distribute evenly. 21. Ignite torch and caramelize the sugar. (Keep flame 2in above ramekin move in a sweeping motion from the perimeter to towards the middle until the sugar is bubbling and deep golden brown.